Conspiracy

ALSO BY S. J. PARRIS

Heresy
Prophecy
Sacrilege
Treachery

S.J. PARRIS

Conspiracy

HarperCollins*Publishers*

HarperCollins*Publishers*
1 London Bridge Street,
London SE1 9GF

www.harpercollins.co.uk

Published by HarperCollins*Publishers* 2016
1

Endpaper image shows detail from 16th century map of Paris
© Bibliothèque Nationale de France

A catalogue record for this book
is available from the British Library

ISBN: 978 0 00 748124 8

This novel is entirely a work of fiction.
The names, characters and incidents portrayed in it, while at times
based on historical fact, are the work of the author's imagination.

Set in Sabon by Palimpsest Book Production Limited
Falkirk, Stirlingshire

Printed and bound in Great Britain by
Clays Ltd, St Ives plc

MIX
Paper from
responsible sources
FSC
www.fsc.org
FSC™ C007454

FSC™ is a non-profit international organisation established to promote
the responsible management of the world's forests. Products carrying the
FSC label are independently certified to assure consumers that they come
from forests that are managed to meet the social, economic and
ecological needs of present and future generations,
and other controlled sources.

Find out more about HarperCollins and the environment at
www.harpercollins.co.uk/green

PROLOGUE

Paris, November, 1585.

'Forgive me, Father, for I have sinned. It has been nine years since my last confession.'

From beyond the latticework screen came a sharp inhalation through teeth, barely audible. For a long time, it seemed as if he would not speak. You could almost hear the echo bouncing through his skull: nine *years*?

'And what has happened to keep you so far from God's grace, my son?'

That slight nasal quality to his voice; it coloured everything he said with an unfortunate sneer, even on the rare occasions where none was intended.

'Ah, Father – where to begin? I was caught reading forbidden books in the privy by my prior, I abandoned the Dominican order without permission to avoid the Inquisition, for which offence I was excommunicated by the last Pope; I have written and published books questioning the authority of the Holy Scriptures and the Church Fathers, I have publicly attacked Aristotle and defended the cosmology of Copernicus, I have been accused of heresy and necromancy—' a swift pause to draw breath – 'I have frequently sworn

1

oaths and taken the Lord's name in vain, I have envied my friends, lain with women, and brought about the death of more than one person – though, in my defence, those cases were complicated.'

'Anything else?' Openly sarcastic now.

'Oh – yes. I have also borne false witness. Too many times to count.' *Including this confession.*

A prickly silence unfolded. Inside the confessional, nothing but the familiar scent of old wood and incense, and the slow dance of dust motes, disturbed only by our breathing, his and mine, visible in the November chill. A distant door slammed, the sound ringing down the vaulted stone of the nave.

'Will you give me penance?'

He made an impatient noise. 'Penance? You could endow a cathedral and walk to Santiago on your knees for the rest of your natural life, it would barely scratch the surface. Besides—' the wooden bench creaked as he shifted his weight – 'haven't you forgotten something, my son?'

'I may have left out some of the detail,' I conceded. 'Otherwise we'd be here till Judgement Day.'

'I meant, I have not yet heard you say, "For these and all the sins of my past life, I ask pardon of God." Because, in your heart, you are not really contrite, are you? You are, it seems to me, quite proud of this catalogue of iniquity.'

'Should we add the sin of pride, then, while I am here? Save me coming back?'

A further silence stretched taut across the minutes. His face was pressed close to the grille; I knew he was looking straight at me.

'For the love of God, Bruno,' he hissed, eventually. 'What are you *doing* here?'

I breathed out and leaned my head back against the wooden panels, smiling at his exasperation. At least he had not thrown me out. Not yet.

'I wanted to speak to you in private.'

'It is a serious offence, to mock the holy sacrament of confession. Not that it would matter to *you*.'

'I intended no mockery, Paul. I did not think you would agree to see me any other way.'

'You always intend mockery, Bruno – you cannot help it. And in this place you can call me Père Lefèvre.' He sighed. 'I heard you were lately returned to Paris. Does the King have you teaching him magic again?'

I straightened up, defensive. 'It was not magic, whatever rumours you heard. I taught him the art of memory. But no, I have not seen him.'

Could he know my situation with the King? Though I could make out no more than a shadowy profile through the screen, I pictured the young priest nodding as he weighed this up, cupping his hand over his prominent chin; the darting eyes under the thatch of colourless hair, the neck too thin for the collar of his black robe, the slight hunch, as if ashamed of his height. He used to remind me of a heron. He must be at least thirty by now. When I knew him three years ago, Paul Lefèvre always seemed too uncertain of himself and his opinions to be dogmatic; he was the sort of man who naturally deferred to more forceful characters. Perhaps that was the problem. Perhaps fanaticism had lent him the courage of someone else's convictions.

'If King Henri has any wit at all – and that is a matter of some debate these days,' he added, with a smug little chuckle, as though for the benefit of an invisible audience, 'he will keep a safe distance from a man with your reputation in the present climate.'

I said nothing, though in the silence my knuckles cracked like a pistol shot and I felt him jump. He leaned in closer to the grille and lowered his voice. 'A word of advice, Bruno. Paris has changed greatly while you've been away. A wise man would note how the wind is blowing. And though you have not always been wise, you are at least clever, which is the next best thing. Find a new patron, while you still can. The King may not be in a position to do you good for much longer.'

I shuffled along my seat until he could feel my breath on his face through the partition. 'You speak as if you know something, Paul. I heard you had joined the Catholic League. Does your intelligence come direct from them?'

He recoiled as if I had struck him. 'I know of no plots against the King, if that is your meaning. I spoke in general terms only. Anyone may read the signs. Look, Bruno.' His tone grew mollifying again. 'I counsel you as a friend. Put away your heresies. Be reconciled with Holy Mother Church, and you would find Paris a less hostile place. There are people of influence here who admire your intellectual gifts, if not your misuse of them.'

I cleared my throat, glad he could not see my expression. I could guess which people he meant. 'Actually, that was the reason I came to see you. To beg a favour.' I paused for a deep breath: this petition was always going to be humiliating, though a necessary evil. 'I need this excommunication lifted.'

He threw his head back and laughed openly; the sound must have rattled around the high arches, leading any penitents to wonder what kind of confession was taking place here. '*Enfin!* The great free thinker Giordano Bruno finds he cannot survive without the support of Rome.'

'It's unbecoming to see a man of God gloating so openly, Paul. Can you help me or not?'

'Me? I am a mere parish priest, Bruno.' The false humility grated. 'Only the Pope has the power to restore you to the embrace of the Church.'

'I know that.' I tried to curb my impatience. 'But with your connections, I thought perhaps you could secure me an audience with the Papal nuncio in Paris. I hear he is a man of learning and more tolerant than many in Rome.'

The fabric of his robe whispered as he crossed and uncrossed his legs.

'I will consider what may be done for you,' he said, after some thought, as if this in itself were a great concession. 'But my *connections* would want some reassurance that their intercession was not in vain. You would need to show public contrition for your heresies and a little more obvious piety. Come to Mass here this Sunday. I am preparing a sermon that will shake Paris to its foundations.'

'Now how could I miss that?' I stopped; forced myself to sound more tractable. 'And if I show my face – you will speak for me?'

'One step at a time, Bruno.'

He could not quite disguise the preening in his voice. It would have been satisfying to remind him then of the many occasions I had bested him in public debate when we were both Readers at the University of Paris, but I had too much need of his help. How he must be enjoying this small power. The boards creaked again as he stood to leave.

'Where will I find you?' he asked, his back to me.

I hesitated. 'The library at the Abbey of Saint-Victor. I take refuge there most days.'

'Writing another heretical book?'

'That would depend on who is reading it.'

'Ha. Good luck finding a printer. As I say – you will find Paris greatly changed.' He lifted the latch; the door swung open with a soft complaint. 'And – Bruno?'

'Yes?'

'I know it does not come naturally to you, but try a little humility. You may have enjoyed the King's favour once, but that means nothing now. I wouldn't go about proclaiming your sins with such relish, if I were you.'

'Oh, I only do that in the sanctity of the confessional. *Father.*'

'And you only do that once in nine years, apparently.'

His laughter grew faint as he walked away, though whether it was indulgent or scornful was hard to tell. I sat alone in the closeted shadows until the tap of his heels on the flagstones had faded completely, before stepping into the chilly hush of Saint-Séverin.

I did not know then that this would be the last time I spoke to Père Paul Lefèvre. Within a week of our meeting, he had been murdered.

PART ONE

ONE

They found him face down in the Seine at dusk on November 26th, two bargemen on their way home after the day's markets. The currents had washed him into the shallows of the small channel that ran south from the shore of the Left Bank along the line of the city wall, close to the Abbey of Saint-Victor; near enough that, being outside the wall and since he was wearing a black cassock that billowed around him in the murky water, the boatmen turned first to the friars, thinking he was one of theirs. It was only when they hauled him out of the river that they realised he was not quite dead, despite the gaping wound on his temple and the blood that covered his face.

I was reading in my usual alcove in the library that evening, a Tuesday, two days after Paul preached the sermon he had promised all Paris would remember, when a young friar flung open the door and cast his eyes about the room in a state of agitation. I watched him exchange a few urgent words in a low voice with Cotin, the librarian. They were both looking at me as they spoke; Cotin's jaw was set tight, his eyes apprehensive. My presence in the library was not entirely official.

'You are Bruno?' The young man strode down the aisle between the bookcases, his face flushed. When I nodded, half-rising, he turned sharply, beckoning me to follow. 'You must come with me.'

I obeyed. I was their guest; how could I refuse? He led me at a brisk trot across the main cloister, his habit flapping around his legs. Though it was not much past four in the afternoon, the lamps had already been lit in the recesses of the arcades; moths panicked around them and the passages retreated into shadow between the pools of light. I followed the boy through an archway and across another courtyard, wondering at the nature of this summons. I had done nothing to attract unwelcome attention since I arrived in Paris two months ago, or so I believed; I had barely seen any of my previous acquaintance, save Jacopo Corbinelli, keeper of the King's library. At the thought of him my heart lifted briefly: perhaps this was the long-awaited message from King Henri? But the young man's evident anxiety hardly seemed to herald the arrival of a royal messenger. Wherever he was taking me with such haste, it did not imply good news.

At the infirmary block, he ushered me up a narrow stair and into a long room with a steeply sloping timber-beamed ceiling. The air was hazy with the smoke of herbal fumigations smouldering in the corners to purify the room – a bitter, vegetable smell that took me back to my own days as a young friar assisting in the infirmary of San Domenico Maggiore in Naples. It did not succeed in disguising the ferric reek of blood, or the brackish sewage stench of the river.

Two men in the black habits of the Augustinians flanked a bed where a shape lay, unmoving. Water dripped from the sheets on to the wooden boards in a steady rhythm, like the ticking of a clock. One, grey-bearded and wearing a leather apron with his sleeves rolled, leaned over the bed with a wad of cloth and a bowl of steaming water; the other, dark-haired, a crucifix around his neck, was performing the Anointing of the Sick in a strident voice.

The bearded friar, whom I guessed to be the brother

infirmarian, raised his eyes as we entered, glancing from me to the young messenger and back.

'Is this the man?' Before I could reply, he gestured to the bed. 'He has been asking for you. They brought him here no more than a half-hour past – your name is the only word he has spoken. To tell the truth, it is a miracle he can form speech at all. He is barely clinging to this world.'

The other friar broke off from his rites to look at me. 'One of the brothers thought he remembered an Italian called Bruno who came to use the library.' His voice was coldly polite, but his expression made clear that he was not pleased by the interruption. 'Do you know this poor wretch, then?' He stepped back so that I could see the prone figure. I could not stop myself crying out at the sight.

'*Gesù Cristo!* Paul?' But it seemed impossible that he could hear me. His eyes were closed, though his right was so swollen and bloodied that he could not have opened it, even if he had been conscious. Above his temple, his skull had been half-staved in by a heavy blow – a stone, perhaps, or a club. It was a wonder the force had not killed him outright. The infirmarian had attempted to clean the worst of it, but the priest's skin was greenish, the right side of his head thickly matted with blood drying to black around the soaked cloth they had pressed over the wound. Beneath it, I saw a white gleam of bone.

'His name is Paul Lefèvre.' I heard the tremor in my voice. 'He's the curé at Saint-Séverin.'

'Thought I knew his face.' The one with the dark hair and the crucifix nodded at his colleague, as if he had won a private wager. 'I've heard him preach. Bit fire and brimstone, isn't he? One of those priests that's bought and paid for by the League.'

From the corner of my eye I caught the infirmarian sending him a quick glance, a minute shake of the head that I was not supposed to see. I understood; it was unwise to express political opinions in front of strangers these days. You never knew where your words might be repeated.

11

'Can anything be done for him?' I asked.

The infirmarian pressed his lips together and lowered his eyes. 'I fear not. Except to send his soul more peacefully to Our Lord. Frère Albaric was already giving the sacrament. But if it is any comfort, I do not think he feels pain, at this stage. I gave him a draught to ease it.'

'Did anyone see anything? Whoever found him – do they know who did this?'

The dark-haired friar named Albaric made a small noise that might have been laughter. 'I don't think you need look much further than the Louvre Palace.'

I stared at him. 'No. The King . . .' I was going to say the King would not have a priest killed just because that priest insulted him from the pulpit, but the words dried in my mouth. I had not seen the King for three years; who knew what he might be capable of, in his present troubles? And even if the King lacked the temperament to strike at an enemy from behind, his mother certainly did not. I wondered what Paul had been doing in this part of town; had he been on his way to see me when he was ambushed? A worrying thought occurred.

'Did he have any letters on him?'

'Why do you ask?' Frère Albaric jerked his head up, his voice unexpectedly sharp.

'I only wondered if he was carrying anything that might suggest why he was attacked. Papers, valuables, that sort of thing.' I kept my tone mild, but he continued to fix me with the same aggressive stare. His skin had an unpleasant sheen, as if his face were damp with sweat; it gave him a disturbingly amphibious quality.

'He had nothing about his person when he was brought here,' the infirmarian said. 'Just the clothes he was wearing.'

'Robbed, one presumes,' Albaric declared. 'All kinds of lawless types you get, loitering outside the city walls. Waiting for traders coming home with the day's takings. They'd have stripped him of anything worth having before dumping him in the river, poor fellow.'

'But he's obviously a priest, not a trader,' I objected. 'Street robbers would hardly expect a priest to carry a full purse.'

Albaric's eyes narrowed. 'He might have been carrying alms to give out. Or perhaps he was wearing a particularly lavish crucifix. Some of them do.'

I glanced at his chest; his own ornament was hardly austere. 'Not Paul. He dislikes ostentation.' Unless he had changed in that regard too, since joining the Catholic League, but somehow I doubted it, just as I found it hard to believe that he had fallen to some chance street robbery on his way to the abbey. Whoever struck him down had done so with a purpose, I was sure.

'Huguenots, then. Wouldn't be the first cleric they've assaulted. They'll take any opportunity to attack the true faith.' Albaric sniffed and turned back to his vial of chrism, as if the matter was now closed. I did not bother to argue. In case of doubt, blame the Protestants: the Church's answer to everything. Though I could not help but notice that this Albaric seemed eager to point the finger in all directions at once.

I drew closer to the bed and leaned as near as I could to the dying man's lips, but found no trace of breath.

'Paul. It's Bruno.' I laid a hand over one of his and almost recoiled; the skin was cold and damp as a filleted fish. 'I'm here now.'

'He can't hear you,' Albaric pointed out, over my shoulder. Ignoring him, I bent my cheek closer. I remained there for several minutes, listening, willing him to breathe, or speak, to give some sign of life, while the friar shifted from foot to foot behind me, impatient to resume his office. Eventually, I had to concede defeat. I had been in the presence of death often enough to know its particular stillness, its invidious smell. Whatever Paul had wanted to tell me, I had missed it. I straightened my back, head still bowed, and as I did so, I felt the cold fingers under mine twitch almost imperceptibly. Albaric was already moving in with his chrism; I held up a hand to warn him off. Under Paul's one visible eyelid, the faintest flicker. His fingers closed around my thumb; his chest rose a fraction as he scraped a painful breath, his frame twisting with the effort. His left eye snapped open in a wild gaze that seemed both to fix on me and look straight through me, into the next world. I gripped his hand tight; he gave a violent shiver and exhaled with his death rattle one final, grating word:

'*Circe.*'

TWO

I hurried back towards the Porte Saint-Victor through a veil of fine rain as dusk fell, keen to disappear into the warren of narrow streets around the colleges on the Left Bank before anyone noticed I had gone. In the commotion after Paul's death I had slipped away from the abbey, knowing they would call in the city authorities; life may be cheap in Paris in these turbulent times, but the murder of a priest was still a serious matter, particularly one with Paul's connections, and I did not want to find myself caught up in their investigation. The friars had asked me, of course, what his urgent last word had been; I told them 'Jesus'. I don't know if they believed me. I was not sure what instinct prompted me to lie; only that it seemed prudent not to divulge anything to people I did not know, especially those in holy orders. Paris was so fractured by divided loyalties that the wrong word to the wrong person could ripple outwards with unintended consequences, and my position was too precarious to place myself knowingly at the heart of a political murder – for it seemed to me that Albaric's first surmise had been correct, that the attack was a direct result of Paul's eloquent rant against the decadence and corruption of the royal House of Valois from his pulpit the previous Sunday.

'Circe', I supposed, must be some kind of code word, intelligible perhaps to his confederates in the Catholic League, but I had no idea what it might mean, or what might be unleashed by repeating it in the wrong ear. Could it be connected to the identity of his killer? Was that what he was trying to tell me? I was not convinced that Paul had even been aware of who I was at the end. Best to keep silent until I could seek the advice of Jacopo Corbinelli, the only man in Paris I dared to trust. Like me, Jacopo was a scholar, an Italian in exile, part of the Florentine entourage that surrounded Catherine de Medici, the widowed Queen Mother. He had been King Henri's boyhood tutor and continued to serve him as advisor and keeper of his library, though he also remained Catherine's secretary, and as such he was uniquely placed to speak in my favour at court. He had taken me under his wing when I arrived in Paris for the first time, four years ago; it was he who had heard me give a lecture on my art of memory at the University and recommended me to the King. I became a regular guest among the Italian thinkers, writers and artists who gathered around Jacopo's supper table in those days and I had hoped, on returning from London, that I might renew the friendship and enjoy again the warmth of that company. But affairs of state kept him busy now between the palaces, or so he told me; I had seen him only twice since I arrived at the beginning of September, and though he had assured me he would persuade the King to grant me an audience, I was still waiting for a word, and it was now almost a month since I had heard anything from him. I decided to send another message to his house and ask to see him urgently. Until then, I would keep my mouth shut regarding Paul's murder; too much about it made me uneasy.

On impulse, I turned north towards the river before I reached the gate, in the direction of the old fort of La Tournelle which stood a squat sentinel over the Seine and its islands, marking the boundary of the city wall. Here, Paris ended abruptly, bustling streets giving way to ploughed fields and orchards, wide unpaved roads built for ox-carts and canals for goods barges from the surrounding farms – all the arteries that kept money flowing in and out of the city. Huddled in the shadow of the old wall, the Faubourg Saint-Victor offered little to passing visitors besides the great abbey that gave the district its name; only a few scattered cottages and cheap inns along the main road out of the city. Mudbanks sloped down to the river, pockmarked with the tracks of gulls; rickety wooden jetties splayed into the water at intervals, their boards slick with weed and splintered like rotten teeth. I walked slowly back along the bank where the inland channel met the broad expanse of the river, scanning the ground to either side. With that head wound, Paul would not have survived more than a few minutes in the water. The current must have washed him into the shallows of the inlet and on to the bank almost as soon as he was thrown in or he would have drowned, which meant he must have been struck just upriver from the channel – in other words, right under the wall of the abbey. It was hard to imagine that Paul would have had any other destination in this part of town; it was reasonable to assume, too, given that he had asked for me by name on his deathbed, that he had come to the abbey looking for me. But someone else had encountered him first.

A wooden bridge crossed the channel, leading directly to the narrow track that passed along the bank at the back wall of the abbey grounds. A few yards further along I found what I was looking for: a patch of churned-up mud, the dark blotch of bloodstains almost invisible now in the fading light against the wet ground. If the rain continued, they would be gone by morning. A chaos of footprints led away from the scene in all directions; though I could see an imprint that might have indicated where a body was dragged to the water's edge, it was impossible to see where the tracks led after that. Even so, this scene undermined Albaric's other theory of street robbers; the route for traders passed in front of the abbey's main gates. No bandit who knew his business would bother lurking on this isolated path in the hope of grabbing a farmer with a fat purse.

I turned slowly, surveying both sides of the river. Only yards from the trampled spot where Paul must have been attacked I noticed a low door set into the boundary wall of the abbey; below it, a set of stone steps leading down to the water, with a rusted iron ring for tethering a boat. I tried the handle of the door but it was locked fast. There was no other living soul stirring out here in the gathering dusk, save a heron flapping its stately line across the row of clouds; at my back the river flowed on, grey and implacable, while beyond the wall, the grand spire of the abbey church and a few plumes of smoke from the cottages stood out against the darkening sky. A lonely place, but in daylight there would be enough traffic on the river to mean that anyone standing here would be visible to passing boatmen. The killer had taken a risk; Paul's death had been a matter of urgency, then. Had his attacker followed him from his lodgings, watching for an opportunity once he realised his target was leaving the city? Or was he already waiting, knowing that Paul would come to the abbey this afternoon?

A staccato exchange between oarsmen out on the river drifted across on the breeze. I turned and watched as two pinpoints of light wavered towards one another, accompanied by the slow splashing of oars. A gust of laughter rippled out as the wherries passed. The boatmen who found Paul must have missed the killer by a matter of minutes; perhaps their arrival had caused him to take flight before the job was finished. It would not be impossible to track down those men and question them, though I supposed that if they had had anything to tell, they would have mentioned it to the friars. It was also likely that they had gone through the injured man's clothes in search of valuables before they realised he was still breathing; life was hard for everyone now in Paris, and even honest men were desperate. If they had found anything worth taking, they would not want to answer questions. I could not help thinking – and it was not a thought which did me credit – that if they had only arrived a few minutes later, he would not have been alive to say my name, and I would not have been the one to hear him rasp out his gnomic last word. My life in Paris was dangerous enough without involving myself in a factional murder and I had an uneasy sense that, with his dying breath, Paul had handed me a thread that would, at the slightest tweak, unravel a mystery better left untouched.

I glanced back at the wall as a new thought occurred; anyone with a key to that door could easily attack a man, push him in the water and disappear again inside the abbey in a matter of minutes. I kicked over the dark stains in the mud and turned towards home.

The gutters along each side of the rue du Cimetière already trickled steadily with the run-off from the roofs, though the rain remained thin and half-hearted. I tilted my head back to look up at the strip of sky between the crooked eaves of houses that leaned in toward one another across the narrow street, like drunks about to fall into each other's arms. Paris was decaying; the years of religious strife had left no money for the upkeep of the streets, where refuse, ashes and shit of every kind banked up around potholes deep enough to break the legs of horses, while the fabric of the crowded medieval *quartiers* crumbled around their tenants, who had long ago resigned themselves to cold and foul smells and the ever-present threat of plague. It was a depressing place to take lodgings, inhabited almost entirely by the poorer students from the nearby Sorbonne and the Collège de France, but I had little choice since my return from London unless King Henri was willing to take me back under his patronage, and with France on the brink of civil war, it seemed he had more pressing

19

matters on his mind than the circumstances of one exiled Italian heretic he had once called a friend.

Hunger, and the desire to delay the gloomy prospect of returning to my rooms alone, drove me to the Swan and Cross at the end of the street, a noisy, amiable tavern where groups of students gathered after the day's lectures to argue philosophy and politics over a jug of cheap wine and exchange flirtatious insults with the working girls they could not afford. The air inside was thick with a fug of wet wool, roasting meat, tobacco and male sweat, but I was glad of the warmth. I turned at the sound of a whistle, to see a round-faced, cheerful whore I vaguely recognised by sight, perched sideways on a boy's lap and winking at me while he chatted to his friends as if he had not noticed her.

'Is it my lucky night tonight, Doctor? You look wet through. Let me warm you up.'

I offered a mock bow. 'Forgive me, mademoiselle, but I'm afraid I'm not stopping.'

She pouted her rouged lips and squeezed her arms together to push up her breasts so that they threatened to spill over her tight bodice. 'You always say that.'

'Because I am always busy. Besides, you have company.'

'Pfft.' She waved a hand over the boy's head. 'Can't be good for you. A man needs pleasure in his life, Doctor. Too much of this—' she tapped the side of her head – 'and not enough of this—' she grabbed at her crotch, an exaggerated, masculine gesture. 'Makes you ill. That's why you're getting thin.'

'You could be right,' I said, almost smiling as I edged by. 'Maybe next time.'

She slapped me on the backside as I passed. 'Well, I won't wait around for ever. *Carpe diem*, Doctor.'

I raised an eyebrow and she grinned.

'I see you've got some Latin out of these students.'

'That's about all I get out of them and their moth-eaten purses, stingy little ballsacks.' She leaned over the shoulder of the boy she was sitting on and drank deep from his beaker of wine; I took advantage of the outcry to slip through the crowd. I could not afford the girls either, though they did not know this; they looked at me and saw well-cut clothes – good leather boots, black wool breeches and a short doublet of black leather with puffed shoulders, tailored in London in the days when I had a little money to spare, and carefully mended since – assumed an income to match and badgered me accordingly. Not that I was tempted by this one or any of her colleagues; still, I found her diagnosis depressingly accurate.

Gaston, the square-shouldered proprietor, appeared out of the fray as he always did, with the lock-jawed expression of a pikeman facing down a foe. When he caught sight of me, he elbowed his way through his customers without ceremony, wiping his hands on his apron and holding them out as if I were a nephew returned from a distant war. I submitted to his embrace as he wrapped me in his familiar smell of garlic and cooking fat.

'Gaston,' I said, finally disentangling myself, 'do you remember a young theologian called Paul Lefèvre, used to come in here three years back when he was at the Sorbonne? Skinny fellow, reedy voice.'

Gaston squeezed his eyes shut and cocked his head to one side, as if listening for the answer. 'That was the lad who went to be priest at Saint-Séverin, no? Adam's apple like a snake swallowing a rat?' He tugged the flesh of his neck out to illustrate the point.

'That's him. He used to take rooms on the rue Macon – do you know if he still had them?'

'Had?' His eyebrow shot up; no sharper eyes or ears on the Left Bank than Gaston's, so they said. 'Why, what's happened to him?'

'I mean – since I've been away,' I corrected, quickly. I needed to act before Paul's murder became common knowledge. 'Was he still living there?'

He shrugged. 'Far as I know. We haven't seen him here for a long time – too holy for the likes of us now.' He gave a throaty chuckle. 'I remember him all right – used to sit there on the edge of the group as if he wanted the courage to throw himself into the conversation. Everyone always talked over him. You know he joined the League? Maybe he got more respect from them.' He sucked in his fleshy cheeks to show what he thought of that. 'He stopped coming in here after he was ordained priest – this would be after you'd gone to England, Signor Bruno. Turned into quite the hellfire preacher, you know, inflaming his congregation against the King and his appointed heir. Me and the wife changed church because of it, must have been a year back. I don't go to Mass for a bellyful of politics. Mind you—' he paused to draw breath, raising a forefinger like a schoolmaster – 'I'm not saying I'd be happy to see some whoreson Protestant wearing the crown of France, but you have to respect—'

'Thanks, Gaston. I have to go now,' I said, patting him on the chest as I turned for the door.

'Got any money for me?' He made it sound good-humoured, but I was stung by guilt; he had given me too many suppers on credit lately, and the bill was mounting.

'I will have it for you very soon, I swear. I just need to – get my affairs in order. Any day now.' By which I meant, whenever the King deigns to send for me.

'Ah, I'm only messing, lad – go on, what'll you have? Put some meat on your bones. You look hungry.'

'Thank you – perhaps later.'

'You say that to all the girls,' he called after me as I ducked between wildly gesturing students to escape, smiling to myself at the way he still thought of me as one of his boys, though at thirty-seven I was probably only a few years behind him. At least the whores and publicans of Paris were pleased to see me back.

The buildings took on a greyish pallor in the deepening

shadows as the rain fell harder. The days were shortening towards midwinter; when the sky was overcast it felt as if night was falling by early afternoon. I wrapped my cloak around my shoulders and pulled the hood close to hide my face as I trudged back towards the river through rutted streets ankle-deep in filth. At the corner of rue Saint-Jacques, I felt a hand reach out and clutch at my sleeve; I whipped around, dagger half-drawn, but it was only a beggar-child, filthy and hollow-cheeked, with staring eyes. I would have thrown him a coin, but he caught sight of the knife and streaked away into an impossible gap between two houses quick as a fish. Paris was full of the dispossessed now; that was another change for the worse. Failing harvests and the constant three-way skirmishes between the Protestant Huguenot forces, the beleaguered royal armies and the swelling numbers of Catholic League troops further south had driven bedraggled flocks of refugees towards the capital, where they begged, stole, sold themselves, or starved to death on the streets.

It was growing harder to resist the melancholy that had crept over me since my enforced return from London. In Paris, as the chill and dark of autumn edged towards winter, I had begun to experience a gnawing homesickness for the blue skies and green slopes of my native Nola, at the foot of Mount Vesuvius, made keener by the knowledge that I might never return. For perhaps the first time since I had abandoned the religious life nine years ago, I was truly coming to understand what exile meant. This rootlessness – living out of a travelling bag, arriving in every town with one eye on the road out – no longer felt like freedom. Now, more than ever, it felt like the reverse. I had thought, for a while, that I might come to call London home, but that did not work out as I had hoped. I had left behind the few people I thought of as friends, and arrived in Paris to find those who had once opened their doors to me turning away, embarrassed. My reputation was becoming a problem, one I entrenched further with each new book I wilfully published. Though every fibre of my being bridled at the forced humiliation, I had no choice but to beg to have this excommunication lifted. At twenty-eight, I had worn it as the proud badge of a free-thinker. Now, at thirty-seven, I was obliged to view it in a different light: as an impediment to any offer of patronage. A man like me could not live without a patron, and no Catholic with a care for his honour will sponsor a known heretic; it was for this alone that I had approached Paul. For now, I belonged nowhere, and it was hard to shake that sense of exclusion.

I clenched my teeth and sheathed my dagger: no more of that. Courage, Bruno, I told myself, as I walked on towards the rue Macon. You have been in worse straits than this and talked your way out and up; you can do so again. I needed to see Jacopo Corbinelli. But first, I had to make sure I could not be further connected with Paul Lefèvre. If he had been carrying letters, they must have been taken from him before he was thrown in the river, but his lodgings would certainly be searched; if there was any correspondence that mentioned me or the favour I had asked of him, I wanted to be the one to find it. I knew too well how it might be used against me. There were those among the extreme Catholic faction here in Paris who knew, or guessed at, my activities in England. If they thought I desired the Church's goodwill again, they would not miss the chance to use it as leverage. Reconciliation in exchange for information – and that was a bargain I was not prepared to strike. I still felt some loyalty to England, even if she appeared to have forgotten me. Beyond that, I had no intention of involving myself in Paul's murder. We had been acquaintances, not friends; I was sorry that he had met such a brutal death, but he would have known he was courting danger when he decided to tangle with religious politics. Besides, I had a good idea that the cynical Frère Albaric had not been far wrong in his surmise about the Louvre, and that was a truth I preferred to leave for others to uncover.

Halfway along rue Macon I met a young woman with a basket of laundry sheltering in a doorway; after we had exchanged complaints about the weather, she confirmed that Père Lefèvre did indeed have rooms in a house opposite, on the first floor. I considered knocking to see if one of his neighbours would let me in, but there were no lights visible in the rest of the house, and it seemed wise to keep my visit discreet. A little careful tinkering with the blade of my knife, and the cheap lock of the front door yielded without much resistance. I latched it behind me, so that I would at least have some warning if someone else had the same idea.

It took a moment for my eyes to adjust to the gloom of the entrance hall, and I wished I had thought to bring a tinder-box and taper. On my left, a crooked staircase ran up to the first floor; after listening for any tell-tale sound of movement from other rooms, I climbed as carefully as I could, though it was impossible to stop the old boards from groaning in protest. My stomach let out a low growl and I clamped a hand across it as if that might muffle the sound; I regretted turning down Gaston's offer of supper. The door to Paul's rooms was also locked, and took longer to tease into compliance; this lock appeared newly fitted, and was of a more sturdy and sophisticated type than the rusted bolt downstairs. Had he installed it out of fear for his own safety, I wondered, or to protect some item of value inside? My fingers had grown stiff with cold; I breathed on them and reminded myself to be patient – a steady hand was vital in the series of minute movements required to persuade a lock to yield without a key. Too much haste and you would break the mechanism or slice your fingers. A strange skill for a philosopher, my friend Philip Sidney used to say, though always in a tone of admiration – but then Sidney found it hard to imagine the life I had led before I met him. As the son of a noble family, he had been taught to duel as a boy by a celebrated fencing master; I had learned to fight with my fists on the streets of Naples.

I picked up additional skills not usually taught to Dominican friars during the two years I spent on the road north through Italy after I abandoned my order: passing nights in barns, or in taverns where men will put a knife in your ribs for a heel of bread, you learn to shift for yourself however you can. My fellow travellers in those years were not aristocrats and poets but criminals, charlatans and itinerants: strolling players, card sharps, defrocked priests, pedlars, jongleurs, whores and heretics. They knew a few tricks about how to survive, and were generous enough to pass them on. I thanked them silently as the lock finally submitted to the point of my knife with a gratifying click.

Paul had liked his surroundings austere; I almost smiled at the painstaking self-denial in evidence as I closed the door behind me. The room smelled of woodsmoke, damp and that stale odour of unwashed clothes that often clings to bachelors. I felt a stab of pity for him; he had allowed himself so little joy in his determination to please God, and look what it had brought him. Perhaps that was the saddest aspect of his death; he had never been a man who cared much for worldly advancement. If he had joined the Catholic League – those hardline religious conservatives determined to restore the purity of the Church, at any cost – it would have been from a genuine zeal to purge France of all that was unholy. Mind you, that was what the Inquisition in my country liked to claim too.

The main room contained only a wide desk under the window and a carved chest, of the kind used to store linen, in the opposite corner. The desk held an inkhorn, a pot containing three quills, a block of sealing wax and a small penknife; to the left of the inkhorn sat a rectangular wooden box, about a foot and a half long and half as much wide, its surface inlaid with intricate patterns in mother-of-pearl and ivory and fastened with a padlock. A mournful Virgin holding an infant with the face of an irascible old man hung on the wall opposite the window. The adjoining room was partitioned off by a curtain, which I drew back to reveal a space that hardly deserved to be called a bedchamber; more an alcove barely wide enough to hold a single bed. There was another, smaller casement here; I peered out to see that it opened on to the yard side of the house, where part of the ground floor jutted out in a sloping roof directly below the window. Above the bed Paul had fixed a heavy crucifix, with a tortured Christ gazing reproachfully, his neck twisted down to one side so that, if you were supine with your head on the pillow, his wounded eyes would stare right into you. *Dio porco*; imagine waking to that sight every morning. I knelt to look under the bed; at first I could only make out a chamber pot and some unidentified shape among drifts of dust. I stretched in, groping towards it until my fingers touched the edge of a wooden casket. I drew it out to find it was secured with a sturdy iron padlock. The keyhole was too small to accommodate the blade of my knife; I cast around the room in search of an alternative, but the best I could do was a poker in the fireplace, with which I forced the padlock until it snapped open and a collection of small items wrapped in cloth tumbled out on to the boards. I picked one up, intrigued; it was tied around with twine and gave off a faint odour of decay and alcohol. I unwrapped the bindings and dropped the object immediately, smothering a cry of disgust as I realised I was looking at a severed human finger, seemingly pickled to preserve it, though with dubious success. The flesh was blackened, the torn end of bone and sinew ragged and stringy. Why had Paul hidden such a thing? I tried to refold it in its cloth wrapping when I noticed a tiny paper label attached to the string. It read 'A. Briant'. The name sounded familiar; I searched the index of my memory as I replaced it in the box and picked up another bundle. This one rattled lightly; scrawled on its label was the name 'E. Campion'. Already guessing what I would find, I untied it gingerly and tipped the contents into my palm, wincing as I looked at a handful of bloody teeth.

The name Campion had sprung the lock of my memory; Father Edmund Campion had been a Jesuit missionary to England, caught and executed for treason four years ago by Queen Elizabeth's government. Alexander Briant was one of the missionary priests executed with him. It seemed Paul had been collecting relics of English martyrs, items highly prized by the English Catholic exiles in Paris, though the trade was illegal. I wrapped the teeth again, intending to push the whole grisly box back where I had found it, when the label of another packet caught my eye. I lifted it and read 'J. Gifford'. My stomach clenched as I untied the string holding it; the cloth weighed almost nothing. Inside was a lock of blond hair, matted with dried blood. I had known an English priest by the name of Gifford once; I had watched him die. It seemed a lifetime ago. The bloodied hair lay in the palm of my hand like a reproach, or a warning. I shivered. Whatever Paul was involved in was not my business; I needed to find what I came for and get as far away as possible. I had been too close to too many deaths, these past few years. I shoved the box back into the shadows under the bed and turned my attention to the desk.

The padlock on the ornamental casket proved easy enough to force; the lid opened to reveal a pile of papers, as I had supposed. I took out the first sheet; it was folded in half to make a pamphlet, and on the front was handwritten 'THE KING OF SODOM' in strident capitals. Beneath this headline was a crude sketch of a crowned and bearded figure bent double and wearing women's clothes, which he had hitched up to his waist to allow another man to take him from behind while wielding a flagellant's whip. I opened the paper; inside was a polemic against the licentiousness of the court, explaining in lurid detail that King Henri III of France could not get an heir because he wouldn't take his prick out of the Duke d'Epernon's arse for long enough. I turned the paper back to look at the drawing. I recognised the style, but the version I

28

had seen before was typeset and printed with a woodcut; one of the many anonymous handbills sold for a sou, thrust at you in the square outside Notre Dame by men who took care to keep their faces covered. You could find these pamphlets, discarded, blowing along the gutter near the colleges on the Left Bank. Even a cursory glance at this draft was enough to see that the author had conflicted feelings about the acts he described with such pious outrage; he had worked himself into such a pitch of righteous fury that in places his pen had scored right through the paper, yet it was impossible to disguise the relish in his lingering and explicit account of what the King and his *mignons* – those louche young nobles who hung about the court to fawn on him – were supposed to get up to in the royal bedchamber. Poor Paul, I thought again, if this were his work.

I lifted out the next paper to find another handwritten draft. The headline on the cover of this one ran: 'An Account of the Most Glorious Achievements and Military Successes of Our Great King Henri III'. Inside, the page was left blank, except for one word in minute letters at the bottom: *Rien*. I had to bite back a laugh; it seemed Paul had possessed a sense of humour after all. This one would have wounded the King far more than any number of drawings of him being mounted by his friends; he had always enjoyed courting notoriety but he could not bear to be thought a failure. It did not surprise me to find that Paul had been providing the copy for inflammatory handbills, given his affiliation with the Catholic League – though I had to wonder why he had kept these incriminating drafts, knowing that the punishment for printing or distributing such libel against the King was execution. I replaced the papers in the box. Perhaps that was exactly what had happened, but without the courtesy of a trial.

A sound from below – a shout, a door slamming – jolted me from my thoughts. I paused, straining to hear, right hand moving instinctively towards my dagger, until I was satisfied

29

that the sound had come from outside. I moved to the window and peered down, keeping to one side so that I would not be seen, but the street appeared to be empty. Again, I caught a faint smell of woodsmoke and glanced across to the small hearth opposite, where the remnants of a meagre fire lay cold in the grate. Paul had not given any indication during our brief conversation in the confessional that he believed himself to be in danger. Rather, he had spoken with the self-congratulating assurance of someone who considered himself favoured by the rising power. He had even hinted that the King was soon to fall. I wondered if he had had time to recognise his assailant before the blow struck, and whether the killer had waited around to see the bargemen pull him out of the water, or knew that he had been taken to the abbey. It would not take long before my presence at his deathbed leaked out; if that became known to whoever had wanted him dead, that person may fear I knew more than I should.

I picked up the poker and prodded the pile of ashes in the fireplace, jumping back as a sudden shower of sparks burst forth from a smouldering ember. The room was cold, yet it seemed Paul had lit a fire here recently; so small, to judge by the remnants, that it hardly seemed worth the trouble for the warmth it would offer. Two or more hours must have passed since the bargemen had brought him to the abbey; perhaps three, then, since he closed the door to these rooms for the final time, leaving the embers to burn themselves out. I crouched and poked further among the ashes, my pulse quickening as I uncovered a few blackened scraps, curling like charred leaves. So he had been burning papers. I hardly dared hope that anything legible might have survived, but I combed further through the cinders and at the very back of the hearth, where a draught must have blown it out of the flames' reach, I spotted a fragment that still showed patches of discoloured writing.

I drew it out and held it between thumb and forefinger, the edges falling away to dust as I lifted it closer to my face, barely breathing lest it disintegrate. Only a few words remained visible between the scorch marks, written in a strong, flowing hand. '. . . *to violate the sanctity of the confessional*', read one line, the remainder of the sentence blackened beyond recognition. '. . . *wrestled with my conscience . . .*' was visible in the line below. Followed by this: '. . . *what harm Circe intends you*'; a gap, scorched away, then '. . . *may God forgive me*'. The only other words I could make out with any certainty were those which caused my chest to tighten: '*Votre Majesté*'.

I stood, still pinching the scrap of paper, steadying myself as the blood pounded in my ears and my mind raced to make sense of these shreds. The first thing that struck me was that the hand was different from the pamphlets I had seen in the box, suggesting that one or the other was not written by Paul – unless he had taken the trouble to disguise his writing significantly, which was possible if he did not want to be associated with the libellous handbills. The reference to the confessional suggested that Paul was the author of the letter, and that he was trying to warn the King of some danger to him from whoever or whatever Circe may be. But why burn it? Perhaps he had had second thoughts about the risk to himself – to break the sacrament of confession would mean the end of his priesthood, not to mention the jeopardy to his immortal soul – or else he had already sent a more polished draft and wished to destroy any possibility of tracing it back to him. I tucked the brittle paper into the pocket sewn into the lining of my doublet; I doubted it would survive, but instinct told me I should keep hold of it. Paul had tried to burn this letter, shortly before he was killed; it was hard to believe the two were unconnected.

If Paul had been destroying incriminating documents, perhaps there were more stashed away in the box on the desk. I returned to it, but as I reached for the papers I caught again the sound of a door creaking and closing, softer but definitely inside this time, and below me. I held my breath and heard the unmistakable tread of feet on the stairs; two pairs, and a

31

muffled exchange in lowered voices. I closed the lid of the box and retreated as silently as I could into the alcove with the bed, pulling the curtain tightly across.

'Unlocked. I don't like that.' The speaker's voice was curiously throttled, as if it were trapped at the back of his throat. He rattled the latch and I heard the door close behind them.

'Perhaps he was in a hurry.' His companion's voice was cultivated, Parisian. There was a sliver of a gap between the curtain and the wall. I edged closer to see if I could glimpse them.

'You think he'd leave his door open for all-comers?' The first man clicked his tongue; the boards squeaked as he paced around the room. His movements sounded off-kilter, as if he walked with a lurching gait. Lame, perhaps. That might make things easier. I eased the catch of the casement free, as quietly as I could. 'Not he. Someone's got here first.'

'Who? Who could possibly know—' The other broke off suddenly; I felt the stillness of them, alert, breath held, only feet away. The faint sound of a board underfoot; the whisper of a weapon drawn from its sheath. One error of judgement here and I would find myself as skewered as Saint Teresa. I sensed them hesitate, deliberating where to strike – just long enough for me to push open the window and roll out at the exact moment a sword's point thrust through the curtain and buried itself deep in the straw mattress where I had been crouching.

I hit the protruding roof of the ground floor at an awkward angle, but dug my heels in enough to slow my fall, so that I was able to clutch at the edge and drop to the ground with a degree of control. A furious cry echoed from the window above, but I did not look up; instead I pulled my hood around my face, brushed myself down – bruises, nothing broken – and scrambled over the back fence into an alley. They would come looking for me in a few minutes and there were two of them, even if one was lame. I glanced left and right: a dead end, the only way out would take me into the street that ran perpendicular to the rue Macon. If I ran towards the river, I might be able to hide along the quay, but if they found me there, I would be trapped, and the dark water and deserted riverbank would be a gift to my pursuers. But if I tried to flee south, I would run straight into them as they turned the corner. I hesitated at the mouth of the alley, expecting to see them at any moment, when I noticed the laundress I had spoken to earlier unlocking the door of a house opposite. I hurtled up behind her just as she was about to close it; she gave a little scream and tried to slam the door in my face, evidently thinking she was about to be attacked, but I was too quick and jammed my boot into the gap.

'Catholic or Protestant?' I demanded, pointing at her.

'What?'

'Don't be alarmed, madame,' I hissed, cutting a glance over my shoulder. 'Are you Catholic or Protestant?'

She looked affronted. 'Catholic, of course.'

'God be praised. There are two Huguenots after me. In the name of the Blessed Virgin, give me sanctuary.'

She was so startled that she relaxed her hold on the door enough for me to push my way in and slam it behind me. I tumbled into a barely furnished room where two small children sat at a scrubbed wooden table, staring at me with their mouths open. I nodded to them, and looked around.

'Get in that corner. If they come near my family, I'll bloody kill you myself,' she muttered. 'What do they look like?'

'I don't know. One of them might be lame.' I retreated into the shadows behind a rickety cupboard.

'Lame? How slow do you run, then?'

One of the children giggled.

'The other one isn't. And they're armed.'

The amused expression vanished; she glanced towards the door, her mouth set tight.

Minutes passed; I heard the children jostling for a place at the window, and a cry from the street. Eventually the woman burst into laughter.

'Huguenots, you say?'

I stepped out, cautious. 'Have they gone? Is there something funny?'

'There were two of them, all right, marching up and down looking for someone. One in a cleric's robes. The other was a dwarf. Were they the ones?'

'They were in disguise,' I said, feeling ridiculous.

She made no effort to hide her smile, but her eyes were gently teasing. 'The dwarf disguise was very good.'

'God will reward you for your charity, madame.'

'I'm sure he will,' she murmured, eyeing the purse at my belt. I drew out a sou and tossed it to the taller of the children, who caught it deftly and beamed at me through the gap in his teeth. 'God be with you, monsieur,' she said, at the door, tucking a strand of hair under her cap. 'You can always take refuge here if you're menaced by dwarves again. I'm a widow,' she added, lowering her voice with a glance at the children, in case her meaning was unclear. I gave a brief nod, embarrassed, and turned towards home, one hand on my dagger, keeping to the centre of the street.

A man in cleric's robes, the woman had said. An educated, well-born priest, by his voice – a friend of Paul's, or an enemy? What had they been looking for? Whatever it was, it must be significant; they had immediately jumped to the conclusion that someone else had been looking for it too. 'Who could possibly know?' the one dressed as a priest had said; did he mean who would know Paul was dead, or something else? I reached inside my doublet and touched the charred fragment of paper with my fingertips. Was this what they had hoped to find? If so, my resolution not to involve myself further in Paul's murder was worthless; I was already up to my neck in it.

I returned to the Swan and Cross, still glancing behind to make sure I was not being followed. The fact that I saw no one in the streets made me all the more uneasy. The tavern was crowded now that night covered its patrons' entrances and exits. Someone had brought out a rebec and struck up a tune; the shrieking of girls and snatches of raucous song carried the length of the street. Gaston spotted me across the room and shoved his way through to intercept me at the door, blocking my view with his wide shoulders.

'Couple of fellers come round just now asking after you,' he said, lowering his voice. 'Said they had an urgent message for you. No one told them anything, so far as I know. Thought you should be warned.'

'A dwarf?'

'Eh?'

'Was one of them a dwarf?'

He laughed, and clapped me on the shoulder. 'What – family, is he?'

It was Gaston's great joke that all Neapolitans are stunted. This apparently never grew any less entertaining, no matter how often he repeated it – despite the fact that he stood only an inch or two above me himself. 'Taller'n you, anyway, mate.' He stopped laughing at the look on my face. He leaned in, his breath hot on my ear. 'These were soldiers, not dwarves. What've you done now, Bruno?'

'I'm not sure I know, exactly.'

A chill prickled up my spine. Word travelled fast in this city; every faction had eyes and ears everywhere. A dwarf and a priest were one thing; if someone was sending professional soldiers after me, the stakes were already higher than I had imagined, and I had no idea who might have sent them. King Henri had troops of Swiss guards under his command, but the Duke of Guise, leader of the Catholic League, had also mustered private forces of his own. It had become fashionable among the nobility to keep dwarves as servants or jesters, in imitation of the royal court. Both the soldiers and the men in Paul's rooms could have belonged to anyone.

I stayed at the Swan until late, drinking little, eyes fixed on the door as I lingered over a bowl of mutton stew that Gaston had insisted on adding to my growing bill, though my stomach was so tight with apprehension that I swallowed less than half of it. When, some time after midnight, he bellowed that he was locking up and the company reluctantly began to stir, I borrowed a lantern and drifted down the street in the wake of a group of students I half knew, all of them too poor to go on to a brothel, who invited me to someone's rooms for cards, eagerly brandishing a bottle of cheap *eau de vie* one of them had concealed beneath his cloak. I was briefly tempted, if only for the protection of their numbers, but I knew how these nights ended: the muddy light of dawn seeping through shutters, a dense head, furred mouth and always a lighter purse, regardless of the hands played. These boys were twenty; I no longer had the stomach for it. I declined and slipped away towards my own lodgings, though I am not sure they even noticed my absence as they reeled away in the torchlight, striking up another catch involving a country priest and a wayward shepherdess, arms slung around one another's shoulders. Someone would throw a chamber pot over them before they reached the end of the street.

Their song still rang in the air as I stopped at the house where I rented rooms on the top floor. I set down the lantern and struggled to unlock the street door with my left hand, dagger drawn in my right. While I was fumbling, two figures unpeeled and gathered shape and substance out of the shadows to either side. I had been so nerved for them that I was barely caught off guard; I stepped back, holding the blade out before me, levelling it between them. They acknowledged it with amused indulgence, as you might a child waving a stick. Each of them held a broadsword, pointed downwards and resting casually against his leg, though I knew the blade could take my head off with one practised stroke before I could get close enough to graze them.

'Are you the Italian they call Bruno?' The taller of the two spoke with a thick Provençal accent.

'Who is asking?'

He lifted his sword a fraction. 'I suggest you put that away, sir,' he said, nodding to my dagger. 'Keep things civilised. We don't want to disturb anybody, do we?' I followed his eyes upwards to the windows. It was true that I preferred not to wake my landlady, Madame de la Fosse, who already had her views on the desirability of a rumoured heretic as a tenant, and she had the hearing of a bat; the first sign of a scuffle and she would throw back the shutters, screaming for the night watch. Although perhaps that would be to my advantage in the short term.

Reluctantly, I sheathed the dagger. 'What do you want with me?'

'We just need you to come with us, sir,' said the second one, in an accent as rough as his colleague's. Clouds covered the moon and I could see little of their expressions in the flickering glow from the light on the doorstep; both were broad-faced and bearded, with grim mouths and unsmiling eyes. The 'sir' was, I presumed, wholly mocking. They wore no livery over their leather surcoats.

'Someone wants a word with you,' said the first, picking up my lantern. 'Won't take long.'

'Where are we going?' I asked, trying to sound calm, as we began walking towards the river, each of them a solid presence hemming me in, so close I could feel the pressure of their shoulders against mine on either side and smell their stale sweat. I knew these streets well enough in the dark, but there was no prospect of running. The one holding the lantern turned his head to offer a sideways grin with missing teeth.

'It's a surprise,' he said, breaking into a low laugh that was the opposite of reassuring.

THREE

'I tell you, he will not rest until he has my head on a spike in the Place de Grève.' Henri folded his arms and nodded vaguely out through the blue-black darkness towards the river, his face cratered with shadows in the torchlight. 'And you roasting on a pyre in the Place Maubert with the other heretics. Crackling like a pig on a spit,' he added, with relish, in case I had failed to picture it.

'Even the Duke of Guise must acknowledge that Your Majesty is God's anointed king,' I said carefully. I was still weak with relief from the realisation, as we approached its walls, that I was being escorted to the Louvre. Even as we twisted up a series of narrow windowless staircases, my fear did not loosen its grip until I emerged with my taciturn escorts on to this hidden rooftop terrace in the oldest part of the palace, under the shadow of the great conical turrets where, by the light of one guttering torch, I could make out the figure of the King pacing, swathed in an extraordinary gown of thick damask silk that must have taken half a convent a lifetime to embroider.

'Must he? *Ha!* Then someone had better explain that to him. Hadn't they, Claudette? Yes, they had.' He bent forward to kiss the quivering nose of the lapdog whose head protruded from the jewelled basket slung around his neck with a velvet ribbon. It yapped in protest; apparently it had not yet learned deference to its sovereign master. This was the newest fashion at court; one of the King's own innovations, he had been proud to tell me: now every courtier who wanted to please him sashayed through the palace with a small dog hanging beneath his chin. Whatever else may have changed in Paris since I had been away, the court's dedication to making itself ridiculous remained reassuringly steadfast.

'The Duke of Guise is of the opinion that, in this instance, God has made a mistake,' Henri continued, tickling the dog between its ears. 'Anyone who tolerates heretics makes himself a heretic, in his view. *Ergo*, I am now a heretic, because I gave the Protestants freedom to practise their religion in my kingdom.'

'Then you took it away again.'

There was no reprimand in my tone, but the words were enough. He rounded on me, nostrils flared. 'God's blood, Bruno – what choice do you think I had? France is rushing headlong into civil war, have you not noticed? The Protestants are massing armies in the south, the Catholic League holds key cities and Guise has turned most of Paris against me. You have no idea – agents of the League go about the city under-cover, swearing the loyalty of dull-brained guildsmen to those who would defend a unified Catholic France against heretics and libertines, when the time comes. Meaning me,' he added, for clarity, slapping his breast with the flat of his hand. The dog jumped in alarm. 'He has priests spouting propaganda against me from the pulpits every Sunday, declaring God's wrath on France for our lack of piety, and the people swallow it whole. *When the time comes* – what do you suppose that means?' He swept his hand out towards the rooftops; a trage-dian's gesture. 'The whole city is poised to rise up and overthrow me at one word from Guise – everyone from the pork butchers to the boatmen on the river, to say nothing of half the nobles at my own table. I fear for my life daily, Bruno, truly I do. But I fear more for France.' His voice trembled a little at the end; I had to admire his stagecraft.

'The people of France would not rise against their sovereign,' I said, aiming to sound soothing, though I was not convinced myself.

He gave a strangled laugh. 'You think not? William of Orange probably thought the same. I tell you, I have not had an untroubled night's sleep since he was murdered. On his own stairs!' He flung out his hands, as if the case were proved, then turned away to lean on the balustrade. The rain had eased, leaving a damp chill in the night wind; violet and silver clouds scurried across the moon, threatening to burst again before morning. Below us, the city lay in darkness. The King shivered and pulled his robe closer around him. 'This is all my brother Anjou's fault, the Devil take him. If he hadn't died last summer, I would not have had to name a Protestant as my successor. That's what threw the taper into the kindling. France won't stomach a Huguenot on the throne, even if Henri of Navarre is the nearest in blood.'

'It was extremely selfish of your brother to leave you in such a predicament.' I kept my face straight and stared out over the ridges of the roofs below. He turned to me slowly, his eyes narrowed. I wondered if I had misjudged. After a short silence, he let out a burst of laughter and rested a hand on my shoulder.

'Ah, how I have missed you, Bruno. No one else would dare talk to a king the way you do.'

Not enough to have troubled yourself to see me in over two months, I thought. To his face, I gave a tight smile. 'Your Majesty is only thirty-four, and the Queen is in good health. You may yet resolve the question of an heir without a civil war.' As I said the words, I thought of the drawing on Paul's pamphlet.

Henri looked at me with a strange expression, as if making

a difficult calculation. 'Well. Perhaps I may,' he said, with an air of enigma. 'My cock is the subject of much learned speculation, you know.' He patted his codpiece with mock pride. 'And I don't just mean the handbills that circulate in the street. I tell you, Bruno – Europe's most senior diplomats scribble frantic dispatches to one another about it. Whether it functions sufficiently for the task, whether it is the right size, whether it might be deformed or poxed – or is it perhaps that I don't know where to put it with a woman?' He gave a dry laugh. 'I ought to be flattered. How many men can boast that their members are the business of council chambers from the Atlantic to the Adriatic?' He scratched the dog's head absently.

'If it's any consolation,' I said, leaning on the parapet beside him, 'the same scrutiny attends the Queen of England and her private parts.'

'I suppose it must. God, to think my brother Anjou almost married her. Imagine having conjugal obligations to that dried-up old quim. Some would say death was a lucky escape.' He laughed again, but his heart was not in it, and his expression sobered. 'Elizabeth Tudor is the last of her line now, like me. Two dying royal houses. And her kingdom will be carved up by factions before she is cold in her coffin, just like mine.' He plucked down his sleeves, straightened the sparkling dog-basket around his neck; the dog let out a small whine in sympathy.

I watched Henri with an unexpected rush of pity. He was never meant to wear a crown, this king; he had a face made for decadence, not statecraft. The full pouting lips, heavy-lidded eyes, the long Valois nose and carefully trimmed triangle of beard all combined to make him, if not exactly handsome, then at least appealingly louche, if that was your taste. He would fix your gaze with a quirk of the eyebrow that always appeared somehow suggestive, even when he was discussing treaties. Even his adoring Italian mother was not blind to the way his effete manner was a gift to his enemies, most of all the supporters of the virile and pious Guise. But Henri was the only survivor of four sons: the last hope of the House of Valois.

'You should have stayed in London, Bruno,' he murmured, after a while.

I looked at him in disbelief. 'I would gladly have done so,' I said stiffly. 'It became impossible.' *You made it impossible*, I wanted to add. *You sent me there to keep me safe from the Catholic League, from those zealots who would bring the Inquisition and all its horrors to France. Then you abandoned me.*

'The Baron de Chateauneuf, you mean?' He waved this aside. 'I had to send him. We needed a robust ambassador who would stand up for France as a Catholic country. The previous ambassador was too concerned with being liked at the English court.'

I continued to hold his gaze; he gave a petulant shrug and looked away. 'Yes, all right, I did it to keep Guise happy. What do you want me to say? Just one of many compromises I have had to make, on my mother's advice. I must prove to France that I am a true Catholic, she insists, otherwise France will find herself a better one. Do you understand?'

'Chateauneuf is a fanatic. You must have known he would not tolerate a man like me under his roof.'

'I thought you might have found yourself a patron in London by then,' he said, still sulky. Then his expression changed. 'Or perhaps you did. There were concerns about you at the embassy, you know.' He lifted his head and gave me a sly look from under his lashes, his lip curled in a knowing smile. 'Some of the household seemed to think there was a breach of security.'

I kept my face entirely blank.

'It was suggested that private letters might be finding their way into the wrong hands.'

He left a pause to see how I would respond. If I have learned one thing in these past years, it is how to conceal every shift of emotion behind a face as neutral as a Greek mask when it matters. I merely allowed my eyes to widen in a question.

'It seems the old ambassador was not the only one who appeared over-familiar with English court circles. Your friendship with Sir Philip Sidney did not go unremarked, for instance. I heard you were sometimes his guest at the house of his father-in-law, Sir Francis Walsingham. Who is called Elizabeth's spymaster, as I'm sure you're aware.'

'Sir Philip and I talked only of poetry, Majesty. I barely knew Sir Francis.'

'Don't play me for a fool, Bruno.' He gripped my arm and his face loomed suddenly an inch from mine, his tone no longer flippant. 'I'm talking about secret letters between the Duke of Guise and Mary Stuart, and the English Catholics here who support her claim to the throne, sent using our embassy as a conduit. Elizabeth wrote to me. She said those letters were evidence of advanced plans for an invasion of England by Guise's troops, backed by Spanish money, to free Mary Stuart from gaol and give her the English throne. Whoever intercepted those letters at the embassy, Elizabeth said, probably saved her life.'

'God be praised for His mercy, then.'

He let go of me and stepped back, eyeing me for several heartbeats in silence. 'Amen, I suppose. Put me in a damned awkward position though.'

'You would have preferred it if Guise had succeeded?'

'Of course not!' He looked appalled. 'But how do you think it made me look? I have been striving for an alliance with England, despite my brother's death and the end of the marriage plan. I send expensive diplomatic missions to flatter the old cow into *entente*, and all the while there's a faction in my own country strong enough to raise an army against her. That I know nothing about! How can Elizabeth have any faith in me as an ally? It makes a mockery of my kingship.'

43

You do that all by yourself, I refrained from saying. 'But it can only inflame the situation to send an ambassador whose first loyalty is to your enemies and who hates all Protestants, including the English Queen.'

He slapped his hand down on the balustrade. 'God's teeth, Bruno – I do not pay you to teach me diplomacy.'

'You do not pay me at all at the moment. Majesty,' I added, holding his gaze. It was a gamble. Henri liked men of spirit who had the courage to speak frankly to him, but only up to a point. His eyes blazed.

'Do I *owe* you? Is that what you think?' He pointed a finger in my face; the dog yelped again. 'I sent you out of danger, at my own expense, and you repay me by taking money from the English to spy on my ambassador.'

'I thought you said those letters came from Guise.'

'Don't cavil, damn you. If you were opening his letters, you were reading everybody else's too. You don't know how hard I had to work to defend myself against the rumours that followed you, after you left.'

'Lies spread by my enemies.'

'*I* know that!' He threw his hands up. 'The people of Paris don't know it. All they hear is that their sovereign king, whom they already believe to be a galloping sodomite and friend to heretics, keeps a defrocked Dominican at his court to teach him black magic. Why do you think I bring you here like this—' he gestured to the night sky – 'in secret?'

'I never understood why I was considered such a threat,' I said mildly. 'Your mother keeps a Florentine astrologer known as a magician in her household, and the people forgive her that.'

'Oh, but the people love my mother,' he said, not bothering to disguise the bitterness. 'Her morals and her religion are beyond reproach. Even so, she's had to banish Ruggieri on occasion to quash gossip, you know that. He keeps his mouth shut at the moment, I assure you.' He grimaced. 'Look – I cannot give you back your old position at court, Bruno. I cannot risk any public association with you while my standing is so precarious – you must understand that. Recognise what you are.'

'I know what I am, sire. But I was also your friend, once.' I kept my eyes to the ground. A long silence spread around us. When I looked up, I was amazed to see tears in his eyes.

'And so you are still,' he said, a catch in his voice. He raised a hand as if to touch my face, but let it fall limply to his side. 'I miss the old days. Those afternoons shut away in my library with Jacopo, talking of the secrets of the ancients. Do you not think I would bring those days back, if I could?' He shook his head and the fat pearl drops in his ears scattered reflections of the torchlight. 'I don't know how it has come to this, truly. The people loved me when I first wore the crown. They crowded the streets to watch me ride by. The processions we used to have!' He turned to gaze fondly into the distance. 'My mother emptied the treasury putting on public entertainments to win their goodwill. And look how they now flock to Guise. Well, let them, filthy ingrates. See if he would give them fountains of wine in the public squares.' His face twisted. The dog let out a mournful whine, as if sensing the mood.

They loved you only because you were not your brother Charles, I could have said. And they cheered him when he was first crowned too, because he was not your brother Francis, and Francis, because he was not your father, the last Henri. That is what people do. Those who now say they love Guise do so mainly because he is not you. Say what you will about the people of Paris, their capacity for optimism seems bottomless, despite all the lessons of history. Or perhaps it is just an insatiable desire for novelty.

'How does your royal mother, anyway?' I asked, hoping to rouse him from self-pity.

'Oh *God*,' he said, with feeling. 'Still convinced she wears the crown, of course. If she's not haring around the country on some diplomatic mission of her own devising, she's leaning over my throne dictating policies in my ear. I fear I shall never escape her shadow. But she refuses to die.' He broke off, looking shocked at himself. 'God forgive me. You know what I mean. She's wracked with gout, but she won't even give up hunting, and she still has more stamina for *la chasse* than any of the men who ride out with her. Sometimes I think I should have sent her to a convent long ago.'

'I cannot picture the Queen Mother retiring without a fight. She lives for political intrigue.' You'd have lost your throne years ago without her leaning over it, I thought.

'True. And she's far better suited to it than I am,' he said, with rare candour. 'She positively thrives on it. Her chief advantage to me is that the Duke of Guise is terrified of her.' He broke into a sudden grin. 'In her presence he's like a boy caught stealing sweetmeats. So I have to keep her around – she's the only one who can negotiate with him. Why can't *I* have that effect on my enemies, Bruno?' The plaintive note had crept back.

If it had been a serious question, I might have replied: because you possess neither your mother's iron will nor her formidable grasp of statesmanship. If Catherine de Medici had been born a man, she would rule all of Europe by now. Instead she has had to make do with ruling France these past twenty-six years from behind the throne of her incompetent sons.

'Few things strike fear into a man's heart like an Italian mother, sire,' I said, instead, but he did not smile.

'All I ever wanted was to bring accord between my subjects, whatever their church, so there would never be another massacre like Saint Bartholomew's night.' He wrung his hands, fully immersed in his own tragedy. 'Now look at us. Three Henris, tearing France apart between us. And my greatest sorrow is that all this strife has parted me from you. I can count the number of true friends I have on the fingers of one hand, and you are among them. Embrace me, Bruno. Mind Claudette.'

He held his arms out to me; gingerly, leaning across the dog, I accepted his embrace. A gust of perfume made my eyes water: ambergris and cedar wood. You learned quickly to take much of what Henri said with a heavy dose of scepticism, but there was no doubting his sincerity at the moment he said it. And it was true that we had been friends – in so far as one can be friends with a king. He may have been weak and self-indulgent, but Henri of Valois was a great deal more intelligent and intellectually curious than his subjects supposed. If there was truth in the rumours about him and his *mignons*, I could not testify to it; he had always treated me with courtesy, and often with the deference of a pupil to his teacher. All that was over, unless I could find a way to have this excommunication lifted, and with Paul dead, my hopes were not high.

I felt him pat my shoulder, just as a wet tongue rasped across my jaw. I jumped back, staring at the King, my hand to my face.

'Claudette, you *are* a naughty girl. You *are*,' he chided the dog, with a mischievous glint, the tears all vanished. 'Well, I am for my bed. Or someone's bed, anyway.' He flashed me a wink, followed by an ostentatious yawn; at the edge of my vision I saw the guards stirring. Was that it, then? Had I been dragged here in the middle of the night so that he could unburden himself of this half-hearted self-justification and wake feeling he had dealt with the problem of Bruno? Beyond the wavering circle of torchlight, the guards hovered at the end of the terrace, uncertain whether to approach, dark shapes in a thicker darkness. Henri pulled his robe closer around himself and the dog, flicked a hand towards the soldiers and moved a couple of paces towards the stairs. 'These gentlemen will see you home,' he said, without looking back at me. 'They belong to my personal bodyguard. Forty-five strong men and true, every one of them scrupulously chosen from the provinces to ensure he has no affiliations in Paris except to me. Simple, loyal and boasting a good sword arm. And I pay them handsomely for their loyalty, don't I, boys?'

The soldiers glanced up and mumbled something before dropping their eyes again to the ground.

'They'll take good care of you. Well, thank you again for coming.' It was the same blithely dismissive tone I'd heard him use to foreign diplomats and government functionaries whose names he'd forgotten. He swept his robe out behind him in a whisper of silk.

'Will I see you again?' I blurted as he reached the stairs, despising myself for it. I sounded like a needy lover.

Henri turned and considered me, as if an idea had just occurred to him. 'You know, Bruno, there is *one* thing you could do for me, if you are still eager for my patronage?'

I bowed my head. 'Your Majesty knows I would be pleased to serve in any way you see fit.'

A satisfied smile creased his face. My jaw tensed. I had walked into this; he had stage-managed the entire scene so that, afraid he was about to leave me with nothing, I would clutch gratefully at whatever chance he offered. I already knew I was not going to like his proposition.

'Good. You there – hold this.' He untied the basket from around his neck and handed it, with its whimpering contents, to the nearest guard, who almost dropped it in surprise. '*Careful* with Claudette – she doesn't like rough handling. Now, stand over there. Watch the stairs.' He motioned them back to their post, steering me with the other hand to the furthest corner of the balcony. I braced myself and tried to assemble an expectant smile.

'Guise means to destroy me. Sooner or later, I fear he will succeed in having me deposed or murdered, whichever proves cheaper.' He leaned forward to clasp me by both shoulders, his face uncomfortably close, his tone conspiratorial. Through

48

the perfume, I could smell the fear on him; after all the posturing, this was real. A succession of unpleasant possibilities chased one another through my head. What was he going to ask of me? Assassinate Guise? It would not be beyond him. Henri pulled at an earring and pressed his lips together until they disappeared. He seemed to be fishing for the right words. 'These priests I mentioned – the ones he sets on to preach against me.'

'What about them?'

'One was a particular thorn in my side – virulent little fellow at Saint-Séverin. Gave me a thorough roasting last Sunday – the hour is coming for the godly citizens of Paris to purge the city of her heretic king, all that.' He let go of me, making a rolling motion with his hand to indicate the monotony of the theme. 'Even the poor harvest is down to my debauchery, apparently.'

I concentrated all my efforts on keeping my face steady. 'I know. I was there. He preached for four hours.'

'Did he really?' He looked at me sidelong, tilted a plucked eyebrow. 'How extraordinary. Even I wouldn't want to talk about my peccadilloes for four hours. I didn't hear it myself, but I have people who keep me abreast of these things. It was the closest any of Guise's puppets have come so far to inciting a mob, I'm told. Dangerous, at any rate.'

I nodded. In this, at least, he was not mistaken; there had been a new mood among the congregation after Paul's sermon: restive, pent-up, angry, a nest of hornets needing only one small prod to explode. It was a miracle there had been no violence; if a Protestant had passed by and happened to say a wrong word, he'd have been torn apart.

'And?' I prompted, since Henri had fallen silent again.

He examined his manicure with apparent indifference. 'It would seem he was murdered yesterday. I'd like you to find out who did it.'

'Me?' I stared at him, wondering if it was a trap.

49

His gaze flickered upwards and rested briefly on me. 'The streets are already alive with rumours that he was killed on my orders, in revenge for his sermon. Guise will seize on this and fan the flames – it could tip the balance of feeling in the city. The League has people wound so tight, it would take only the slightest provocation to spark a riot or another massacre. An attack on a priest is a direct attack on the Church – people are superstitious about that sort of thing, and it will be seen as further proof of my disregard for the Catholic faith. I assume that's why he did it.'

'Who?'

He frowned, irritated. A nerve twitched in his cheek. 'Keep up, Bruno – you're supposed to be the finest mind at my court. Guise did it, obviously, to inflame the people against me.'

'Killed one of his own supporters?' I could not quite disguise the doubt in my voice. It was a plausible explanation, but less convincing than the simpler version, which was that Henri had done exactly what the rumours claimed. I thought of the burned scrap of letter inside my doublet: the words *Votre Majesté*. The same cold sensation tightened my throat again.

'Precisely.' Henri rubbed the back of his neck, stretching from side to side. 'He can find himself twenty more hellfire preachers like that one. But the chance to lay the murder of a priest at my door – that serves him beautifully. Wouldn't that sway any pious citizens unsure about where their loyalties should lie in the event of a coup? So, you see, I need to clear my name before Guise tortures some poor wretch into saying publicly that I put him up to it. I want you to find the man who did this, with evidence that will convict him before all Paris. Justice must be seen to be served. If you can tie the killer to Guise, all the better.'

'You don't ask much.' I moved away to lean against the balustrade. 'With respect, sire – why me?'

He smiled. 'Ah, my Bruno. Do you think Francis Walsingham

50

is the only one who has informers at his beck and call? You kept yourself busy in England, I hear. It seems you have quite the knack of sniffing out a murderer.'

Sidney used to use the same turn of phrase, I recalled – as if I were a trained wolfhound.

'Your Majesty has enough lapdogs, surely.' I returned the smile through my teeth, while my mind ran through a list of all the people who might have been spying on me for Henri over the past three years. I wondered what else he knew, and how he might choose to use it. 'Besides, if you believe this killer belongs to the Duke of Guise's circle, how am I supposed to get near him? They all know me for an enemy.'

'I dare say you'll find a way, Bruno. You could pretend you are looking for a new patron. Or claim you wish to be reconciled to the Church. That might get his attention.'

He held my gaze, unwavering, that smile still playing around his lips.

'Guise finds you interesting,' he added. 'He always has. I'm sure you can talk your way into his confidence.'

It was difficult to tell when Henri was mocking; he tended to smirk even when he was sincere. Did he know anything of my conversation with Paul, or was his reference to reconciliation mere coincidence? And if he did know, had he learned it from a letter found in Paul's lodgings or on his battered body? I thought again of the priest and the dwarf, and who might have sent them.

'Guise is not a fool,' I said.

'Neither am I.' His expression hardened. 'I won't force you to do this, Bruno. I'm offering you an opportunity to return to my service. It's the only position I have available, so it's your choice.' He turned his back to make the point: I guessed that if I refused, I could say goodbye to any prospect of future patronage. Spots of rain blew against my face. I tried again.

'I'm not convinced I am the man for this job, Your Majesty.'

'Please yourself, then.' He affected indifference and moved

51

towards the door, before glancing over his shoulder. 'Oh, a funny coincidence – almost slipped my mind. A friend of yours from England called on me a while back. Wanted to sell me a book.'

He knew immediately from my face that he had hit his mark.

'A man with no ears?' I asked. 'In August, was it?'

'No ears? A common criminal, you mean? Certainly not. Goodness, what company have you been keeping, Bruno?' He feigned shock. 'No, this was last summer, more than a twelve-month past. An exceptionally pretty boy. Ah, I see you know who I mean.' His lips curved slowly into a smile. He had saved his best card till last. I cursed him for it silently.

'And, what . . .?'

'The guards sent him on his way at first. There are so many hawkers at the gates, as you may imagine. But this one was remarkably persistent. Came back day after day, saying you'd told him to bring me this volume. Claimed it was both valuable and inflammatory. Eventually Ruggieri heard about it. He has spies all over the palace.' He rolled his eyes, to show that this was one more trial he was obliged to endure. My heart dropped. For more than a year I had been clinging to one last shred of hope that the book in question might have found its way to the court in Paris. To learn that it should have come so far, only to fall into the hands of Cosimo Ruggieri, that Florentine serpent, was galling. He would never give it up willingly to me.

'Ruggieri brought the boy to you?'

'Of course not. You think he'd get his hands on a book like that and offer it to me? I knew nothing of it until later. But it seems he was sufficiently convinced that he persuaded my mother to buy it. You know how easily she's seduced by the prospect of anything esoteric.'

'It was a book of magic, then?'

'Ruggieri seemed to think so. He talked her into paying

fifty écus for it. I suspect she was robbed. According to her, it's written in cipher – meaningless, unless you know how to read it. Your young friend must be laughing himself sick now, to think he's duped everyone twice over.'

Twice over. 'Did you meet him?' I asked, trying to keep any trace of eagerness from my voice. Henri gave me a sly smile.

'Alas, no, though I wish I'd had the pleasure. Ruggieri took him directly to the Tuileries to see Catherine. She only told me about it afterwards. Well, it turned out—' here he widened his eyes, relishing the performance – 'this boy wasn't a boy at all – imagine! Ah, but you knew that. No – she was apparently a girl trying to disguise herself. But quite beautiful either way, I'm told. She swore you had insisted I would want the book. That was what piqued their interest.' He watched me carefully. I said nothing. 'Lover, was she?'

'Acquaintance.' I clenched my jaw.

Henri laughed. 'You're a most adept liar, Bruno, like all Dominicans.'

'I am no longer a Dominican.'

'But you've learned their lessons well. Did you give her the book as a love-token?'

'I did not give it to her at all.'

'So she stole it from you? I did wonder.' He laughed softly. 'Bruno outwitted. Well, well. A most resourceful young woman, by the sound of it. Pity she disappeared. I asked my secretary to make enquiries but no luck so far. Perhaps I should ask him to try a little harder.'

'If the Queen Mother would let me examine the book—'

'I'll tell you what, Bruno,' he said, all brisk and amiable, 'you can see the book when you bring me some information about this priest. And perhaps by then there'll be news of your girl as well. How is that for a deal?'

I took a deep breath and bowed. 'I am yours to command, Majesty.'

'I do hope so. I have faith in you, Bruno. Don't let me

down.' He patted my shoulder, his attention already drifting now that he had what he wanted. 'His name was Père Paul Lefèvre, by the way. The dead priest.'

'I know. I knew him.'

'Oh?' He brushed raindrops from his cheek and looked at me, surprised. 'Well, that should give you an advantage, then.'

'Did you?'

'What?'

'Know him? Did he . . .' I hesitated, 'ever correspond with you, perhaps?'

Henri frowned, as if he didn't understand the question. 'Of course not. You think I have time to exchange letters with every malicious little shit-flinger?'

'I only wondered if he might have written to you,' I said, choosing my words carefully. 'Urging you to repent, warning you, something of that sort.'

He snorted. 'I might have given him some credit if he'd had the courage to address me directly. But they're cowards, these Guise lickspittles. Let's get out of this rain.'

One of the guards picked up the torch from the wall bracket and they followed us in to the staircase at a respectful distance. Our shadows flickered like giant carnival grotesques over the clammy walls as we spiralled down.

'He was killed outside Saint-Victor, so I was told,' Henri said, as we reached the first landing, taking out a key to unlock a small door set into the wall. A secret way back to his chambers, no doubt – this old part of the Louvre was full of hidden passages, as if it had been built expressly for spying and adultery. 'I'd start there if I were you. I think we can safely say I don't have many supporters among the religious orders. Those friars are all in Guise's pocket.'

I nodded, and made a non-committal noise. I still had no idea whether the King was lying to me; I hoped he did not intend to direct my steps throughout. I had accepted a poisoned chalice, however I chose to look at it, and my motives for doing so were precisely the two things that had undone me before – a book and a woman. *That* woman. I should have been wiser.

Henri held out his hand so that I could bow and kiss his signet ring, a gentle reminder of his power to command. 'One last thing,' he said, pausing in the doorway. 'My mother's putting on one of her grand entertainments next Friday. Improve morale. If our popularity's flagging, put on a show – you know what she's like. Remind people of the old days. You must come.'

'I thought I couldn't be seen at court?'

'Ah, but that's the beauty of it – you won't be. It's a masked ball. Everyone will be in costume, faces hidden, no one will have the faintest idea who you are. Say you'll come. Her *women* will perform too, if you need more persuading. I'd wager you don't see anything like that at Elizabeth's court.' He poked the tip of his tongue between his teeth and wiggled it, an impish glitter in his eyes.

I could think of few places I would feel more exposed than the Tuileries palace during a masked ball, but the door had closed behind him and the key turned before I could protest. His departure seemed to suck all the force from the air; I felt my body sag with the weight of my tiredness. If the guards had allowed me, I would have curled up in a corner of the stone staircase and slept right there.

The ghost of Henri's perfume followed me down the stairs. I left feeling deeply uneasy on several counts, hoping that I had not just made a pact to disguise a murder for my own advantage.

FOUR

I woke late the next morning, opening my eyes to a dusty grey light with a lingering sense of dread. Easing myself on to my elbows, I registered the bruises along my shoulder and hip from my plunge the day before, but it took a moment longer for my mind to struggle through the fog of sleep until I could be sure that I had not dreamed my nocturnal audience with the King and its unwelcome conclusion.

So she had fled to Paris, as I had suspected. Sophia Underhill, the woman I had known in Oxford and Canterbury. The King was right; she had bested me, and the memory of it still burned. Like a fool, I had thought myself proof against the wiles of women; the self-discipline I had learned in thirteen years as a Dominican served me well enough to withstand the cynical and obvious seductresses of the French court, but nothing had prepared me for a woman like Sophia. Educated, spirited, hungry for life, knowledge, independence, she had found herself ceaselessly frustrated by the constraints placed on her by her sex. Life had not been kind to her, and those scars had lent her a lean and wary look, and an edge of ruthlessness in her determination not to be duped. She made it a matter of principle to strike first, before you could touch her; she trusted no one. That was a bitter lesson, and one I had learned too late. I had done my best to excise her from my heart and my memory, but the agitation I now felt at the possibility that she might still be in Paris suggested I had not succeeded. I tore a comb through my hair and examined my face in the glass to judge how much I had aged since she last saw me, all the while cursing her under my breath. Now I would walk every street searching the crowds for her face, despite myself.

Outside, the rain had relented but a thick mist lay over the streets, rising in curlicues from the river; it would not burn off now, with the air so cold and dank. Resting one hand on my dagger beneath my cloak and darting frequent glances over my shoulder, I followed the rue Saint-Jacques north towards the river, picking my way through hoof-churned mud and waterlogged wheel-ruts as the damp seeped through the soles of my boots. A bell tolled sullenly nearby; students hurried between the faculties of the Sorbonne, urgent voices carrying out of the mist before they emerged like rooks, robes snapping around dirt-spattered ankles, deep in earnest debate. I kept my head down, but my senses alert. No one appeared to pay me any attention, for which I was grateful.

The church of Saint-Séverin squatted on the corner of Saint-Jacques and rue des Prêtres, one street away from the river, a sprawling mongrel of styles and stones jumbled together over four centuries. Gargoyles leered down from its buttresses. I was surprised to find a crowd of at least a hundred gathered in the churchyard, clustered around a tombstone on which a man with grey stubble and fiery eyes stood shouting with his legs planted wide and a fist raised. I wondered first if he was mad, but as I drew closer I could hear his voice ringing out clear and purposeful, as if he were accustomed to oratory; some among his audience were clutching sticks and pokers and bellowing their agreement. The mood felt as edgy and dangerous as it had the previous Sunday, after Paul's sermon.

'The House of Valois believe they can defy all the laws of

God and man without consequence,' he cried, to an appreciative roar. 'For years they have been stained with incest and murder, sorcery and heresy.' (More roaring.) 'Now our king allows heretics to flourish in France and we all know what is coming, don't we, my brothers and sisters?' (A frantic chorus of agreement.) 'When the Huguenot Navarre is king, the Protestants will take their revenge for Saint Bartholemew's night. They will rise up and cut us down in our homes. The streets of Paris will run red with Catholic blood, yours and mine, brothers and sisters!' (A scream of 'God have mercy' from a woman in the throng.) 'God has turned his face from France. Our harvests have failed, our armies are defeated, children and widows starve in the gutters. And what right have we to expect otherwise, when we allow ourselves to be governed by a king who is a blasphemer, a sodomite and a murderer, and his witch mother?'

The crowd almost lost control, roaring and brandishing their weapons; I stepped back in alarm as a man near me swiped a butcher's cleaver through the air. I began to wish I had stayed away; there would be blood spilled before this was over.

'Our dear curé, Père Lefèvre, has been murdered in cold blood for daring to speak out against the decay and corruption of the royal line. Thus the Valois show their contempt for the Church, for the laws of God and for human life. There will be no justice for him unless we the people demand it. We must march on the Louvre! Justice for Père Lefèvre!'

The crowd erupted in a cacophony of righteous fury; 'Death to the King!' and 'Justice for Père Lefèvre!' rang in the damp air. I took the opportunity to scurry away to the church. The main door was locked, but I followed a path around the back and found a side door that had been forgotten. It was a relief to step into the cool gloom of the empty nave. Despite the mist outside, a pearly light filtered through the high windows, painting faint jewel colours over the delicate arches of the vaults and the worn faces carved on the capitals. Here the air was cold and clear; the mineral smell of old stone cut through lingering traces of beeswax and stale incense. It seemed a lifetime ago that I had listened to the echo of my footsteps on these same stones on my way to corner Paul in his confessional. The dust swirling in ribs of light might have hung in the air for centuries. I stood before the altar, casting around as if I had lost something, until I attracted the attention of a young curate crossing one of the side aisles, a red-haired man in his mid-twenties with a preoccupied air and a tic in his left eye that gave the impression he was frantically winking at me.

'The church is closed, monsieur. How did you get in?' He sounded frightened.

'I'm not one of them,' I said, jerking my thumb towards the door. 'I was a friend of Père Lefèvre.'

'May God have mercy on his soul,' he muttered, crossing himself. 'A very sad business. But I can't help you. The doors are supposed to be barred until they disperse.' He chewed his lip and pulled at a thread on the cuff of his cassock.

'I only wondered if anyone knew what had happened. I heard him preach on Sunday. It's been a terrible shock.'

The young curate bit his thumbnail. 'I understand there was an accident.' His gaze flicked past me to the pillars of the ambulatory and the recesses behind. 'He was attacked outside the city walls, they said.'

'That doesn't sound like an accident.'

Another sideways glance. 'I don't know any more than that.'

'He seemed anxious recently. Something was troubling him.' I left this hanging, neither quite a question nor a statement. This young man, for all his twitching, appeared shrewd; if he worked with Paul every day, he would surely have noticed any unusual behaviour.

Recognition sparked in his eyes for a moment, before it was replaced by the shadow of suspicion.

'*Who* did you say you were?'

I searched his eyes again. A man in a priest's robes, the laundress had said. Not this one; the voice was wrong. But there would be other curates here, potentially his friends or confederates.

'I've known Paul – Père Lefèvre – for a long time. Before he was ordained. We were at the Sorbonne together.'

'Before he joined the League, then.' His tone gave nothing away. I had the sense that he was testing me. I decided to take a further risk.

'Yes. Back when he was still human.'

The young curate's face visibly relaxed. 'I did not have that pleasure. I have only been here six months.' He fixed me with a look that seemed intended to convey what he felt he could not voice. 'I don't think I have seen you here before?'

'I did not attend often. I found Paul's sermons increasingly hard to swallow.'

'You were not alone there.'

Little by little, I thought, I could coax some truth out of him. 'He was a difficult man to get along with,' I said.

He shrugged. 'He was sincere in his beliefs, at least.'

'Not in itself a virtue. The Pharisees were sincere. Luther and Calvin were nothing if not sincere.'

'True.' He liked this; a faint smile chased across his lips. He glanced past me again, down the aisle towards the door, and dropped his voice another notch. 'I say nothing against the League, you understand. They may be right on some points. Many points, even. But I believe a priest's role is to preach the word of God, and to bring harmony where there is discord, not to fuel more discord. Our duty is the cure of souls, and there is a high price to pay for disregarding that.'

'And you think Paul paid that price?' I said.

The twitch in his eye intensified and his face closed up. 'You have heard the crowd out there. They have already delivered their verdict. I'm afraid I must ask you to leave now, monsieur, so that I can lock the doors.' He paused as another animal roar rose up from the churchyard. 'When they are inflamed, they tend to break things.'

He turned and began to walk away through the ambulatory. I hurried after him as he slipped between the rows of carved columns, and caught at his sleeve.

'But you *had* noticed that he seemed troubled lately, Father?'

He walked on a few more paces then stopped and turned to face me, anxiety knotting his features. 'I don't know who you are, but for the sake of Saint-Séverin, leave this alone. Let us mourn him quietly. His death is tragedy enough without it becoming more ammunition for one side or the other.'

'It is already too late to escape that, I fear.' I gestured in the direction of the noise outside. 'Please – if you know anything about his death, it may help to prevent more violence.'

He regarded me a moment longer, then drew me by the elbow into an unlit side chapel, out of sight.

'You are right that he was not himself lately,' he said, in a voice that barely reached a whisper. 'It began no more than a month ago. He seemed all of a sudden – uncertain.'

'About what?'

'Everything.' He circled a hand to encompass the chapel, the altar, the crucifix above it. 'He grew more and more withdrawn – I might almost say fearful. He was often absent – he turned up to celebrate Mass, but between times none of us knew where he was. Once he stopped me and demanded out of nowhere to know why I had desired to be ordained, and if I still felt the same.' He shook his head. 'I had witnessed something similar with a fellow ordinand when I was in the seminary. If it had been anyone else, I would have said . . .' He let the sentence tail off.

'That he was losing his faith,' I offered. I had seen it too, when I was taking holy orders; no one who has entered the religious life could fail to recognise a crisis of belief in a brother. 'But it did not show in his sermons.'

The young curate's eyes narrowed. 'I thought you said you did not attend service here?'

'I came on Sunday. He invited me in person.'

He weighed this up and nodded. 'You are right. It was quite the opposite, in fact – the more he seemed to be unravelling in private, the more of a demagogue he became in the pulpit. As if he could drown out his doubts by shouting his convictions in public.'

'And you have no idea what prompted this – unravelling? Was there a confrontation, perhaps?'

A guilty flicker across his face; the eye tic quickened. I waited.

'Four weeks ago,' he said, so quietly the words barely escaped his lips, 'the first day of November, we had celebrated the Mass of All Souls. I stayed late after the service to clear up and lock away the silverware. I thought everyone had left, but when I came back to the ambulatory, I heard raised voices from inside this chapel. Père Lefèvre was arguing with someone.'

'Did you hear what they said?'

'Père Lefèvre called him Judas. The other man laughed, and said Lefèvre should be more careful with his words. I wanted to get home but I didn't want them to think I'd been listening, so I made an obvious noise outside and they fell silent immediately. They must have thought they were alone. The other fellow slipped away down one of the side aisles and Lefèvre walked out and tried to greet me as if nothing had happened. But I could tell he was upset.'

'Did you see the man he was arguing with?'

'I did not catch sight of his face, but I saw what he wore.' He hesitated, biting his lip again. 'The black habit of the Augustinians.'

'A friar from Saint-Victor, then?'

He seemed about to reply when I thought I caught a slight movement outside the chapel; I whipped around, but when I poked my head out, there was no one in sight in either direction. The curate had heard it too; his eyes darted around the walls like a cornered animal.

'You must leave now. I have to lock the church.'

He chivvied me out into the damp air. When I turned the corner by the apse, I saw that the crowd had grown; people stood on tombs and jostled for position along the wall as the man with the stubble, his voice now hoarse, whipped them on to cries of bloody vengeance against the King. The mood had darkened; they brandished makeshift weapons and turned black stares on those who did not join in with the chorus of slogans.

'Death to the House of Valois,' I muttered, to placate a murderous-looking blacksmith who was eyeing me while pounding a hammer into his fist. The mob had knotted tightly around the churchyard gate; it would be impossible to fight my way through without injury. I knew how these protests ended, too; shop windows smashed, carts and houses set on fire, people bloodied and wounded in the confusion; then royal troops called out to quell the crowd, shots fired, more injuries or even deaths, which would stoke the anger further. I only wanted to get away as quickly as possible. I decided I would have to climb over the wall, though it was hard to see a place where it was not jammed with eager spectators. I glanced to my left and noticed a tall man of about my own age standing on the fringe of the crowd, his arms folded, watching the growing frenzy with an air of detachment. His clothes were expensively tailored, his neat pointed beard and chestnut hair carefully barbered, making him conspicuous in this rabble of rough-clad tradesmen and apprentices. I wondered if he was an informer. He glanced across and caught my eye with a frankness that implied recognition. I half-expected him to address me, but his look seemed neither friendly nor hostile; he merely observed me, making no attempt to hide it, before returning his attention to the man

63

still delivering his impassioned speech from the plinth. Unease needled up the back of my neck. A quick check through my memory assured me that I did not know his face, though he had seemed to know me. I turned and walked briskly the way I had come, away from the mob, conscious of the stranger's eyes following me until I was out of sight.

It was a relief to escape the churchyard; the mood of the crowd promised violence before too long. I realised I had not eaten since the night before and my stomach was pinched with hunger. On the corner of rue Saint-Jacques I bought a galette in a greasy paper from a street vendor and demolished it in two bites. The noise from Saint-Séverin carried through the chilly air; the vendor shook his head and began to pack up his wares, anticipating a riot. Over my left shoulder, the façade of Notre Dame gazed downriver towards the Louvre, serene and implacable on its island.

The rabble and its leader clearly held the King responsible for Paul's death, or were content to use it as an excuse, though I concluded that I had no choice but to proceed as if Henri were telling the truth: that he had nothing to do with the murder and that the Duke of Guise, having encouraged Paul to attack the King in his sermon, had then had him murdered with the sole purpose of inflaming further outrage against the House of Valois. If that were the case, it meant I was looking for evidence that would link the murderer to Guise, who already had more than enough reason to want me dead, if he too suspected that I had been instrumental in disrupting his plans to invade England. Guise had no firm proof that I had intercepted those letters in London, but that hardly mattered; since I was the only known enemy of the Catholic Church living in the French embassy at the time the conspiracy was uncovered, it hardly took advanced powers of reasoning to point the finger in my direction. As I had already observed, Guise was no fool. If the Duke found out I was trying to expose him a second time, he would have my balls roasted on a skewer, while the King looked the other way and studied his manicure. In that light, it became clearer why Henri had asked me to undertake this business and not one of his usual fixers: he considered me expendable.

I passed under the Porte de la Tournelle and paused in the shelter of the tower wall to wipe my forehead where the mist had condensed in cold droplets on my hair and brows. Behind me, under the shadow of the arch, I thought I glimpsed someone else stopping too. I twisted around, but saw only the usual stream of hawkers and goodwives, mules and hand-carts, ragged children and dogs, all spattered with mud and weighed down with bales of cloth, coils of rope, barrows of vegetables or baskets of eggs, making their way in and out of the city to barter or beg. No one obviously loitering or watching me; and yet, after nine years of living in exile, one eye always open for anyone who might want to arrest me or knife me in a back alley, I had developed a finely tuned instinct for being followed, and now it quivered like a cat's whiskers. I pulled up the hood of my cloak and moved on along the road away from the Porte, straining to catch any unexpected movement through the grey air.

The abbey church of Saint-Victor reared up in the distance behind its boundary wall and orchards, its spire a bony finger poking through a shroud of low-lying mist swirling up from the river. A lone crow called into the empty sky, as if announcing my arrival. I shivered, wondering if the night's rain had washed Paul's blood away from the track along the bank behind the abbey, by that small door in the back wall. Now there was a man in a friar's habit to add to the picture, and I wished the curate's testimony had not pointed me here again.

Saint-Victor – or at least its opulent library – had become a kind of sanctuary for me since my return to Paris. Four years ago, before I left for England, the old abbot had been pleased to grant me free access to the library, despite the misgivings of some of his brothers over my writings, but that was when I had the distinction of being a Reader at the Sorbonne and personal tutor of philosophy to the King, before the rumours of magic trailed after me. The new Abbé was deeply conservative in matters of religion and learning, a public supporter of Guise and the Catholic League; though Frère Guillaume Cotin, the librarian, had welcomed me back as a friend, we had kept the arrangement between ourselves. But I had come to depend on the library, and not merely because it would be impossible for me to finish my next book without access to its manuscripts. In all the turbulence of the last few months, I had come to find in its stillness and its smell of old books, polished wood and candles, a comforting sense of order. I did not want to lose my one refuge in Paris, nor did I wish to cause any trouble to Cotin, after his generosity to me. If Paul's killer came from the abbey, he would have powerful men protecting him, and they would not welcome the intrusive questions of an ex-Dominican known to be a friend of the King.

An ominous silence hung over the scriptorium with its rows of chained manuscripts; at the hour of None, most of the friars would be in church. Two who must have had special permission to miss divine service were still working at desks under the west windows; they glanced up with mild curiosity as I entered. Cotin bustled across to intercept me. He had evidently been waiting.

'Bruno! I thought you weren't coming today. I feared—' He glanced across the room at the two young copyists, who had turned to whisper to one another, and nodded me towards a spiral staircase in the corner. This led to an upper gallery, which in turn opened on to a series of connecting rooms, each with a locked door guarding the volumes considered either too valuable or too inflammatory for public display. Cotin unlocked the first of these doors from a key ring on his belt and pulled me inside, closing it behind him.

'They've been looking for you,' he said, breathless. He was well into his sixties by now; short and broad, with tufts of white bristle sprouting from his ears and nostrils and a bushy greying beard, as if all the hair had migrated south from his flaking scalp. Without his eyeglasses, his face appeared undefended, his pale blue eyes squinting and anxious, as if fearful of missing some vital detail. 'There's been a lot of talk, since yesterday, that business with the priest. What's going on, Bruno?'

I shook my head. 'Who's looking for me?'

'The Abbé wants to question you. They know the priest asked for you before he died, and spoke some words that you refused to share. The Abbé called me in to see him last night – gave me quite an interrogation. How long you had been coming here, which books you asked for, what you were writing. He was not happy that I had let you return without seeking his permission.' He paused and grimaced, pulling the cloth of his habit away from his neck as if it was chafing.

'I am sorry to have caused you trouble. I never anticipated—'

He tutted the apology away, glancing over his shoulder. 'The Abbé is a pompous fool. I have learned to accommodate him. But there is a great commotion over this death, Bruno – apparently the priest was a close associate of the League, and the Duke of Guise regards his killing as a personal attack. The Abbé wants to know what secrets he whispered to you on his deathbed.'

'I see. Prompted by his love of justice, of course.'

Cotin gave me a long look from under his brows. 'The Abbé has his eye on a cardinal's hat. He thinks Guise is his surest route to one. And he has no choice but to concern himself with this murder, since the priest died inside the abbey walls.'

'He was attacked only yards from your back gate, too,' I said. 'I'd be surprised if that was a coincidence.'

His face contorted with distress. 'God have mercy on us all. There is something I must show you, Bruno. You are the only man I dare tell.' He stopped abruptly, laying his hand on my sleeve, head cocked as if listening. I thought I caught a sound from the room behind us. 'Follow me. The servant on the gate will have told them you're here by now. We'll go out this way.'

He unlocked the far door and led me through a further succession of rooms until we emerged from a tower in the west side of the courtyard beyond the cloisters. Cotin motioned to me to keep back inside the doorway until two friars had passed, carrying a basket between them. When he judged we were safe, he led me along a passageway between stone walls and out into the gardens behind the abbey's complex of buildings. Here we were exposed, though the dense mist offered a useful cover; Cotin pulled up his hood and I followed his example as we hurried across the open space to the shelter of the orchard beyond.

Fruit trees loomed in twisted shapes, the fog lingering clammy between them, but Cotin ploughed on, ducking under branches and around trunks with a dogged sense of direction, despite the absence of any path that I could make out. I glanced back to see if we had been followed, but saw nothing through the web of mist except the knotty outlines of bare trees.

After a good ten minutes' walking we reached the far side of the orchard and the solid mass of the boundary wall appeared, twelve feet high around the perimeter. Gulls circled above, harsh calls echoing over the river on the other side. I had not been to this part of the abbey grounds before; there had been no reason for me to venture so far from the main cloister and the library. I now saw that a row of low buildings lined the inside of the perimeter wall. There was no sign of any living soul out here. As we approached the outbuilding at the end of the row, Cotin selected a key from the ring at his belt and as he fiddled with the lock, I noticed a narrow path running along the inside of the wall. I followed the line of it as far as I could see and realised that it led straight to a small wooden door, set into the wall. This must be the gate I had seen from the towpath on the other side, where I had found the evidence of Paul's death. I wondered what Cotin could want to show me here with such urgency.

He ushered me through the low doorway, peering back into the mist to make certain we were still alone. Once inside, he took down a lamp from a high shelf behind the door, drew out a tinder-box from inside his habit and struck the flint, lighting the stub of candle, before pulling the door closed behind us. Rodent feet scuttled away into the corners at the sound. As the flame took hold and flickered up the walls, I saw that we stood in a low, windowless storeroom, with wooden crates stacked along one side, casks and sacks piled up at the far end.

'You say the priest was attacked close to the abbey gate,' Cotin whispered, glancing around again as if we might be overheard.

'I saw his blood on the track out there, by that door that leads to the jetty,' I said.

He nodded, absorbing this, then gestured to a pile of crates in the far corner of the room. 'My predecessor acquired over the years all manner of books and manuscripts from private collections. The most valuable went straight to the library, but the remainder could not be housed in the library archive, there was not the space. He died before he had a chance to catalogue them, so when I became librarian I inherited all these boxes that no one has looked through in perhaps thirty years.' He swept a hand to encompass the volume of material. 'Slowly but surely, I am working my way through, deciding which are worth the cost of repair. The answer is precious few, to my lasting regret – time has not been kind to them and many are suffering the ravages of damp, this place being so close to the river, even though they were packed in treated skins. At least the mice have spared them. But whoever decided to keep them in here should be thrown in the Bastille, in my view.'

He folded his arms and glared at the door, as if the culprit might appear at any moment. I motioned for him to continue. Intrigued as I was by the prospect of crateloads of forgotten manuscripts, with the Abbé already combing the grounds for me, I wanted him to come to the point.

'And?'

'Well.' He twisted his hands together. 'I came in yesterday after supper to make a start on the next pile. The atmosphere among the brothers was sombre after the death of the priest, you may imagine, but I had not thought – I mean to say, it was supposed that the poor man had been attacked by brigands on the road . . .' He broke off to set the lantern down. Then he lifted off the topmost of the boxes, placing it on the floor before rummaging through the books in the crate beneath, from which he retrieved a bundle of rough brown cloth. 'I pulled those boxes out and found this stuffed behind them. My first instinct was to leave it, since whoever put it there would surely come back to dispose of it more permanently. But my conscience . . . I don't want to be mixed up in this business, Bruno,' he said, his eyes bright with fear, 'but if someone in this abbey . . .' He shook his head and handed over the cloth, as if that were explanation enough, holding up the light so that I could see it more clearly.

The bundle was heavier than I had expected; I unfolded it carefully and understood the source of Cotin's distress. I was holding a rough woven cloak, such as the abbey servants might wear; wrapped inside it was a statue of a saint, about eighteen inches high – Saint Denis, to be precise, staring up at me with blank eyes from the severed head he carried tucked under his own arm, his expression serene. He was carved from a block of white limestone, discoloured with age, the same stone as the walls and pillars of the abbey church; the sculptor's art had once teased delicate details into the folds of his robe, the curls of his hair and beard and the braiding on his mitre, but his shoulders and the halo surrounding his empty

70

neck had been smoothed and effaced by time and weather, and one of his feet was chipped away. Denis stood on a solid cuboid base, its edge stained with gobbets of bloody matter and a few strands of hair. I balanced it in my hands; it was easily heavy enough to strike a killing blow. I held up the cloak with the other hand; the front was spattered with dark blotches, now dried to a rust-brown crust. There could be little doubt as to the significance of these items. I looked up and met Cotin's fearful gaze.

'I haven't told the Abbé. Do you think—'

'Was this statue taken from the church?'

He shook his head.

'Originally. But it has been in here for as long as I can remember. Those crates at the back there are full of bits and pieces from the church awaiting repair. Reliquaries, masonry, statues, candlesticks, glass. Anything that is no longer fit to glorify God is put here to be mended or else given away or the materials sold, though in practice it just gathers dust waiting to be sorted.'

'Whose job is that?'

'The sacristan's.'

'Could one of the servants have come in here and taken it?' I asked, indicating the cloak.

'Almost certainly not. This storeroom is kept locked, only three of us have a key. Some of those sacred objects are valuable. The servants are not allowed to enter unless they are helping one of the brothers to move things.'

'Then who has access?' I asked, eyeing the ring at his belt.

'Myself, for the books. The almoner, Frère Joseph – he keeps the dry goods here that we distribute to the poor once a week at the back gate. And the sacristan.' He paused, reluctant. 'Frère Albaric. I believe you met him.'

I recalled that prickle of distaste I had felt on encountering Frère Albaric in the infirmary; his snide expression and shiny skin, the impatience with which he had tried to nudge me away from the dying priest's bedside as he administered the last rites. *Dio cane* – had that been because he was afraid of what Paul might say to me? I looked down at the bloodied mess on the base of the statue. I must not jump to conclusions just because I had taken a dislike to the man.

'And this Frère Joseph,' I said. 'What kind of man is he?'

Cotin snorted softly. 'One that should not be in holy orders, in my view. The usual story – surplus son of a wealthy family. The one they give back to God, but no less full of worldly ambition for that. Joseph is a cold man. He barely troubles to disguise his contempt for the poor – hardly a desirable quality in an almoner. Of course, that may be why the Abbé appointed him,' he added. 'He has a reputation for frugality. The abbey's profits have certainly improved since he began to review the distribution of alms to the needy.'

'What age is he?'

'A little younger than you. Not yet thirty-five, I think.'

'Which family?'

'His name is de Chartres. Parisians. He's a cousin of the Duke of Montpensier. Well connected.'

'Ambitious, you say. Is he – let me speak bluntly – a man who might be persuaded to take a life if he thought it would help advance him?'

'I could not swear to that, Bruno. Who knows what any of us might do, given the right incentive? By temperament, perhaps . . .' He hesitated, looking at the statue.

'But?'

'Joseph has an affliction of his right hand. Some weakness from a childhood illness, he says. He can do everyday tasks competently enough with his good arm, but he lacks the strength for manual labour.'

'So . . .' I held the statue by the neck with my left hand and attempted to swing it through the air as if striking a blow. Paul Lefèvre was a tall man; if he had been standing when he was first hit, the assailant would have had to raise the

72

statue above shoulder height before bringing it down. Saint Denis was heavy and unwieldy when held aloft with one hand. A strong man might be able to muster enough force for a killing blow one-armed, but it would be difficult to aim with any precision. Paul's attacker could not have afforded to miss and risk the priest trying to fight back – especially if he lacked the strength to fight.

'And Albaric?'

'Two good arms, as far as I know.'

'I meant, is he ambitious too? Political?'

Cotin looked unconvinced. 'I do not know him well enough to say. I'm not sure anyone does, though he has been here eight or more years. He is devout in his duties, and that is all I can tell you, except that he guards his privacy, as far as one can in a community such as this. If he has political interests, I have no idea what they might be.'

For all that, he is certainly not politically naïve, I thought, recalling Albaric's throwaway remark about looking to the Louvre to find the killer. It had struck me as an odd comment, given that at first Paul was assumed to be the chance victim of street robbers. He had known who Paul was, too, though he had affected only a vague recognition.

'What about the back gate? Who has the key?'

'All the senior officials whose work concerns deliveries to the abbey,' he said. 'Various goods come in by river to be unloaded at that jetty. So the two I have mentioned, but also the cellarer, the bursar, the infirmarian, among others. But it is not impossible that copies have slipped into other hands over the years.' He allowed himself a half-smile. 'In my day it was not unknown for younger friars to find their way out at night.'

'In my day, too,' I said, remembering my own nocturnal sorties in Naples. I looked back at the statue in my hands. 'But why did he – whoever he was – not simply throw these in the river so they would not be found?'

'Perhaps he was interrupted,' Cotin suggested. 'If a boat came too close and he needed to hide himself, he may not have had time to throw the statue into deep water. Or perhaps he was afraid it would be noticed missing. He may have meant to clean it later and return it to its place.' He dragged a hand across his beard, covered his mouth. 'God have mercy.'

'Either way, he will be back for it,' I said. 'I am going to wait for him.'

He peeled his fingers away from his face and his mouth pinched. 'You should not involve yourself in this any further, Bruno.' He sighed. 'By which I mean, I would prefer not to find myself in any more trouble with the Abbé as a result of your meddling. I have already defended you once.'

'Defended?'

'The Abbé advanced the theory that the priest had spoken your name repeatedly not because he was asking for you, but because he was trying to accuse his killer. I insisted that was impossible, that you had been sitting under my nose in the library all afternoon. Even then I'm not sure he was persuaded. Either way he wants you questioned.'

'Thank you.' I wondered who had planted that helpful idea in the Abbé's mind. 'But listen to me, Cotin. What are your choices? Will you go to the Abbé and tell him what you found here, or will you keep quiet in the knowledge that one of your brothers is a killer?'

The old man looked stricken. Neither prospect held much appeal. 'It could have been a servant,' he faltered. 'A stolen key—'

I clicked my tongue, impatient. 'Whoever struck Paul Lefèvre did it on behalf of someone more powerful, you can be sure. I'd be surprised if that person would have entrusted such a task to a servant. The Abbé will not thank you for drawing his attention to the scandal, if it was one of his friars. He may even have an interest in protecting the murderer. No one was supposed to find this evidence—' I lifted the statue into his line of sight. 'If you speak up about it, you may put yourself in danger. That's why I should be the one to confront whoever comes back for this. Once I know who he is for certain, it will be for others to deal with and no one will connect it with you.'

He rolled his eyes. 'Don't be absurd, Bruno. Everyone will know I let you in here.'

'You just said yourself, a key might be stolen. Supposing you had left yours unattended in the library? I might well have helped myself. It's the sort of thing they would expect of me.'

I cocked an eyebrow, waiting to see if I had convinced him. He regarded me with a tired smile.

'You are relentless, Bruno. You propose to conceal yourself in here until he returns to dispose of the evidence. Then what? Will you accost him yourself? By whose authority?'

'You can guess,' I said quietly.

He pulled at his beard, looking doubtful. 'You know the religious houses outside the city walls have their own jurisdiction. Unless you are carrying a royal seal, Henri's name will not mean much here. It will be your word – a known heretic who has broken into abbey property – against that of a senior official of the order. Do you think the Abbé will meekly send for the royal guard at your request? Or is it more likely that you are the one who will end up detained?'

I sucked in my cheeks. He had a point. 'Then I will not confront him. I will merely make sure I can identify him beyond doubt, and report what I know. It will be in the King's hands after that. You'll need to give me the key to the back gate, so I can escape.'

'And by the time you have passed on what you know and the King's guard arrives, that evidence will be gone, if you do not intervene.' He spread his hands to indicate helplessness. 'So it will be your word against the perpetrator's once more. Henri will not send his soldiers barging into a powerful abbey

75

and accusing a friar of murder without proof, not with rumours already flying that it was he who had the priest killed in the first place.'

'Damn you, Cotin – you are right again.' I closed my eyes for a moment while I considered. 'Very well – we will do it this way. You must send a message to the Louvre palace as soon as possible. Address it to Jacopo Corbinelli, sign it from me. Tell him to ask the King to send two of his strong men, the two that know me, have them wait outside the abbey gate after Compline tonight. I don't think our man will come looking for this until he can be sure he won't be seen. Tell them to be discreet, and I will deliver the killer into their hands, with proof. I can pay you,' I added, seeing his discomfort, though I knew that was not the issue.

'I don't want your money.' He tutted, turning his head away. 'This is your notion of keeping me out of it, eh?' He hunched his shoulders, weighing up the price. 'I know you need the King's favour again, Bruno, but tell me – can you be certain he is blameless in this?'

I passed a hand over my face. 'I can be certain of nothing, Cotin. Except that it seems beyond doubt that Paul Lefèvre was bludgeoned with this statue by someone who has access to this building and your back gate. That man is the only one who can tell us the truth about this business, and I mean to find him.'

'I would face severe discipline if the Abbé learns I was part of your escapade – which he will. I could lose my position. I know I owe you, but . . .'

He lowered his eyes. He did not need to say more; I knew what the risk meant to him. When I had first met Cotin, during my last stay in Paris, he had dreaded losing his office as librarian; too proud to admit that his sight was failing, he did his best to hide his deficiency from his brothers, living in fear of the day he could no longer read his beloved manuscripts. Through my friend Jacopo's connections, I had had made for him a pair of eyeglasses that could magnify the smallest script; not such a great expense for my pocket at the time, but a luxury beyond the means of a friar sworn to a life of poverty. The instrument had restored Cotin to his work; now I was the one threatening it again.

'I will not persuade you against your better judgement,' I said, affecting unconcern. 'Only consider this: how will it feel to look across the chapel every day during the office and catch the eye of one of your brothers, knowing he killed a man in cold blood?'

'God's tears, Bruno.' He made a soft noise that might have been a curse, or a rueful laugh. 'You know how to pluck at my conscience. Where do you want to hide yourself, then? I had better hurry with this message – they will be ringing the bell for Vespers any minute.'

I gripped his shoulder. 'God will reward you, my friend. Or at least, I will, when I get the chance. Let us pile up those crates at the back and I'll squeeze in behind them. That would give me a view of the door between the two stacks, providing he has a light with him.'

I indicated a recess at the back of the storeroom; together we pulled away misshapen sacks of root vegetables and shifted the crates of old masonry and ornaments into a stack the height of a man to cover it. I pressed in behind the boxes and the wall; cobwebs moulded across my mouth and nose and there was barely space to expand my lungs, but I would be concealed from anyone searching in the opposite corner behind Cotin's boxes of books.

'You're well hidden,' he said, standing back. 'Now you just have to stay there for as long it takes, without needing a piss or falling asleep. Rather you than me.' He eased a heavy iron key from the ring at his belt as I scraped out from the recess. 'That's for the back gate. For the love of God, don't lose it. And you'd better take this one for the door here, in case your fellow locks it behind him when he leaves.' He shook his head again. 'I don't like this, Bruno. If you should be caught off guard – this man is a killer, after all.'

'I can put up a fight against any friar. Wouldn't be the first time.' I grinned, bending to show him the knife hidden in my boot; no weapons were permitted inside the abbey precinct, but the gatekeeper was usually too lazy or too bone-headed to bother with more than a cursory check of my belt. Cotin jumped back in alarm.

'For Jesus' sake, try not to shed more blood inside these walls. Come.' He replaced the statue of Saint Denis, carefully wrapped in the cloak, in its original hiding place behind the boxes of books in the opposite corner. When it was secure, he opened the door a crack and held up his lantern, peering out and listening for any movement. 'Quick.' He nodded towards the path. 'All quiet for now.'

The mist had thickened – or perhaps it was just that the light was already failing. It must be close to four in the afternoon. If I was right, and the killer would wait until the abbey was asleep, I could be standing behind those crates for six hours or more. I had survived worse, I told myself. By the corner of the outbuilding, I unlaced my breeches and relieved myself in a steaming stream on the grass, trying not to think that it might be my last opportunity for some time, while Cotin kept his eyes trained on the trees ahead. I nodded to him when I was ready, and he waited until I had taken my place again in the recess behind the crates.

'I'll stay in the library tonight after the lights go out,' he said. I could just make out the shape of him through the gap between the stacks. 'I have special permission to work there if I am unable to sleep – they will see nothing unusual in that. If you have any trouble, you will know where to find me. Pray God you'll have no need. Get what you came for and leave quietly. I will find you at the Swan tomorrow after dinner to fetch the keys – best you stay clear of this place for a while. And take care of yourself,' he added over his shoulder, his voice gruff to disguise his concern.

I smiled to myself in the shadows. The door closed behind him, leaving me in darkness as the lock clicked into place. I fidgeted until I found a position that allowed me to lean my weight against the wall and settled back to wait, reminding myself that the discomfort would be worth it, that in a matter of hours I would deliver both murderer and evidence into the King's hands. After that, how they chose to persuade the man to implicate the Duke of Guise would be Henri's concern. I allowed myself to dream a little of how the King might choose to reward me for my service.

Perhaps if I had been less cocksure about my ability to apprehend the killer single-handed, so that I could prove myself to the King and take the credit, the night would have unfolded differently and another death might have been avoided. But I run ahead of my story, and it does no good to speculate on what might have been.

FIVE

Muffled by fog and distance, the church bells of Saint-Victor tolled the passing hours, summoning the friars to observe the holy offices first of Vespers, then of Compline. The temperature dropped as darkness enfolded the abbey; in my coffin-like space behind the crates, my limbs grew so chilled I felt I was being paralysed from the inside out, my feet so frozen that hot currents of pain began to needle through them and up my legs. My back developed a fierce, dull ache; from time to time I dared slide out and stretch or stamp to restore some blood to my extremities. Despite the discomfort, I must have dozed, waking with a start each time I began to tilt sideways, wrenched from monstrous dreams of being buried alive. I wished I had asked Cotin to leave his lantern; I could have passed the hours looking through the boxes of forgotten manuscripts. But that was folly; I would not have had time to conceal myself if the door opened, and the smell of candle smoke would give me away. Instead I remained hidden in the darkness, listening to the squeaks and pattering of rats and the slow creak of old timbers, reviewing what I thought I knew.

Paul Lefèvre had intimated to me during our conversation in the confessional that he believed the King would not hold power for much longer. Though he had quickly tried to deny that he meant anything specific, it seemed likely that he had some concrete intelligence of a planned coup by the Duke of Guise and the Catholic League. But a priest like Paul would be small fry to Guise; useful while he could be persuaded to attack King Henri from his pulpit, but hardly someone to whom Guise would have confided plans for an act of treason. So Paul must have come by that knowledge another way; the burned scraps of letter in his hearth suggested that he had heard something in the course of a confession that had disturbed him so greatly he had considered breaking the holy seal of the confessional in order to warn the King. Some terrible harm planned by someone or something known as 'Circe'. Whatever he had learned had troubled him so much that it had been the last thought to pass from his shattered brain to his lips as the life bled out of him. But here my theory foundered on a lack of certainty. There was no way of knowing whether Paul had sent a copy of that letter to the King, or whether he had changed his mind but someone had still felt he needed to be silenced.

The nature of the letter also puzzled me. Paul was a zealous supporter of the Catholic League; you would suppose that he would support any plot to topple the degenerate King and replace him with a righteous Catholic. What could be so terrible about the harm intended by 'Circe' that it could have induced the fervent Paul to consider betraying not only the sacrament of confession but his loyalty to the entire cause of the League? And who could have confessed such a conspiracy to him? I did not have the answers to these questions. I could only guess that, somehow, the Duke of Guise had anticipated betrayal and taken measures that he hoped would prevent it. But if so, that meant he must also know about the confession; presumably that person too would have to be silenced. Perhaps the killer would be able to shed more light on the plot once he was in the custody of the royal guard.

I was jolted from my theorising by the sound of a key in the lock. Wedged tight into the recess, I leaned across to make sure I could see through the narrow gap between the two stacks of boxes. Ignoring the pain in all my joints, I held myself still, terrified that the slightest sound would give me away and ruin my advantage. Despite what I had promised Cotin, I had no intention of allowing the killer to leave and hide his evidence. I was confident that, with surprise on my side and the help of a weapon, I could easily overcome him and force him at knifepoint to the gate, where the King's soldiers would be waiting.

The door creaked open and a faint circle of light appeared; behind it, the outline of a figure, the cowl of his habit pulled up over his head. I heard the door click shut and the light brightened; I realised he had draped the lantern with a cloth to dim it on his way through the grounds. I held my breath, every fibre tensed. He crossed immediately to the boxes of books, set down his light and crouched to pull away the first crate. Silently, I eased out from my hiding place and drew my knife. The light from his lantern puddled on the floor; I caught a glimpse of his profile as he straightened, clasping the bundle with the statue to his breast with both hands like a Madonna holding an infant. I stepped forward; the movement startled him and he whipped around to face me, frozen with surprise.

'Keep quiet, don't move, and you won't come to harm,' I said, holding the point of the knife towards him. 'I need you to come with me. Bring that with you.'

His face was still hidden in shadow, but I saw his eyes flick down to the statue, as if he had forgotten he was holding it. In an instant he seemed to recover his power of thought; he leaned back and, with considerable force, hurled the statue at me so that it struck me in the chin. I staggered backwards, touching my fingertips to my face, and in that unguarded moment he swung a punch that connected with the left side of my jaw. I dropped the knife; my mouth filled with blood as I struggled to recover my balance, but he reached out and pulled at the stack of crates beside us so that it toppled forwards. I managed to jump back as boxes of stone, glass and metal crashed across the floor, trapping me in the corner. I was fortunate that no flying debris struck me, but by the time I had clambered over the heap, he had already grabbed the lantern and plunged me into darkness as he closed the door behind him.

Cursing, I stumbled blindly across the room, spitting blood, relieved to find that he had not locked me in. Outside the mist was so thick now that I could not see more than four or five feet in front of me, but the lantern was barely visible as a pinprick of fuzzy light between the bent shapes of trees ahead. I lurched after it, tripping on clumps of grass, branches clawing at my clothes, damp skeins of cobweb clinging to my face as trunks loomed out of nowhere and the light bobbed and grew fainter. Moonlight barely silvered the layers of vapour that hung heavy as smoke in the air. After a few paces I could no longer see the lantern at all. I thought I heard a low laugh from just behind my left shoulder, though it might as easily have been a magpie. I realised he had led me into the orchard deliberately to confuse me. There was no sound now but the stillness of the night and my own blood thudding in my chest. Turning again to what I believed was the direction of the path, I moved with caution, but before I found the edge of the trees I glimpsed the light again, jouncing up and down a few yards ahead. I ran towards it, only to see it disappear as I heard the sound of a gate slamming and the key turning in the lock.

'*Merda*,' I muttered. A few feet further on I found the path leading to the door in the wall; my quarry had slipped out while I was stumbling among the trees. I hesitated, trying to decide my best course. I had Cotin's key; I could pursue him, but he might have hidden himself along the river track with the idea of ambushing me if I followed. He had already shown himself unafraid to kill a man on that path; I did not want to go the same way, and I was unarmed now. Besides, I thought, brightening – if all had gone smoothly, he would have run straight into the arms of the King's soldiers. I hoped they would have the wit to hold him until I caught up with them. But there was still the matter of evidence; while he was away from the abbey, this was my chance to see if there was anything more than the cloak and statue that would serve to condemn him beyond doubt. Perhaps he had kept some correspondence hidden in his cell that would make explicit who had set him on to kill Paul – any such letter would be a thousand times more valuable than a bloodied statue. It was worth a try. I ran my fingers gingerly over my swollen lip; though I had still not had a clear view of his face, I could be fairly sure that punch was not thrown by a man with a crippled right hand. If Cotin was right, there was only one other friar with a key to the storeroom. At least that meant I had an idea of where to start.

I turned my steps away from the gate and followed the path back to the outbuilding. Feeling along the shelf behind the door where Cotin had found the lantern, my fingers closed over a stub of candle. I drew my tinder-box from the pouch at my belt and fumbled with frozen and trembling fingers to strike a spark from it. The room was a chaos of broken stone, metal and glass, strewn over the floor where he had pulled the crates down to slow me. Scrabbling one-handed while I tried to hold up the feeble light, I found my knife, then unearthed the statue, still tangled in its cloak, and bundled it under my arm.

The damp air snuffed my candle as soon as I stepped outside. After a couple of attempts to relight it I was forced to concede that I did not have the time to lose; I would have to rely on my sense of direction. If the King's guards had not stopped my attacker, there was always the chance that he would run around the perimeter of the abbey wall and try to enter another way, but the main gate would be barred at this hour and surely he would not want to wake the gatekeeper and explain himself. My guess was that he would wait and return eventually through the back wall in search of the statue. I had no idea what time it might be by now, but I must not be found sneaking around the abbey when the friars were awakened for the office of Matins at two o'clock. I could not afford to end up wandering lost in the mist. From the store-house I set out through the trees away from the wall that separated the abbey grounds from the river path and tried to steer myself in a straight line. As a novice, I had been taught to recite certain Psalms as a means of measuring time without the need for clocks or church bells, and though I no longer spoke them in worship, I still had them all by rote, and they proved useful when I needed to mark the passing time. So it was that, after around ten minutes of determined walking, one step after another, into the white blankness, I saw the bulk of the abbey church against the sky a hundred yards ahead. Relieved, I quickened my steps towards it and the cloisters that lay beyond; in my haste I collided with a tall figure who reared up out of the mist, arms outstretched over me. I stifled a cry and jumped back, dropping the statue and grabbing for my knife as my heart hammered at my ribs, but my assailant did not move. After a moment, my shoulders slackened and I let out a panicked laugh at my own folly. I had run into a stone angel, wings spread, empty eyes raised to heaven. Taking another step back I almost fell over an object at knee height; I turned to find a moss-covered cross and realised I had wandered into the abbey cemetery. Picking my way through the graves, I found a path that I could follow as far as the church. There had been plenty among my brothers at San Domenico who would have been gibbering prayers to the Virgin and all the saints had they found themselves alone in a mist-shrouded graveyard at this hour, but I had never shared that monkish fear of the unquiet dead. It was only the living who would creep up on silent feet and put a blade in your neck.

There was no trace of light from the windows of the library, but the door was unlocked, so I slipped in as quietly as I could and lit my candle. Shadows leapt back and I felt a pulse of affection at the sight that greeted me; Cotin had fallen asleep at his desk with his head on an open book, resting on the crook of his arm, his lamp burned down beside him. I crouched and shook him by the shoulder.

'Wha—?' He jerked awake, turning unfocused eyes on me. I motioned for him to be quiet.

'Where's Albaric's cell?'

'Eh? Dear Lord, what happened to your face?'

'Not important. I need to look in Albaric's cell. You have to show me which one it is.'

He levered himself up, wincing at the complaints of his joints. 'I had hoped not to see you again tonight.' He eased his neck from side to side.

'My apologies. We need to hurry.'

'Why, what hour is it?'

'No idea. But he could return any moment.'

'It is him, then? You are sure?'

'No. But it seems the most likely possibility. He had a key and there was nothing wrong with his hand.' I ran my tongue along my swollen lip and tasted blood. 'That's why I want to see his cell.'

Cotin eyed the statue under my arm, muttered a half-hearted protest and motioned for me to follow. At the door, he blew out my candle, in case the light gave us away to the night watch, and we both pulled our hoods around our faces. Keeping to the shadows against the walls, he led me around the arcades of the cloister and into the courtyard behind. The friars' dormitory, directly ahead, was a long building of unadorned stone with rows of individual cells on two storeys facing one another across a wide corridor. I followed him up the first flight of stairs to the upper level. From the recess of the staircase, he pointed to the left-hand row of doors and held up four fingers. My eyes had begun to grow accustomed to the dark; I handed him the statue and left him hidden on the stairs while I crept along until I came to the fourth door. I glanced about me to either side before putting my hand to the latch. The atmosphere was oddly silent here, not even the usual snores or grunts you might expect from a house of sleeping men. It was as if every friar were holding his breath in anticipation. All the doors I could see appeared to be closed fast, but in my experience that did not necessarily mean no one was looking.

I let myself into Albaric's room without a sound, keeping my hood up, and struck my tinder-box until the damp candle caught flame. By its light I saw a plain table against the wall by the door, with a large leather-bound book lying on it. That would be a place to start, at least; letters might be hidden between pages or inside bindings. I picked up the book, trying to hold the candle steady, but the volume was too large to lift with one hand, and as I was shaking it by the spine it slipped from my grasp and landed with a loud slap on the table. I froze, every muscle taut and trembling, eyes fixed on the door as I waited to see if the noise had disturbed anyone.

'What in Jesu's name—?' said a voice behind me.

I whirled around with a gasp, to see Frère Albaric sitting up on the mattress against the far wall, tangled in a woollen blanket. He stared at me, equally amazed, his eyes dazed and puffy with sleep. His hair stood up in tufts around his tonsure; one cheek was marked with a crease from his sheet and I could see that he was wearing a linen nightshift. His face bore the naked vulnerability that comes from being jolted out of deep sleep. I had been so convinced that he must have been the man in the storeroom I had no more than glanced at the bed to register a heap of blankets. I recovered my presence of mind before he did and blew out the candle as I slipped

87

back into the corridor, hoping he had not had a chance to see my face.

A hand shot out from the darkness and grabbed my arm as I emerged; I jumped again, but it was Cotin, pressed up against the wall.

'Frère Joseph is not in his cell,' he whispered, pulling me by the sleeve and pointing me to a door on the opposite side, towards the far end. I scuttled along, hoping that Albaric would conclude he had imagined a figure from his nightmares and fall back to sleep without feeling the need to raise an alarm.

I eased the door of Joseph's cell shut behind me and leaned against it, trying to slow my breathing. When I had managed to light the candle again, I saw that the almoner's room was laid out much as Albaric's, though the few furnishings were more obviously expensive: a mattress on a wooden pallet under a small arched window, set high in the wall opposite the door; on the right-hand side, a table and on the left, a wooden trunk. At least this time the bed was empty; from the tumbled sheets it looked as if Joseph had left in a hurry. The table was also bare, save for a branched silver candlestick, but to my relief, the chest was not padlocked. I opened the lid and began to pull out whatever I could find: good quality linen undershirts; a pair of leather shoes; a rosary of amber beads, smooth as glass; a tortoiseshell comb . . . but nothing more. Not in a trunk open to anyone; I should have realised. I cast around to see where else he might have hidden personal effects. The room held no other furniture, no cupboards, no drawers. Where had I squirrelled away the writings I wanted to keep from prying eyes when I was a friar? My eyes lighted on the mattress.

I fixed my candle into the silver holder on the table and set it down by the bed so that I could grope along the underside of the mattress until I felt a split in the seam, just large enough to slip a hand inside; through the lumps of horsehair my scrabbling fingers closed around a sheaf of papers. I drew them out and untied the ribbon binding them as I brought them closer to the light. The topmost sheet was instantly recognisable; another crude sketch of King Henri mincing in women's clothes while two sly-looking young men with lascivious pouts wrapped their fists around the sceptre he held erect in his lap, above a set of satirical verses about the Queen Mother's desperate recourse to witchcraft to secure a Valois heir. The paper beneath was more unusual: it showed a series of drawings depicting a variety of imaginative forms of torture and execution, while a queen looked on, the name 'Elizabeth' emblazoned above her head. The text was an impassioned plea, shorn of all ribald jokes, urging the people of France to consider the plight of their fellow Catholics in England, and to rise up and exterminate heresy before they too suffered the same fate at the hands of the Protestants. The writer ended his polemic by calling on true Catholics to finish the work begun on the glorious night of Saint Bartholomew's – an extraordinary exhortation for which he would certainly be executed, if his authorship could be proved. The style – and I could almost swear the handwriting – were identical to the ones I had found in Paul's room. That, at least, was evidence of a connection between Frère Joseph and the murdered priest.

But there was another paper beneath, of better quality and written in a different hand. As I read, I felt my eyes widen.

Your fingerprints your mouth your tongue burn my skin long after you are gone. Only you know the secret places of my body, the way I ache for you, in the knowledge I should not. Yet for all the judgement and scorn arrayed against us, for all the punishment that might befall us if it were known, I would not have given up one single hour in your embrace. You consume me. My desire wills me to you like a hawk towards home.

89

Followed by more in this vein, though it was neither signed nor dated; hot words for a friar who had taken a vow of celibacy. Joseph was running a great risk in keeping such an inflammatory letter, but perhaps his high birth gave him immunity from routine searches. I held the paper up to my face and sniffed it; faint traces of perfume lingered behind the smell of stale horsehair. The writing was distinctive, the letters embellished with elaborate flourishes; an educated hand, but belonging to someone with a taste for ostentation. I decided to keep the note; Joseph de Chartres may be well connected, but proof of a forbidden love affair might make him vulnerable. I was not sure how much could be achieved without a signature to the letter, or any means of identifying his correspondent, but it would surely make him nervous to suspect that someone else had it in their possession, and that might give me leverage.

I tucked the papers carefully into the secret pocket sewn into the lining of my doublet – an alteration I had had made to all my clothes when I lived in London, for just such a purpose. Reaching again into the mattress to check I had not missed anything, I rummaged around until my fingertips touched another object; this time a leather purse, tied with a drawstring. I opened it and tipped the contents into my palm: two gold écus and a torn strip of paper, on which was scribbled, in the same hand as the pamphlets, *Brinkley, 28 11 4h.*

Was it a code? Who or what was Brinkley? It was an English name, if I was not mistaken. Many of the émigrés who had fled to Paris rather than renounce their faith under Elizabeth had established connections with the Catholic League; if Joseph de Chartres was involved in distributing propaganda against the King, he might also be collaborating with the English Catholics – the anti-Elizabeth pamphlet among his papers suggested as much. Or perhaps Brinkley was a reference to the mistress, and the money was for her. As I stared at them, it struck me that perhaps it was not a cipher at all, but a far more obvious explanation – 4h could mean simply a time, *quatre heures*, in which case the other numbers might be the date. The 28th of November was tomorrow. A rendez-vous, then? Even if my guess were correct, I had no way of knowing where or with whom, but at least it was one more thin thread I could follow, now that I was certain that Joseph must be Paul Lefèvre's killer. I touched a thumb to my bruised mouth. Evidently he had exaggerated the limitations of his crippled hand.

I was crouching to return the money to its hiding place when the cell door juddered open and light flooded the walls. I whipped around, startled; a figure filled the doorway, lamp held aloft. He appeared to be fully dressed, despite the hour.

'Put down the weapon,' he said, in a voice accustomed to giving orders.

I stood and held out my hands, palms up, to show I was not armed. He eyed the purse.

'The one at your belt,' he said, with a touch more steel. He was a solid man, tall and broad, nearing sixty but still possessed of a vigorous energy apparent in his florid cheeks and quick, sharp eyes under bristling brows. His abbot's robes were trimmed with fox-fur and patterned in gold thread that winked in the light; a jewelled crucifix hung from his neck, so large it almost reached his belt and would have made a lesser man stoop. 'Let us see, now,' he continued, as I unstrapped my knife and dropped it to the floor, 'carrying a weapon inside the abbey precincts – that is an offence in itself. Unlawful intrusion, theft, violent assault—' he gestured to the blood on my lip. 'Quite a list of charges to be going on with.'

'It was I who was assaulted,' I said.

He raised an eyebrow. I realised I would do better to affect a degree of humility.

'Father Abbot – I can see how this must look. But I can explain. If you send someone to look outside the gate, you will find soldiers from the King's personal guard who will vouch for me. My name is—'

'I know exactly who you are, Doctor Bruno,' the Abbé said. His look suggested this knowledge was not going to work in my favour. 'As for the soldiers – there *are* armed guards here, but not, I fear, the ones you requested in this letter.' He flicked his wrist up to show a piece of paper held between his first and second finger. My heart dropped to my stomach. 'Do you imagine I allow messages in and out of this abbey without knowing what they contain? Especially ones addressed to the Louvre. Cotin should have known better. But perhaps he stood to gain as your accomplice.'

'Father Abbot, you must listen. I believe you have a murderer in your abbey.' I looked him in the eye and spoke solemnly. If I betrayed a hint of alarm, I would be giving him the confirmation he wanted.

'I have a *thief* in my abbey, that much seems beyond doubt.' He sniffed.

'I am not a thief, Your Grace, I swear.'

'That is your money, is it?'

We both looked at the purse in my hand.

'I pray you, send to—' I hesitated. Not the King. Cotin was right – Henri would not risk inflaming further ill feeling among the religious orders by coming to the defence of a heretic accused of theft in defiance of a powerful abbot. As I had already worked out, he had chosen me precisely because he could dissociate himself from me if things became awkward. But I still had one friend with a degree of influence. 'Jacopo Corbinelli, at the palace. You must know him – he is secretary to the Queen Mother and the King's librarian. He will vouch for me.'

'No doubt. You Italians always stick together. Though he would be a fool to soil his hands in this instance. And in any case, I am not your messenger boy.' He crushed the letter Cotin had written for me in his fist and turned in the doorway, motioning to someone out of sight. Still believing I might negotiate my way out of the situation, I dropped the purse on the bed and picked up the candle. Without thinking, I bent to retrieve my knife – it was valuable and I did not want to leave it behind if I was to be escorted out under guard. But the Abbé glanced back as I was reaching for it and cried out with as much drama as if I had stuck the blade in his ribs. Before I could surrender the weapon, he had retreated and two men armed with pikestaffs barged into the room; one seized me by the hair while the other twisted my arm behind my back and wrenched the knife from my grasp. In the commotion I let go of my candle, which caught the edge of Joseph's bedding; a small conflagration erupted and the man holding my arm yelped and let go, flapping his hands at his leg where the flames had singed his hose. I took advantage of the confusion to tear myself away from the other one, leaving a clump of my hair in his fist. I hurled myself towards the door and out into the corridor; by now most of the cell doors stood open and a row of pale, awed faces stared at me.

The Abbé stood blocking my way to the stairs; there was no sign of Cotin and I could only hope he had had the sense to vanish with the statue before anyone had seen him.

'Stop that man!' the Abbé thundered. I glanced back, in time to see the arc of a pikestaff descending, a moment before I felt the impact of the blow and my knees buckled beneath me. I tried to speak but no sound emerged; my sight blurred as the soldier crouched over me and the world turned black.

It remained dark when I opened my eyes some time later, to find I was lying on my side, face pressed to the ground. My senses were still dulled from the blow to my head, though not sufficiently to block out the fierce smell of excrement that assailed my nostrils as soon as I was conscious. Where was I? I raised my head an inch as pain seared up the back of my skull like a hot needle. Under my cheek, the prickling of dried straw. A stable, perhaps? But it was not the clean, grassy smell of horse dung making me retch; this stink was human. Mine? I could hardly tell. When I tried to roll over, I found I could not move my arms; my wrists had been bound together behind me. I struggled to my knees and twisted my right shoulder up to try and wipe the dirt, or caked blood, from my eyes on my sleeve, but it made no difference to the darkness. There was no source of light in the room. I was frozen through, shivering so hard that my teeth clattered together and I was in danger of biting my tongue. I slumped back on to my heels, rolled my shoulders to ease the pain and tried to join the jolted fragments of memory. I had drifted in and out of consciousness after I was struck; they had put me on a horse, or had I imagined that? With a hood over my head, so I had no idea where they had taken me. I forced myself to my feet, feeling the world tilt and sway unnervingly as if I were at sea. I could at least stand upright. Despite the filthy air, I breathed slowly and deliberately, in and out. The pain in my head advanced and receded, making my eyes swim. When I was reasonably certain that I was not about to faint or vomit, I called out.

'Is anyone there? Hey!'

From somewhere behind me came an answering moan that sounded as if it had been loosed by one of Dante's lost souls. I let out a cry, startled to find I was not alone. Dear God, what was this – a dungeon? The darkness was so thick you could almost feel it sliding across your face. I staggered forward, step by halting step, until finally I collided with a wall, slimy to the touch. Facing away, I groped along the stones with my bound hands as far as I could, until I met a corner. I followed that wall too, battling my rising fear that there was no door here, no way out. I stood still and shouted again for help, stamping my feet on the stone floor, though this produced no effect at all. The formless lament from the depths of the room grew louder and more agitated the more

I yelled for someone to come, until the pitch of it made the wound on my head throb as if it would burst open—

'For the love of Christ, will you stop that? I'm trying to make myself heard here.'

The tortured noise broke off abruptly. I peered into the darkness but could make out nothing. In the silence I heard a shuffling in the straw and a soft trickle of water, which could have been the damp running down the walls or my companion relieving himself. I put the thought from my mind and resumed my shouting.

'They won't come.' The voice from the corner scraped like a rusted hinge, as if it had not been used in years.

'Where are we?' I cast around in the dark, desperate. 'Who are you?'

There was a rasping sound, a cough or possibly laughter, followed by the wet spatter of a gob of phlegm ejected on to the wall or floor. 'I don't remember.' A pause. 'That's why we're here. They forget you, then you forget yourself.' More hacking, as if he were amused by his own joke.

Forget yourself. *Dio mio* . . . 'An oubliette? Is that where we are?' The deepest pit of any prison, underground, where they throw those who will never see the sky again. Those best forgotten, as my unseen companion pointed out. Panic surged through my veins; I resumed my stamping and shouting with renewed urgency, fighting the insistent voice in my head telling me it was likely that no one who could help me knew I was here. My fellow prisoner took up his wordless keening again, softly this time, as if exhausted by his own grief. After another prolonged bout of yelling until my throat was raw with the effort, I began to understand why his voice sounded so broken. Presumably he, too, had screamed himself hoarse at first in the belief that someone would respond. I stopped to gather my breath, and was rewarded by the sound of a metal bolt rattling overhead.

A hatch swung open above me and a greasy yellow light

swept around the walls, revealing a low-ceilinged, windowless pit. I squinted, turning my face away; though it was only one candle in a lantern, the glow was still shockingly bright after the long spell in darkness. Once my eyes had adjusted, I was able to peer upwards to see the lower half of a face, veiled in shadow, looming through the opening.

'You listen. I'm only here to tell you that if you keep up that fucking noise, I will come back and shut your mouth for you.' I could make out stumps of teeth and a prominent growth on the man's stubbled cheek. 'Understood?'

'Wait,' I managed to stammer, 'there's been a mistake. I shouldn't be here.'

The gaoler cackled. 'That's right, friend. You and all the others. Never met one yet that thought he should.' He withdrew, and the light with him.

'Please! I need to send a message to my friend. I will pay you handsomely if you help me.' I lurched a step closer to the opening. The man leaned down, cocking his head as if he were considering the offer. His expression suggested he doubted my ability to deliver on this promise.

'Tricky. See, someone's already paid me to keep you in here.'

'I will pay you more.'

'Wouldn't be so much use to me without a head, though.'

'That won't happen. Please – just send a message to the Louvre, that's all I ask.'

'Oh, is that all?' In the light from the lantern his face contorted into a grotesque grin. 'Friend of the King, are you?'

'In fact, yes. Only let me prove it.'

He let out another bark of laughter. 'You'll be right at home here, then. Among the nobility. You all right, Monsieur le Comte?' He lowered the light through the hole and I turned to see the creature in the corner raise his head with a frightened whimper. I could not suppress a gasp; my fellow prisoner was hardly recognisable as a man. He was so emaciated that he seemed little more than a corpse. Blistered yellow skin stretched tight over his skull; wisps of long grey hair cobwebbed over a face that would have been hideous, had it not been so pitiful. The man tilted his nose up like a mole, sniffing the air, and I could see that his eye sockets were empty, the rims livid with scar tissue. He was almost naked, save for a few scraps of rag, the remnants of clothes that had rotted away. Unlike me, he was not restrained with ropes or manacles; perhaps he was so destroyed there was no need.

'Not pretty, is he,' the gaoler remarked, with a cough. 'Best you're in the dark, so you don't have to see him. Stay here long enough, you'll look like that too.' He backed away from the hatch, still laughing.

'No – please!' I cried, feverish with desperation. 'Send a message to the palace for me – I beg you.'

'Tell you what – I'll put a word in next time I'm taking dinner with the King. In the meantime, you keep quiet and I might throw you something to eat later if you behave.'

'No, wait—'

But the flickering circle of light vanished and the wooden cover dropped back into place with terrible finality; his laughter was still audible as the bolt was shot into place. I called a few more times, but it was evident that he was not coming back. It was only now that I realised how painfully hungry and thirsty I felt; I was torn between the need to try and negotiate with him, and the fear of jeopardising my prospects of food. And possibly those of my companion, I thought, and I could not risk that; he looked as if one more day without eating might be the end of him – although perhaps that would be a kindness. I crawled across the straw in the direction of the poor wretch in the corner, making reassuring noises to disguise my own fear. I could hear him moving away from me as I approached.

'Don't be afraid,' I whispered. 'Listen. Your hands are free. Can you untie me?'

His only response was a choked sob. Curbing my impatience, I tried again.

'I won't hurt you. Will you help me? Please. I can't think clearly with this pain in my arms.' I shuffled closer on my knees until I heard his ragged breathing beside me. The stink coming off him made me retch; not just of his own filth, but the rotting odour of infected flesh from the sores and lacerations I had seen all over his body. It was a wonder the man was still alive. I turned my back and lifted my bound hands until my fingers made contact with him. I waited, breathing through my mouth – though that made little difference. After a long moment, a bony hand clasped my wrist. I gritted my teeth; those who fear the dead walk out of their graves to visit the living on All Hallows' Eve must imagine just such a touch as this. But with surprising gentleness, those claw-like fingers began to pick at the knot on the cord holding me.

'Are you really a count?' I asked, as he worked. For a while he didn't answer. I could tell the task was costing him considerable effort; it must have been painful to bend his fingers.

'I had that name once,' he croaked, when I no longer expected a response. 'Now I am no one.'

'Why are you here?' I was determined to keep up a conversation, though he seemed to find speech difficult. But only this meagre human contact could keep me from despair, I knew, though it was probably too late for him.

Another long silence elapsed; I could not tell if he was ignoring me or merely concentrating.

'Saint Bartholemew's,' he whispered, at last, and his voice cracked as he spoke. At the same time, I felt the rope slacken slightly around my wrists. I tried to pull them apart; he laid his hand on my arm. 'Patience,' he murmured, and resumed his plucking at the knot.

'Saint Bartholemew's night? You are here because of the massacre?' I flinched, despite myself.

He remained silent as he eased the rope away from my

hands and rubbed at the raw patches on my wrists where the bindings had broken the skin. Gingerly, I raised one arm and touched the back of my head; there was a tender lump where I had been struck, and my hair was crusted with dried blood, but the wound was no longer bleeding. The massacre of Saint Bartholomew's happened thirteen years ago. Had he been here all this time? My mind baulked at the thought.

'They came for the wedding,' he said eventually, in a distant voice. 'From the south. All Huguenots, you see. They were guests in my house.'

'Who?'

'My cousin. His wife. The little girls. They had new gowns for it.' His voice faltered and his breath hiccupped again. If he had had eyes, they would have been shedding tears. I reached out and through the dark I found his hand. Swallowing down my revulsion, I let him fold those dreadful skeletal fingers around mine and gradually his distress appeared to subside.

No one in France could fail to shiver at the mention of Saint Bartholomew's night. The twenty-third of August, 1572, when Catholic mobs rampaged through the city, putting every Protestant they could find to the sword. The Seine ran crimson with blood for days after. Catherine de Medici had tried to force an end to the wars of religion by marrying her wild and beautiful daughter Margot to the leader of the Huguenots, the Protestant Henri of Navarre. The marriage was not approved by the Pope, and many devout Catholics were furious at the prospect of such an alliance, but Catherine pushed ahead with the wedding regardless, inviting the most prominent Huguenot nobles in the country to Paris for the celebrations, more extravagant and decadent than any of her famed entertainments. After three days of feasting, dancing and pageantry, the bells of Saint-Germain l'Auxerrois rang out at midnight – a prearranged signal for Catholic troops to kill all the Huguenot leaders in Navarre's entourage, off guard, undefended, many of them in their bedchambers. No one, even now, could say for certain who planned the assassinations or gave the initial command, but the bloodlust spread quickly through the streets; anyone known or suspected to be Protestant was cut down where he stood, or dragged out of bed to be murdered along with his family. Women, children, babies, grandmothers; corpses piled up in the gutters and clogged the river.

I was still in Italy at that time, but my friend Philip Sidney had been living in Paris and told of barricading himself into the English embassy along with Sir Francis Walsingham and his young family as the mob tried to break down the doors. Neither ever forgot the horror of that night: the screaming, the smell of blood, the sight of heads, limbs, entrails scattered in the streets the next morning as if on a battlefield. The shovelling up of corpses, so many that there was not room in Paris to bury them all, the unclaimed dead left to rot along the banks of the Seine. The memory of it drove every decision Walsingham made with regard to the defence of England; he believed the same horrors would come to London if Catholic forces invaded. When King Henri talks of an uprising, it is another Saint Bartholomew's that he fears – as does every citizen of Paris, Catholic or Protestant. It is a fear that the Catholic League has learned to exploit, as the pamphlet I had found in Joseph's room made clear.

'What happened to your cousin?' I asked the Count.

'It was *her* doing,' he said, with unexpected vehemence, clutching at my hand. I felt his spittle fleck my cheek. 'The soldiers came, demanding I give them up. I said I had not seen them. But they broke the doors down and ransacked my house. They found them all. Even their servants.' He paused to draw a rattling breath. 'I said I had not *seen* them,' he repeated, in a hollow voice.

'So you were punished,' I murmured, understanding. 'For not seeing.'

'He took my eyes. And I thanked God, because then I was spared the sight of the little children lying in their gore. Would he had taken my life too. But he will not let me die. Nor will he let me live. He says he still has a use for me in here.'

'Who do you mean? Who blinded you?' I asked.

He heaved a great sigh. 'You *know* who. Young Henri.'

'The King?' I drew back, staring.

'No. You are confused, boy. *Charles* is the king.' The old man gripped my hand tighter. 'I mean Henri Le Balafré.'

The Scarface. The popular nickname of Henri, Duke of Guise, on account of his prominent war wound.

'But you said it was *her* doing. Whose? Do you mean Catherine?'

It was asserted as fact by many that the Queen Mother had issued the order for the Protestant leaders to be killed, to isolate her new son-in-law and ensure he knew where his loyalties now lay. In her defence, people said, she had not anticipated how the flame of murder would catch and consume the entire city, and spread through France until perhaps seventy thousand Protestants lay slaughtered. But the uncomfortable fact remained that, before the bells rang out at midnight, someone's agents had slipped silently through Paris, marking every Protestant home with a white cross, ready for the Angel of Death. There were plenty of others, of course, who pointed the finger at Guise.

'No more now,' the Count said, his voice drained.

I let go of his hand and felt him slump against the wall beside me. He had been in this pit for so long he had no idea King Charles was dead, and his brother now on the throne. But his memory seemed sharp enough when it came to the terrible events that had brought him to this place. If it was true that he was being kept here by the Duke of Guise, then we must be in a Guise prison, and I had no prospect of sending word to anyone with the influence to save me. Another wave of panic overwhelmed me; I had to stand and pace the limits

101

of that confined space before the pounding in my chest and head would subside. Perhaps after some weeks the King would notice I had disappeared, but would he make the effort to find me? Would he dare to confront Guise for my liberty, if I were still alive by then? I forced myself to cling to the gaoler's words about food; if I was to be fed, they surely did not mean to kill me immediately. Cotin had said that the Abbé wanted me questioned about Paul Lefèvre; it was no great leap to suppose that it was Guise who was interested in the answers, and that the Abbé had handed me over. Perhaps I was only here as a prelude to interrogation – a thought which did not bring comfort. When I had brought my breathing under control again, I crouched beside the Count.

'You were at court when Charles was king?' I asked.

'Another kind of prison,' he murmured. It appeared he had not lost all his wits, then.

'Did you ever hear mention of Circe?' It was a long shot, I knew; the man had been shut away from the world for thirteen years. Much had changed at court since then, but perhaps not that much.

'Circe.' His voice drifted off again, as if he were searching his memory. He let out a bitter laugh. 'I know that name.'

A small flame of hope flickered. 'What does it mean? Is it a person? A woman?'

He took a long time to answer.

'She is a witch,' he said, at last. 'A temptress. You must know this. She robs a man of his will, until he is no better than a beast.'

'I know the story from the Odyssey, yes,' I said, trying to hide my disappointment. 'The enchantress who turned Odysseus's men into pigs. But is there another Circe? Someone in Paris?'

'A temptress,' he said, again, more forcefully this time, his voice weighted with contempt. 'But they all are, behind the mask. They bewitch you, then betray you. You will learn, boy.'

He fell silent. I could not tell if he was speaking of Homer's mythical enchantress, or someone specific, or women in general. If the latter, he need not have feared; I had already learned that lesson the hard way.

Perhaps I slept; it was difficult to tell down there in the unchanging dark. I tried to keep my mind occupied, anything to steer it away from the edge of despair. I had no idea how much time had passed before I was jolted back to awareness by the sound of the bolt and the sudden intrusion of light from the hatch.

'Oi. You. The foreign whoreson.' The gaoler leered into the opening; I could see only his mouth and chin. 'Seems Dame Fortune is smiling on you tonight, my friend.'

'I can't remember when I felt luckier,' I said. I guessed from his sarcasm that things were about to take a turn for the worse.

'Shut your mouth and get on your feet against that wall while I fetch the ladder. Governor's orders. Someone's just paid your bail.'

SIX

The gaoler bundled me up the steps and out of the pit, a thick wooden club in one hand in case I thought to cause trouble. I was prodded along a dank corridor and up another spiral staircase. With every step away from the bowels of the building I felt better able to breathe.

'You're lucky you weren't left there any longer,' he said conversationally, as he jabbed me in the back with the club. 'Last feller they threw in with him died of fever inside a couple of days. When I went to get the body out, there was only half of him left.'

'What?' I turned to stare at him; he grinned and mimed a man gnawing a hunk of meat. 'The Count *ate* him?'

'Reckon he had a few bites. Unless there's rats the size of dogs down there. Keep moving.'

'I wouldn't have thought he had the teeth for it.'

'You'd be amazed what desperate men can do. I've seen it all, believe me.'

The sky was still dark outside when we emerged into a cobbled courtyard lit by torches in wall brackets. Though the mist persisted, I could make out the elegant white façades of the surrounding buildings, rising to pointed turrets at the corners and realised where we were: the Palais de Justice, the former royal residence on the Ile de la Cité, now home to the Parlement, the law courts and a small village of ramshackle stalls built around the walls. Ahead was the filigreed roof of the Sainte-Chapelle, its spire vanishing into the smoky air. No one looking from outside would have supposed such a fine place to contain anything as foul as that dungeon among its foundations.

The sound of hooves rang out on the cobbles; I turned to see a handsome chestnut horse with a cloaked rider approaching from the gate. I could not make out his face in the shadows of his hood, and my throat dried. I had been so relieved at my release that I had allowed myself to believe the gaoler had been swayed by my promise of a reward and sent a message to the Louvre after all. Now I realised that he could hardly have had time to do so, still less to have received a response. Another possibility was that somehow Cotin had managed to send a message to Jacopo after I was arrested – but how would Cotin have known where I had been taken? There was only one other possibility, I thought, as I watched the hooded figure spring from his saddle with the agility of a practised horseman: that I had been taken out of the frying pan only to fall into the fire, like the fish in the fable.

The rider led his horse towards us across the courtyard, sweat steaming from its flanks. He walked with the loping stride of a tall man, straight-backed, with an athletic frame; a description that fitted Guise. Would the Duke bother to come for me in person? I lowered my eyes as he approached, steeling myself.

'Give him back his belongings before he dies of cold,' the man said, in an accent that caused me to jerk my head up and stare at him. 'And hurry up about it, you streak of piss, I'm freezing my balls off here.' The gaoler mumbled something and scurried away, leaving us alone. The horse's breath clouded around us as it stamped and shook its head.

'But – you're English,' I said stupidly, in French.

'Correct.' My rescuer pushed his hood back from his face and I recognised the man I had seen watching me from the edge of the crowd in the churchyard of Saint-Séverin yesterday. He smoothed a hand over his sprightly hair and looked me up and down, his face creased in distaste. 'The state of you. Are you injured?'

I touched the lump at the back of my head. 'A little. Not too serious. Who are you?'

'Think of me as a well-wisher.' He gave me a thin smile, and my fear came flooding back. I opened my mouth to ask another question, but he held up a gloved hand. 'All in good time. Let's get off this bloody island first. Are you fit to ride?'

'I think so.'

The gaoler returned and handed me my cloak and, to my great relief, my dagger, glaring at me as if this humiliation was my doing. The Englishman mounted without another word and reached down a hand to pull me into the saddle behind him.

I clung on as he wheeled the horse around and urged it out of the gate. He slowed as we met the Boulevard de Paris, where a man I took to be a servant stood waiting with a flaming torch; he led the way to the Pont Saint-Michel and we followed at walking pace. Even so, the jolting motion sent waves of pain up my spine to the bruise on my head.

'Did Jacopo send you?' I asked, in English, when it seemed he would not speak. The houses ranged precariously along the bridge remained dark, though I thought I glimpsed movement behind the windows; people evidently roused by the sound of the horse's hooves, curious – or afraid – to know who was abroad at this hour.

'Jacopo Corbinelli? No, he didn't. Why – were you expecting someone?'

'I thought – then who? How did you know where to find me?'

'Oh, I've been keeping an eye on you for a while,' he said cheerfully, over his shoulder, ignoring the first question.

'Spying,' I said. I should have guessed. How naïve to think I could have lived quietly in Paris for the past two months without anyone watching me.

'Well, you're the expert there.' He did not say it unpleasantly; more in the spirit of making conversation. But the remark alarmed me further; the only people in Paris likely to accuse me of spying – apart from the King – were those who considered me an enemy. And there might be more of those than I knew; Paris was full of English Catholic exiles now, either banished by Elizabeth's government or fled illegally, many of them rallying to the banner of the Scottish Queen Mary Stuart, whose ambassador here was at the heart of the conspiracies to free her with the help of the Catholic League. My name would be known to anyone who had been party to the most recent of those plots, the one uncovered – as the King had rightly said – by letters intercepted at the French embassy in London. It was quite possible, I now realised, that my rescuer was one of their number.

'I have never seen you before yesterday, in the churchyard.'

'Naturally you haven't. I do have some skill in this business.'

'So why now?'

'I thought it was time we were introduced.'

'Who do you work for?'

He flashed a smile over his shoulder. 'I serve God, Doctor Bruno. How about you?'

Merda. Only a Catholic would give an answer like that. I decided it was best to say nothing. On the far side of the bridge he turned left on to the Quai des Bernardins and it became clear that he was not taking me to my lodgings.

'I can walk home from here, if you let me down,' I said, trying not to betray my anxiety in my voice.

'I don't think so,' he said pleasantly. 'You can barely be

trusted to get yourself to the end of the street without someone's soldiers carting you off. Besides, it's gone three in the morning – we don't want to disturb the redoubtable Madame de la Fosse at this hour, do we? And – forgive my candour – but I'm afraid you do smell quite unforgivably of shit. You need a bath and a hot meal before you're fit to go home. A few more hours won't hurt.'

I fell silent again as the horse continued its steady pace along the quai, the servant with the lamp plodding doggedly ahead, a wavering pool of orange in the grey air. The fog condensed on my lips with a taste of earth and smoke. This man was clever, that much was certain; in one response he had managed to convey how much he knew about me, down to the name of my landlady and my visit from the King's guard the night before. I could only assume that he was taking me to Guise. I leaned out and looked at the ground; the horse was moving slowly enough that I could slip off without too much damage, but I would be unlikely to outrun him and his servant.

'I wouldn't jump if I were you,' he said, without turning. 'Francis is easily startled. He might very well trample you before I could stop him, and then I'd have paid out all that money for nothing. You didn't come cheap, you know.'

'Is Francis the horse or the servant?'

'The horse. Named for my favourite member of the Privy Council.'

'You named your horse after Walsingham?'

'He's really quite intelligent. For a horse.'

I could not help a burst of laughter, despite myself. I felt his shoulders relax.

'Who the devil *are* you?' I asked.

He considered the question for a few moments. 'My name will not be unfamiliar to you, just as yours is not to me. We have a number of acquaintances in common – not all of them well disposed to either of us. So it may be that you have heard things about me which are partially or entirely untrue. In any case, I urge you not to overreact.'

'For God's sake,' I said irritably.

'Very well. My name is Charles Paget.'

I let go of him instantly and pushed myself backwards over the hindquarters of the horse, landing hard on the ground. I heard him pull the horse around, barking a command in French; before I could scramble to my feet or reach for my dagger, the torch-bearer loomed over me, his response surprisingly swift for such a lumpen man. He took hold of my arm in a grip that was not worth arguing with and dragged me to my feet.

'Now, you see, I call that an overreaction,' Paget observed from above, holding the horse on a short rein as it stamped on the spot. 'If I wished you harm, I would have left you where you were, would I not?'

I said nothing. There were worse harms than being left in the Conciergerie; I feared that was about to become all too apparent. My free hand crept across to my belt.

'Don't touch the knife, Bruno, or I shall regret my generosity in returning it to you. You can walk if you choose, but it would be easier for everyone if you stop being a bloody fool and get back in the saddle.'

I planted my feet and looked up at him. 'I'm not going anywhere unless you tell me where, and why.'

He let out a theatrical sigh. 'Very well – let us continue with this pretence that you have some agency here.' The horse danced its feet forward and back in a square and snorted. 'I am taking you to the English embassy. Happy? Now get on the horse.'

'I am not stupid. You mean to kill me.'

He laughed at this. 'How dramatic you Italians are. I don't know where you got that notion. If that were my intention, I could have managed it before now with a lot less trouble. And I'm afraid you can be remarkably stupid. For a man with so many enemies, you don't look over your shoulder nearly as often as you ought.'

This needled me, because I knew he was right; I had allowed myself to grow careless.

'Why should I trust you?'

'Be*cause*—' and there was an edge to his voice now – 'I've just handed over a hefty purse of money to free you from that hole. I didn't see any of your friends from the Louvre queuing up to get you out.'

'Who sent you?'

He rolled his eyes to Heaven. 'Who do you think?'

I shook my head, blank. The only people I could think of who would send Charles Paget after me wanted me dead. He slapped the horse's neck twice and gave me a meaningful look. My eyes widened.

'Walsingham? But—'

'Let's not discuss it in the middle of the street, eh? For the last time, Bruno, get on the damned horse.'

He reached down and the servant crouched to give me a forceful shove in the backside with his shoulder, as my arms were too tired to heave myself up into the saddle. Exhaustion crashed over me; I slumped against Paget's back and could not even muster a smile when he said, 'On, Francis, good fellow,' nudging his mount's flanks with his heels. He was right; I had no choice in the matter.

'Is Walsingham here in Paris?' I asked, as we rode along beside the river.

'All will become clear,' he replied, enjoying his enigmatic act as much as it was infuriating me. I tried again.

'But you work for the Queen of Scots. You are still secretary to her ambassador, unless I am mistaken?'

He hesitated; I waited for him to deny it.

'Our Lord Jesus Himself said a man cannot serve two masters,' he replied, after a while. 'I venture to suggest He had little experience of intelligence work.'

110

He was so pleased with that answer that I did not bother to reply. We reached the grand, four-storey houses of the Quai de la Tournelle, with their wide leaded windows overlooking the river. The torch-bearer stopped outside one with a heavy studded front door, and knocked. There was no response. He pounded again; after some time the door was opened by a harassed-looking servant, who regarded us with understandable outrage. Paget's man exchanged a few words with him, gesturing up at us; the servant appeared to be protesting, until finally he nodded and closed the door in our faces.

'They are all abed. Let me go home,' I said to Paget, when it seemed we had been turned away.

'Wait.' He pointed to a high double gate at the side of the house. After some minutes, it swung open and he clipped through into a cobbled stable yard. A boy came forward to take the reins; Paget hopped down lightly and held out a hand to assist me. I ignored it and slid to the ground. I could not help but notice that the boy seemed nervous. He may have been skittish at being roused from sleep, but I did not think that was the case; he was dressed in outdoor clothes and seemed alert, his eyes flitting past us as he led Paget's horse towards the stables. Following the direction of his gaze, I saw a fine black stallion tethered to a post in the yard, a handsome creature with four white socks, saddled up with expensive tack, as if someone had that moment arrived, or was about to leave. There was no distinguishing badge or livery on the harness or saddle cloth. The horse turned its head to regard us with dark liquid eyes and I noticed a pink scar running along its nose and down one cheek.

We were met by the servant who had answered the front door, who led us, apologising, through a tradesmen's entrance to a stone-flagged scullery and on into a spacious kitchen, where a fire burned in a hearth large enough to accommodate an entire cow on a spit; Paget gently urged me towards it and I crouched by the embers, shivering violently, grateful for the heat but conscious of the prison stink rising from my clothes.

'The ambassador will be with you shortly,' the servant said, as he craved our pardon once again for the wait. Paget nodded graciously, as if the fulsome apologies were no more than he was due; I found this curious, since we were the ones who should be sorry for disturbing them at this hour.

'God's teeth, you smell like a leper,' Paget remarked, pacing the kitchen, slapping his hands together in their leather gloves. 'You should get those clothes off and burn them as soon as possible. Probably infested with all kinds of vermin. I'll bring you replacements tomorrow.'

'Thank you, but there is no need—'

I broke off at the sound of voices; Paget had heard them too. We both turned to look at the interior door of the kitchen; from beyond it came an urgent, whispered exchange, two men speaking, one angry, the other mollifying. The conversation stopped abruptly and the door swung open. A short, mouse-haired man entered alone, wearing a woollen robe over a sombre grey doublet and hose and rubbing tired eyes with the heel of his left hand. In his right he dangled a quill pen and a pair of spectacles. I had the growing impression that whatever we had interrupted here, it was not a household asleep.

'This is damned inconvenient, Paget.' The man sounded irritable, but I thought I detected an underlying note of fear. He polished the eyeglasses on his sleeve, replaced them on his nose and glared at Paget, who crossed the room in a couple of long strides and bent to murmur in the man's ear.

The short man squinted past him and took in my appearance with evident antipathy. 'Oh dear,' he said, wrinkling his nose, as if someone had pointed out to him a damp patch on the ceiling.

'I have no wish to inconvenience you, sir,' I said, darting a glance at Paget. 'I will gladly be on my way, if—' I did not manage to finish the sentence; tiredness, or perhaps hunger or the effects of the blow to my head brought on a wave of dizziness that caused my legs to buckle, so that I stumbled back and almost lost my footing. Paget dived forward and thrust a stool under me.

'I think Doctor Bruno needs food and rest, Ambassador,' Paget said smoothly, as if he were accustomed to taking charge.

'Of course,' the ambassador said, with a hint of impatience. 'No inconvenience at all. Geoffrey!' He turned to the servant standing discreetly in the doorway. 'Light a fire in the blue chamber. Warm some wine and stew for our guest and have the girl heat some water. Doctor Bruno—' he stepped forward and held out a hand, then thought better of touching me, withdrew it and offered an awkward smile instead. 'I am Sir Edward Stafford. It has long been my hope that I would one day welcome you to Her Majesty's embassy as my guest, though I confess I had pictured more orthodox circumstances. I am truly sorry you should have been subjected to such an ordeal tonight. But – well, these are unruly times. I pray you take your ease for now and when you are rested we will speak further. Do not hesitate to ask my steward, Geoffrey, if you have need of anything. I bid you good night.' He paused in the doorway. 'I mean no offence, but I would prefer if you did not come any further into the house until you have washed and removed your clothes. They may carry some pestilence from the gaol. Geoffrey – fetch Doctor Bruno a robe and take his things outside.'

'I can dispose of them on my way out,' Paget offered, ever helpful. I wrapped my arms tighter around my chest and felt the crackle of the papers inside my doublet. Was that why everyone was so solicitous to relieve me of my clothes – so that they could search me?

'I think I can manage to undress myself. I thank you, gentlemen,' I added, to soften the reproach.

Paget exchanged a glance with Stafford. 'As you wish. You will have the opportunity to thank me tomorrow, Bruno. Give you good night.' He gave a cursory bow to the room in general and turned as if to leave.

'Paget. A word, before you go.' Stafford nodded towards the door into the house. 'Wait in my study, would you?'

I noticed Paget's face twitch at this peremptory tone, but he merely inclined his head and did as he was asked, closing the door behind him. Stafford rubbed the back of his hand across his forehead. He seemed relieved that Paget had gone. I had heard a little about the English ambassador from Walsingham, but he was younger than I had expected, no more than mid-thirties, though his worn expression and fussy mannerisms lent him the look of a middle-aged academic. He peered at me now as if I were yet another problem to be solved.

'I have letters for you,' he said, lowering his voice.

My heart leapt. 'From London?'

He answered with a curt nod. 'They will keep until tomorrow. We will discuss it all then. Give you good night, Doctor Bruno.'

'Thank you, sir. For everything.' I was so tired now I could barely raise my head, but I knew I could not afford to let my guard slip. 'And do not fear – I will reimburse you as soon as I can.'

He frowned. 'For what?'

'What you paid in bail.'

He shook his head. 'That was none of my doing. If money was paid out, you must take that up with Paget.'

Now it was my turn to look confused. 'But why would—'

He held up a hand to stop me. 'All I know is that a fort-night ago, when these letters arrived, I asked him to find you and deliver the instruction to call on me, at Walsingham's behest. I did not ask him to bring you to my house in the middle of the night smelling like a plague pit.'

'I apologise for that. It would not have been my choice to arrive like this either.'

Stafford looked uncertain; he seemed about to speak further, when he glanced at the door and his jaw tightened. 'If you will excuse me.'

I knew I had only a moment alone before the steward returned and demanded my clothes. I reached inside my doublet, drew out the pages I had taken from Frère Joseph's cell and smoothed them flat on the floor as best I could. They were badly creased, and damp with sweat in places, but still legible. I pulled off my boots, rolled the papers together and stuffed them inside. I had just placed the boots by the hearth when the steward, Geoffrey, entered with a dark red woollen robe draped over his arm; in one hand he carried a large sack and in the other a silver tankard, steam rising from its surface. A young maidservant followed carrying a pail of water, her face drooping with fatigue. Geoffrey handed me the drink; I breathed in the scent of spiced wine, took a sip and felt its welcome warmth spread through me.

'You may bathe in the scullery when the water is heated,' he said, his tone civil but detached. 'If you would put your clothes in the sack, I can take them out to the yard.'

'They are good wool, made by English tailors,' I said, unbuttoning my doublet one-handed. 'Take them outside if you must, but do not destroy them. I will take them away with me tomorrow and have them laundered.'

'I fear, sir, you will not be rid of that smell easily.'

'Well, it is worth a try. And my boots I will keep with me.'

He looked doubtful. 'I fear they may have absorbed some contagion. At least allow me to clean them.'

'They stay with me,' I said firmly. He inclined his head, knowing better than to insist. But he watched me closely while I undressed, marking every item of clothing as I dropped it into his sack; I guessed he had been instructed to make sure I was not hiding anything. I was at last left alone to wash myself in the scullery, the maid leaving fresh pails of hot water outside the door. I plunged my head into the bucket, rubbing hard at my hair; as I raised it, water coursing down my face, I heard a sharp exchange of voices from the yard outside, followed by the clatter of a horse's hooves. It could have been Paget leaving, though I remembered that unmarked horse with the scar tethered outside. Perhaps Stafford's nocturnal visitor had preferred not to be seen and slipped away through another door.

I dreamed that night of the Count. His cadaver's face looming, eyeless sockets staring, rotting breath gusting in my face as he hissed the word 'Circe' over and over. I woke with a cry into a chilly light, covered with a sheen of sweat though I was wearing only an undershirt beneath the blankets. It took me several minutes to recover my bearings; enclosed in the blue canopy and curtains of my bed, I had the sense of being underwater. I sat up, running through a tally of my injuries and their severity as I attempted to move. My wrists were bandaged with clean strips of linen; Geoffrey had applied a salve and wrapped them himself the night before with a sure touch, polite but inscrutable. He had bathed the wound on my head and made a poultice that had done much to reduce the swelling, I realised as I reached up to check. Drawing back the bed curtain and swinging my legs gingerly to the floor, I was pleased to find that, though I was well decorated with cuts and bruises and every part of me ached, none of it was severe enough to keep me from walking. I was fortunate that those soldiers at the abbey had not been more energetic in my detention.

I crossed the room and opened the shutters with a loud creak. My window overlooked the river, busy with boats. Yesterday's mist had lifted and patches of blue showed through a high gauze of cloud; I guessed the morning was already well advanced. I needed to be on my way. Shivering, I pulled on the robe I had been given the night before and wondered what I was supposed to do about clothes. All I had were my

116

boots. I glanced around the room and realised immediately that they were not where I had left them, by the door. I crouched to look under the bed; perhaps I had misremembered. But a brief search confirmed that the boots were no longer in the room. Someone had been in while I was asleep and taken them – and with them, the draft pamphlets and the love letter I had taken from Frère Joseph's cell. I stood by the window, weighing up what to do. Not only were those papers proof of a link between Joseph and Paul Lefèvre, they could be a danger to me; to print and distribute treasonous words against the King was a capital offence, and protesting that I was not the author would be a flimsy defence if I was caught with them. I wondered if anyone here could have taken them to use against me. I did not trust Paget to do anything without ulterior motive, including the bail, and Stafford's furtive manner was hardly more reassuring.

There came a brisk knock on the door, as if someone had been waiting outside for the first sign of movement. I called '*Entrez*,' then remembered I was in an English household. 'Yes?'

The door opened to reveal Geoffrey, wearing his impeccable smile, a suit of clothes over one arm and an earthenware bowl in his hand.

'Good morning, sir. I trust you are rested. I've brought you some warm milk with honey, and some spare clothes of the ambassador's clerk to try on. You are of a similar size, I think. Sir Edward awaits you in his study when you are ready.' He laid the clothes on the bed – a plain but serviceable grey doublet and breeches, with good woollen hose and a linen shirt – and backed away towards the door with a neat bow.

'I cannot seem to find my boots,' I said, giving him a pointed look.

'Ah, yes. We have done you the service of cleaning them, sir,' he said, in that same deferential tone that gave nothing away. 'You will find them in the kitchen, warming by the fire. If that is all?'

I could not object to his taking the boots without revealing that I had something to hide, so I shook my head and muttered my thanks.

'I will tell the ambassador to expect you shortly, then,' he said, and closed the door.

The clothes fitted well; not bothering to lace the doublet, I raced down the stairs in my stockinged feet to find my boots, cleaner than they had been in months, waiting as he had said in the hearth. They were, as I had feared, empty. I turned to ask Geoffrey what he had done with the papers, but he had conveniently disappeared. A kitchen girl pointed me to Sir Edward's study. I knocked on the polished wood and entered.

The ambassador sat behind a wide desk piled high with bundles of documents tied up in different-coloured ribbons. His casement overlooked a tidy garden at the rear of the house, the other side from the river. It was a companionable room; shelves of books lined the walls and a large globe in a mahogany stand dominated one corner beside a smaller desk where a pale young man sat copying letters. Stafford pushed his glasses up his nose and snapped his fingers for his clerk to leave the room as I entered. 'And see that I am not disturbed,' he added, as the young man gathered up his papers. 'Bring one of those stools for my guest on your way out.' The boy moved a stack of books from a stool by the fireplace and carried it over to Stafford's desk, before bowing and closing the door behind him. Stafford gestured for me to take a seat opposite. The stool was lower than his own chair; I could see he was pleased with the advantage.

'Well, you smell better than you did last night, at any rate. You have slept well?'

I inclined my head. 'I must apologise again for intruding in such a state, and at that hour. It was not my idea.'

He waved this away. Replacing his quill carefully in its stand, he folded his hands together and gave me a long look over his glasses.

'Let us deal frankly with one another, Doctor Bruno. I have had a communication from Master Secretary Walsingham urging me to make use of your talents now that you are here in Paris. He says that for courage, loyalty and cunning I will not find your equal.'

'That is generous of him.' I could barely hide my surprise; Walsingham was famously grudging with his praise. I had been of use to him while I was in England and resident in the French embassy, with access to their communications, but I had felt this past summer that, if he had truly valued my abilities, he would have done more to enable me to stay in London. He had assured me, when it seemed inevitable that I must return to France, that he would recommend me to Stafford, but as I had heard nothing, I had come to believe he meant it only as a courtesy. I should have had more faith in the old spymaster.

'I know that you were instrumental in preventing the success of that conspiracy two years past, now known among the Queen's councillors as the Throckmorton Plot, and that you rendered further services to Her Majesty during your time in London. I am only sorry I have not acted sooner, but things have been rather fraught of late. Now listen.' Stafford leaned forward and fixed me with a serious expression. 'We have good intelligence that the Duke of Guise and his supporters are planning a coup against King Henri.'

I laughed, assuming this to be some kind of straight-faced English humour. 'Every tavern-keeper and laundress in Paris has that intelligence. People talk of little else.' I stopped when I saw his expression.

'You think it is a laughing matter?' He pushed his eyeglasses up his nose again, indignant. 'France in the hands of the Catholic League would be calamitous for England. There would be nothing then to stop France and Spain joining forces to invade us. We could not repel such an attack, especially if those Catholics remaining in England were to support them and take up arms – it would be death for Queen Elizabeth and the English Church. The murder of this priest could be the spark that starts the whole conflagration.'

'If people think King Henri is responsible, you mean?'

'Guise intends to denounce a man publicly as an assassin hired by the King. The people will be incensed.'

'What man?'

'I don't know – that hardly matters. Some wretch who will have been tortured and threatened until he says whatever Guise needs him to say.' He picked up the quill again and turned it between his fingers. 'There was a riot yesterday outside the priest's church of Saint-Séverin. It was only put down when the King sent a company of archers to disperse the crowd. At least one person severely injured, which has made matters worse. With a sufficient mob at his back and popular feeling in his favour, Guise would have the strength to march on the Louvre. If he succeeds in toppling Henri, he will not rest until the Protestant Church in France is torn up by the roots and cast into the fire. It would make the Saint Bartholomew's massacre look like a children's game.' He pressed his lips together until they disappeared in a white line.

'How do you know all this?'

He shot me a look over his glasses, as if to say I should know better than to ask his sources. But before the question was even out of my mouth, I had answered it myself: Charles Paget. I recalled his comment about serving two masters; was he now selling Guise's secrets to the English? And what did he stand to gain by it?

'You were friends with this priest, I understand?' Stafford continued.

'I would not say that, exactly. I knew him a little from the university, some years ago.'

'You had a secret meeting with him shortly before his last sermon. And you were there at his deathbed.' He rearranged some papers on his desk as he said this, not looking at me, his tone matter-of-fact.

'Only by chance. And the time before I was making my confession.' Paget had been keeping a keen eye on me, it seemed.

Stafford clicked his tongue, impatient. 'You are excommunicate, Doctor Bruno, you are not permitted the sacrament of confession. So you must have had other business with him. In any case, the Duke of Guise is under the impression that the priest told you some secret with his dying breath. He will no doubt be concerned lest that information undermine the version he wants people to believe. Lefèvre belonged to the League. It is my view that he must have been killed because he knew more than he ought, or because his loyalty was suspect. Guise clearly fears that he confided something to you. So I am asking you plainly what you know of the matter.'

I took a deep breath, considering how much to lay before him. While I could not deny I was excited by the prospect of working for Walsingham again, especially if there was a stipend involved, I was not at all sure how far to trust Stafford.

'Am I to consider myself in your employ, then, Sir Edward?'

He tutted, as if the commercial side were beneath him, but after a short pause while we looked expectantly at one another, he reached down and unlocked a drawer in his desk. From it he withdrew a small chest and took out a purse, which he laid on the table in front of me.

'If I consider your intelligence worthwhile, it will be rewarded.'

I smiled. 'You are a shrewd negotiator, sir. But it would be no fault of mine if you judge what I tell you to be worthless, when it may have value to others. I would like nothing better than to help preserve England's freedoms, but a man must eat.'

His mouth twitched again, but after a moment he nodded and shook out two gold écus on to the papers. 'Walsingham said you were a sharp man. Very well. If you are agreeable, I will pay you a small amount for the gathering of information, and more if what you bring is valuable to England.' He pushed the coins towards me. 'Would such an arrangement be satisfactory to you?'

'Paul Lefèvre hinted that he had knowledge of an imminent plot against the King,' I said, picking up the coins and ignoring his sarcasm. 'When I pressed him on it, he said he spoke in general terms only. But I believe he may have had second thoughts about his complicity. He may even have considered warning Henri.'

'What makes you think that?'

'Hints he gave.' I decided not to mention the burned letter until I had a clearer idea of whether or not the King had received a copy. 'In any case, my guess is that the League had come to feel he could not be relied upon to keep his mouth shut.'

'As I thought. So they shut it for him.' Stafford nodded. 'Especially if they knew he had been talking to you. You are still a confidant of the King, I understand?'

I shrugged. 'Not as I once was.'

'But he sent for you the night before last.'

'Sir Edward . . .' I paused, chinking the coins in my palm. 'How long has Charles Paget been watching me?'

He blinked. 'I asked him to find you a fortnight since. Beyond that, I cannot account for his movements.'

'He seems on very familiar terms with you,' I said carefully. His eyes grew guarded.

'That surprises you, does it? Because he is a Catholic?'

'With respect, sir, he is not just any Catholic. He was a principal architect of the conspiracy against Queen Elizabeth two years ago. He was the main contact between Mary Stuart's supporters here and the Catholic nobles in England. It was he who arranged safe harbours and provisions for Guise's invading army.' I broke off, aware that my voice had risen.

Stafford brought his palm down on the desk, his expression stony. 'Precisely. Paget is a uniquely valuable source of information, with access to the inner rooms of all our enemies.' He counted off on his fingers. 'He is secretary to Archbishop Beaton, Mary Stuart's ambassador here. He has the ear of the Spanish ambassador. He is trusted by Guise and his sister and knows everyone of interest among the English émigrés. It is quite an achievement to have turned him, believe me.' He allowed himself a preening expression. 'Look closely at this whole tangled web of religious and political alliances in Paris and you will find Paget at the very heart.'

'Forgive me, but – why would a man like Paget switch loyalties? When only two years ago he risked his life in a plot to assassinate the Queen and invade England?'

Stafford glared at me. 'Because he craves the Queen's pardon. He does not want to spend his life in exile. You of all men should understand that.' There was an edge to his voice; a twist of the knife. Clearly he did not like having his judgement challenged. 'I suspect the fates of his co-conspirators have greatly frightened him – he wishes to distance himself from them through loyal service to England, in the hope of one day returning to court. And because, like the rest of us, he needs money.'

If you believe that, I thought, you are the greatest dupe on either side of the Channel.

'We both know that his friends are dead or in prison because of me,' I said. 'You will understand, then, that I am not convinced his feelings towards me are entirely benign. And I find it hard to believe that a man like that would give up his religious allegiance so easily.'

'Nonetheless, if it were not for him you might be sitting across from the Duke of Guise this morning, answering his questions instead of mine.' Stafford flashed a thin smile that did not reach his eyes. 'And I doubt he would have offered you breakfast. Not that this is any of your business, but Paget has already given me several pieces of intelligence from the Catholic side that leave me quite satisfied as to his integrity. Tell me why you were at the abbey of Saint-Victor last night?'

I realised the discussion about Paget was closed. 'I believed Paul Lefèvre's killer came from among the friars,' I said. 'One of them fled when I tried to accost him.'

Stafford nodded, more relaxed now that we were back on less fraught ground. I did not envy him his position here, trying to juggle all the competing factions in Paris and second-guess which of them might rise to power so that he could move to his sovereign's best advantage. Or indeed his own. No wonder he was willing to take a man with Paget's rich connections without probing too closely. No wonder either that he looked older than his years.

'And these?' he asked, pushing a crumpled sheet of paper across the desk. I saw that it was one of the draft pamphlets I had taken from Joseph's room and hidden in my boot. There seemed little point in protesting about him looking through my belongings while I was asleep.

'I searched the friar's cell after he fled. If he wrote these polemics it suggests he was actively involved with the League. The Abbé interrupted me before I could find anything more conclusive. He didn't appreciate my intrusion. Hence the Conciergerie.'

He nodded. 'Abbé Renaud of Saint-Victor is ultra-conservative in religion and politics, that is well known. He would not want one of his friars accused of murder, especially if he could be linked to Guise. You were lucky to escape with your life.'

I agreed. A thought occurred. 'Do you know anyone called Brinkley? It is an English name, I think?'

He looked startled. 'Yes indeed – Stephen Brinkley, a printer, originally from Oxfordshire. He spent time in the Tower for printing Jesuit books in '81, fled here when he was released. He has a small shop by the Palais de Justice. We keep an eye on him – he's been smuggling Papist works and we suspect he's a link in that filthy trade in martyr's relics coming out of England. Why, do you think he has something to do with this business?'

'A printer. Would he print propaganda for the League?'

'This, you mean?' He tapped the pamphlet with a forefinger. 'Yes, I would not be surprised. The English Catholics here are a tight community, and most of them look to Guise and Mary Stuart as their best chance of restoring their fortunes. They often use the printers' shops as meeting places with their League contacts.' He curled his lip. 'Look into it, by all means, if you can be discreet. And, ah – there was also this.'

He slid another paper towards me. I saw that it was the love letter I had found in Joseph's mattress.

'Something else I am investigating. It may or may not be important.'

He gave me a long look. 'I wondered if it might be your personal property.'

'I should be so fortunate.' I held his stare, but could not help a roguish tilt of one eyebrow, just to keep him guessing.

'Hm. Well, then.' He gave the letter a little shove with his finger and gestured for me to take it. 'I am more interested in the news you might bring us from the Louvre. My audiences with King Henri are infrequent these days, and unhelpful when they do occur.' He rubbed the back of his hand across his forehead again. His appearance suggested he had not slept much. 'I think Catherine de Medici dislikes me.'

'Don't take that to heart. She dislikes most people, including her own family. Apart from Henri.'

'True. In any case, you are better placed to know the King's mind than I, and that is information that would be of great value to Walsingham.' He patted the chest from which he had taken the coins. 'We will work out an arrangement. In the meantime, if you want to speak to me, you can always send a message or call in here. Preferably not at three in the morning.'

'No – I see you entertain other visitors at that hour.' I had meant it as a light-hearted aside, but Stafford's head snapped up and his eyes burned into me.

'You overstep the mark.' He pointed his quill at me. 'You should understand that some embassy business needs to be conducted away from public view.' He dipped the nib in the ink and with a show of ceremony turned his attention to the pile of papers before him. It appeared that my audience was at an end. 'Geoffrey will see you out. You can return my clerk's clothes in due course.'

'You said you had letters for me, from England,' I reminded him. He gave a small, impatient exhalation and reached into another drawer, from which he withdrew two folded papers, both sealed with plain wax. One bore my name on the outside in Sidney's exuberant hand; the other was blank, save for a small symbol inked in the bottom left corner: the astrological sign for the planet Jupiter. The sign I always used to validate my correspondence with Walsingham. I reached for the letters, feeling that old kick in the gut, the anticipation of the chase. A quiet life: I had tried so hard, these past two months, to convince myself that I could be satisfied with that. Avoiding risk, keeping my head down, invisible among my books; I was a philosopher, after all, and the business of putting my ideas into print was dangerous enough. But the fierce, pure thrill that surged through me at the sight of that symbol made me realise I could not go on pretending. Walsingham had asked for me. That exhilaration that came with intelligence work; the giddy sense of walking a knife-edge with every step – it was hard to give up, once you had tasted it. Only now could I acknowledge how adrift I had felt without that sense of purpose. I ran my thumb over the smooth wax seal. It looked suspiciously pristine.

'Have you read them?'

'One is in cipher,' Stafford replied, without looking up.

'So you *have* read them.'

126

He raised his head this time, and had at least the grace to look embarrassed. 'I don't possess the code. I presume you do, or it will remain forever a mystery.' He scrawled a flourish and scattered a pinch of sand across the lines he had written. 'Philip Sidney's had a daughter, though,' he remarked, blowing the excess away.

The throwaway delivery angered me; I would have liked to hear that news direct from Sidney's pen. But I kept my face straight and thanked him as I tucked all the papers inside the borrowed doublet and fastened it tight.

'One piece of advice, Bruno,' he said, as I reached the door. 'The Duke of Guise is still looking for you. You would be wise to make a friend of Paget.' He held up a hand before I could protest. 'I can see you do not trust him, but his intervention saved you last night, which should be proof enough that he is true to England's cause. He has Guise's ear, and he could be useful to you, if he chose.'

I murmured a vague agreement and took my leave. I could not argue with Stafford's assertion that, without Paget, I would likely still be in the Conciergerie, or facing questions from the Duke of Guise, quite possibly at the end of a hot poker. It appeared that Paget had already chosen to be useful to me, whom he had every reason to hate, and the question was – why?

SEVEN

Gaston seemed more effusive than usual when I arrived at the Swan shortly after midday.

'Jesus, boy, what's happened to your face?'

I touched a finger to my swollen lip. I had not seen myself in a mirror yet. 'I was involved in an altercation.'

'That right?' He seemed impressed. 'One of your philosophical debates, was it?'

I grinned, and winced at the pain. 'My opponent put forward a robust defence of Aristotle.'

He clapped me hard on the shoulder.

'What can I get you, then? How about a dish of the beef, now that we have a clean slate, so to speak?'

'Clean slate?'

'I don't know how you do it, Bruno. You could charm your way out of Purgatory, I always say. Not that it was a problem—' he held up a hand – 'you know I've never chased you for it, but I take my hat off to you all the same, I really do, you've the luck of the Devil.' He shook his head, indulgent. 'Will I bring you some wine with it?'

'Gaston – what are you talking about?' I never ordered beef at the Swan; he knew my purse did not stretch that far.

Now it was his turn to look puzzled. 'Your debt, my friend.

Feller come in this morning and paid off the lot. Said he owed you a favour.' He looked stricken. 'Maybe I wasn't meant to tell you.'

I sighed. 'An Englishman?'

'That's right.' He brightened. 'Friend from London, he said. Very generous of him, I thought. I mean, I don't want to remind you how much it'd crept up to, but—'

'Then don't.' I preferred not to think about actual figures. I had no doubt that my benefactor would make clear the extent of my debt in due course. 'He is generous, no question.'

'Well, don't look too happy about it. Some of us'd be glad to have a friend like that.'

'Make it the beef, then. But leave the wine.' All I could think of was the old adage that with friends like Charles Paget, one has no need of enemies.

While Gaston disappeared to bellow my order through to the kitchen, I closed my eyes and mulled over the letter from Walsingham that had just taken me the best part of an hour to transcribe, before committing it to memory and burning it.

My skill at deciphering had grown rusty and the cipher Walsingham had given me before I left England was devilishly complex, disguised as four unique alphabets of letters, numbers and symbols and hidden in separate books so that no one, happening upon only one of the papers, would hold the complete cipher in his hand. The exact combination of the four keys to unlock any text was not set down anywhere in writing, but existed only in my memory. But with patience, Walsingham's brisk, direct voice had emerged from the impenetrable jumble of signs on the page. He must have been confident that the cipher was beyond Stafford's capabilities, since much of the letter concerned the ambassador and his new protégé:

It has come to my attention that Charles Paget has once again offered his services to England in the hope of buying a pardon for his past treasons – an offer he has made to me several times and which I have repeatedly refused. But I fear Stafford is taken in by him, for he has a most plausible manner and was born to double-dealing. Be assured – Charles Paget is a most dangerous instrument, and I wish for England's sake he had never been born. While Stafford congratulates himself, you may be sure that Paget is steering their alliance to his own advantage. Do not be fooled. Paget takes money from many hands, but he serves only himself.

Stafford believed he was engaging my services, at Walsingham's instruction, to bring him intelligence from the royal court as to where the King intended to make alliances, either with the Huguenots or the Catholic League. But that was only half the story. The old spymaster's real intention, he explained, was to give me a reason to visit the embassy on a regular basis so that I could keep an eye on Stafford, and particularly his dealings with Paget. All secret correspondence concerning them was to be sent via a trusted messenger, an agent of Walsingham's in Paris who would make himself known to me in due course, and would place my letters directly into Walsingham's hands, so that Stafford would not suspect I was watching him.

Fresh reports from Rome said that Pope Sixtus had issued a new bull, the lead still soft on its seal, confirming and re-inforcing the excommunication of Queen Elizabeth and denouncing her as a bastard, a heretic and a schismatic – justification enough for a patriotic Catholic to feel he was doing a service to God and England by dispatching her. This bull, Walsingham feared, might be the spark that lit the fuse under the powder keg. Mary Stuart's supporters in Paris had recovered from their defeat two years ago and he had reason to believe that another substantial plot was brewing, making Paget's overtures to Stafford all the more suspicious for, as Walsingham said, no conspiracy worth the name would unfold in Paris without Paget at the heart of it. Meanwhile it appeared that Paget had also been watching me, for reasons as yet known only to him, but which were unlikely to be to my advantage.

I let my head drop into my hands as a wave of giddiness washed over me, blurring the edges of my vision; the bench seemed to tilt beneath my weight, as if the reed-strewn floor of the Swan were the deck of a ship. I blinked hard and pressed the heels of my hands into my eyes until the sensation passed. Perhaps the blow to the head had affected me more than I realised. I had wanted this, I reminded myself: to be taken back into Walsingham's service. The strain of leading a double life was the price of admission.

'Doctor Bruno?'

I jerked my head up and focused on the eyes of a young man across the table, peering into my face as if he feared I might need a physician. I took in his appearance, tensing at the realisation that he wore the Augustinian habit. I had not seen Frère Joseph's face last night, and this man appeared to know me. Slowly, I slipped one hand under the table to feel for my knife. I saw from the flicker of his eyes that he had noticed.

'You look unwell,' he observed, with an uncertain smile.

'Just a few scratches,' I said, hoping the waves of dizziness would hold off if I had to fight.

He looked at my face, then shrugged. 'Frère Guillaume sent me, though he wasn't certain you'd be here, after last night. He said you had something to return to him. He was unable to come himself.'

I peered more closely, squinting to focus my blurred vision on him, and realised why he seemed familiar; he was the one who had first come to find me in the library when Paul had asked for me at Saint-Victor. I let my shoulders relax, and unhooked Cotin's keys from my belt.

'Is Frère Guillaume all right?'

The young friar looked pensive. 'He's been confined to his cell for a few days while the Abbé considers how to discipline

131

him. He asked me to tell you not to worry about him, and that Denis was safe and well, if you needed him. He said you would know what that meant.' He hesitated, his eyes expectant. When I only nodded, he continued: 'He also said you'd be interested to hear about Frère Joseph.'

'What about him?' I kept my face neutral.

'He's missing. No one has seen him since last night. The Abbé is worried. He has people out scouring the city for him, the brothers are saying.'

'Really? What else are they saying?'

He lowered his voice. 'The talk is that it has something to do with you.' He hunched forward with an air of complicity. 'Some of the brothers said you were arrested last night stealing money from his cell.'

'There was a misunderstanding. As you see, I am not in custody.' I held up my wrists to prove the point. The young friar looked dubiously at the bandages and back to the cut on my lip.

'Were you spying on him?' He seemed intrigued by the idea. 'The rumour in the abbey is that Joseph is the Abbé's go-between. That he carries secret letters.'

'To whom?'

He shrugged. 'No one knows. It is all speculation. Some say the Duke of Guise, some say the Queen Mother, others say Navarre.'

'Well, that covers most possibilities. So the Abbé is concerned that Joseph might have disappeared with letters in his possession?'

'I suppose. Where do you think he is?'

I eyed him, weighing up how much to say. This boy could not be much more than twenty, and he had the same harried air that had struck me when he came to summon me to the infirmary. Perhaps that was his habitual manner. I noticed his fingernails were bitten down raw to the quick. Cotin evidently trusted the boy enough to send him; still, I needed to be careful.

'No idea. What are the guesses at Saint-Victor?'

He considered. 'Joseph comes from a noble family – he is related to the Duke of Montpensier. I suppose the Abbé is trying all those connections. Also—' he glanced up to make sure he had my attention, and a faint colour stained his cheeks – 'there were rumours he had a mistress.'

I sat up at this. 'What, a courtesan?'

'No one knew for certain. Some said a married noble-woman.' He lowered his eyes, abashed. 'I don't know if there is truth in it. But friars like to run with that kind of gossip.'

I thought of the love letter I had found in Joseph's mattress, with its suggestion of forbidden desires. Doubly illicit, if his lover were married, though abbey rumours were hardly a reliable source of information.

'Oh, I know how friars love the smell of scandal. The way crows love carrion.'

He gave me a shy smile. 'Frère Guillaume said you were once a friar too. Though you abandoned your order.' I saw the shine of admiration in his eyes. 'I envy you your liberty,' he added, lowering his voice.

'You should not envy me anything, Frère . . .'

'Benoît.'

'What may appear liberty to you—' I broke off, seeing the way he twisted his features and turned his gaze to the window. I remembered all too well being his age, staring down the years into a lifetime of cloistered confinement, picturing your youth and vigour withering, unused; what right had I to tell him how to feel? 'Is there anything else you can tell me about Frère Joseph?' I asked, to change the subject.

He shook his head and returned his attention to the table. 'But if I hear anything, I can bring you word. We are not a closed order, as you know. I come into the city to study theology with one of the doctors at the Sorbonne. We could meet. I should like to talk further with you . . .' He looked up with a hopeful expression; his boyish eagerness made me sit back, as if he had encroached too close. I hardly felt worthy to be anyone's advisor at present.

'I would be glad if you could bring me any word of how it goes with Cotin,' I said, a little formally. 'Gaston here usually knows where to find me. Tell Cotin I hope he is soon restored to his liberty.'

'Liberty,' Benoît said, in a voice loaded with scorn. At that moment a serving girl arrived with a steaming plate of beef stew and a roll of fresh bread; the smell rising from it made my stomach lurch and I tore into the food with my fingers, barely raising my head to mumble farewell to Benoît as he took his leave.

The bells were striking three as I finished my meal. I left some coins on the table for Gaston, guilt sitting uncomfortably heavy in my stomach along with the stew. I had been able to eat well today thanks to Paget, I had my freedom thanks to his purse, and I could not shake the feeling that I was already compromised by taking his money. Not that he had given me any choice in the matter, but I needed to extricate myself from that debt as soon as possible, before he demanded something in return, and my only hope of doing so was to find this Frère Joseph de Chartres and hand him over to the King. With Stafford's information about Brinkley, it seemed most likely that a rendezvous was scheduled at the printer's shop for four o'clock this afternoon, and there was a chance that Joseph might turn up, or that I might catch a glimpse of whoever he was intending to meet. It was worth a try, at least; I had no other paths to follow.

A sharp wind had whisked away the mist and cloud of the previous day, revealing a pale wintry sky. The surface of the river whipped into small peaks, crested with foam on the mud-coloured water as I crossed the Pont Saint-Michel. I kept my cloak tight around me but my hood down, alert for any movement at the edge of sight. Paget's criticism – that I did not look over my shoulder as often I should – had stung me, though it had also sounded like a subtle warning. I had believed myself to have developed some skill at this shadowy craft over the past three years, but he had made me feel like a boy playing at soldiers. Perhaps that was how he saw me. 'Born to double-dealing', Walsingham had said, and it was not just a figure of speech; I knew that Charles's father, Lord Paget, had been spymaster for King Henry VIII of England. His sons had swallowed intrigue with their mother's milk. It irritated me that Paget now occupied so much of my thinking, but I could not escape the sense that he was toying with me, and that I needed to raise my game if I were to spar with him as an equal.

As the round white towers of the Palais de Justice rose into view behind the houses of the bridge, I tried to order my unruly thoughts. My guess was that Frère Joseph authored the pamphlets against the King while Paul Lefèvre collected and delivered them to the printer. I had assumed in my ignorance that Paul had come to Saint-Victor on the day he was killed looking for me, but the propaganda leaflets offered a new interpretation; if he had a regular rendezvous with Joseph at the abbey, it would have been an easy business for the almoner to arrange to meet him outside the back gate as usual, attack him while he was off guard and push his body in the river. If Joseph had returned to the abbey by now, he would have learned that the draft pamphlets had been taken from his cell. There was no knowing whether he would take the risk of turning up at the printer's to explain, but I had the papers tucked inside my doublet; if Joseph did not show his face, I could pretend he had sent me in his stead. It was a gamble, but I could learn much, if I could gain the printer's trust.

The Palais looked elegant, if shabby, in the grey light; a maze of spires and towers in white stone, some three hundred years old, occupying the western-most tip of the island. Inside, the business of governing France was conducted at the highest level: the Parlement, the Chambre des Comptes, the Cour des

Aides and the Cour des Monnaies. Outside, all around the buildings and courtyards, ramshackle shops and stalls filled every available space, reminding me of the yard around Saint Paul's church in London. Some were no more than market barrows, with coloured canvas awnings snapping in the wind; others were substantial wooden workshops with painted shutters built against the stone walls of the Palais. Here you could find merchants and printers of all varieties; stationers; bookbinders; food stalls selling sausage, bread, pies, roast chestnuts; letter-writers; poets and troubadours for hire; working women, parading self-consciously in their high wooden shoes, waiting for the clerks and officials to finish work; errand boys, beggars, pickpockets, skinny dogs and feral children, who would stare at you with wild, ravenous eyes.

Soldiers in royal colours guarded the doors into the Palais; others patrolled the courtyards in pairs, chatting, hands resting casually on sword hilts, eyes raking the crowds for any signs of trouble. The whole place buzzed with activity and purpose. Just as in London, people gathered in the aisle of Saint Paul's to meet, gossip, barter, flirt and argue, so here in the Grande Salle, with its vast marble columns, the citizens of Paris congregated, overseen by the ranked statues of long-dead kings. It was hard to believe that somewhere beneath all this bustle and life and colour there could exist an oubliette as dark and silent as the one I had found myself in last night. I thought of the Count, slowly losing his mind down there in his own filth for thirteen years, for the crime of trying to protect his family, and my fists bunched at my sides. When this business with Frère Joseph was over and I was back in the King's favour, I would petition him to do something about the poor wretch.

The English printer's occupied the ground floor of a house in a row of buildings that stood along the boundary wall of the Palais. It appeared to be one of the better-kept premises; the front windows were glazed behind their wooden shutters and a painted sign swung outside. I peered in; my breath misted the glass, but I could make out a neat shop with rows of printed books displayed on shelves behind a counter where a man in his shirtsleeves bent over an open volume by the light of a candle. As church bells across the river struck the hour of four, I stepped back and ducked into the shadow of a wooden shed opposite, where I could remain half-obscured with a view of anyone approaching Brinkley's shop.

I did not have long to wait. At about ten minutes past four, a figure in a dark cloak hurried past the windows and entered the printer's, slipping around the door as fluidly as a cat. He had worn his hood pulled up; I had not seen his face but his furtive manner made clear that he did not want to advertise his presence there. I flexed my fingers and checked my knife as I crossed to Brinkley's door, ignoring the voice in my head that questioned whether I was fit to fight two men at once. Perhaps I would do better to wait until the friar came out, but I was so close now to taking him, with evidence of his treasons; if I could catch him exchanging documents with the printer and bring him alive to the King, he would soon be persuaded to reveal his part in Paul's murder and perhaps the wider conspiracy.

At the sound of the door, both men snapped their heads around immediately with faces as guilty as adulterers. The one in the cloak had drawn down his hood and was looking at me with a startled expression, fixed in the act of passing over a packet. I stared back at him; he was younger than I had expected, no more than mid-twenties, blond and rangy, with pale skin and sharp features dusted with freckles. He did not have the tonsure of a friar; more than that, there was no hint of recognition in his eyes. I had not seen Frère Joseph's face last night and I was not sure how clearly he could have seen me, but I would have expected my appearance to excite some reaction, given that he knew people were looking for him. This boy seemed nervous, but not necessarily on my account.

'May I help you, monsieur?' The older man behind the

counter addressed me in French with a blunt English accent as he took the packet from the boy and tucked it under the counter in one brisk movement. I assessed the room with a quick glance. The ground floor was divided in two by a partition wall; through the open doorway that connected the shop with the room behind I heard the rhythmic clanking of a printing press. The only way out was the main door; as long as I did not allow either of them to get behind me, I would have a clear escape. I smiled, attempting to recover an air of normality, though my presence was clearly unwelcome.

'I beg your pardon, gentlemen,' I said, in my best English, offering them a slight bow. 'I did not mean to interrupt. Please – finish your business.'

'We are finished, sir,' the printer said, his voice hard. 'And what is *your* business?'

I was tempted to observe that his manner of dealing with customers could do with a little refinement, but the boy was still staring fixedly at me.

'Forgive me,' I said, addressing him, 'but have we met? You seem familiar.'

He looked even more alarmed. 'I do not believe so, sir.' Despite his evident unease, his voice was firm and educated. It was also unmistakably English.

'I beg your pardon, then. It must be that you remind me of someone.' I inclined my head by way of apology and turned back to appraise the man with the rolled sleeves. Middling height, sandy hair receded so far that he had apparently decided to cut his losses and crop what remained so close to his skull that he appeared almost bald. Perhaps nearing fifty, though thickset and muscular, with the air of someone who knows how to throw a punch.

'I was told this was the place to find a good selection of books translated from English into French,' I said. 'Books that are not widely available, if you understand my meaning. Ask for Master Brinkley, I was told.' Immediately his face tightened.

'I am Brinkley. But it would depend which titles you are looking for. I don't think we have had the pleasure of your custom before, monsieur? I would be interested to know who recommended my shop. I have only a small clientele, as you can imagine, and they are Englishmen for the most part. But you are not French either, I don't think?' I noticed his eyes flicker to the outer door.

'Oh, do not let me disturb you, if you are expecting somebody,' I said, following the direction of his gaze.

'Not at all – I am expecting no one.' But his face had grown wary.

'In answer to your question – I am Italian, and it was an old friend, Père Paul Lefèvre, who suggested I visit you,' I continued. 'He told me a great deal about you and spoke highly of your shop as a place where one might find all manner of hidden treasures difficult to obtain elsewhere.'

Brinkley was struggling to hide his confusion. 'Is that so? God rest his soul. You have heard the news, I suppose?'

I composed my face into a solemn expression and lowered my eyes. 'Diabolical. That anyone could strike a man of God in cold blood like that. Huguenots, we must presume.'

'That would be the most convenient theory,' the young man broke in, hotly. Brinkley shot him a warning glance.

'And I see you do not believe it. But convenient for whom?' I turned to him, but it was Brinkley who answered.

'If he was your friend, you will know where he has been making enemies of late.' He came out from behind his counter, arms folded across his chest, gently intimidating. I took a step back towards the door.

'Ah. I see your meaning.' I mimed a mincing walk in imitation of the King. This obviously pleased him, because his face relaxed a fraction and he almost cracked a smile. The paper rustled inside my doublet as I moved. 'If that is the case, then we are all in danger,' I said, dropping my voice and sending him a complicit look.

He had regained his composure now and was not to be drawn. 'I'm not sure what you mean by that, monsieur, or who you regard as *we*?'

'I mean—' I leaned in – 'that if the royal family will strike at anyone who speaks ill of the King, there can be few people in Paris who would escape that charge.'

'Only you know your own conscience there, monsieur. For myself, I do not speak ill of the King or his appointed heir. Has someone suggested otherwise?' He held my gaze, impassive. He was waiting for me to slip up, give myself away; clearly he suspected I was a spy. I would have done the same in his place.

'Of course not. I spoke in general terms only.'

'In any case,' he said, shifting half a step towards me, arms still folded, 'I barely knew Père Lefèvre. He may have come in once or twice but he was not a regular customer. Why don't you tell me which books interest you and I will see if I stock them?'

I nodded. 'But I believe we may have another acquaintance in common. A friar from Saint-Victor by the name of Joseph de Chartres?' I glanced at the door. 'I thought I might run into him here today.'

'I know no one of that name. I told you – I trade with Englishmen, for the most part.' Brinkley's glare grew more concentrated, but I detected a flicker of anxiety across his brow. It was impossible to tell whether he was speaking the truth. Behind me, a shadow passed across the shop window, blocking the light for an instant. I made a decision; a reckless one, but I felt I had to act, or we would be dancing around one another until nightfall.

'Master Brinkley – may I speak frankly with you?' I met his gaze full on.

'I wish you would, monsieur,' he said, running a hand across his stubbled scalp, though the crease between his brows deepened.

'Paul Lefèvre was supposed to deliver something to you today,' I began.

He gestured to stop me and turned to the young man. 'Come back later.'

'But—' the boy tried to protest; Brinkley jerked his head sharply towards the door. Reluctantly, with a last reproachful look at me, the boy left.

Brinkley crossed and recrossed his arms and planted himself squarely in front of me, but his eyes darted constantly to the door.

'Who are you?'

'My name is Filippo. You are expecting this, I think.' I took the two écus that Stafford had given me from my purse and tossed them on to the counter. Brinkley jumped and backed away. If anything, the money had made him more suspicious.

'Who sent you?'

By way of answer, I reached inside my doublet for the pamphlets. Before I had a chance even to unfold them, Brinkley's face stiffened, eyes wide; he raised a hand as if to ward off a blow. We continued to stare at one another, each waiting for the other to speak, when the silence was broken by the click of the latch behind us. Brinkley started as if he had been stuck with a knife. I whipped around and my heart dropped.

'Ah. Afternoon, Brinkley. Doctor Bruno – what a surprise.' Paget, immaculate in a fur-trimmed cloak of plum velvet, ducked his head to enter and took off his hat, brushing non-existent dust from the brim and smoothing its feathers. He stopped, taking in the guilt and confusion on our faces, and his eyes locked immediately on to the paper in my hand. 'What have you there?'

Before I could react, he leaned forward and whisked it from my grasp, uncreasing it and scanning the first few lines. I could feel the pulse beating hard at my throat.

'I don't know this man, sir. He just turned up here and shoved these at me.' Brinkley was still backing away, as

141

if putting his counter between us might afford him some protection. He appeared to be scared of Paget; this did not surprise me.

Paget flicked a hand in his direction as if to dislodge a fly, his eyes still running over the page. Eventually he lifted his head and fixed me with that infuriating expression of amusement. 'Dear me, Bruno – this is not the sort of thing one should be waving around in public. Very dangerous. Did you write this?'

'Of course not.'

'I believe you, naturally. I'm not sure others would, though.' He looked at me with a level gaze; I saw Brinkley flinch. 'Imagine if you were caught with such a tract. People might not understand.'

Before I could stop him, he took two long strides across to the fire and threw the paper in. I watched in silence as it curled and blackened in the flames, cursing my impatience. I should have watched and waited; now Paget had destroyed the only evidence linking Joseph to Paul Lefèvre. He looked up at me and smiled.

'There. Wouldn't want you or Master Brinkley compromised, would we?' He turned to the printer. 'Don't worry about this man. We go back a long way.' He clapped me on the shoulder. Brinkley continued to scowl at me, unconvinced. 'Do you have my order?'

'Oh – yes, sir.' Brinkley reached under his counter and produced the package the young man had handed over when I arrived.

Paget tucked it under his arm without offering payment. 'Is that your money there, Bruno?' he said, gesturing to the coins I had thrown on the counter. 'Buying some of Master Brinkley's fine books?'

'I changed my mind,' I muttered, scooping up the coins as the printer followed them with his angry gaze.

'Not to worry – you can buy me a drink instead. Good day, Brinkley. Let me know if you come across anything you think I would enjoy reading.' He cocked an eyebrow at the printer, replaced his hat on his head and swept out, holding the door for me to follow. I could feel Brinkley's stare burning into my back even after I left the shop.

Paget strode away from the Palais without looking at me, though he clearly expected me to accompany him. After a few paces he turned, his face pinched with anger. 'Perhaps you'd like to explain what in God's name you hoped to achieve by frightening Brinkley with that pamphlet.'

'I owe you no explanation,' I said. As soon as the words were out I regretted my choice of them.

'No? Would you like to talk about what you do owe me, Bruno? An explanation would be the very least of it. I hope you enjoyed your dinner at the Swan today, by the way. You're welcome. But if you were hoping Joseph de Chartres was going to turn up and walk into your arms, I shall be disappointed in you – I was led to believe you were an intelligent man.'

'What makes you think I was looking for Joseph?' I said, falling into step beside him. I was not going to give him the satisfaction of thanking him for a debt I never asked him to repay.

He glanced at me from the tail of his eye. 'You were caught stealing from his cell last night. He is still missing. I deduced that you found those papers and reasoned he might have intended them for a printer.'

I guessed Stafford must have told him about the pamphlets, and about Brinkley.

'So you knew Brinkley was printing propaganda for the League?'

'I make it my business to know everything that goes on through the English presses here.' He lengthened his stride deliberately so that I had to half-run every few steps to keep up; a subtle humiliation. 'This will do,' he added, indicating a dim tavern leaning crookedly on the corner of the Boulevard de Paris.

Paget's clothes and air of entitlement drew sharp glances and whispers from the other drinkers, mostly the lower ranks of clerks from the Palais, to judge by their dress, though he appeared not to notice as he pushed through the tap-room without apology and eased himself behind a table by the window, calling for a jug of hot wine.

'How could you be so certain that Joseph would not come to the printer's today, if you knew about their arrangement?' I asked, sliding in beside him.

'Because he is not an idiot. Though I fear you may be.' He leaned in, his face close to mine, hissing through his teeth. 'What did you think you would get from Brinkley, showing him those papers?' He reached out and gripped my arm hard; it was meant to hurt, but I did not flinch. He had bought me, for now, and this display was a reminder. Besides, for all his studied elegance, I suspected he would prove more than competent in a fight, even without a sword. His eyes never left mine.

I said nothing, though I pulled my face back from his hot breath. I was embarrassed to admit that I had panicked; I had hoped to frighten the printer into giving something away and instead I had only succeeded in destroying the evidence. We glared at one another for a long moment, eyes locked – I determined not to look away first – until eventually he made a noise of contempt and let me go.

'All you have achieved is to put Brinkley and all his associates on their guard,' he said, pouring the wine. 'They will go to ground now, or find another meeting-place. That hardly serves us well. Any of us.'

'You will forgive me if I express some doubts about who exactly you mean by *us*,' I said. 'I find it hard to believe we are working to the same ends.'

He leaned his head back against the wooden panelling, took a sip of his wine and laughed softly. He was a handsome man, I could not help noting, with a pinch of envy; chestnut hair swept back and barely touched with grey, a strong jaw framed by a neat beard and curling moustaches, lively brown eyes implying an impish spirit that belied his years. A most dangerous instrument, Walsingham had said. I must remind myself of that.

'Well, you are right to question my feelings towards you, Bruno,' he said, stretching out along the bench, a half-smile still playing around his lips. 'A number of my closest comrades have suffered greatly as a result of your actions. Two of them cruelly executed. Others jailed, lost everything. Years of planning turned to dust in our hands. Men I counted on fled into hiding, scattered through France and Spain, including my own brother. I freely confess there was a time I would gladly have disembowelled you myself.' He raised his tankard to me.

'Where is your proof that any of this was my doing?'

'Oh, come now – we're beyond such delicate pretence, surely? Guise had his spies in the French embassy too, you know. Nothing you did there was as secret as you thought.' He took another drink, watching me over the rim. 'I heard you tried to seduce the ambassador's wife.'

'She tried to seduce me, in fact.' I lifted my cup and put it down again, untouched; better to keep a clear head around Paget.

'I'm sure she did. You can spare me the details. The point is that I recognise a worthy adversary when I see one. Since your victory two years ago I have been curious to meet you. Walsingham imagines he has a nose for ingenious men, but in truth many of his informers are no better than hired hands, easily won over with a better coin. You are a different prospect, I think. You are motivated by *higher aims*.' He ran a finger along the edge of his cup, smiling as if he found the idea charming and quaint.

'You concede we are adversaries, then.'

'Times change, Bruno, and a wise man bends with them. I spend a good deal of time at the English embassy now. Stafford has finally accepted that I am well placed to be useful to England.'

I thought again of Walsingham's letter. 'And what do you gain from it?'

He heaved a long sigh and his shoulders slumped as he peered into his drink, as if it might hold the answer. 'Eventually, I hope, a pardon, if I can prove my worth to Her Majesty. I am sick of exile. Aren't you?' He raised his head and fixed me with a frank look. 'You must be nearing forty. We are of an age. The time of life when a man wants a home, a hearth, a sense of his place in the world, not this rootlessness. Wouldn't you choose to go back, if they would pardon you?'

I glanced away to the early dusk, the grey November street. A sudden image of sunlight on lemon trees flashed through my memory. 'You are guilty of treason.'

'You are guilty of heresy. And yet here we both are, begging to be taken back, any way we can. You hope to petition the Papal nuncio, I understand.'

I tried not to show any reaction. 'Did Paul tell you that?'

'Doesn't matter how I know. Just reminding you again that your secrets don't stay hidden for long. Well, we shall see. Walsingham has pardoned worse offenders than I, if they make sufficient amends. And I'm sure His Holiness has pardoned greater heretics than you.' He paused, stroking a drop of wine from his moustache with a swipe of his forefinger. 'Can't think of any at present, but one must always live in hope.' Another calculated hesitation. 'And have I not proved that I can also be useful to you, Bruno, these past days?'

'What is it you want from me, Paget?' I folded my hands around the tankard and concentrated on the rough wood of the table, its whorls and gouges.

'It seems to me,' he said, pouring more wine for me, though I had not yet touched what I had, 'that we are both looking for the same thing. We want to know who killed Paul Lefèvre, and why. I'm assuming Henri has set you to find out.'

'What is your interest?' I took a slow sip, keeping my eyes on his face.

'Paul was a significant conduit between the Catholic League and the English émigrés. He was entrusted with a great deal of confidential information from both sides. Naturally, a number of people have a stake in discovering who ordered his death.'

'Try asking Joseph de Chartres. Or your friend the Duke of Guise.'

'Guise was keen that I ask you.' He flashed a wolfish smile.

I took another small draught of the wine to cover my reaction. 'So you still work for him?'

'I would not be much use to England if I did not maintain the appearance of intimacy with Guise and his faction,' he said, not meeting my eye. 'You see, at first it was supposed by the League that the King was behind Lefèvre's death, because of his preaching. It seemed the most obvious explanation.'

'Not to the King.'

'He would hardly admit to it. But since it became known that the priest asked for you on his deathbed, the Duke has naturally become curious to know what he so urgently needed to impart to your ears.'

'If Guise has cause to fear what Paul might have said, that surely suggests he had an interest in keeping him silent.'

'You might be forgiven for thinking so. But as far as I can see, the Duke is deeply alarmed by this murder. More so since he learned that your enquiries had led you to Frère Joseph de Chartres.'

'I imagine he would be, given that Joseph writes pamphlets for the League.'

'It's more embarrassing than that. De Chartres is a cousin of the Duke of Montpensier, who is the stepson of Guise's sister.' He arched an eyebrow to convey the difficulty.

'Then the connection seems obvious.'

'But Guise is adamant that he has had no direct contact with Joseph over League business, much less given him orders to kill anyone. I have known the Duke for some years now, and I would swear he is telling the truth. He is therefore keen to know who else Joseph might be involved with.'

'Then he should probably address that question to Joseph himself.'

'Joseph has disappeared, as you know.'

'Perhaps Guise should ask around among his relatives.'

'I imagine he is making enquiries. But he fears that any day the King will press some wretch into declaring publicly that he, Guise, was behind it.'

I gave a dry laugh. 'Has he not planned to do the same to the King?'

'I dare say. But he would prefer to find out the truth. From what I can see, he is worried.'

'So he thinks it would be quicker to threaten me.'

'Has anyone threatened you?' He held up his hands to prove his innocence. 'I admit, that would likely have been his preferred method, if I had left you in the Conciergerie last night. I felt that was not the most effective way to proceed with a man like you. I would guess you are stubborn enough to make it a point of honour to resist hard questioning.'

I looked away. Wouldn't we all like to believe we have the strength to maintain our firmness of purpose in the face of rigorous interrogation? Though I had been roughed up and imprisoned for my public teachings in Rome and Geneva, I had chosen to flee rather than test my resolve at the hands of the Inquisition. I fear pain like any man.

'So,' he said, in a brisker tone, 'why don't you thank me for sparing you the Duke's methods by telling me what Paul Lefèvre confided to you before he died? That is what everyone wishes to know.'

I turned my cup between my hands, nodding slowly. 'So you can pass the information to Guise? Though you now say you are working for England's interests.'

'It *is* in England's interest.' He clicked his tongue. 'Let us say rather it is a question of trading information with Guise.

148

I am only of use to England so long as Guise and his people have confidence in me. Just as your value to Walsingham lies in your intimacy with Henri. This is all one great game, Bruno – all of us playing one another off against the others. The trick is choosing which cards to hold and which to show. I should not have to explain that to you.'

He sat back and tipped the dregs of the jug into his own cup, watching me with an expression that hovered between amusement and anticipation. Born to double-dealing, murmured Walsingham's voice in my ear.

'Paul said nothing intelligible. I already told the friars that.'

His face tightened, all traces of humour vanished. 'Of course you told the friars that. I want you to tell me the truth. You are doing yourself no favours.'

'There is nothing to tell.' I looked him in the eye as I drained my cup and stood. I never had the patience for the gaming table, to Sidney's enduring disappointment, but I did at least have the face for it. Paget was furious, I could see, though he too was trying to show nothing; it was concentrated in the way he pressed his nails into the wood of the table, the ends of his fingers white. I threw down the gold écus on the table. 'There is a downpayment on your trouble. I will bring the rest as soon as I possibly can. Then I will be out of your debt.'

Paget laid a hand over the coins and contemplated this. 'I wish it were that simple, Bruno. Very well then – but you cannot complain later that I did not ask you nicely. I wonder which of us will find Frère Joseph first?' He made it sound as if he were declaring a contest. I offered him the briefest bow and turned my back, though I could swear I heard him chuckling as I left. Somehow he always managed to give the impression that I had behaved exactly as he had predicted, that I was playing a part he had written for me in advance.

EIGHT

I returned to the Left Bank, breath clouding in angry puffs around me as I stamped home, as if I might outpace the humiliations of the past hour. My face burned against the cold air, flushed with wine and fury as I counted again all the ways in which I had been a fool. I had lost the papers that would have linked Joseph to Paul Lefèvre; I had set the printer Brinkley on his guard and gained nothing by it, and I had made an enemy of Paget – not that I now supposed him to have been anything else. I did not believe for a moment in his change of heart, his declaration of loyalty to England, nor his surprising willingness to make an ally of me, who he still held responsible for the ill fortunes of his friends and fellow conspirators. And yet part of me had responded when he spoke of the yearning for home with a frankness that struck such a familiar echo in me; I could almost have been duped into trusting him by the desire to believe that he too understood my particular loneliness. But Paget was clever; he had recognised that tender spot and aimed straight for it. At least I had not allowed myself to be flattered into giving him anything useful.

I wondered again who could have confessed to Paul and what they could have said that had made him break the seal of the confessional. It must be this that the Duke of Guise feared he had confided to me. The key surely lay in whoever or whatever Circe might be, but I could think of no one in Paris I trusted enough to ask, except Jacopo Corbinelli. Working as secretary to Catherine de Medici offered him a comprehensive grasp of court intrigue, and he was the only one I could count on to keep a confidence; I had left it too long to share this business with him. I determined to visit him that evening. The decision raised my spirits; at least with Jacopo I could lay out the whole story, rather than the partial truths I had been dealing to Stafford or Paget.

It was dark by the time I reached rue du Cimetière, though still too early to find Jacopo at his home on the rue des Tournelles, even supposing he were to return there today; he usually stayed at the palace until Catherine had taken her supper, and she often called on him for company in the evenings, increasingly these days as she grew more troubled by her son and her gout. Frequently Jacopo stayed in his own rooms near her apartments at the Tuileries in case she summoned him. I would try his house later; in the meantime, I decided to take my filthy clothes to the laundress in the rue Macon who had helped me to hide from the men searching Paul's lodgings, one of whom I was now certain must have been Frère Joseph de Chartres. It occurred to me that she alone had seen the two men close to, and that, since she had seemed well disposed to me, she might be able to give a more detailed description. I also realised that it would likely take flattery or bribery to persuade any laundress to touch those clothes, such was the general fear of plague or gaol fever, and that as the woman had helped me once she might be convinced to repeat the favour.

She appeared disconcerted when she opened the door to me, but she patted her hair into place and smiled, pulling the door to behind her and wrapping her thin shawl tighter around her shoulders against the night air.

151

'Monsieur. Dwarves after you again tonight?'

'Not this time. I am sorry to disturb you so late, madame, but I have some items here that urgently need washing. They may require more effort than usual,' I added. 'For which I will pay extra, of course.'

Lips pursed, she took the sack from my hand and opened it to peer inside; she recoiled, suppressing a slight retch.

'Mother Mary! Did you fall in a privy?' From the look on her face, I guessed whatever appeal I might once have held was rapidly diminishing.

'Something like that.'

She rubbed her nose with the back of her hand; the skin on her fingers was cracked and raw.

'I will pay well,' I said, again, wishing now that I had not thrown those gold écus to Paget.

She considered, then gave a brief nod. 'I'll need to look at them in daylight. Give me a few days – they won't dry quick in this weather anyway.' She hesitated, tucking a loose strand of hair back into her ragged bun, and darted another glance into the house.

'Thank you. There was something else I wanted to ask you. Those men you saw – the ones who were looking for me. You said one was a cleric.'

She frowned. 'He wore a black robe. Looked like a religious. I saw him again today.'

'The same man? You are sure? Where was this?'

'Here, in the street. Around noon – I was on my way home to give the children their dinner. I wouldn't have paid any attention but I recognised his face under his hood. He was going into one of the buildings.'

'Which one?'

'The house you asked me about before. Where the curé lived, the one from Saint-Séverin.'

I ran a hand through my hair. So Joseph – for it must have been him – had been back to Paul's lodgings today. He must

152

still be looking for whatever he had come in search of the first time, when he and the dwarf had almost caught me, and it had to be important, for him to risk being seen here again now that he knew he was suspected of Paul's murder, despite his powerful friends. Some evidence, then, which might connect him with Paul or with a bigger plot. Perhaps he would have left traces behind that might indicate what he needed to find.

'Did you see him leave again?'

She shook her head. 'I was out delivering laundry all afternoon. You could ask the old widow who lives downstairs in that building, she might remember.'

I thanked her and walked down a few houses to the door of Paul's lodgings. The bells had not yet struck six but the street was empty; a few windows showed the glow of candle-light through gaps in shutters, and voices carried from inside, the noises of evening meals ending and families settling for the night: a clatter of plates, an infant's thin wailing, a woman's voice singing, the words indistinct. Frost crunched under my boots in the ruts left by carts. The houses were sunk in shadow; only a thin rind of moon and a scattering of stars behind drifting clouds offered light and there was no one but the circling gulls to watch me slip my knife into the lock of the street door. At least, so I hoped.

I closed it behind me as soundlessly as I could manage but was certain I caught the click of a latch from inside. The small entrance hall by the stairs was darker than the night outside, but I sensed a tension, as if someone were holding his breath. I could not see if the door into the ground-floor room was open. I paused briefly, wondering if I would do better to knock and speak to this old woman the laundress had mentioned, rather than risk being caught breaking in like a thief, but decided against it; with so many people interested in Paul's death, it was quite possible she had already been suborned by somebody to report on anyone prowling around the dead priest's rooms. I climbed the stairs slowly, wincing at every

153

creak and groan of the old wood that echoed around the ceiling. Unless the woman was stone deaf, I might as well have flung the door wide and announced myself.

The door to Paul's rooms was locked, suggesting that Frère Joseph had been in possession of a key and sufficient time to have conducted his search without being disturbed. I strained to catch any sound but could hear nothing from within the room, and when I peered through the keyhole I saw, to my relief, that the key had not been left in the lock. After some work with my knife, the bolt yielded and I slipped inside the room once more. The air was cold; a sharp draught chased around my legs and the curtain closing off the bedchamber billowed as I closed the door behind me. I rummaged in my bag for a candle stub and tinder-box; once it was alight, I kept it shielded with my hand and turned slowly so that I could take in anything that struck me as different from the last time I had seen this room.

The smell of old woodsmoke still lingered, overlaid with a new scent, delicate and noticeable only in patches, as if it were shifting just out of reach: perfume, spicy and rich, a scent that made me think of Henri and the rarefied air of the court, not the austere rented rooms of a dead priest. Turning towards the desk, I noticed a heap of cloth on the wooden chair. I lifted it to see that it was a linen undershirt and silk hose, folded neatly. I bent and sniffed the shirt; it smelled faintly of sweat, but no trace of perfume. Perhaps Joseph had come here to change clothes; one of his friends or relatives could have arranged to meet him with an outfit less conspicuous than the habit of a religious, and he might have applied the perfume as part of his altered image. This idea brought a jolt of panic; suppose he had changed his appearance in order to leave Paris until someone else was hanged for Paul's murder and he was no longer under suspicion? Once he was out of the city, the chances of finding him or holding him responsible were as good as

154

non-existent. But if he had swapped clothes, where was his friar's habit?

The candle flame snapped and shivered in a sudden gust as the curtain across the partition flapped again and I realised that the small casement in the alcove must be open. Had Joseph escaped that way, to avoid being seen in his new disguise? I pulled back the drape and stifled a cry at what I saw in the instant that the wind snuffed out the candle.

A man lay prone on the bed, naked, his face turned away from me, his skin white and disturbingly luminous in the gloom. Though I had sprung back by instinct, in the same moment I knew already that he would not be woken. I reached out a tentative finger to make sure; the flesh was cold and unyielding. I leaned across and pulled the window shut; it took a few moments before I could reignite the tinder-box and steady my breath. The crown of his head was tonsured; I had little doubt that this was Joseph de Chartres, who only the previous night had landed such a forceful punch to my jaw and outrun me through the fog. Now he was lying dead and naked in the bed of the man I supposed him to have murdered.

Attached to the wall above the bed was a fixture for a candle; I fitted the light into the bracket so that I had both hands free to turn the body on to its back, half-dreading what I would find. But there was no blood; his skin had the flaw-less white sheen of a waxwork, an impression aided by his fair complexion and sparse body hair. I laid him out with as much gentleness as I could manage, given the weight of his body; whatever a man may have done in life, it is a basic human courtesy to treat his corpse with dignity. I lifted his right arm and felt along its length. The time I had spent as a young friar assisting the brother infirmarian at San Domenico had given me a basic knowledge of human anatomy in various states; it had always interested me to note, as we prepared the body of a deceased brother for burial, the different stages of stiffening in the limbs, how quickly the discolouration would appear on the skin. The ability to judge such matters had proved unexpectedly useful more than once over the past few years when confronted with unnatural death. With Joseph the rigidity was only just beginning to set in; I estimated that he had been dead not much more than four or five hours. That fitted with the laundress's story that she had seen him arrive here around noon.

I looked more closely at the face. He would have been an attractive man in life; now his lips had taken on a bluish tinge and he stared at the canopy of the bed from glassy eyes. I lifted the candle down for better light. Though it was cheap tallow and the flame coughed out an oily smoke, I could see in the dim light that the whites of his eyes were flecked with scarlet pinpricks. I clenched my jaw, fought down my distaste and prised open his mouth to find the tongue swollen, the inside of his mouth darkened with discoloured patches, all signs suggesting that he had been strangled. A faint brown mark ran across his throat, almost too indistinct to suggest a ligature. Soft material, then, whatever the killer had used; not a rope. Leaning in, I noticed livid scratches down the side of his neck where the skin had been gouged. I checked his right hand again. Three of the fingers were slightly misshapen – perhaps this was the source of his claim to have a crippled hand. It had not hampered him from hitting me; I could see bruises across the top of the knuckles where he had made contact. More significantly, I found traces of dried blood under the fingernails. He must have been scrabbling against the ligature as it tightened; the killer had taken him by surprise. How, though? Had he been waiting here to ambush Joseph, knowing he would come back eventually, or was it someone he had arranged to meet – someone he knew and trusted, but who needed to dispose of him now that his part in Paul's death was suspected? But that still did not explain why Joseph was naked. I shone the candle along the length of his body

156

and stopped when I reached the shrunken penis in its furze of pale hair. The light picked out a faint pearly sheen across the crease of his groin. Reluctantly, I looked more closely, touching a fingertip to the skin, where a dried film cracked and peeled. So he had ejaculated recently; this could happen to a hanged man at the point of death, I knew, but I was not certain if the same occurred with strangulation. Or was there another, more obvious explanation – that he had met the lover Benoît mentioned and been killed while he was off guard?

I fixed the candle back in the wall bracket and rolled Joseph on to his side once more to examine his back. There I found what I had missed at first: two bruises between his shoulder blades, suggesting that someone had knelt on his back to hold him down while they tightened the ligature. With the force of their own body weight bearing down and a strong cord or tie, even a weaker person – a dwarf, or a woman – might easily subdue a bigger man while he was prone once the ligature was around his neck. It occurred to me that I should speak to the old widow downstairs after all; if she had been watching me, she would likely also have seen anyone who had entered the building earlier.

I crouched with the candle to look under the bed in case anything else had been taken. The small chest containing the grisly martyr's relics was still there. As I reached in to check whether the contents had been disturbed, my hand brushed against a hard object just under the edge of the bed that had half slipped between the floorboards. I lifted it into the light and saw that it was a slim penknife, the kind used to sharpen quills, about six inches long, the handle made of solid silver and decorated with a delicate tracery of vines and leaves. I drew it from the sheath and pressed the blade against my finger. It was sharp enough, though small and neat; it would hardly be much use as a weapon. But it had not been here the last time I searched under this bed, so it was likely that Joseph or his killer had dropped it. The friar had not been cut anywhere, as far as I could see. Had he grabbed for it in self-defence? I peered at the blade as the candlelight danced along its edge. One side was engraved; at the top, just below the handle, a maker's mark stamped in the shape of a single crenellated tower. An expert would know what this emblem signified – where the knife came from and which guild the silversmith belonged to – but it meant nothing to me.

I tucked the penknife into the pocket in my doublet. For now I needed to make sure I left the building unseen while I decided who to inform about Joseph's murder. I supposed that the King ought to know before anyone; he would not be happy. To have come so close to taking the man who could have explained the reasons for Paul Lefèvre's death, and then to lose his confession at the last minute, would strike Henri as a gross failure on my part, I had no doubt. Now there was another murderer to find, higher up the chain, and I might well find myself charged with that task too, as a punishment. I rolled the body back to its original position, glad that I could no longer see those bulging eyes with their wild death stare. It seemed I had won Paget's challenge to see who would find Joseph first, I thought, as I reached to pull the curtain across, and the realisation made me freeze in the act.

He had been so certain that Joseph would not turn up at the printer's shop this afternoon. I closed my eyes and tried to recall the tone, the expression on his face, as he speculated on which of us would track down the missing friar first. All I could picture was a mischievous twist of a smile, an impish suggestion of mockery behind the words, but perhaps I was imposing imagination on memory. Even so, I could not ignore the question: had Paget known what had happened to Joseph all along?

I let my hand fall to my side and remained at the bedside, staring at the corpse, running through everything Paget had said to me that afternoon. I was still lost in thought when I heard a creak of boards, the click of the latch. In one motion

I blew out the candle, leapt up on to the bed beside the body and crouched in a corner behind the drape. I dared not attempt to draw it across lest the movement attract attention. As silently as possible, I slid my dagger out of its sheath. The door closed and footsteps – one pair – advanced a few paces across the floor as the wavering light of a lantern lurched along the far wall. I leaned forward, muscles tensed, ready to spring with the knife as a tall figure came into view and the light was held aloft. From behind its glare a familiar, aristocratic voice spoke in carefully enunciated English.

'Good Lord, Bruno. I'm not sure even I can get you out of this one.'

NINE

The same glint of amusement flickered in his eyes, as if this were still a great game. I felt too tired to humour him by playing along. He was right; he had caught me in an impossible position. I climbed down from the bed and sheathed my knife. He was alone and his own sword hanging at his belt; I did not think he meant to attack me. Not by such an obvious means, anyway.

'I see you've won our little wager, then,' he said casually, moving a few paces nearer to stand by the bed, where he tilted his head and regarded Joseph with professional interest.

'I don't recall agreeing a wager.'

'Perhaps not explicitly,' he said, 'but the stakes are high nonetheless, don't you think?' He turned to me with a victor's smile. 'Whatever have you done to the poor fellow?'

I ignored the question. 'How did you know to find me here, Paget?'

'Process of deduction. You're looking for de Chartres because you think he killed Lefèvre. You're methodically checking all the places you think Joseph might visit, as we saw this afternoon. Presumably you have a reason for thinking he would have come here, or else someone claims to have seen him. A helpful washerwoman, perhaps.' He peeled off his gloves with precision, finger by finger, and gestured with them towards the body. 'You must admit, Bruno – it doesn't look good. Finding you crouched over the naked corpse of the man whose room you broke into last night.'

I swallowed, trying to keep my voice level. 'Since you're obviously still following me closely, you'll know that I've only been here twenty minutes at most. This man has been dead for hours – look at the limbs.'

'Hm.' Paget tucked his gloves into his belt and gave the body a cursory prod. 'The widow downstairs is extremely observant, you know. People up and down these stairs all afternoon, according to her. She's naturally alarmed by so much activity in the rooms of her murdered neighbour. I've had to leave one of my servants to reassure her.'

My heart dropped. So he had brought reinforcements; of course he had. He had planned this with care.

'What an undignified way to go,' he remarked, still looking at Joseph's naked back. 'How was he killed?'

I turned to him. 'Why don't you tell me?'

'I?' He held my gaze. 'I am not a physician.' I continued to look at him in silence; after a few moments he nodded, as if making a concession. 'Very well. I will hazard a guess.' He leaned over to examine the dead man's face, pulled up one of the eyelids, shone his candle on the throat. 'Garrotted, I would say.'

'With what?'

He raised a shoulder. 'How should I know? Something broad and soft, there's not much of a mark. A scarf, perhaps, or a stocking.'

I stared at him. 'Wait.' I lifted the shirt from the chair and drew out the silk stockings that had been left folded in the pile. I held them up to the light. They were long, the kind held up around the thigh with a garter. More usual under the velvet or satin breeches of a court dandy than beneath a friar's robe, but I recalled that at San Domenico the aristocratic young brothers had liked to indulge in finery under their habits as a reminder of their status – the inverse of a hair shirt. Most striking about this pair, though, was that a knot had been tied approximately halfway along.

'He tried to pull at the ligature as he was strangled – he made his neck bleed. There – look.' I pointed; the stockings were spotted with blood and snagged, where the fabric had been torn by frantic nails. 'I'll be damned. Killed with his own stockings.' I stretched them between my hands at either end; there was not much give in the material. 'You'd think they'd be too flimsy,' I murmured, half to myself.

'Not necessarily,' Paget said, taking them from my hands and studying them. He appeared to be giving the matter serious consideration. 'Not if you had a stick.'

'A stick?'

'To make a tourniquet.' He held his fingers about six inches apart to indicate. 'A stick or baton, this sort of length. Get the loop around the victim's neck, twist the ends together, insert the stick and turn it. Tightens instantly without the killer needing to use much force. Then the knot crushes the windpipe.' He wound a stocking once around his wrist and mimed a rotating action with a finger.

I looked at him, almost impressed. 'You seem very familiar with the technique.' The distance between his fingers was about the length of the penknife I had found.

He gave a dry laugh and tossed the stockings back to me. 'I dare say you and I are both conversant with skills that might surprise polite society. One has to learn certain tricks to survive, in our business.'

'How to garrotte a man with a tourniquet?'

'Not something I've put into practice, but I understand the theory.'

'So it seems.'

A silence elapsed. 'Oh, I see,' he said, eventually. His moustache twitched with a smile. 'You think *I* did it?'

162

'You knew Joseph was not coming to Brinkley's shop this afternoon.' I spoke slowly to give myself time to formulate my thoughts. 'I wondered how you could have been so sure. You've coordinated all this. Did you arrange to meet him here, with the promise of helping him escape?' I laid the stockings on the chair and continued to back away from him, towards the door. 'Was that why you got me out of the Conciergerie last night – because you were planning for me to take the blame all along?' I could hear the pitch of my voice rising and broke off; I must remain in control. I was acutely aware of the danger I was now in. Paget laughed.

'I'm flattered that you think I'm so capable, Bruno, but I must say you're beginning to sound a little overwrought.' He took a step back, so that he blocked my way to the door. 'I knew Joseph would not come to Brinkley's because I understand how those networks operate. Lefèvre was the go-between. Joseph would never have turned up himself – that's not how things are done. But you're right to think that you are in serious trouble. I could send for the watch right away. You'd be arrested like that.' He snapped his fingers and grinned. 'Especially with him naked. Everyone knows what you friars are like.'

I didn't smile. 'So what is stopping you?'

He leaned his weight on his right foot, allowing his hand to rest gently on the hilt of his sword as he eyed me with apparent indifference. 'Because I know that you know more than you are telling, and this death means I cannot afford to indulge you any longer. It's time you and I paid a visit.'

I could guess where he had in mind.

'And if I refuse?'

He shook his head, as if my answer had disappointed him. He placed two fingers between his lips and produced a short but piercing whistle. The door opened instantly to reveal the burly servant who had accompanied him the night before, still holding his club in his hand. I could see that he also

163

carried a large hunting knife at his belt. He closed the door behind him and stood against it, his eyes fixed on me.

'It's surprising how sharp an old woman's memory can be when jogged by a little incentive,' Paget said, not acknowledging the servant's presence. 'The neighbour will make a valuable witness. She says someone came up here earlier this afternoon, shortly after the friar arrived.'

'What time? Did she get a look at him?' I thought of the unseen gaze I had sensed in the dark of the hallway downstairs. She would have seen the killer. I wished again that I had thought to speak to her first.

'I have an awful feeling that, if pressed, she'd say he looked exactly like you,' Paget murmured, smoothing his hair. 'Let's not waste any more time, Bruno.' He jerked his head towards the door.

'What about him?' I glanced towards the bed.

'He's not going anywhere. We can discuss what to do about him later.'

'And the widow? She might call the watch. If someone else finds him—'

'I don't think she'll do that.' He patted his purse. 'They drive a hard bargain, these widows. I'll leave one of my men outside – tell her it's for her own safety. She won't try and look in here.'

He nodded to the man by the door, who held it open and waited for us to pass. Paget led the way down the stairs, stopping at the door of the ground-floor rooms to exchange a few hurried words with someone inside. I heard the servant's heavy tread behind me and felt a sudden flush of fear. If I were to be accused of murder, only the King could possibly come to my defence against the testimony of men like Paget and the Abbé of Saint-Victor. Would Henri rouse himself to save me from a false accusation? I supposed it would depend on whether he was implicated. As the street door opened and I felt the slap of cold air on my face, I realised everything

164

now turned on the outcome of the encounter I had been hoping to avoid since I arrived in Paris.

Firelight flickered in restless patterns over the face of the man who stood with his arm resting on the great mantel at shoulder height, staring in silence into the flames. It silvered the scar snaking down his right cheek and hid his deep-set eyes in shadow. In every corner of the chamber, banks of candles gave out a bright glow, their lights constantly in motion, like sun on water. The grand salon at the Hotel de Montpensier lent the occasion a ceremonial air, its high ceiling bright with gilded panels of biblical scenes and plump-cheeked putti, the oak-lined walls hung with antique tapestries of hunting scenes. From every ceiling boss and capital the Montpensier coat of arms gleamed forcefully. No one had spoken since we had arrived. All eyes were on the scar-faced figure by the fire. Paget had settled himself on a stool near the hearth, legs stretched out and crossed at the ankles, casting from one to the other of us with the alertness of a spectator at the Colosseum. I stood, stupidly, in the centre of the room, as if by keeping still I could avoid making a wrong move.

Just as it seemed he had forgotten I was there, the man by the fireplace stirred and lifted his head in my direction. I drew myself up, set my shoulders back and met his appraising stare. If he expected me to grovel to him, he would be disappointed. The face I looked into was refined but hard, an impression emphasised by the scar but implicit in the sharp cheekbones, the pointed beard, small mouth and, most of all, the unblinking eyes, cold as stone. A face weathered by battle, making him appear older and more world-weary than his thirty-six years. Unlike his namesake the King, Henri Duke of Guise did not wear earrings or perfume or shirts of embroidered lace. He smelled of sweat, leather and horses. Despite that, *le Balafré* was reported to be irresistible to women; if half the rumours were true, there was barely a wife or maiden at court who hadn't been willingly conquered by that ruthless manner. I could not see it myself.

'Who do you think killed Joseph de Chartres, then?' The question was addressed directly to me in a voice that belied his appearance; low and resonant, almost musical, the voice of a man assured of his own authority. It was there in his bearing, too; a quiet self-possession distinct from Paget's more obvious swagger. You might almost say that, unlike the King's, the Duke's poise was instinctively regal.

I watched him, trying to gauge what answer he might be expecting. 'I think you did,' I said, eventually.

One corner of his mouth moved a fraction; I could not tell if it was a smile. 'And yet I was not the one discovered crouching by his naked corpse with a knife in my hand. Well – let us suppose for a moment that you are correct. Why did I do it? I am interested to hear your theory.'

I hesitated. The smirk vanished in an instant; the eyes glittered. 'Don't try my patience,' he said, his tone just as measured and elegant as before, but with an edge of flint. 'If you disappeared tonight, Giordano Bruno, who would miss you?'

I did not reply. I had already assumed that I had been brought to the house of his sister, the Duchess of Montpensier, in order to distance him from whatever might happen here. He removed his elbow from the mantel and folded his arms.

'Not King Henri. Nor your English connections, I fear. You are friendless in Paris,' he continued, in the same low voice, 'and that is a dangerous state for any man in these days, all the more so an excommunicate heretic with such a gift for making enemies.'

He was waiting for a response. I inclined my head by a tiny degree to show that I acknowledged the truth of his words. Otherwise I intended to give him nothing. But he had cut through to my greatest vulnerability, and he knew it.

'It would be to your advantage to make new friends, one would think.' He brushed an invisible speck from his sleeve.

'You have been a thorn in my side for some time now, Bruno. You destroyed a project in which I had invested heavily. I have considered having you killed, obviously.'

The logs spat and hissed in the hearth. He lifted his chin as if daring me to answer back. We looked at one another in silence.

'Is this where I graciously thank you for having decided against it?'

'Decided against it, *so far*.' The corner of his mouth twitched again. 'On reflection, I felt that for the present you were more useful alive.'

'And now you wish me to be your friend? That is quite a change of heart.'

'The royal family are not your friends, no matter how much you wish to believe otherwise. You may soon be glad of influential allies in Paris. Let us raise a glass to new alliances.' He picked up a small bell from the mantelpiece and rang it. At the clear note the door opened, though as far as I could see no one had entered, despite the sound of laboured breathing. I peered over the back of a chaise longue and started at the sight of a dwarf in a black velvet suit embroidered with tiny pearls, who crossed to execute a bow towards Guise.

'A jug of hot wine for our guests,' the Duke said, hurrying him out with an impatient gesture. The dwarf turned and moved towards me with his strange, bow-legged gait. It was difficult to judge his age, but he was not a youth; his tightly curled hair was touched with grey at the temples, as was his beard. He returned my stare with open contempt; as he was almost past me he pulled his lips back and bared his teeth. Did he recognise me, or was that merely his way of greeting all visitors? I did not think the dwarf in Paul's rooms had seen me any more than I had seen him; it was impossible to know whether it was the same man, but his appearance had only sharpened my sense of the danger I was in. I was tired of being a source of entertainment.

167

'What is it you want from me, my Lord of Guise?'

The Duke appeared surprised by my bluntness. He tilted his head and considered his answer. 'Good, then, let us be direct. I did not order the deaths of Paul Lefèvre or Joseph de Chartres. You may choose to disbelieve me, but it is the truth. And I want to know who did.' He pulled at the point of his beard, not moving his eyes from my face. 'At first I assumed Lefèvre's murder was Henri's doing. But de Chartres's death complicates matters. If he killed Lefèvre, he would not have done it for Henri, I am certain, not for any price. So something else is at work here. Paget is under the impression you could shed light on it.'

I glanced at Paget, who smiled as if he had done me a favour. 'Did Joseph work for you?' I asked.

Guise frowned. 'He served God and his Abbé, in that order.'

'Who is also your supporter. The Abbé, I mean – I cannot speak for God's allegiance. There are enough people in Paris already who claim to do that.'

This time Guise allowed a brief smile. 'It will not be news to you by now that both the dead men were active on behalf of the Catholic League. De Chartres was a relative of my sister's by marriage and the family will take his murder hard. It is not in my interest to have my name dragged into the business. It would be extremely convenient for me if you took the blame for de Chartres's death. And – let us be frank – you have served yourself up on a platter, and the King with you.'

'I can see that,' I said, fighting to keep my voice even. 'But you know I did not kill him.'

'Ordinarily, that would be no reason not to have you arrested for it.' He tapped his thumbnail against his teeth. 'Except that you know something about this matter. Lefèvre confided in you – don't pretend otherwise. You are going to tell me, one way or another, before I hand you over to the authorities.'

I took a deep breath. Though I was far from convinced that Guise was telling the whole truth, instinct born of experience told me that his uncertainty over the murders was genuine. Beneath the commanding demeanour I thought I caught a hint of anxiety in his eyes, in the way he continued to worry his nail against his teeth. Some element of his network had escaped his control, and it troubled him. I guessed that it had something to do with the conspiracy Paul had hinted at; one or both deaths had taken him by surprise and he needed to discover how much had become known, and by whom. The dwarf returned with a jug of wine and handed me a glass, nailing me with the same hostile glare from beneath his wild brows. I thanked him, hoping he would speak so that I could see if I recognised his voice, but he only showed his teeth again and shuffled away.

Guise gave an impatient cough. Realising that I had no choice, I ran through a brief, carefully edited summary of my reasons for pursuing Joseph, the links I had found between him and Paul, without mentioning Cotin's name, and my conclusion that Joseph had killed Paul on someone's orders and been killed himself once he had served his purpose. The Duke watched me keenly as I spoke, stroking his scar with the tip of his finger, his eyes never straying from my face; it was the same penetrating look that Walsingham trained on his agents when he questioned them, and I had no doubt that Guise was as well versed in how to read the signs of deception. I had never been more conscious of the need to appear entirely without emotion. I did not mention Circe, nor the burned letter I had found in Paul's fireplace; if they were connected with the plot Guise was concerned about, it was better he remained ignorant of the fact that anyone else knew. Other lives might be in danger – mine chief among them. I kept my version concise, and told him no more than I suspected he had already heard from Paget. When I had finished he nodded and turned back to the fire.

169

'But you still haven't answered my question. *Why* were they killed?'

'We cannot know that without knowing who killed them.'

'Speculate, then. Let us imagine, as you say, that I ordered it. What were my reasons?'

'I would suppose that Paul Lefèvre, as an active supporter of the League, was privy to information that someone felt he could no longer be trusted to keep safe. He was urged to preach a ferocious sermon denouncing the King, after which it would appear that his death was a retaliation from the Palace. Very neat – silence a threat and inflame the people against Henri in one move.'

He nodded, still watching the fire, pulling at the point of his beard. 'A logical hypothesis, one I presume the King favours. And what do you suppose this secret was, that Paul Lefèvre knew and could not keep?'

'That is beyond my powers of guesswork. My lord,' I added, lowering my eyes.

He gave a soft laugh, directed towards the glowing logs. 'Let me put it another way. What did he tell you the day you made your confession at Saint-Séverin?' The voice was knife-edged again, the smile evaporated. A chill spread through my gut. If Guise believed our meeting had been prearranged, that Paul had betrayed him to me, and that I was spying for the King, it would mean my impetuous visit to the confessional was directly responsible for the priest's murder. I swallowed, but my throat was dry.

'He told me nothing. It was I who approached him, to confess my sins.'

'Is that right?' A quick, pitying smile flickered across his lips. Without warning, he took one long stride across the room and struck me forcefully across the face with the back of his hand. I felt the stones of his rings tear open the wound on my lip; I clenched my teeth against the pain and managed not to cry out. My hands trembled from the shock; I clasped them hard around my cup of wine so it would not show. A warm trickle of blood ran down my chin and dripped on to my collar. I did not reach up to brush it away.

'You are supposed to be a master of the art of memory. Perhaps yours needs refreshing. The way your friend Walsingham had to refresh young Throckmorton's memory in the Tower. Surprising how much a man can recall with a little prompting.' He rubbed the knuckles where he had hit me. 'If you had been confessing your sins, Bruno, you would still be there. You would be there till Candlemas. So let us try again. Why did you meet Paul Lefèvre in the confessional?'

'I needed to ask him a favour.' I glanced up; he nodded for me to continue. 'I wanted him to speak to the Papal nuncio on my behalf. To petition for my excommunication to be lifted.'

I had expected mockery; instead Guise studied me, his eyes thoughtful. 'What was his response?'

'He said he would see what might be done, if I showed some evidence of contrition. He insisted I hear his sermon last Sunday. He also urged me . . .' I hesitated, swallowed again and tasted blood, '. . . to consider my future and where my loyalties were best placed, if I meant to stay in Paris.'

'Interesting. What did you take him to mean by that?'

'I think he meant to suggest that the King could not be relied upon as a patron in the future.'

Something – recognition? – flashed across Guise's eyes. 'What else?'

'That was the sum of our conversation, my lord. He did not give me absolution.'

'I'm pleased to hear it.' Guise sucked in his cheeks. He seemed to be deciding whether to accept this testimony. 'And later – at the abbey, as he lay dying? I understand he called for you by name to impart something urgent. It would be wise for you to tell me of your own volition what that was.'

I tried to keep my voice level, hoping he could not hear how my mouth had dried.

'I do not know why he asked for me. Perhaps he wanted to tell me who attacked him. But by the time I arrived he was past the point of rational thought or speech. He made one sound only before he died, but it was incomprehensible. Most likely it was the name of Our Lord.'

I looked him straight in the eye, unwavering, as I spoke. He took another step towards me and flexed his knuckles; I flinched, a reflex response before I could stop myself, and he laughed again.

'This is where I begin to suspect you are playing false with me, Bruno,' he said, in a soft voice that managed to contain more menace than any explosion of rage. 'Because whatever he said sent you scurrying straight to Henri that same night.'

'No!' I heard the note of panic in my voice. 'That was co-incidence. It was the King who sent for me, on a different matter.'

'You can see why I might struggle to believe that.' He was standing close to me now, his voice little more than a whisper, almost seductive. I revised my opinion; I was beginning to see exactly how he might manipulate a woman's interest. 'Since I know that immediately after your visit to the Louvre you began making enquiries about Lefèvre and his activities. You are keeping something from me, Bruno, and I will prise it out of you, one way or another.'

'My lord, I have told you everything I know.' I felt my gut constrict. If he chose not to believe me, I had no doubt that he would be prepared to use torture. His casual reference to Francis Throckmorton had been a less than subtle reminder that, in his eyes, I still owed him an unpaid debt. I would not have been surprised to learn that there was a room with the necessary instruments somewhere in this house, and he was right to suppose that no one would come looking for me. But behind the rapid wingbeats of fear in my head, I registered something else. Guise believed I had begun investigating Paul's death the day after my visit to the King. Meaning he did not know that I had been to Paul's rooms the same afternoon he was killed. Meaning, then, that Joseph and the dwarf could not have been sent by Guise that day, or they would have told him straight away that they had surprised a third party there, and by now he would have put two and two together and guessed that it was me. But if Guise knew nothing of that visit, then it seemed he must be telling the truth, at least as far as Joseph was concerned, and that Joseph and the dwarf had been searching for whatever they hoped to find at someone else's behest. I looked at the glass in my hand. So the Duchess of Montpensier had a dwarf who served her, and she was also related to Joseph.

'But why was he *naked*?' Guise said suddenly, addressing the room, as if this question had been needling him all along. I breathed out; it appeared that, for now, he had decided not to push me any further.

'Changing his clothes in order to escape?' I offered.

'Or he'd been fucking,' Paget remarked, from his place by the hearth. I noticed Guise frown at the crude expression; for all his soldierly manner and his reputation with women, the Duke liked to present himself as pious in matters of decency, as a contrast to the dissolution of Henri's court.

'What makes you say so?' he asked.

'The garrotte.' Paget held out his palms as if it were obvious. 'It's not easy to take a tall man by surprise with a ligature around his neck, if he's standing. He would have struggled. If, on the other hand, he'd been lying down and willingly allowed it, he might not have realised it was no longer a game until it was too late.'

The Duke's brow knotted. 'Game? What are you talking about?'

Paget cleared his throat discreetly. 'Some gentlemen, I understand, find pleasure is enhanced by a simulation of choking during the act of love.'

Guise looked faintly appalled. 'Do they? Is that what people do in England?'

'I don't believe it's exclusive to any one region. I'm sure it goes on in Italy, for instance – does it not, Bruno?'

'Everything goes on in Italy,' Guise said darkly, giving me a look.

'I cannot be held responsible for all of it,' I said. Guise harrumphed and I saw Paget suppress a smile. In that moment he almost felt like an ally.

'Sounds like the sort of thing the Valois would get up to,' Guise said, with evident disgust. I guessed his own dealings with women did not allow for much variety or imagination in the bedchamber. On your back, straight in and out, as God intended. I thought of the trace of ejaculate I had seen on Joseph's skin. Had he gone there to meet his mistress and instead walked into his murderer? Were they one and the same?

I turned to Paget. 'Didn't you tell me the old neighbour downstairs saw someone going up to the room?'

He nodded. 'Three people, she says. The first around noon in a friar's habit, the second, shortly after – she says she could make out only a dark cloak and hat. According to her, the friar left again an hour or so later, but she didn't see the second person leave, though she heard nothing. The third, we must suppose, was you, Bruno.' He rubbed a hand across the back of his neck. 'Though I have to say I would not rely too heavily on that woman's testimony. It's pitch-dark in that hallway and her eyes are failing, though she can see the glint of a coin readily enough.'

'She didn't see the second person because they had put on the friar's habit,' I said, animated again despite myself. 'And she didn't hear anything because the original friar – Joseph – was already dead.'

The Duke's stare burned into me. He appeared to be calculating. 'You will find this person in the cloak and hat for me. But be discreet about it. My sister had a family connection with de Chartres – I do not want her honour compromised.'

174

I blinked at him, taken aback. 'Me?'

He inclined his head. 'I am assured by various sources that among your dubious talents is the ability to find out a murderer, especially one who thinks he is clever enough to have hidden his tracks. I need to know who killed these men and why. If, as I have suspected from the beginning, it is someone at the Louvre, my reach is limited. There are doors there closed to me and anyone known to be connected with me. Whereas you . . .'

'You are mistaken, my lord. The doors of the Louvre are firmly closed to me too – I am banished from court.'

'Officially, perhaps. But Henri trusts you. You have Corbinelli's ear. You could learn much that is hidden from me, if you were to apply yourself.'

'You want me to spy on my friends for you?'

He let out a laugh, sharp with contempt. 'Your friends? Do you not listen to anything I tell you? What has Henri given you?' He spread his arms wide to indicate emptiness. 'Do you not think he would wash his hands of you without a backward glance, if anything you did proved awkward for him? Besides – if you spy on him for the English, why not for me?'

I lowered my eyes. He knew very well that every word was hitting its mark, true as an arrow. He made an impatient noise.

'It's very simple. If you do what I ask, I will not have you arrested for Joseph's murder. If that is not a sufficient incentive, I offer you this – the Papal nuncio Ragazzoni is a frequent guest to this house. Find this killer for me and I will arrange an audience. I have no need to be so generous, you know.'

I kept my teeth clenched. I did not trust myself to speak.

'Look at yourself, Bruno,' Guise said, his voice soft and lulling again. 'What is your future? The English didn't want you. Perhaps they could tell you are not really a Protestant, any more than you are a Catholic. Indeed, what *are* you?'

'I am a philosopher, my lord,' I said quietly, when it became

175

clear that the question was not rhetorical. 'I believe God has given us reason and understanding to query what we know and consider new ideas based on new discoveries, so that each generation can build on the knowledge of the past,' I added, since he seemed to expect more.

'Mm. I should rethink that answer before you meet the Papal nuncio.' He steepled his hands together and touched the tips of his forefingers to his lips. 'Prove yourself useful to me, Bruno, convince me you have repented of your heresies, and you may yet have a future in France. And the English girl will come to no harm.'

I snapped my head up and stared at him. 'What English girl?'

He seemed pleased with the reaction.

'Come now, Bruno. A beautiful girl appears in Paris, fresh off the boat, knocking at the gates of the Louvre brandishing your name like a royal seal – do you not think I would come to hear of it sooner or later?'

'So she is still here?'

His mouth curved into a smile, making the scar twist. 'Let us say I would know where to find her. You will report anything you uncover to Paget – I don't want you seen here again. If I hear that you have taken any information to Henri before me, the girl will lose her pretty nose. And her hands. She would have to go and beg with the lepers.'

'What makes you think I would care about saving her skin?' I asked.

'The look on your face when I mentioned her,' he said. He lifted the glass left for him by the dwarf and raised it first towards me and then to Paget. 'The two of you will work together. With your combined connections, something must come to light. And you will say nothing of Joseph de Chartres's death yet. I must decide how to arrange that before it is known.'

'He cannot be found in the priest's rooms, my lord,' Paget said briskly. 'It will make the connection between them explicit.

And since that connection is the League, it would be preferable if his body turned up elsewhere.'

Guise looked pensive. 'Must he be found at all?'

'If he simply disappears, it will be assumed that he has run away because he is guilty of murder.'

'Which he is,' I pointed out.

Paget darted a look at me from the corner of his eye, irritated. 'And if his guilt is assumed *in absentia*, it will point to my Lord of Guise as the author. So he must be found, but nowhere that will imply any connection with the death of Paul Lefèvre.'

Guise waved this aside. 'Leave that to me. Let us drink to unlikely alliances.' He nodded to the glass in my hand. 'And to a unified, Catholic France, free from heresy.'

'A unified Catholic France,' I mumbled, lifting the glass and forcing myself to swallow a drop. All I could taste was my own blood.

'Have you ever tried it, Bruno?' Paget asked, over his shoulder, as we rode back across the river to the Left Bank. He had offered to take me home on his horse, prompted more by a desire to ensure I did not detour via the Louvre than from any concern for my well-being, I guessed.

'Tried what?'

'Being throttled.'

'No. Not for pleasure, anyway.'

'Ah.' He jabbed the horse gently with his heels and it picked up its pace as we approached the Pont de Notre-Dame. 'Your English girl not up for that sort of thing?'

'She's not my English girl.'

'Hm. Still. Pretty creature, though.'

I knew he felt me tense against him in the saddle and grip the fabric of his cloak tighter. He meant to provoke me and I was determined not to give him the satisfaction. We rode on without speaking, as I willed myself with every jolt not to ask any questions. Lamps had been lit in the windows of the houses along the bridge and smoke gusted from chimneys. The air smelled of damp and soot; the cold worked its way inside my clothes. My fingers were frozen and my lip throbbed dully. The only sounds were the gulls, the brisk ring of the horse's hooves and an occasional shout from a boatman below on the dark water. I longed more than ever for the warmth of Jacopo's parlour, his quiet attention and wise counsel, but I thought it likely that Paget would still have someone tailing me. I would have to wait.

'Do you believe him?' I asked, in an effort to steer him away from the subject of Sophia.

'Guise?' His voice echoed off the walls of the houses on either side. 'About the murders, yes. I wasn't sure about Lefèvre at first, but I would swear he had nothing to do with de Chartres's death – it comes too near his own family. He's worried.' Paget leaned back so I could hear him more clearly. 'Guise doesn't dirty his hands with anything so grubby as propaganda. It's his sister who directs all that. The Duchess of Montpensier. You know what they call her?'

'The Fury of the League,' I murmured.

'Ever seen her?'

'No. She's a widow, I believe.' I pictured a pinch-faced woman in a black veil, thumbing through pictures and descriptions of the King's sexual misdemeanours, eyes burning with religious zeal and frustration.

'But only thirty-two. And a beauty.' He whistled. 'Not short of suitors, as you may imagine. No interest in men, though – all her energy goes into promoting her brother's cause. She'd do anything for Guise. De Chartres was a cousin of her late husband – I expect that's how she recruited him. She's the one who pays all those pamphleteers. The King's tried to have her exiled from Paris, but he won't enforce it because her stepson, the present Duke, is neutral and Henri doesn't want to alienate him.'

'Then perhaps the Duchess knows something about the murders, if they both worked for her.' An idea struck me. 'Guise implied that she was close to de Chartres. You don't suppose they could have been lovers?' I closed my eyes and pictured the words of the letter I had found in Joseph's mattress. A frisson chased through me. An illicit affair between a high-born friar and a young widowed duchess – that would certainly offer the edge of danger hinted at by the letter writer.

'The Fury?' Paget sounded offended. 'That would be quite the scandal. She is famously chaste. You're not seriously suggesting the Duchess of Montpensier murdered de Chartres this afternoon?' He gave a shallow laugh. 'I wish you luck pursuing that line of enquiry. She'd burn a man like you on the spot if you stood still long enough.'

'You said yourself she'd do anything for her brother. In any case, I thought you might be better placed to investigate there,' I said.

'I hardly think Guise would thank us for pointing the finger at his own sister.' He plainly did not like the idea of being directed by me. 'He made it clear he wants you to look at the court.'

'Perhaps that's because he already suspects his sister's involvement.'

'You seem to be jumping to conclusions rather prematurely, Bruno. And not ones that will earn you anyone's favour.'

I was too tired for any more verbal sparring with Paget. We rode on in silence and emerged on to the Left Bank.

'So you know her, then?' I said, eventually, despite myself.

'The Duchess? Of course.'

'You know who I mean. The English girl.'

I could not see his face, but I could hear the smile in his voice.

'Guise asked me to find her. He'd heard mention of her from one of his informers at the Palace, as he said. An associate of yours from England, demanding an audience with the

179

King – naturally he was curious. I tracked her down to the Eagle. That's the tavern where the restless young Englishmen gather. The ones Walsingham would like to get his hands on.' He chuckled.

'I know the place. Conspirators, you mean.'

'Well. That's how they'd like to think of themselves, no doubt. Most of them are just students with too much time on their hands. Angry dispossessed boys who blame Elizabeth for their family's losses. They drink too much, they talk of being ordained, going to Rome, overthrowing the English government. Some of them might get as far as carrying a few letters back and forth. Most are too disorganised to do more than curse and sing rebel songs, then pass out in the street and do it all again the next day. I keep a weather eye on them. Occasionally one proves firmer of purpose than the rest. Curious choice of company for a young woman travelling alone, though.' He slowed the horse as we reached the rue Saint-Jacques to allow an ox-cart to pass. 'But then she was a curiosity altogether. Yours wasn't the only name she was throwing around.'

'No?' I tried to think who else Sophia might have been looking for in Paris.

'She was trying to find associates of someone she had known in Oxford. A name that would not be unfamiliar to you, I think. I thought it best to make her acquaintance.'

I nodded, understanding. 'So where is she now?'

'In gainful employment.'

'Working for you, I suppose?'

'Not at all. As a governess to one of the English families. I quickly realised she was unusually well educated, for a woman of her birth. I introduced her to a Catholic gentleman who had fled early with his wife and daughters and enough of his fortune to keep a decent household in Paris. I hear the girls make excellent progress with their lessons and would be lost without her.'

180

'And what do you get out of it?'

'My dear Bruno,' he said, half-turning in the saddle to shine a smile over his shoulder, 'your opinion of me is quite unflattering. You are going to have to learn to trust me a little more, now that we are working together.'

'I trust you precisely as much as you trust me. And now we are both supposedly working for Guise while our true loyalties lie elsewhere, so we are hardly exemplars of integrity.'

He laughed. 'Well, you and I of all people should know better than to trust a spy. They have a tendency to betray people for profit.' He kicked the horse again and it broke into a trot; all my bruises jolted together as I gripped his back. 'The art of dealing with Guise is to make him think you are doing what he wants, while making sure you use the situation to your own advantage.'

'That is the art of dealing with anyone, surely?'

'Ha! Spoken like a true cynic. We have more in common than you might imagine. I think perhaps I shall enjoy our partnership after all.'

I lacked the energy to dispute this, so we rode the rest of the way in silence. He let me dismount at the corner of rue du Cimetière and told the servant to see me to my door with the torch.

'One more thing,' I said, as I turned to go. 'This English family. What is their name?'

He pushed back his hat and looked down with the smile of one better versed in the ways of the world. 'Ah, Bruno. I dare say if she wants you to find her, she will let herself be found. Softly, softly with a woman like that, you know.'

So you have tried, I thought, and fought down an urge to pull him out of the saddle and punch his smirking face. Surely Sophia would have the wit to resist a man like Paget. Wouldn't she?

'I have a suggestion for you, Bruno, before you go. Talk to the women.'

He was still looking down at me with his knowing smile. The horse stamped on the spot, its nostrils steaming.

'Which women?'

'The Flying Squadron, of course. You want to find out what's going on at court, they know everything. That's their *raison d'être*. And you're a handsome man, when your face isn't looking like a plate of tenderised beef, even if you are on the short side. I'm sure you could cajole a few confidences out of them. That's where I'd start digging, if I were you.'

'And why aren't you following your own good advice?'

'Oh, they know me too well by now. They're wary. You, on the other hand – you've been away. They won't know where your loyalties lie. They'll consider it a challenge to find out. You might learn something. In more ways than one.' He flashed a grotesque wink. 'You could make a start at the Queen Mother's ball next week.'

'What makes you think I'd be invited?'

'Bruno.' He shook his head, disappointed. 'You don't need an invitation. If you can't find a way to insinuate yourself into a masked ball, of all places, I shall have a very low opinion of your abilities. *Le tout Paris* will be there.' He jerked his heels and wheeled the horse around, gobbets of mud spraying from its hooves. 'I'll be seeing you soon.'

I did not doubt it.

The Flying Squadron. *Dio porco.* As if I weren't in enough trouble already.

PART TWO

TEN

'Giordano Bruno, you old scoundrel! I haven't seen you in – what is it, three, four years? Where have you been? Come here, let me look at your face. *Madonna*, what have you been doing with yourself, my friend – fighting in the streets? Well, I would expect no less of a Nolan.'

Without pausing for breath or answers, Francesco Andreini threw himself on me and wrapped me in an embrace that crushed the breath from my ribs, kissing me loudly on both cheeks. Though he was right, it had been some years since we last met and I could hardly claim him as a close friend, I felt a rush of affection for the young actor from Milan and grasped him as if he were a lost brother. Not so young now, I reflected; he was born the same year as me, though his close-shaved face, with its thick brow and supple features, appeared endlessly mutable, unfixed by age. He could play a pinched miser of eighty winters or a dazed *inamorato* in the first flush of young love and convince you utterly, without recourse to wig or beard. He and his troupe, *I Gelosi*, were so loud and colourful, so gloriously Italian in the way they all talked over one another with defiant gestures, as if every exchange were a matter of life or death, that if I closed my eyes I could imagine I was back in the grand Roman palazzo where I had first watched them perform their distinctive variety of the Commedia years ago, instead of here in Jacopo Corbinelli's house in the rue des Tournelles.

Jacopo's large front parlour had been transformed into the dressing room of a theatre. On all sides open trunks disgorged a landslide of frothing fabric: gowns in delicate taffeta, rippling swathes of velvet that shimmered in the light, rustling silks, thick furs and exquisite floating lace; painted leather masks lay on every surface, leering or simpering with their hooked noses and hollow eyes. Quick hands arranged elaborate hairpieces on stands or whisked them away from candles. Between these trunks and their apparently infinite contents, the ten members of the company darted and feinted around one another in their shifts and undershirts, men and women alike, candlelight gilding naked shoulders and arms as they plucked robes, belts, stockings or necklaces from the mouths of boxes as required, avoiding collision as skilfully as if they had rehearsed each move many times over. The air smelled of beeswax, powder, perfume and the faint mustiness of old cloth.

'So – Jacopo says you have come to join us?' Francesco released me, stepped back and grinned. He was half-dressed in the costume of his usual role, the Captain.

'Just to get inside the gates. I promise you will not be obliged to suffer my lack of skill on stage.'

'Too modest, Bruno! You are renowned throughout Europe as an orator. Granted, that might be because you end up in prison every time you open your mouth—' he broke off into guffaws as I cuffed him on the arm. 'Give me a week, I could train you as a player. I would put money on it, if I had some to spare.'

'How is business?' I asked, when he had stopped laughing. The spark in his eyes dulled.

'Huh.' He gestured around the room as if that answered the question. 'We keep working as long as we keep moving. You know how it is.'

186

'You don't go home?'

'*Home.*' He pronounced the word as if it offended him. 'No. We have the same problem you have now, my friend.'

'Which one?'

He snorted. 'What do you think? There is only one, in Italy. The Church.'

'But people love your shows.'

'That is the trouble.' He grimaced. 'The Commedia has grown too popular. Certain cardinals decided to take an interest. They have concluded that we are corrupting the common people.' He threw his hands up. 'Why – because we show human nature in all its naked folly? Because we acknowledge that people shit and fart and fuck as well as pray – yes, even priests and bishops? Because we are not afraid to say cock and cunt on stage, because these things are not offensive, and instead we say that what is truly offensive is hypocrisy and oppression? Tell me – is that corrupting the people? Is it not more corrupt to deny them a few moments of fun, or truth, or the chance to laugh at those who have puffed themselves up with power?'

His voice had grown in pitch and fervour; by the time he reached the end the rest of the room had fallen silent and the company burst into a spontaneous round of applause. Francesco looked gratified, gave a mock bow and waved them back to their duties.

'I see why you're on the wrong side of the cardinals,' I said. He smiled, but there was a sadness in his eyes that I recognised.

'So.' He swirled a peacock-blue cloak around his shoulders. 'In Italy now they say that in every town, we must submit a script of our play to the censors before we can be granted a licence to perform.'

'But your shows are extemporised.'

'Exactly. So we say we have no script. Ah, then we are sorry, they say, we would like to oblige, but without a script, our hands are tied.' He crossed his wrists and held them up as if bound. 'And I will not drain the lifeblood from our work by committing it to paper and letting them take their pens to it – what would be left of us?' He shook his head. 'But we are lucky – while it pleases King Henri to continue his patronage, we find enough work in Paris.' He flexed and clenched his fist a couple of times, then picked up a pair of leather gloves. 'We perform at the Hotel de Montpensier the day after tomorrow. A small, private entertainment, but exclusive, and they will feed us well.'

'For the Duchess? You will have to mind your language there – I hear she is a most pious Catholic lady.'

'Aren't they always the ones who love a bit of filth?' He made a crude thrust of his hips, grinning. 'Though it is her stepson, the Duke, who has invited us. I believe his tastes are a little broader. But we shall test our material tonight. Performing for one of Catherine de Medici's entertainments is not the same as playing an inn yard. They still want the dirty stuff, but we must dress it in fine words.'

'What do you perform tonight?'

'Two pieces,' he said, stretching the gloves out finger by finger. 'At different times. And I'm told that Catherine's women will perform a masque of their own devising too. Heh.' He nudged me with an elbow. 'The Flying Squadron. We will have a hard time competing with that, I think. But at least we won't have to make ourselves heard over the rustling of silk from all the gentlemen furtively frotting inside their breeches.' He burst out laughing again and slapped me on the back, so that I almost stumbled into a slender young woman who had appeared unseen at my shoulder.

'*Ragazzi* – stop your clowning and get dressed or we will be late, and you do not keep a king waiting.' Isabella Canali interposed herself between us and slapped Francesco sharply on his backside with a sly smile at me. Francesco's wife was the acknowledged star of the *Gelosi*; the one who had taken the docile character of the Inamorata and turned her into a mischievous, knowing and feisty young woman in her performances, which were risqué enough to make the censors sweat even more under their clerical collars. She was also an accomplished acrobat, turning her lithe body in cartwheels or backbends that provoked further shock; more radical still was the fact that she managed the company's business with her husband as an equal partner. I tried to pretend I had not noticed that she was only wearing a thin linen shift. She leaned on my shoulder and whispered close to my ear. 'Too busy dreaming about the Flying Squadron, eh? And *you* had better behave yourself,' she added, turning to Francesco with a scolding finger. 'I'll be watching you. Keep your hands in plain sight.' But her eyes were laughing as she said it.

'What is this Flying Squadron?' A tall young man with dark curls held back by a scarf turned to ask the room as he applied the white face of the clown Pedrolino, in a looking glass propped against a pile of books on Jacopo's table. A low ripple of male laughter spread through his colleagues.

'Poor Ercole,' Isabella said, nodding to the young man. 'He is new to us. He doesn't know what he's letting himself in for. The Flying Squadron are Catherine de Medici's secret weapon,' she told him, *sotto voce*, with a wink at me. 'They're like the Sirens. We'll have to tie you to the mast.' The boy looked alarmed beneath his facepaint, but the others only chuckled and shook their heads, as if to say he would have to learn for himself. I said nothing. I had experienced the dangerous allure of the Flying Squadron before.

Isabella turned back to me and held up a black hooded robe. 'Here, Bruno – I thought this for you? It would hide most of your face.'

'An advantage, with a face like his,' Francesco remarked, strapping on a belt.

Isabella gave him an affectionate cuff on the back of the head before helping me to fasten the robe with a pin. She passed me a three-quarter mask. 'Try it.'

189

I took the mask and turned it slowly between my hands. 'Ah. *Il Dottore.* The pompous philosopher, puffed up with his Latin quotations, so stupid that he cannot see what goes on under his nose. Not sure I approve your choice of character.'

'Whatever made her think of that, I wonder?' Francesco said, with his deep-chested laugh.

She rolled her eyes at me in complicity. 'Jacopo said something that would cover you as much as possible. This is the best costume to hide behind.'

I looked down at the mask. I had never liked these faces – the bulbous brows and cheeks, the curved beak of a vulture in place of a nose, the painted lips pulled back in a grimace or a sneer; there was an implicit malice in their expressions, a grotesque exaggeration of baseness. But she was right; it would conceal my identity sufficiently, I hoped, to allow me to roam the Tuileries undetected. The ruse had been Henri's suggestion, according to the letter I had received from Jacopo the previous day instructing me to arrive at his house this evening; with a troupe of costumed Italians expected at the palace gates, who would notice one more among their number? Apparently the King was delighted with his ingenuity. I shrugged on the Doctor's black cloak and glanced around, my gaze resting on Isabella as she eased a cascade of silk over her narrow hips, the smooth muscles of her back rippling as she twisted to fasten the skirt behind her. Francesco caught me looking and threw me a grin; I darted my eyes away, embarrassed, before it occurred to me that, if he objected to people looking at his wife, he would not be in this business. I leaned back against a chair. For all its frantic energy, there was a sense of serenity in this room that I had not experienced for a long time, and which was not solely to do with relaxing into my own language. I would have given much to spend the evening here with them instead of piling into a boat for the palace.

A draught chased through the room as the door was flung

open; the candle flames ducked and shrank in concert. In the doorway stood a figure in a blue and silver gown, peering around the company from the suspicious eye-slits of a white mask with rouged cheeks, its mouth a twist of bitterness.

'I am Pantalone,' the figure cried, in a strong Florentine accent, 'and I have come to stop you stealing my silver and looting my chests of gold!' An accusing finger stabbed towards Francesco. 'Turn out your pockets – I know what you Milanese are like. Yes, and you Nolans.' This last was addressed to me, as the pinched face turned in my direction. I smiled politely, but the fixed grimace unnerved me.

Pantalone pushed his mask on to his forehead to reveal the neat grey beard and mischievous eyes of Jacopo Corbinelli, creased with laughter. 'What's the matter, Bruno? You don't like my performance?'

I laughed, a beat too late. 'Pantalone is a stubborn, ignorant miser. It seems to me a poor choice of costume for one who is known to be wise and generous.'

'Now I know you flatter me.' He put an arm around my shoulder and drew me away from the players, lowering his voice. 'Is everything all right?'

'I have sent you messages this past week asking to meet. I began to fear you were avoiding me, Jacopo.' I tried to keep my voice light, but the anxiety was real; I had wondered if he had been instructed to keep me at a distance. He looked away, though I thought I caught a flash of guilt in his eyes.

'I know. One reached me, late, and the rest I suspect not at all. Too many open eyes and deep pockets between the palace gates and my rooms. I'm sorry I have not had a chance to see you this week,' he said. 'The Queen Mother has kept me at court the whole time with preparations for tonight. She has been preoccupied—' He broke off, as if he had thought better of sharing royal troubles. 'Henri has you chasing after this priest's killer, I understand?'

I glanced behind me, but the players were too busy with

191

their costumes to take any interest in us. 'He wants me to find proof it was a Guise plot, before Guise fabricates proof against him. He seems to think it would be a simple matter.'

Jacopo frowned, his hand still resting on my shoulder. 'Henri always thinks it will be simple for others to solve his problems. But you should not be mixed up in this, Bruno.' He slid his fingers under the mask and scratched his head, where one stubborn tuft of silver-grey hair survived in the middle while the rest receded like a tideline. His brows remained defiantly black, so they looked as if they had been stuck on for a disguise. Though only midway through his fifties, there was a gravity to Jacopo that lent him the air of an elder statesman; he, too, understood the pain of exile. Catherine de Medici had brought him to France as a young man after he was banished from Florence due to a series of ill-judged political allegiances by his family. His expression now was one of paternal concern.

'What choice do I have? I cannot refuse the King.' I stopped, wondering if this was a coded warning. 'Why, do you know something I do not?'

Jacopo shook his head. 'Only that whoever had the priest killed is more than likely to strike again to protect himself, if he fears someone is coming close to the truth. A business like this rarely finishes at one corpse. You know, the young almoner of Saint-Victor was found dead last week.' He raised an eyebrow, leaving a space for me to expand on that, if I chose.

'I heard,' I said carefully. 'But he was discovered in an alley behind a gaming house, was he not? Is it supposed the deaths are connected?'

He pressed his lips together and lowered his voice further. 'You tell me, Bruno. Word has it you were caught rifling through the man's room a couple of days before he died. The Montpensier family do not accept that he was killed in any gaming-house brawl, at any rate, and they are powerful. You are lucky not to have been arrested.'

I turned the mask over in my hands. I knew this already; young Frère Benoît had come hotfoot to tell me on the last day of November, the day Joseph's body was officially discovered. Guise's people must have moved the body the night after I found him in Paul's bed. Now the death was public knowledge, and plenty among the friars at Saint-Victor had seen me dragged out of his cell the night he fled; there was no doubt that the family would have heard too, and drawn their own conclusions. If they had not moved against me, it could only be because Guise was holding them in check. I still did not understand his motives; since our encounter I had grown increasingly anxious, wavering between the conviction that Guise was covering for his sister, and the belief that he genuinely did not know who had killed Joseph and expected me to discover the truth. The fact that I had not yet been arrested lent weight to the latter theory, which itself did not exclude the possibility that the Duchess of Montpensier had acted without her brother's knowledge. These past couple of days, I had taken to keeping my shutters closed just in case, and freezing behind the door, dagger drawn, whenever I heard footsteps on my stairs.

'All the more reason for me to find the real killer,' I said, not meeting Jacopo's eye.

He let out a heavy sigh. 'Let me speak to Henri. You are a philosopher, Bruno, and he should give you his patronage as such. You know I do not always agree with your ideas, but the world should have the chance to hear them nonetheless. He should not have you chasing around the city on the heels of killers.'

'Will he listen to you? It seems he has not so far,' I added, unable to resist the implicit accusation.

'Ah. Well.' He folded his hands and looked at the floor. 'My influence with Henri is not what it was, but if I catch him in the right frame of mind, he will sometimes recall the respect he once felt for his old tutor and give me his ear.' He shook his head sadly. 'He was always wilful, even as a boy, but he was also eager to learn. Now he pitches between these fits of melancholy and debauchery, it is hard to steer him back to equilibrium. But he still holds you in great esteem, you know, though he may not show it. I pray you, Bruno – do not pursue this matter of Lefèvre's death any further. Henri has left you undefended, and you are not without enemies in this city.'

'I know it,' I said, with feeling. 'But listen, Jacopo – the reason I wanted to see you so urgently this past week. There is something I need to ask, in connection with this business, that I dared not commit to paper.' I glanced again at the players. 'Have you ever heard of—'

'Signor, the boat is ready.' A boy in the Queen Mother's livery appeared in the doorway and delivered his announcement with a stiff bow. A babble of commands went up from the players, as they began bundling props into baskets and arguing over who had last seen Arlecchino's hat.

'Later, Bruno.' Jacopo squeezed my arm. 'Our friends are expected at the palace. Time to hide our real faces.' He reached up and pulled his Pantalone mask over his eyes.

'I do that all the time already,' I muttered, threading the ribbon around the back of my head. The Doctor's mask smelled of stale breath and damp leather.

'So do we all,' Jacopo said darkly, his voice muffled.

ELEVEN

Torches blazed along the length of the landing stage outside
the river gatehouse of the Tuileries. Boats with curtained
canopies glided into place, hauled in by boys uniformed in
Catherine's colours, who held the crafts steady for guests in
fur-trimmed cloaks and jewelled or feathered masks as they
extended their gloved hands and stepped out on to the jetty,
slippers crunching on a carpet stiff with frost. The biting wind
of the past few days had dropped, leaving the night clear and
still; ice glittered on the trees and the sky was a high dome
of ink-blue, studded with bright stars and a new-minted moon
like a silver écu, blurred at the edges. They said Catherine
had borrowed half a million écus from the Gondi bank to
finance tonight's extravagance, so that every ambassador
would moan over his dispatches tomorrow morning, resting
his pounding head on a fist as he wrote to his master of how
the Valois court could still dazzle, how the royal house stood
firm and laughed at the rumours of ruin.

Despite the December cold, people would spill into the
gardens later in pairs, or perhaps more than pairs, seeking
the shadows of trees and hidden bowers behind hedges. I had
only been on the fringes of Catherine's entertainments on one
occasion, but I knew how these nights ended; solitary revellers

in drooping costumes stumbling through corridors, masks dangling limp from one hand as the torches burn themselves out, asking forlornly if anyone knows where their husband or wife might be. Best make your way home without them, or find a substitute. For all her stern piety and stiff widow's attire, Catherine knew how to make sure her festivities were remembered. From behind the walls I caught the rising sound of pipes and viols, gusts of laughter and raised voices. I drew the hood closer around my face. My breath condensed on the inside of the mask and grew clammy.

We pulled up at a plainer landing stage further downriver, for tradesmen and workers. Jacopo stood and exchanged a few words with the official who waited by the entrance, checking names off on a list; after a cursory head count, he waved us through. I was given a box of stage properties to carry; the rest of the players had kept their masks on too, save Francesco, who had pushed his back to talk to the man with the list. No one gave me a second glance.

We processed through a maze of back corridors, where uniformed servants with fixed expressions scurried in silence, arms laden with silver dishes, boxes of candles, glass bowls, stacks of velvet cushions, musical instruments or gilt chairs, until at last we were ushered into a small room and told to wait for the Master of Ceremonies. I stood uncertainly, holding my box, as the players moved efficiently around me, until the white-faced boy Ercole took pity on me and lifted it out of my arms.

'This might be the moment for you to slip away, Bruno,' Francesco murmured, strapping an imitation sword to his belt. 'Ah – this reminds me.' He rummaged in a box of stage weapons and pulled out my knife, which he had had the sense to make me hide there before we arrived, so that I would not be disarmed at the gate. 'No one will notice you now, among the guests. Go, drink your fill and make merry with these notorious Frenchwomen, and whatever else you came for. Don't forget to cheer the loudest when we take our bows.'

I pushed the mask up on to my head and strapped the dagger to my belt, making sure it was tucked away under the cloak. Now that I was here in the heart of the court, I had little idea of why I had come. Talk to the women, Paget had said. I had only one way into that secret world, but I did not know if she would be willing to talk to me after all this time. Besides, tonight every man would be trying to get close to Catherine's women. And if it should reach the Queen Mother's ears that I was skulking incognito in her halls, being kicked into the street on my arse would be the kindest response I could hope for.

I looked around for Jacopo, but he had vanished to other duties somewhere along the warren of corridors. I was about to wish the *Gelosi* good luck for their endeavours, but before I could speak, the door opened and a slender, dark man entered the room with a brisk handclap. I twisted my face away and pulled down the mask, hoping he had not seen me. This was Balthasar de Beaujoyeux, the Master of Ceremonies – another of Catherine's Florentine imports, who had adopted the French version of his name when he arrived in Paris twenty years earlier to take charge of the artistic performances at court. He must be in his early forties by now, though he was still in fine shape; he had been a celebrated dancer in his youth at the court of Catherine's cousin, the Grand Duke of Tuscany, until an injury had forced him to leave Italy and turn his talents to teaching and choreography. Now he marshalled these great *magnificences*, as Catherine liked to call them – their extensive casts of dancers, singers, players and musicians, their extravagant staging and special effects – with the fierce discipline and cool head of a military strategist. We had crossed paths a few times when I last lived in Paris; though he had always been courteous to me in the past, I did not wish to attract his attention tonight for fear of word reaching his mistress. He stood in the doorway, neat and wiry in a grey silk suit and velvet slippers, elevating himself on his toes and scanning the room as if checking off each player against a list in his head. As he reached me, his gaze lingered and the echo of my breathing seemed to grow louder inside the mask, but he gave no sign of recognition as his eyes flickered down to the pages he carried.

'Welcome, friends,' he began, in Italian, tucking the paper under his arms and clapping his hands again to ensure he had their full attention. 'The timing is tight tonight so I need you on and off as quickly as possible. Let's go through the running order. Your first piece will be straight up after the *castrati* – with luck the audience might still be sober.'

Isabella laughed. 'Always the optimist, Balthasar.'

He flashed her a brief smile. 'Regardless, my mistress will be sober all night, so consider yourselves to be performing for her and keep it tasteful. Now then, Andreini—' he beckoned Francesco over to look at the list. 'I want you in position in the antechamber before the *castrati* go on. Is this your full company?'

'All of them – but let me see again where we come in?' Francesco slipped an arm around Balthasar and turned him away from the door as he leaned over the director's shoulder to examine his schedule; I took the opportunity to edge past him before he could ask the company to identify themselves.

Outside the dressing room, a brief lull, the corridor unexpectedly empty. I leaned against the wall and adjusted the mask, pulling the hood of the Doctor's cloak over my head. As long as I kept my mouth shut, I would remain invisible in this crowd, cut loose from my name; there was an undeniable frisson in this thought. The sound of singing voices carried from somewhere close by, tightly wrapped harmonies over the layered instruments of an *air de cours*. Laughter rippled outwards. I followed the sound along the corridor, head lifted like a dog after a scent. A boy appeared around a corner, skin dark as varnished wood against the blue and gold of his velvet suit. He carried a tray of marzipan sweetmeats fashioned in the shape of scallop shells. I asked him the way to the Grande Salle and he jerked his head in the direction he had just come; I helped myself to a shell as I thanked him. He didn't stop me, only blinked his large black eyes, impassive, and continued on his way. The passageway ended in a door which opened on to a larger, broader corridor where lugubrious Valois faces in oils glared down from the walls at a procession of men and women in lavish costume strutting their way towards the heart of the palace. I slipped in behind a group and allowed myself to be borne along in their wake, my fingers and tongue still sticky and sweet from the marzipan.

The Grande Salle had been decked out like an enchanted castle from a chivalric tale. Two storeys above us, the vast carved ceiling was hung with a canopy of dark cloth embroidered with the constellations and figures of the zodiac in gold and silver thread, with paper models of the Sun, Moon and planets suspended at varying heights; if their arrangement lacked cosmological accuracy, it compensated with colour and exuberance. At one end of the hall a wide wooden stage had been erected, surmounted by a painted backcloth depicting a pastoral landscape and bordered by real trees in great earthenware pots at either side. Here five singers dressed as shepherds and a group of musicians were working valiantly through a series of chansons by Claude le Jeune, though their efforts were largely drowned out by the chatter of the guests. Along the side walls, tiers of seating faced one another, the wide space of tiled floor between them strewn with dried petals. Banks of candles glittered at intervals along the walls, pitching wavering shadows up the tapestries and embroidered cloths that hung the length of the hall; more candles flickered in the chandeliers that had been lowered from the ceiling so that they would not singe the cloth of the heavens.

Opposite the stage, at the other end of the room, was a raised dais spread with crimson velvet and shaded by a canopy of the same, three gilded thrones placed in the centre with less ornate chairs to either side. Garlands of evergreen branches and dried fruits decorated every window embrasure; the air was fragrant with the scent of pine resin, cloves and orange, and something else, heavy and spicy, like the smell of burning incense. In one corner a fountain carved with nymphs spouted wine into fluted glass bowls. Braziers of scented wood had been lit in corners to warm the vast space, whose stone walls and high mullioned windows would otherwise have lent it the chill of a cathedral this December night.

The effect was magnificent. But it was the people milling around between the banks of seats who compelled the eye. Three hundred already, at a guess, and more still pouring through the main door, in every conceivable disguise. Cardinals and Venetian senators jostled with Greeks and Trojans, knights, Harlequins and Saracens for the attention of milk-maids and Amazons, fairy queens, Turkish concubines or damsels from ancient tales, who swirled and billowed in satins and velvets of sapphire, plum and emerald; candlelight glinted on silks woven with gold and silver thread, capes of glossy fur and bodices shimmering with seed pearls. Headdresses of ostrich and peacock feathers bowed and swayed as their owners curtseyed or bent their heads to whisper behind their fans of ivory and tortoiseshell at the appearance of some newcomer. Earrings, pendants and jewelled belts flashed like knives. And every face hidden behind a mask: painted, trimmed with lace or elaborate embroidery, studded with precious stones or hung with strings of glass beads, some topped with crests of feathers or draped with veils, all lending the allure of anonymity, the promise of throwing off inhibition for the space of a few hours. The air crackled with anticipation.

I felt a presence beside me and looked down; a dwarf had appeared noiselessly at my side, holding out a tray of glasses filled with some amber liquid. How long had he been there? I could read nothing in the dark eyes that stared out of the slits in the black mask he wore, but instinctively I took a step

200

back. Then, thinking I should not draw attention to myself by acting with undue suspicion, I inclined my head and took one of his drinks, though not the one nearest me. He nodded and slipped away, unnervingly silent for such an ungainly man, and I sniffed my glass; it smelled like a fermented fruit punch, though powerfully strong. As I raised it to my lips, I glanced up and noticed a tall woman with a tiara of white feathers hovering at the back of the crowd on the other side of the hall; her face was almost completely obscured by a mask of ivory silk painted with silver spider webs, but it seemed she was watching me. There was something familiar about her bearing. I moved along the wall for a better view, but people drifted across in front of me and when a space cleared between them, she had vanished.

I sipped the punch and felt it burn my throat and roar through my veins. It would not surprise me if something had been added to it, some secret ingredient to hasten intoxication. Feeling suddenly reckless, I took another, longer draught and rolled my shoulders back as the tension began to melt away in the heat of the drink; excitement flickered in the pit of my stomach and deeper in my groin at the idea of moving through this company unrecognised. Emboldened, I peeled myself away from the wall and crossed the floor between the banks of seats, half looking for the mysterious woman in white. From this side of the room a door behind a thick curtain led out to a torchlit terrace overlooking Catherine's famous gardens. Though the night air was cold as glass, people had already drifted outside to take advantage of the dark, or perhaps just to escape the cloying scent of the incense. I wrapped my cloak tight around me and stepped out, thinking a gulp of icy air might sharpen my senses; much as I wanted to, I could not afford to succumb to the temptation to forget myself here.

I walked to the edge of the terrace, shivering as I watched a couple steal down the steps to the gardens, pulling one another urgently along a path towards a complicit spread of darkness beyond the reach of the torches that flickered along the paths, spilling pools of uncertain light that served to make the shadows between more impenetrable. I swallowed the rest of the punch and placed the glass on the stone balustrade in front of me, tucking my hands inside my sleeves. Almost immediately, a gloved hand placed another full goblet beside it. Jolted out of my thoughts, I snapped my head around to see the woman in the white mask standing to my right, only a couple of feet away, looking at me. She held a fan over the lower half of her face, but I could tell she was smiling. Her height was her most remarkable feature; I could not place her and yet neither could I shake the sense that I had once known her, in another context. She seemed to think she knew me, too; it could be the only explanation for her intent stare, her air of amusement. Though lean, her frame was large, her shoulders broad for a woman, her hands disconcertingly strong and solid in their lace gloves. It was only as I looked more closely at her hands that understanding began to dawn. I raised my eyes and met her mischievous stare again. She gestured towards her drink, offering it to me. I shook my head. She let out a soft laugh, her breath escaping in plumes behind the fan, held my gaze for a few moments longer, then lowered the fan slowly so that I could see her mouth. Despite the ceruse and the painted lips I saw now where I had met her before. She dropped into a deep curtsey with unexpected grace.

'Buona sera, Signor Bruno.' She spoke with a lisp, in a half-whispered little-girl sing-song.

'Good evening, Your Majesty,' I replied, with deliberate forbearance.

The mask was lifted with a squeal of delight. 'You've got to admit, from a distance it's convincing,' King Henri said, in his own voice. 'Even close up, if you're not too choosy. The Marquis de Tours has been giving me the eye since he arrived, short-sighted old goat. It's my feet that give me away, though.'

He lifted an oversized dancing slipper from beneath his skirts and pointed his toe in a show of daintiness. 'What did you think, Bruno – were you tempted, even briefly?'

I should have remembered this favourite game of Henri's. The pamphleteers barely had to stretch their imaginations where he was concerned. 'I prefer women with a less obvious beard line, sire.'

'For shame.' Henri ran his fingers along his jaw. 'I had myself shaved twice today, you know. And a woman did my make-up, so she ought to know what she was about. I have to avoid my mother, of course. I'm supposed to take part in this masque she's devised. Another heavy-handed allegory where I save France from ignorance and perdition. I'm tempted to do it in this get-up just to see their faces, hers and my wife's.' He sighed. 'Though Louise has been sick this past week, poor creature. I don't know if she'll manage to haul herself out of bed for the evening. I suppose she'll be too afraid of my mother to do otherwise.'

'I'm sorry to hear it.' I gave him a cautious look. 'Although, if she is sick, perhaps it may be happy news?'

'Well, if it is, it's a holy miracle. None of my doing,' he said, brusquely. 'Now listen.' He took my elbow and led me to a corner of the terrace, shadowed by the wall of the palace. 'What of this priest? I had hoped to hear from you sooner. It's been over a week.'

I hesitated. I had been putting off any contact with Henri partly because I had wanted to speak to Jacopo first about Joseph's death, and the meaning of 'Circe', but mostly because I was afraid that Guise would know immediately if I tried to see the King. I did not think his threats to harm me or Sophia were made in jest.

'Forgive me, Your Majesty – I was following leads that needed to be verified. These things take time—'

'We don't have time. I expect you've heard – there's been another death. The almoner at Saint-Victor. The Montpensier bitch is up in arms about it, he's a relative. Is it connected to our priest?'

'I believe so,' I said. 'I think the almoner killed Père Lefèvre on someone's orders to silence him and was then killed himself for the same reason.'

He stiffened. 'Silence him about what?'

'That's what I'm trying to find out. They both worked for the League. The almoner wrote pamphlets against you and Lefèvre carried them to the printer. That's how they knew one another.'

Henri clenched his fist. 'Then it all points to Guise, as I said all along. Can you prove it?'

I thought of the papers Paget had thrown in the fire at Brinkley's. 'Not at present. But they used an English printer by the name of Brinkley at the Palais – you could order his shop to be searched. He might talk if you have him questioned forcefully.'

He swatted the suggestion away with his fan. 'He wouldn't know anything that could implicate Guise directly. The Duke is too careful for that. Though perhaps I will bring this printer in anyway, to make his friends sweat – these English League supporters could do with a sharp lesson. I give them asylum in Paris and the next minute they're plotting with my enemies. But why was the priest killed in the first place – what secrets were they afraid he might spill? Some conspiracy against me?' He glanced about him with a theatrical shudder before poking me in the shoulder.

'It's possible—'

'It must have been. So you need to find out who killed the almoner. And do it quickly. Joseph de Chartres is not some parish priest of no name. He came from a noble family and they will seek justice for him by whatever means serves their purpose.' He tapped his fan on the balustrade, his body tense.

I cleared my throat. 'I think the family may try to blame me for his death.'

Henri turned, eyebrows arched. 'You?'

'The Abbé of Saint-Victor caught me searching his cell last week, the night before he died. I was looking for papers that might tie him to Guise or Lefèvre.'

'And?'

I looked at the ground. 'Nothing.'

He puffed out his cheeks and let his breath escape in a sharp laugh. But when he turned to me, his eyes were hard. 'Damned stupid of you. How could you let yourself be caught? Abbé Renaud is a notorious tyrant. And no friend to heretics, nor to me. You were lucky he didn't have you thrown in gaol.'

I considered, briefly, the consequences of telling the King what had happened that night, but to recount the business of the Conciergerie would oblige me to explain how I had been rescued, and Henri was agitated enough without giving him reason to believe that I now owed a debt to a notorious English conspirator and ally of his greatest enemy. It seemed wiser to say nothing.

'It will be assumed that you are working for me, of course. The Abbé will make sure the Montpensiers believe that. Christ, Bruno – I thought I could rely on you to be discreet.' His voice was tight; he picked up his glass and for a moment I feared he might crush it in his fist, or dash it to the ground. Instead he took a sip, winced and shook his head. I lowered my eyes and tried to look contrite.

Henri wrapped his arms around himself and stared out over the frosted garden, his face sombre beneath the gaudy make-up. From somewhere beyond the reach of the torches came the staccato moans of a woman copulating. He nodded towards the sound. 'Not even eight o'clock yet. At it like foxes. No wonder my court has a reputation. What can you expect, when my mother deploys a squadron of harlots to spy for her?' He lifted his head as if to pick up the scent. 'Did you ever succumb, Bruno, when you were here before? I do recall they took a keen interest in you.' He turned and gave me an enquiring look. I did not reply. A triumphant smile spread slowly across his face, causing his white paint to crack as he wagged a finger in affirmation. 'You did! I remember now – the de la Tour girl, wasn't it? That was the talk anyway. The one who broke down your iron resolve. Was there truth in it?' He jabbed me again in the shoulder, playfully this time. 'I command you as your sovereign to tell me.'

'Only the once,' I said, looking away. 'The flesh is weak. But there was very little conversation. I knew what she really wanted from me, and she didn't get it.'

'Huh. She wanted to find out if you were teaching me magic, I suppose? My mother was determined to know.' Henri laughed. 'They have talent, those women, no denying it. They know ways to loosen a man's tongue far more efficient than anything dreamed up in my prisons. You look at my mother and you think, what could that desiccated crone in her widow's weeds possibly know of such matters? But I tell you, Bruno, she is the subtlest and shrewdest madam in France, as well as the greatest intelligencer. Not an image one would wish to have of one's mother, but we must be pragmatists. She knows men's weaknesses better than we could hope to understand ourselves.' He picked up his glass and turned it by the stem, considering. 'You should tell that to your friend Francis Walsingham,' he added, with a sideways look. 'Tell him he'd learn more by employing nubile young women than men like you.'

'What makes you think he doesn't?'

He smiled. 'Get him to send some over here, then. I'm sure we'd relish the challenge of resisting them. What's that look for, Bruno – you didn't think that would be my taste?' He leaned against the balustrade. 'I took a mistress recently. Does that surprise you?'

I was glad he could not see my face behind the mask. 'A little.'

'Don't believe everything you read in street pamphlets. All

that "King of Sodom" – it's a convenient stick for my enemies to beat me with. Which is something else I'd enjoy, if you believe the pamphlets. But in truth, you know, my tastes are far more catholic.' He paused to chuckle at his own joke, as if it were expected of him, then looked thoughtful. 'It's more that, once the business is over, I would choose the company of men over that of women. Would not you? Would not any man?'

'Surely that depends on the woman, sire.'

He lifted his chin and grunted a grudging acknowledgement. We stood a moment in silence, considering.

'Is she still at court?' I asked, after a while.

'Who? My mistress?'

'Gabrielle de la Tour.'

'Ah.' A sly look crossed his face. 'Thinking of trying your luck again? Yes, I believe she came back last year.'

'Back?'

'Retired discreetly to the country for an interval. Usual business – got herself a full belly and my mother sent her away before it started to show. Catherine likes to preserve the appearance of decorum, at least.' He added this with a brief, dry laugh.

'When was this?' An odd tightness had crept into the base of my throat.

'After you'd gone.'

'How long after?'

'*I* don't know, Bruno, you can't expect me to remember every – oh. I see.' He glanced at me, understanding. 'You'd have to ask her. She'll be dancing in the masque later on. But try to keep your presence quiet – my mother will have you stuffed and hung from the ceiling with her crocodiles if she finds you.'

Female laughter gusted out behind us; I glanced back to see a group of costumed revellers emerge from the door to the Grande Salle, jostling one another and shrieking. The King pulled his mask down and nudged me further along the terrace, lowering his voice.

'You had better find this killer before the Duchess of Montpensier has you arrested for de Chartres's murder and tries to bring me down with you. Whoever he is, I will make him talk. I will expose the Duke of Guise before all of Paris as a man who murders loyal Catholics to serve his own ends.' He gripped my cloak in his fist, his masked face eerie as it loomed close to mine. As he stared into my eyes, his resolve seemed to falter. 'What is it, Bruno? What are you not telling me?'

'There is always the possibility, Majesty, that it was not the Duke of Guise who ordered the murders.'

'What?' He let go of me abruptly and I stumbled back. 'What makes you say that? Who else would be plotting against me?'

I held out my hands, empty. 'I only say that we should keep an open mind. I have made contact with some of Guise's associates, as you suggested. It seems the Duke is also concerned to find out who was behind the death of de Chartres.'

Henri grunted. 'A bluff on his part, no doubt. You be careful, hanging about with his people. Nest of vipers. They'll tear you apart in a heartbeat if you give them the slightest cause, and I won't be able to protect you.'

'I am well aware of that,' I said, giving him a pointed look, but the effect was lost behind the mask. I thought again of the burned scrap of paper in Paul's hearth, and of something Jacopo had said earlier, about messages disappearing inside the palace gates. 'Who takes care of your letters these days?'

'Writing them?'

'Delivering them. Any letters that arrive for you at the Louvre, I mean. Whose hands must they pass through to reach you?'

Henri made a face that implied he had never given any thought to such procedures. 'Official correspondence is usually sent by private couriers, who are instructed to put it directly into the hands of my secretary or his representative. As for unsolicited petitions and the like, I suppose they would come to the guards at the gatehouse, in the first instance. Then I imagine some household official collects them and passes them on to my secretary, who decides which are significant enough to warrant my attention. Why?'

'And your secretary has never mentioned seeing any letter warning you of a plot against your life or your throne in the past month? It would almost certainly have been unsigned, but clearly written by an educated man.'

He pursed his lips. 'As I understand it, my secretary burns scores of communications every day from righteous Parisians predicting my imminent downfall and informing me that I am bound for Hell to join the rest of my family. We heat an entire wing of the Louvre with them.' His tone grew serious. 'But anything that spoke of a specific danger he would have brought to my attention immediately.'

'You are certain? You trust him?'

The mask twitched as he frowned. 'Are you impugning the loyalty of my household? What is this, Bruno? Do you know of such a letter?' His voice had risen; I held up a hand to calm him and dropped my voice to a whisper.

'I found a burned draft of some correspondence in the priest Lefèvre's lodgings, warning of danger to Your Majesty. That a fair copy never reached you does not mean one was not sent. Any number of people along the way might have intercepted it and decided to find their own solution without your knowledge.'

'Including people close to me, you're implying.' Henri pressed a palm over his mouth under the mask, trying to compose himself. 'People who chose to keep it from me.'

'Not necessarily. As a League supporter Lefèvre would likely not have risked being seen near the Louvre himself – he could have sent a messenger who read the contents and thought to profit by putting it into other hands. But it may be that it came as far as the Palace and was read by someone there. I

209

only wondered if there was anyone with access to your letters whose integrity you were not entirely sure of.'

'Christ, Bruno – is one ever entirely sure of anyone's integrity?' He reached under his hairnet and scratched at the back of his neck. 'Everyone has his price. I dare say Guise makes it his business to find out what will buy those nearest to me. So, no – I cannot vouch for all my household servants. But I can vouch for my secretary. His loyalty to my family is undisputed.'

'Who is your secretary now?'

He laughed. 'Of course – you have been away. I appointed Balthasar de Beaujoyeux. He serves both me and my wife as *valet de chambre*. My mother thought it politic to surround me with her people. She hasn't always approved my choice of confidants.'

I thought of the handsome young *mignons* that Henri had appointed to positions of power over the years, many of them unfit for the job and several of them actively working against him, it had later turned out. Small wonder Catherine had decided to assert her control.

'Of course, it may be that Lefèvre never sent that letter at all,' I said. 'I have no way of knowing. But somebody surely found out he was thinking about it – I'm certain that's why he was killed.'

'What about this de Chartres?' Henri looked into his glass, as if the answer might be divined in its depths. 'Since you believe he killed Lefèvre. Suppose the priest confided in him, or asked him to carry the letter to me – he read it, decided to make sure the priest didn't talk.'

'But then who did Joseph tell? Who decided – at considerable risk – that he could not be trusted either?'

'Well, you know my answer to that. Our friend Le Balafré.'

'Perhaps. But the Duke of Guise did not kill de Chartres with his own hands, I am certain of it. Whoever did that is the link in our chain. He – or she – will lead us to whoever is conspiring against you.'

'Then find him – or her, if you insist,' Henri hissed. 'Because until you do, this plot may still be active. Suppose it is meant to unfold tonight?' He reached out for my arm again. 'All my enemies are here, at my mother's invitation. She calls it diplomacy – but a masked ball? What possessed her? Anyone could approach me – I wouldn't know them. What better place to put a blade or a bullet in me and disappear?' He whipped around as if an assassin might be lurking behind the nearest ornamental shrub, but we saw only the gaggle of women, defeated by the cold and retreating, still shrieking with laughter, back to the hall, pulling their fur capes around them. When they had cleared, I noticed a tall man standing further off along the terrace, looking out over the darkened lawns, his silhouette in profile against the light of a torch. He wore a tricorn hat and a dark red floor-length cloak. When he turned his head for an instant, I saw that he wore a blank white full-face mask, such as the chorus would wear in a Greek tragedy. The effect was unnerving. He turned back; though he was too distant to have heard any of our conversation, and he kept his gaze fixed straight ahead, I had the sense that he was aware of us, and that we were the reason for his presence.

'You should be on your guard tonight, sire,' I whispered. 'Drink only from the common bowl. Do not go walking in the gardens alone.'

'If I take a turn in the gardens, Bruno, I would hardly bother to go alone.' He smiled, but it died on his lips. 'What did it say? That letter you found. What danger did he want to warn me of?'

'There was almost nothing left of it,' I said. I laid my hand over his; he was trembling, or perhaps just shivering, it was hard to tell. 'He wrote only of possible harm, from . . .' I hesitated, taking a deep breath. I had carried this name in my head for eleven days, since Paul had rasped it out with his death rattle, not knowing what further danger I might unleash by repeating it. But Henri was right: if the threat of which Paul had written remained imminent, I had no choice but to see if he understood the dead priest's mythical allusion.

'From whom, damn you?' Henri rubbed his hands together, impatient, his breath clouding in the cold.

'Someone called Circe.'

'*What?*' He pushed the mask back on to his head and stared at me as if I had slapped him. 'How would he—?' He broke off and continued to gape at me, his jaw working soundlessly as if to form words.

'Majesty? You know who this is?' A curious sense of relief washed through me; if the name meant something to Henri, perhaps the mystery was solved, and he would know how to deal with it without my further involvement. The changing expressions on his face – from shock to fear to anger and back – suggested that my revelation had not improved the situation. He looked like a boy sledging across a frozen lake who had just been told the ice was not strong enough to hold him.

'That is not possible,' he said, after a long pause, though he sounded uncertain, and it was no longer clear whether he was speaking to me or thinking aloud. His gaze roamed the air behind me for a moment before his eyes snapped on to mine again. He grasped me by both shoulders and shook me. 'Where did he get this name?'

'It was written on a letter he subsequently burned. He spoke of the confessional. That is all I know.'

Henri lowered his head, still leaning on my shoulders for support, breathing hard as if he had been running. When he looked up again, his expression was bewildered. Hairline cracks had appeared in the white lead of his face.

'He said that Circe confessed the intention to do me harm?' His eyes searched mine for reassurance. 'I don't understand. What else?'

'Nothing else, sire. I understand no more than you. Less, it seems.' I recalled what Jacopo had said – that Henri always

212

wants someone to solve his problems for him – and briefly pitied him. 'Who *is* Circe, sire?' I prompted, gently, but at that moment I felt him start, just as a presence materialised out of the dark at our side. I looked down to see a dwarf in a black mask bowing discreetly. The same one who had approached me earlier? It was impossible to tell behind his disguise.

'To the Devil with you – what is it?' Henri barked at the man.

'Your lady mother wishes to speak with you urgently, Your Majesty.' His voice was thick and guttural. It reminded me of the man I heard in Paul's rooms, but I could not be certain – perhaps it was a quality particular to dwarfs, like the rolling gait. I stared at him and he acknowledged me with an insolent glance.

Henri clicked his tongue. 'Tell her I will be there presently.'

The dwarf did not move. 'She has instructed me to return with you in person, sire.'

The King threw his hands up. 'Does she think I need a nursemaid?' It was not clear whether he expected an answer; the dwarf and I remained silent. 'Very well. But there is someone I must see first.' He pulled the mask down over his face and turned back to me. 'Do not leave here tonight without my permission. We will speak further on this matter.' He patted me absently on the shoulder and walked away, his steps pinched and awkward in his woman's slippers, the dwarf compact and silent at his side. I glanced along the terrace; the man in the tricorn hat had disappeared. Henri had left his glass behind; shivering, I picked it up and raised it to my lips before recalling my own advice. I replaced the glass on the balustrade without drinking, pulled my cloak around me and returned to the Grande Salle.

213

TWELVE

The song of the *castrati* rose up to the canopy of the heavens in layers of shifting harmonies, fluting, unearthly – unnatural, to my ears. I had always been disturbed by the sound of those soft-bodied, hairless creatures, trapped in perpetual limbo between boy and man. Under cover of their music I slipped between masked guests at the back of the hall, behind the raised dais with the thrones – still empty – in search of a vantage point where I could watch both the stage and the crowds unobserved. As I passed behind two women talking in strident, aristocratic voices, I caught a phrase in their conversation which caused me to slow my step and hover, straining to listen.

'The Fury of the League,' said one, letting a snigger escape behind her fan. 'Who'd have thought?'

'Fervour like that, you can always be sure it's hiding something,' her companion remarked. 'Wanting the world to think she's some kind of saint. And all the while – incest and murder!'

'Hardly incest, *chérie*,' said the first. 'He was her husband's cousin, not hers.'

'Family by marriage, it's all one,' the second woman said, adjusting her lace shawl over bare shoulders. The general noise of conversation in the hall was so great she had to lean in and shout. 'And he was still a man in holy orders, cousin or no. I wouldn't be surprised if she did it herself.'

'Stabbed through the heart, I heard.'

'Really? Henriette said his throat was cut.'

'How would Henriette know?'

'She knows people.'

'Could a woman do such a thing, do you think? A duchess?'

The second woman rippled her fan and shuddered. 'That one could. She'd stab you with a look if she had the chance.'

'Keep your voice down – I heard she's here tonight. Could be right behind us, for all we know.' She glanced around; I looked quickly at the floor and shuffled a few paces away. The woman's gaze slid over me without interest behind her scarlet mask. 'Anyway, she's a Guise by blood, what do you expect?' she continued, when she was satisfied that their subject was not within earshot. 'Her brother the Duke's had most of the women in this room. Apart from me,' she added, in case of doubt.

'At least he's only had the women,' the second one said, at the same volume. 'Unlike the King.' She gave a merciless snort of laughter.

'It's Queen Louise I pity,' said the first, in a sympathetic voice. 'Imagine being married to that. If I were her I'd drink poison.'

'If *I* were her, I'd bed the nearest courtier, tell the King it was his. Solve everything at one stroke,' the other whispered. 'I'm surprised she hasn't had the wit to try it before now.'

'She probably did, but the courtiers were too busy bedding each other.'

They collapsed into a fit of malicious giggles, clutching one another's arms. I moved away before they noticed me. So gossip had already declared that the Duchess of Montpensier was behind Joseph's murder, because they were lovers. I wondered how long those rumours had been in circulation, and where they originated. I recalled Frère Benoît saying that the abbey gossip declared Joseph's mistress to be a married noblewoman, and thought of the passionate note I had found among the almoner's papers, now carefully hidden in a box with my most dangerous writings behind a loose rafter in the ceiling of my lodgings. I knew better than to draw any conclusions from hearsay, but the same unease that had dogged me since my meeting with Guise grew sharper. What meagre scraps of information I had gathered all suggested that the Duchess had a greater motive than anyone – save Guise himself – to silence both Paul and Joseph. I had no idea whether she was a woman who could kill in cold blood, as the gossips claimed, though Paget had remarked that she was ruthless in her brother's cause. Was it possible that she could have organised both murders – even carried out one of them – without the Duke of Guise knowing? There was also the manner of Joseph's death to consider, and Paget's suggestion that he had been killed by his lover while he was naked and off guard. But if that were the case, how would Guise respond if my investigation appeared to be leading towards his own sister? I could answer that too easily; he would be all the keener on his original plan of blaming me for de Chartres's death as an agent of the King.

I slunk away to the side of the hall and found myself a spot by a pillar with a view of the stage and the dais with the thrones. To my right, a brazier coughed out its scented smoke, stinging my eyes and the back of my throat, though at least it gave off some warmth. I wondered again what herbs they were burning; already I felt a little light-headed and was grateful for the solidity of the stone at my back. The *castrati* reached the crescendo of their song, though their voices were barely audible by now over the hum of conversation. In the smoky air and torchlight, the crowd of guests appeared garish and alien, with their exotic colours and the blank or distorted expressions lent them by the masks; a host of half-human creatures risen up from a subterranean world for their demonic

216

revels. Every time someone looked at me for a heartbeat too long I imagined malice in their eyes, and was rocked by the fear that they could see through my disguise, that I alone was standing naked and exposed in a hostile crowd. I shook my head and blinked hard; I needed to stop this and keep my wits about me. It was still early and the King had ordered me not to leave without his permission, though I was not sure what more he wanted from me. The name 'Circe' had visibly upset him, that much was clear, but I had no idea why unless he deigned to explain further.

A woman dressed as a milkmaid drifted towards me in a gown cut low in the bodice so that her breasts were almost spilling out. She looked at me sidelong from under her mask; for a moment I thought she meant to speak, but as she moved past with uncertain steps I saw that her eyes were glazed, unfocused. An empty glass – not her first – dangled from her hand. She might have been the Duchess of Montpensier for all I knew. Those women had speculated that she was here; the one thing I might usefully do tonight would be to watch her under cover of my Doctor's costume, but first I would need someone to identify her, and that would require me to find one of the few people at the ball to whom I could reveal myself.

The *castrati* took their bows to polite applause, though only those nearest the stage showed them much attention; the rest of the crowd remained intent on their own conversations at a volume that filled the hall like the roar of a cataract. Piqued, the eunuchs stalked off stage and I drew myself up straighter, eager to see Francesco and his friends make their entrance. Instead, the cold, clear note of a trumpet cut through the noise; a deferential silence descended and the guests fell back on either side to create a path through the room for the royal party.

She entered on an open litter borne by four strong men dressed as Saracens, naked from the waist up and walking at a stately pace, the timing of their steps impeccable despite the veins straining in their muscled arms and the sweat beading their brows and chests. Catherine de Medici sat in her chair proud as a martial statue, head erect, eyes fixed straight ahead. She had made no concession to the demands of a costume ball. Instead she was dressed, as always, in a high-necked gown of black velvet with a neat white ruff and a black collar fanning stiffly behind her neck, her hair scraped back under a black hood and draped at the back with a black lace veil, the sober widow's uniform she had worn since her husband was killed in a joust a quarter-century ago. Her heavy-jowelled face was bare of cosmetics, though I noticed her brows had been artfully plucked, and she wore no jewellery except her wedding ring and a signet ring. I bowed the knee along with the rest of the company as she passed, sneaking a glance at her marble composure. Here was a woman who truly deserved to be called ruthless, though I could not help but admire her: she had fought to preserve the throne of France for her sons with the ferocity of a she-wolf defending her cubs, and the strain of those twenty-five years showed in the furrows of her brow and the pouches beneath her eyes. If, at sixty-six, she was losing her appetite for the fight, you would never guess it from her demeanour, just as you would never know the constant pain she suffered from gout and rheumatism; she rode through the crowd with her face set like a general riding into battle, as consummate a performer as any of the acts who would appear before her on stage.

Walking behind her, Henri's neglected wife Queen Louise cut a sorry figure; she had never been a robust woman, but she seemed to have faded since I last saw her, perhaps as a result of the endless fasting and pilgrimages she undertook in the hope of bargaining with the Blessed Virgin to give her a child; all wasted efforts if it was true that her husband never visited her bed. She was dressed tonight as a lady from a chivalric tale of centuries past, in a high-waisted green gown

218

which accentuated the angles of her spare frame. Her shoulders and collarbone jutted sharply through the fabric; the tall conical headdress with its drifting veil appeared too heavy for her slender neck. She walked as if it pained her to lift her head and her eyes were ringed with purple shadows. Three young women carried her train, all pink-cheeked and vital by contrast with their mistress, who stumbled more than once in her progress toward the thrones like an old woman, though she could not be much above thirty. I thought of the gossip who had said she would take poison if she were married to Henri. One might be forgiven for thinking Queen Louise had been doing exactly that. Of her husband the King there was no sign; I presumed his mother had sent him to get changed.

The silence lasted until the royal party had settled themselves into the thrones on the dais, with a gaggle of courtiers and ladies strewn artfully on cushions at their feet. Catherine rose with some effort and stood at the front of the platform; as if on cue, the assembled guests erupted into rapturous applause and cheers, which she accepted with a nod and an inclination of her head to either side. When she had taken her seat again, the guests arranged themselves with an unnecessary degree of fuss and argument on the tiered stands ranged along the sides of the hall. Finally, Catherine raised her hand and the musicians struck up a tune as the players of *I Gelosi* took to the stage and assumed their poses.

I had my reservations about the Commedia in general – there were limitations, I felt, to how much of human nature could be shown in its stock characters and scenarios – but Francesco and Isabella and their companions were so skilled in their stagecraft, so finely tuned in the physical comedy of their storytelling, that, watching them, I found myself laughing with sheer delight in their invention along with the rest of the audience, so absorbed in the performance that I did not notice any movement in the shadows behind the pillar until I felt a hand close around my arm.

'Almost like home, eh?' Spoken in Italian; a soft voice, sibilant, Florentine accent. I turned to see Balthasar de Beaujoyeux at my side, casually holding my arm, his lists and running orders bunched in his other hand. He did not wear a mask; it made his face look startlingly undefended among the disguised guests. Behind my own mask, my breathing sounded unnaturally loud. He gestured with his papers towards the stage.

'For my money, Isabella Andreini is the finest performer in Italy – though Italy is too blind to see it. You have heard the bishops want to ban women from the stage altogether?' He clicked his tongue, indignant. 'Their loss is Paris's gain, do you not agree?'

I stole a sidelong glance at him, saying nothing. He was still holding my arm with a grip firm enough to make a point. His close-cropped black hair and beard were flecked with grey; there was a severity to his good looks, and his dark eyes missed nothing. I had not known him well the last time I was at court, before I left for England, but I had never sensed that he was one of those courtiers who resented my friendship with the King, or had actively pursued my downfall – unlike Cosimo Ruggieri, the Queen Mother's astrologer. On the few occasions we met, Balthasar had treated me with courtesy and even a degree of warmth. But he held himself generally aloof, as if he believed that his position at court was uniquely elevated; he may be working as Henri's secretary now, but he was always Catherine's man, and I had no idea if he was trying to trick me into revealing myself so that he could scurry to inform her that a *persona non grata* had entered her halls. There was an outside chance he had taken me for someone else, though the fact that he had addressed me in our shared language argued against that.

'Come now, Giordano Bruno,' he whispered, as if reading my thoughts. 'Do you think I lack eyes to see?' But he did not speak unkindly. 'I did not spot it immediately, I admit,' he continued, when I still refused to speak. 'But I have known the *Gelosi* since they first came to Paris. I knew you were not their usual Dottore. Besides, I can count above ten. They have never before brought an understudy. I only realised who they had smuggled in when I saw how you avoided my eye. But you always did like to flirt with danger.'

'What will you do?' I said eventually.

He lifted one shoulder, non-committal. 'Your presence is of no consequence to me, as long as I will not be blamed if she discovers you.'

'She will not, if no one tells her. It was the King's idea.'

'That does not surprise me.'

'I hear you are his secretary now.'

He allowed a small pause; I sensed he was weighing up his words. 'I serve His Majesty and Queen Louise. These are difficult times – so much potential for betrayal. And Henri has not always exercised good judgement in his choice of intimates, as you know. Catherine wished him to be served by a close circle whose loyalty she can vouch for personally.'

And who will report back to her on the King's every move, I thought. 'It must give you less time to spend on all this, though.' I gestured to the stage, the decorations overhead. He inclined his head with a wry twist of his mouth.

'Truth to tell, there have not been many entertainments since you left, not the way we used to have. The coffers have been emptied to arm the troops. This is the first on such a scale in three years or more.' He sighed. 'I still teach the girls dancing most days, but you are right – I have missed it. I am more at home chivvying players and musicians than copying dispatches – for all the nerves it gives me.'

'I will not keep you from it, then.'

'No – I must go.' He pursed his lips. 'Well, I shall forget I have seen you. But take care you don't run into Ruggieri. He won't miss the chance to do you harm.'

'True. Ruggieri has always hated me.'

Balthasar smiled. 'Because your reputation as a magician eclipsed his.'

'That was more slander—'

He held up a hand to stop me. 'I have no quarrel with you, Bruno. You are my countryman, whatever they say about you. Personally, I always felt you rather livened up the place. Not that this court has ever wanted for incident,' he added, with a hint of pride. He tightened his grip and pulled me closer, conspiratorial. 'I warn you only because if I have recognised you, others may too, and there are plenty here who are not your friends. The Queen Mother is in a particularly unforgiving temper with the strain of this entertainment. I would not count on Henri to take responsibility, if she finds you here.'

I nodded, though my eyes were drawn again to the stage, where Isabella had stretched herself over backwards, her body arched so that only her feet and palms touched the ground. She lifted one leg, toes delicately pointed, followed by the other, balanced for a moment on her hands, then allowed her legs to scissor above her head and down to the boards behind her, slowly and with perfect control, so that she was upright once more, her body describing two fluid curves in the manoeuvre. This was an innovation of her own but the audience seemed to appreciate it; they erupted into whistles and applause, as much for the glimpse of lean stockinged thigh the move had afforded them as for its daring.

'She is quite something, isn't she?' Balthasar murmured. 'But wait until you see my girls dance their masque. Holy Mother – I must go and rally them, we are next. You'll enjoy this one – the Masque of Circe.' He let go of my arm and levered himself forward from the pillar with a little bounce before setting off around the back of the stand.

'Wait!'

I had raised my voice too far, and in Italian; a few guests standing nearby turned their heads to look. Balthasar spun on his heel and gave me a hard look.

'The Masque of Circe, you said?' I caught up with him, clutching at his sleeve.

'That's right. The enchantress who deprives men of their reason and turns them into beasts. Well – you know your Homer. Allegorical, naturally. France lulled into complacency by the Protestants, rescued by our gallant king.' He arched an eyebrow to acknowledge the irony. 'But you will spend yourself in your breeches when you see our Circe. I must go.'

'One more thing. Is Gabrielle de la Tour still among your dancers?'

He broke into a knowing smile.

'Ah. *Cara* Gabrielle. One of my finest, though by rights she is past her prime. Do you have a particular interest to declare?'

I made the calculation; Gabrielle would be no more than twenty-eight, at most. A cold sensation prickled up the back of my neck, despite the rising heat of bodies and braziers in the room.

'Is she . . .' I hesitated. 'She is not dancing the part of Circe?'

'You will see for yourself in a few moments. I would not wish to spoil the surprise.'

'Will you tell her . . .' Again I paused; this was truly a risk, to reveal myself to a woman I had not seen for more than three years, and who had no reason to show me loyalty. But Gabrielle was my only point of access to the secret life of the court, as Paget had intimated, and if I did not take my chance now it may not come again. 'Tell her I am here, and I would be glad to speak to her, if she is so inclined.'

Balthasar twisted his mouth; he seemed uncertain.

'If you think that wise. But she will not be free until after the masque, and it may be that others have a prior claim on her time . . . Still, I will convey your regards, in any case.'

'I will be in your debt.'

'I know you will.' He nodded, turned again and disappeared through clusters of standing spectators with his sprightly gait. I did not entirely trust him to keep my secret; I could only hope that his anxiety about being implicated in having allowed me to enter with the *Gelosi* would keep his lips sealed as far as Catherine was concerned.

The Masque of Circe. I turned the phrase over and over, my feet rooted to the floor as my mind raced. It was like trying to assemble shards of a broken mirror; a few fragments now appeared to fit together and I had begun to see a jagged, if partial, reflection. Paul's letter had warned of some harm to be perpetrated by 'Circe', a threat I had to assume he was trying to reiterate to me with his dying breath. I had supposed it was a code name for an operative of the Catholic League, but after what Balthasar had told me, it seemed possible – likely, even – that Paul's last word had a less cryptic meaning; surely it could not be a coincidence that the women of the court were to present the story of Circe tonight? Henri had already observed that many of his adversaries were in attendance at the ball; still others might have slipped in uninvited. Where, then, did the danger lie? In the masque itself? In the person of 'Circe'?

I became aware that the guests had broken into applause and cheering. I forced myself to focus and saw that Francesco and his troupe were already making their bows, blowing extravagant kisses to the audience. At each side of the stage, servants had taken up positions ready to shift scenery and replenish the candles for the next act. The masque would begin shortly. I felt a sudden wave of dizziness; my knees buckled as all the sounds of the hall receded, falling away like a retreating wave, and I was overcome by a terrible premonition. Something was going to happen to Henri during the masque, I felt sure of it. That was what Paul had been trying to tell me. Sitting there in the centre of a raised platform for all to see, relaxed, guard down, his attention on the dancing girls – the King would be an easy target. One lead shot in the chest from close range would be all that was needed; though there were guards armed with halberds positioned around the dais, they would not be able to move fast enough to prevent a hit. It would be suicide, of course; the assassin could not hope to escape in such a public place, but Paris was not short of fanatical Catholics who would willingly martyr themselves for the chance to rid France of her heretical monarch.

I glanced across to the royal party; Henri's throne was still empty. Another possibility occurred: that the King had been lured into an assignation in the gardens – he had hinted earlier that he intended a tryst tonight – where some violence would befall him while the guests and his attendants were distracted by the masque. It might be supposed that a sovereign who knows himself to be the target of an active conspiracy would not agree to a rendezvous in a dark garden, but I was not convinced that even Henri's instinct for self-preservation was strong enough to override the promptings of his loins and the impish desire to defy his mother when the mood took him. I suspected he would relish the idea of sneaking out in disguise, without his bodyguards. Given what he called his 'catholic tastes', the potential assassin could be anyone – man or woman, duchess, lord or servant. I needed to warn him; he may be walking towards a flashing blade in the dark even at this moment.

Jacopo Corbinelli had taken a discreet seat at the back of the royal platform, behind Queen Louise's right shoulder, still cheerful beneath his Pantalone mask. If I could get word to him, he would surely know what to do; he would be able to rally the King's armed men and search for him in the gardens.

I edged nearer to the dais through the standing spectators, those who had not managed to find a seat on the tiered benches. Two guards stood at either side of the stage to prevent anyone from encroaching too closely on the royal party, but their presence appeared to be more for show; they held their weapons loosely and their concentration was all bent on the stage at the far end, where the women of the Flying Squadron were expected to appear at any moment in their notoriously revealing costumes. I moved a few steps closer until I was within Jacopo's eyeline and coughed loudly. One or two people nearby turned with disapproving looks, but Jacopo was leaning forward to speak to Queen Louise and appeared not to have heard. I took another step nearer and coughed again, but this had brought me out of the fray of the spectators so that I stood exposed near the dais, too close for the liking of one of the armed guards, evidently, as he immediately jerked his attention back from the stage and stepped towards me, brandishing his halberd.

'You! Get back.'

I held up my hands to show that I meant no harm, but unfortunately he had barked his order during a lull in the general conversation, so that a number of heads turned in my direction.

'I said back,' he repeated, louder this time; I had already retreated several paces, not wishing to draw further attention, but the man clearly wanted his royal employers to know he was doing his job, so he jabbed the weapon towards me again and I realised that the party on the dais were now peering across to see the cause of the fuss. I caught Jacopo's eye but was unable to make any signal to him as I was distracted by the sight of Catherine de Medici staring straight at me with eyes like arrowheads. I saw her incline to her right, still watching me, and whisper to the attendant standing by her chair, a masked dwarf clad in black velvet. The dwarf bowed his head once, and promptly vanished. When he moved I noticed, among the spectators standing on the far side of the dais, the tall man with the tricorn hat and the Greek mask, his blank face fixed on me, or so it seemed; the candlelight and shadows could play tricks at that distance.

I was spared any further scrutiny by another commotion at the back of the hall, heralding the breathless and apologetic arrival of King Henri himself, dressed this time in more manly attire of doublet and breeches, though of a startling violet satin with legs and arms puffed. His doublet hung open to show his unlaced shirt and his cheeks were flushed, traces of white lead paint still visible in the creases of his ears and chin. He wore a purple feathered mask pushed up on to his forehead. Flinging himself into the central throne, he stretched out his long legs and leaned across to mutter to his mother, who responded with a sour look as the assembled courtiers swept off their hats and bowed to their sovereign. Henri waved a hand as if such affectation were unnecessary and pulled his mask down over his face. I was greatly relieved by his arrival, not just because he was clearly very much alive, but because I appeared to have been forgotten in the excitement.

I scanned the audience on both sides; most of the guests were busy in conversation, animated by drink and anticipation. There were enough cloaks and voluminous costumes among them to make it easy to hide a weapon, I thought; I had concealed one myself under my doublet. But it was too late to do anything now; the musicians struck up a new tune and servants hastily snuffed some of the candles at our end of the hall, so that all the light was concentrated on the stage where the masque was about to begin.

An expectant hush fell over the room. Eight young women, bare-legged, their skin gleaming with oil, in short costumes of animal skin and wearing masks intended to represent wolves and lions, danced on to the stage and proceeded to circle one another in formation, hands clawing the air to indicate ferocity. The audience emitted a low, male murmur of appreciation. The wild animals were followed by eight more girls, this time dressed as nymphs, their hair loose and woven with garlands of leaves, their gowns made of some clinging, diaphanous fabric that emphasised the curves of their thighs and breasts, so thin that the outlines of their nipples, stiff with cold, were clearly visible. The nymphs undulated down the length of the hall in the space between the two stands, towards the royal

227

platform, weaving in and out of one another in movements carefully choreographed to give the seated spectators an uncompromising view of their bodies, before and behind. With more suggestive gyrations, the nymphs skipped prettily back towards the stage, where the lions and wolves affected to attack them, pawing unconvincingly at their clothing in a manner that clearly delighted the onlookers, to judge by the whistles and stamping that greeted this performance. Then the music shifted tempo to become slow and menacing; the nymphs stopped their frolicking and fell back into two lines, heads bowed; a breathless silence descended on the crowd, and Circe appeared.

THIRTEEN

Her appearance was met with a collective intake of breath from the audience. She entered perched on the shoulders of two Herculean young men, both dressed in animal skins and wearing lion masks. Each of them held her around the upper thigh, their steps perfectly matched to the music, which had darkened and slowed suggestively. She wore a serpentine eye mask of green, shimmering fabric and a gold circlet in the shape of a snake around her brow. Thick, dark hair was coiled and pinned up on her head, loose tendrils falling across her bare shoulders, but this was not her most arresting feature. She was dressed in a gown that made the nymphs look nun-like by comparison, of gauzy blue cloth fixed over one shoulder with a gold brooch, and so entirely transparent as to leave her as good as naked.

I was relieved to see that it was not Gabrielle in the part of the enchantress, though I did not recognise the girl. She was a voluptuous young woman, strong and full-figured: her breasts taut, with large dark nipples grazing the fabric, her thighs firm and rounded. She sat with her legs primly crossed at the knee, a position that made her balance precarious but served teasingly to hide her mound of Venus from sight. She held both arms aloft, a gesture which lifted and emphasised the shape of her breasts; in one hand she clasped a goblet, in the other a golden staff. Her mouth was full and wet, the tip of her tongue poking pinkly between her lips in concentration as her sturdy lions set her carefully down before the curtseying nymphs. Despite myself, I felt the reflex stirrings of desire and recalled Balthasar's crude boast that I would spend myself in my breeches at the sight. As Circe passed her cup and staff to two of the nymphs and proceeded to gyrate languidly, in a style that involved drawing maximum attention to her attributes, a quick glance around the room at the slack jaws and lust-clouded eyes of the male spectators told me every man present – even the elderly and infirm, I guessed – was feeling the old heat in the blood and surreptitiously adjusting a cockstand.

Despite the distracting pressure in my breeches, I grew alert as she progressed down the hall towards the royal dais. On her high-backed chair Catherine sat upright, following the performance with an expression of grim approval, but it was Henri who caught my attention. He was leaning forward in his seat, hands gripping the carved armrests so that his knuckles turned white, his face rapt. Even with his half-mask, I could see there was something unusual in his expression, beyond lust or mere appreciation for beauty. Was it apprehension? Fear, even?

With that thought, my eyes flicked back to Circe. She was level with me now and facing the royal platform, dancing solely for the King, like Salome, while her nymphs cavorted in symmetry behind her. Her cheeks were flushed from her exertions, her lips parted, but there was a strange intensity in her look as she fixed her eyes on Henri, as if she were aware of no one else, or else trying to communicate wordlessly with him; her face seemed illuminated, feverish almost, with an expression of urgency or compulsion. It looked for all the world as if she truly had the King under some enchantment.

Watching them, I felt as if another significant shard of the mirror was within my grasp. When I had told Henri that Circe meant him harm, had he assumed I was talking about this woman? He had declared it to be impossible, but the way he was sitting now, every sinew taut as a bowstring, suggested he had taken the warning to heart; more than once I noticed his eyes dart sideways to the armed guards by the dais. I wondered if she could be the recent mistress he had mentioned. I found that I too was braced for any sudden movement on her part, though I was fairly certain she was not concealing a weapon anywhere in that dress. Across the hall I noticed the man in the Greek mask and the tricorn hat had advanced a few paces, so that he now stood between the front left corner of the royal platform and the edge of the tiered benches. He kept his cloak wrapped tight around himself, his arms hidden from view. As far as I could tell, his gaze was fixed on the King. Bodyguard or potential assassin? My fingers flexed; he and I were equidistant from the royal dais. If he were to dart forward, I would have to match him for speed and precision if I were to have any hope of stopping him, and if he were concealing a pistol I would surely die.

But then the music changed tempo again – lighter this time, less sinister – the spell was broken and Circe pirouetted once, gave Henri a last piercing glance and danced her way back to the girls dressed as animals on the stage, her magnificent hips swaying in mesmeric rhythm as she passed, to further lascivious cheers from the audience.

The rest of the masque unfolded as a confused patchwork of stories, in which more women scantily dressed as Greek warriors fell under Circe's bewitchment and were turned to swine, then rescued by the cunning of a tall, slender girl in the guise of Odysseus, who was in turn seduced by the sorceress in an erotically charged ballet between the two women, requiring intercession to Heaven by the Four Cardinal Virtues. The highlight was the arrival of a giant painted wooden eagle descending from the gallery via an impressive system of ropes

231

and pulleys, with a girl dressed as the god Jupiter balanced precariously astride it, to a swelling choral accompaniment. Jupiter took the serpent-crown from Circe and, with a great show of solemnity, strode the length of the hall to kneel and present it to the King, who accepted it with a suitably grave expression and held it aloft to cries of '*Vive le roi!*' from the dancers, quickly echoed by the audience in the stands. The whole was an absurd, overblown piece of flattery and self-mythologising by the Valois, but as a spectacle it was undeniably arresting; there must have been at least thirty young women on stage in varying states of undress, and a good deal of that Gondi money was evident in the construction of the eagle. I had been so intent on watching the man in the Greek mask that it had taken me some moments to recognise the young woman playing Odysseus, costumed in a short tunic with her long legs bare and her hair pinned up under a battle helmet. With the recognition came a small jolt of anxiety: Gabrielle de la Tour, the only one of Catherine's women to have defeated my resolve when I was last in Paris.

Every man at the French court knew the stories of the Flying Squadron and their purpose, and yet it never ceased to amaze me how foolishly they – *we* – fell for their wiles, each of us wilfully deceiving himself that in his case it was different, that the girl's desire must be genuine. Henri was right: his mother knew exactly how to exploit the weaknesses of men. She selected and cultivated an entourage of the most beautiful and accomplished daughters of noble families, to be in name her attendants, and in practice her spies. She made it her business to know the particular tastes and predilections of every man she considered worth monitoring, and without compunction would direct the girl most suited to his fancy to seduce him, win his affection and, in return for her liberal favours, draw from him his deepest secrets, particularly those concerning his political and religious loyalties. Catherine's detractors put about that she trained up her girls in the debauchery of Florentine

232

harlots, the better to win confidences from their enthralled targets; it was also said that she had her magician Ruggieri prepare spells and philtres that would ensnare a man's wits and rob him of discretion and wisdom. I did not think I had been bewitched, though the night I spent with Gabrielle had revealed innovations I had not previously encountered in my dealings with women, so perhaps there was truth in the former accusation. Whatever her methods, it was certain that the Flying Squadron had proved itself a highly effective operation: some years ago, when Henri's brother Charles was on the throne, Catherine had intercepted a coup against him because one of the conspirators had unwisely murmured his plans in his beloved's ear in a moment of post-coital intimacy that had cost the pretender and his comrades their heads.

I watched Gabrielle now, as the women removed their masks and curtseyed prettily to rousing cheers and stamping feet, smiling to the spectators on either side. She had set her sights on me at the time when Ruggieri was trying to turn Catherine against me; Gabrielle had not been the first of Catherine's women to approach me, so that when she did I was in no doubt as to her intentions. She, for her part, knew this perfectly well, but that had become part of the game and we had derived a good-humoured amusement from seeing how long I could maintain my resistance as she was obliged to become ever more creative in her efforts to lure me to her bed.

To look at her now, tall and lithe in her boyish tunic, you would not guess that she had been bustled away from court to deliver an inconvenient child – an occupational hazard for the women of the Flying Squadron, but not one that need impede their position at court if their skills were valued. At the thought, that same falling sensation came over me, as if I had missed my footing on a stair. But there was no point in dwelling on that – I told myself, sternly – until I could ask her exactly when her child had been born.

The cheering continued long after the girls had left the

stage. I realised I had been distracted by the appearance of Gabrielle for so long that I had taken my eye off the man in the Greek mask; now I saw that he had disappeared, and I felt an unpleasant prickling in my palms at the thought that he was no longer in sight.

The King stood, followed by his wife and mother; at this cue the assembled guests also rose to their feet and bowed, while Henri formally thanked them for their presence and invited them to join him for the fireworks in the gardens. Attendants dashed forward holding out heavy fur-lined cloaks and hats for the royal party; the armed men by the dais moved in formation around them as they stepped down and processed the length of the hall to the door leading to the terrace. In the swarm of people that followed them I lost sight of the King, and could only pull my cloak tight around me and allow myself to be carried along in the crowd.

It might be regarded as folly to stage a firework display outside at the beginning of December, but Catherine was not deterred by such considerations; braziers had been lit the length of the terrace to give a faint semblance of warmth to the spectators, and the sky was still startlingly clear, the stones glittering with frost. Her guests wrapped themselves tight in furs, huddling together, though I noticed a few were already taking the opportunity to slip away in pairs from the crowd and melt into the deep shadows on the far side of the lawns, where winding paths led into arbours, copses and carefully cultivated wildernesses. Servants passed among the masked figures with pitchers of hot wine. I helped myself to a cup and drank it off almost immediately, the rush of warmth a welcome, if brief, defence against the biting cold.

While the fireworks fizzed and exploded in bright starbursts overhead to a chorus of gasps and cries, I edged my way around the periphery of the crowd, scanning it for any sign of the man in the Greek mask. Against the palace wall, a couple grappled with one another in the shelter of a window embrasure, the man's hand thrust under her skirts, his face pressed into her neck as she arched her head back and moaned softly. I moved away, though I doubted they had even been aware of my presence. At the rear of the terrace, I found a step on which I could stand in the shadows to survey the guests as they watched the fireworks. Henri was right, I thought, as I sought him out in his furs at the front of the spectators; it would be the work of a moment for a masked man – or woman – to slip up behind him and put a blade between his ribs, despite the bodyguards. Perhaps his mother felt that to appear in a crowd like this as if he had nothing to fear would look like a show of strength.

I was musing on this when I noticed a hooded figure sidling towards me along the palace wall, half hidden in the dark. My right hand crept inside my cloak, feeling for my dagger. The figure stopped a few feet away and darted a furtive glance in my direction. I could see nothing of its face. Our breath clouded around us, leaving trails in the air. I waited, fingers closing around the handle.

'*Buona sera, Dottore*,' said a woman's voice, after a while.

I breathed out, and let go of the knife. 'Gabrielle?'

A soft laugh. 'It *is* you,' she whispered, in French. 'Thank goodness. You are not the only one wearing the Doctor's costume tonight, you know. I have already approached the wrong man once. He thought it was his lucky night.'

'I bet he did.'

'I should have known you'd be the one standing apart from everyone else. You always did prefer your own company.'

'Not always,' I murmured.

She drew her hood back a little so that I could see her mischievous smile. The top half of her face was covered by a jewelled mask of midnight blue silk, but her eyes held a knowing sparkle, seeming in that moment so familiar it sent a jolt of affection through me. Her look implied complicity;

though I knew her loyalty was always to Catherine first, it warmed me to think there might be one more person in this city who was pleased to see me. Though immediately I had to remind myself not to take anything at face value where Gabrielle was concerned.

'When Balthasar said you were here, I could hardly believe it,' she said, keeping her voice low. 'You know Catherine has forbidden the King from seeing you. I should have guessed you would contrive to defy her, between you.' She sounded amused.

'Will you tell her?'

'Give me one good reason why I should not.' Her tone was teasing. She was still looking at me from the corner of her eye.

'Because you are secretly in love with me, and you have been praying since I left that I would come back and marry you and take you away from all this,' I said, straight-faced.

She laughed aloud, a pleasingly unladylike snort. 'Still the same high opinion of yourself, I see.'

'I must hold myself in high regard, madam – no one else in Paris will.'

'Oh, I wouldn't say that. You still have a certain roguish appeal for the ladies of the court. And one or two of the men, I don't doubt.' She flashed me an impish smile, holding my gaze boldly until I shook my head, laughing. Gabrielle was never an obvious beauty, not in the provocative way of the woman who played Circe; her allure was all in the way she carried herself, with a natural elegance and an insouciance that suggested she didn't much care if men paid her attention or not – an attitude which, naturally, made their interest all the keener. She was tall, with long limbs, dark-gold hair and a strong-featured face whose natural expression in repose made her look as if she had just remembered a filthy joke. It had been difficult to resist her for as long as I did, and she knew it.

'It's good to see you,' I said, falling back on understatement. 'You look well.'

'I'd like to say the same, but I can see nothing of you under that disguise.'

'I can't take it off in public view.'

She raised an eyebrow. 'Are you suggesting you take it off somewhere more private?'

Flustered, I began to mumble some excuse, but she only laughed again and nudged me with her elbow. 'Even if what you said earlier were true, Bruno, and not just your wild fantasy, I'm afraid you're too late. I'm already married.'

There was no logic to the fleeting stab of disappointment I felt at this announcement, but I was aware of it nonetheless.

'Congratulations,' I said, without conviction.

'Hardly. She had me married off to the Comte de Ligny. It's not a bad arrangement. One has to be practical. It was very good of him really, in the circumstances.'

'Ah. I heard . . .'

'I'm sure you did. But Catherine has ways of managing these things. I went away before anyone could do more than speculate. The Count is my daughter's father as far as the world is concerned and I am returned to court an honourable wife. People can say what they will, but decorum has been preserved and everyone is satisfied.' She pressed her scarlet lips together. 'Apart from my father, of course, but what did he expect? He sent me to Catherine with his eyes open.'

'Your daughter,' I repeated, softly. I had to look away. 'Is she . . .?'

'In Ligny, with her nursemaid. I'm told she thrives. Two years old last month. Pretty little thing, last time I saw her.'

'Two. So—' I calculated rapidly in my head – 'she was born in November of '83?'

'That's right.' It seemed she meant to say more, but she fell into silence.

'Then . . .?' I turned back to her. The question seemed to catch in my throat.

She hesitated for the space of a breath, and laid a hand on my arm. 'No, Bruno.'

'But – we were together in the January. Could it not be—'

'The dates do not match.' She did not meet my eye, though her hand still rested lightly on my sleeve.

'It is possible to miscount the dates. Or so I understand.'

'You know nothing of these matters, Bruno.' She spoke gently, but it felt like a rebuff. 'I'm sorry. Besides,' she added, sounding weary, 'what difference would it make?'

'It would make a difference to me,' I said, with a vehemence that surprised me. I was aware that I had raised my voice. 'Just to know.'

'Really? Would it not rather be a kind of torment? She is the Count's child now. You could never see her. Even if she were yours, I mean,' she added quickly.

'It will be more of a torment to be always wondering,' I said. 'To think there might be a sliver of doubt.'

'Then take my word for it.' She squeezed my arm before removing her hand to pull her cloak close around her throat. 'There is no doubt.' But still she would not meet my eye.

'Is she dark or fair?' I was not sure why I was persisting, as if I might press the truth out of her one way or another. Given the life she led at court, it was entirely possible that she could not say for certain who the child's father might be; I was not so deceived as to think I had been the only one, but I imagined there might be some clue in the child's looks as to which of her lovers was responsible.

'She looks like me.' She pressed her lips together again. It appeared the subject was closed, and I knew better than to go on forcing it; she would only walk away, and I still needed her help. We stood in silence for a while, watching the colours explode against the dark backcloth of the sky. She shivered, and I slipped an arm around her, rubbing her shoulder to keep her warm. She remained very still, neither quite a rejection nor a welcome of my touch. 'I must go,' she said, eventually, with – it seemed to me – a note of reluctance. 'There is someone waiting for me inside.'

'Your husband?' I removed my arm.

'God, no. No, the Count detests Paris – it's one of his most appealing traits. He likes to stay on his own estates, devising ways to be more productive with *agriculture*.' She made this sound like an outlandish fetish. 'But I could meet you later,' she said, dropping her voice. 'Once I have fulfilled my obligations.'

'I would like that,' I heard myself say, though every shred of reason told me it would be the purest folly. Gabrielle was Catherine's spy, had only ever been Catherine's spy, whatever may have passed between us; there was no reason to suppose she regarded me now with anything other than professional detachment, and to make an assignation with her was most likely to be a trap. And yet the warmth of the drinks, the scent of her perfume, the slight pressure of her shoulder against my arm, together with the throbbing in my blood from the memory of the women dancing, all conspired to produce a more powerful effect than the promptings of reason. Perhaps I was no better than Henri when it came to resisting the stirrings of the flesh.

'If you follow the left-hand path down from the terrace,' she said, quietly, 'and pass the fountain and the ornamental gardens, you come to a sort of wilderness beyond with a stretch of woodland. There's a clearing there. Give me an hour.'

I nodded. I felt obscurely as if the power of choice had been stripped from me, and all I could do was to follow orders. 'But I must ask you something before you go,' I said, recovering my wits enough to remember why I had wanted to speak to her.

'Be quick, then.' She wrapped her arms around herself and shivered again. Her eyes behind the mask darted from one side of the crowd to the other, as if she were looking out for someone in particular, or afraid of being caught.

'The girl who played Circe – what can you tell me about her?'

She stiffened. 'Ah. You have your eye on her now, do you?' Her voice sounded pinched. 'I don't suppose you can be blamed, after that display. But take my advice – keep well away. That one is not for you.'

'That was not my meaning,' I said, realising my lack of tact. 'I am not interested in her for myself. I only want to know more about her.'

She turned to me, curiosity quickening in her eyes. 'You cannot expect me to be satisfied with that.' She ran her thumb across her lower lip; I could see her calculating. 'So you want information about Circe. What will you trade me for it?'

'Well – what do *you* usually trade for information?'

She laughed. 'I don't think my currency will work for you, Bruno. Here are my terms – when you meet me in the copse, I will tell you what you want to know about Circe, and you will tell me why you are asking about her.'

'Very well.' I reasoned that by then I would be able to think of something. 'But at least tell me her name.'

She sighed. 'Her name is Léonie de Châtillon. Youngest daughter of the Marquis de Châtillon. Widow of the Comte de Saint-Fermin. But everyone at court knows her as Circe. Not always as a compliment.'

'Because she has played the part before, or because she is known to enchant men?'

Gabrielle made a noise that sounded like derision. 'She became notorious dancing it half-naked at the marriage of Queen Margot to the King of Navarre.'

'The night before the massacre,' I murmured. 'Thirteen years ago.'

'She's older than she looks,' she said, with a gleam of

pleasure. 'Childless, of course – that's how she can still get away with it. So far, anyway.'

It was not clear whether she meant Circe was childless so far, or had got away with it so far.

'And is she—' I was silenced by her finger laid across my lips.

'I said I would trade with you, Bruno. Information for information. Look how much you have pried out of me already. No more until later.'

She clutched her hood around her face and turned to leave.

'One more question,' I said, pulling her back by her cloak. 'Unrelated.' A flicker of irritation crossed her face, but I cut her off before she could refuse. 'Do you know the Duchess of Montpensier?'

This evidently wrong-footed her; she looked first incredulous, then amused. 'You will have even less luck there, Bruno. I know her by reputation, of course. Chaste and devout guardian of the flame of true religion. You may safely assume our paths do not cross often.'

'Have you seen her here tonight?'

She nodded. 'Why?'

'I will tell you later, if you can tell me what costume she is wearing.'

'I see you are learning to barter.' She reached up and stroked a finger along my jaw. 'Very well – but you must promise to tell me everything about your interest in these other women. I want to know what you are up to.'

'I promise,' I said, reasoning that a promise to Gabrielle need only be as binding as one of hers.

'Good.' She glanced over her shoulder, then leant in and planted a kiss on my jaw below the mask, just where she had touched me. 'She is dressed as Jeanne d'Arc, in silver chain mail. You will know her – skinny like a boy, with the Guise chin. Now I must go. Try not to get yourself into any trouble. I will see you in an hour.' She reached down inside my cloak

241

and ran a practised hand up the outside of my thigh to my belt, like an ostler checking a horse. She stopped when she encountered the sheath of my dagger. 'What a bad boy you are,' she murmured. 'So you came prepared for trouble.'

'I always travel prepared,' I said. She stepped back a pace.

'Until later, then.' A note of wariness had appeared in her voice; I wished I had thought to conceal the dagger better. Perhaps she now feared that I had tricked my way into the palace with some malicious intent. I hoped she would not feel the need to warn anyone.

'I look forward to it,' I said, though I was already harbouring doubts about this meeting. She turned and disappeared into the crowd just as the final fireworks flared brightly before falling in a shower of sparks that faded quickly to black.

The next hour passed in a blur. The crowd dispersed, drifting back into the warm, and I followed, looking out for a woman in silver chain mail, or the man in the Greek mask. I took another drink from a tray and swallowed it down. Inside the Grand Salle, the light seemed dimmer as the banks of candles had begun to burn down and the smoke from the braziers hung thicker in the air, blurring my vision. Musicians were playing, dark, urgent pieces a long way from the airy tunes of the earlier singers; the drink and the incense were already having a visible effect on the inhibitions of the guests. On the floor between the stands of tiered seating, dancers whirled in frenzied steps, bodies pressed together, and in every alcove and behind every drape I saw couples entwining themselves with little regard for privacy. Through the haze and the milling outlines of people I thought I glimpsed a woman in silver chain mail; I followed her out of the Grande Salle and into a maze of dimly lit corridors and galleries lined with guests seeking darker corners. I wandered a room full of mirrors, starting each time I saw my own shape swaddled in the hooded cloak with the twisted mask of the Doctor leering back at me. A distant clock chimed.

I followed the sounds of the music back to the hall and stumbled out to the terrace. On the far side, by the wide stone steps to the gardens, the oily flames of torches revealed two figures, heads bowed together in earnest conversation: a masked woman in the costume of Joan of Arc, light rippling on her silver chain mail, and the tall man in the tricorn hat and the Greek mask. My blood quickened; I pressed myself back into the shadows by the palace wall and crept closer to see if I could catch what they were saying. They gave no sign of having seen me, and I was certain that I had been silent, but when I was a few feet away they drew apart with no warning, the woman walking quickly with her head bowed back to the hall, the man slipping down the steps to the gardens without a backward glance. I hesitated briefly, but decided my best option was to follow him; his behaviour had already given me cause for suspicion, and now I had caught him in intimate conference with a woman who matched Gabrielle's description of the Duchess of Montpensier, I had all the more reason to watch him closely. This was not so easy in practice. The man in the Greek mask either had the night vision of a cat or knew the layout of the Tuileries gardens by heart; though he had taken no lantern, he walked quickly, with sure steps, through the formal borders where the paths were lit and on into the darkness beyond.

I hurried after him, with the uneasy sensation that he knew very well he was being followed and was deliberately leading me on. Frost crunched under my boots; I gulped in cold air as if it were spring water, feeling my head begin to clear as I left the palace behind. The torches along the path burned low, giving out little light; I took one from its bracket and held it before me. To each side I encountered more couples barely concealed among the bushes, oblivious to the cold. In the lee of a box hedge, a woman stood with her bodice unlaced and

243

her head thrown back, one man behind her caressing her breasts, while from beneath her skirts emerged the legs and haunches of a second, his head and torso swallowed up by her petticoats. None of them gave any acknowledgement of my presence; I turned away, adjusting myself, irritated by the old familiar ache of desire. I wanted to forget the man in the Greek mask, and instead to find Gabrielle in the velvet darkness of the woods and take some fleeting satisfaction in her embrace, like before.

As if in silent complicity, the man in the mask appeared to have melted away into the shadows while my attention was distracted; I could see no sign of him against the line of trees ahead. The woods bristled with night noises: the call of an owl, the uncanny screech of a fox – though that might just as easily have been the sound of an amorous couple, as might the scufflings and rustlings of brittle leaves underfoot that caused me to pause every few steps as I strained to listen for the sound of anyone approaching. As the trees thickened, the path dwindled until I was no longer sure I was following any marked trail at all, or perhaps I had wandered from it long before, but I pressed forward, trying to keep the torch flame away from the bare twigs, hoping I would soon stumble on the clearing Gabrielle had mentioned.

Presently, I became aware of a curious noise, one I could not recognise at first, but which sounded like the muffled whimper of a wounded animal. I slowed my steps, afraid of startling the creature, but as I listened I realised it was the sound of a woman crying. My first thought was of Gabrielle in distress; I moved as carefully as I could manage towards the sobs until I emerged unexpectedly from the trees into a small hollow. On the far side, I made out the figure of a woman sitting on a fallen trunk, bent over, a flickering lantern at her feet. At my arrival she jerked her head up, swiped a tear from her cheek with a savage gesture, and lowered her eyes again.

'You came, then. I had almost given up. I cannot do it,' she said, without preliminary, in a tone that dared me to argue. I almost did not recognise her, now that she was no longer wearing her mask. I opened my mouth to reply but she held up a hand to stop me. 'No – let me speak. What you are asking of me – I cannot. Before God, I cannot. If I continue, I am damned. Surely you see that? And so are you,' she continued, fiercely, before I could say a word, 'for your hands will be as dirty as mine in God's sight.'

Her voice trembled and she broke off in a gulping sob. She was turning something over and over between her hands. It glinted in the light; a coin, perhaps, or a ring. I coughed and moved a step closer.

'Say something, then,' she urged, 'or is your conscience quite dead? Will you not release me?' There was no mistaking the desperation in her voice. The best thing I could do now would be to turn and leave, rather than add to her distress. Instead I took a few steps closer.

'Madame – I fear you have mistaken me for someone else.' I held the torch nearer to my face so that we could see one another clearly. She peered forward and I lifted my mask on to my head. I did not know what prompted me to do so, except some desire to reassure her, she looked so vulnerable. She stifled a little scream, pressing a hand over her mouth, and I found myself looking into the wild frightened eyes of Circe.

'I was expecting someone else too,' I said, moving cautiously forward another pace, as you might approach a spooked horse. 'This is a popular meeting place, it seems.'

She said nothing, only continued to stare at me as if I were an apparition from the grave. She was wrapped in a white fur-trimmed cloak. Her shaking fingers scrabbled at the object she held, keeping it in constant motion.

'Madame, is there anything I can do to help you?' I asked, as gently as I could. The import of her words when I first appeared, before I identified myself, was not lost on me; if I could only judge this right, she might reveal the answers I was seeking. I felt the tension I experienced when picking a lock: absolute precision was required. One tiny slip of the hand could mean the difference between the mechanism yielding or breaking beneath your fingers so that it remained shut for good. 'If you are afraid of someone, I could wait with you—'

I took another step nearer, holding out my hand to her; the movement seemed to wake her from her shock and she scrambled to her feet, backing away from me with an arm raised to cover her face. I made soothing noises, but she cried out as if I had struck her, then turned and crashed through the trees into the darkness beyond the reach of my torch. My first instinct was to go after her, though I knew that might alarm her further, but I saw that in her haste she had kicked over her lantern and the candle had fallen out on to a pile of leaves that were beginning to smoulder. I rushed across to stamp them out and as I did so, I noticed a glint on the ground. Bending, I picked up the metal object she had dropped in her panic. In the dying light of my torch I laid it flat on my palm. It was not a coin but a medallion, slightly larger than a gold écu, with a dolphin engraved on one side and the Valois coat of arms on the other. I could not understand what it might signify, but it was evidently valuable in itself, so I slipped it into the pocket in my doublet. For a few minutes I stood in the clearing, straining to listen, wondering if she might return in search of the medallion, or the man she had expected to meet, or if Gabrielle would come to find me as agreed. The thought of Gabrielle made me hesitate – was it coincidence that she had directed me here, only for me to stumble upon the very woman I had been asking about? Anything was possible with Gabrielle; I had been half-expecting to turn up and find Catherine's guards waiting to arrest me.

As I stood considering whether I should pursue the girl,

wait for Gabrielle or return to the palace and report to Henri what Circe had said, the torch in my hand guttered and died. There seemed little hope of finding her in the dark; in the thin wash of moonlight silvering the clearing I stumbled back to a track at the edge of the treeline, hoping it was the path towards the palace. After a few yards I rounded a corner and saw the flame of a torch approaching; there was no time to hide myself, and I could only wait as the person carrying the light drew nearer. He was almost level with me when I realised it was the man with the Greek mask and tricorn hat. He slowed his pace, eyes fixed on me; my hand stole instinctively inside my cloak in search of my knife, and I almost drew as I saw him raise his right arm, but I froze in the act when I understood his gesture. Without speaking, he tapped his mask and pointed to my head; I realised in that moment that I had forgotten to pull down my own mask. He continued past me towards the trees, as nonchalant as if he were out for a summer afternoon stroll. I watched him, paralysed by indecision. I had encountered him too many times already this evening for it to seem an accident; if he had suspected who I was, I had just given him confirmation through my own carelessness.

The flame of his torch had almost vanished into the night; I could hear him whistling a refrain from one of the chansons the musicians had been playing earlier. This show of insouciance needled me and I felt myself in the grip of a sudden reckless fury. He had seen my face; why should I not see his? I hastened after him; in a few paces I was close enough to strike. I thought I had moved silently, but just as I drew my knife, he whipped around and, using his torch as a club, swung it and struck my outstretched arm before I had a chance to react. I cried out and dropped the knife as soon as the flame made contact with my skin; holding the torch before him, like a shepherd keeping a wolf at bay, he drove me back until he could put his boot over my fallen weapon. We stood, facing one another, breathing hard, he still keeping the torch

247

pointed at me as he crouched and picked up my knife from the ground.

'Who are you?' I said. My voice sounded unnatural, ringing out through the clear air.

He made no answer, only began to back away, the torch and the dagger held out towards me in case I should make a sudden movement. I pressed my left hand hard over the burn that throbbed along the ridge of my right thumb as if that might tamp down the pain, watching for an opportunity to lunge at him, when a woman's sharp cry somewhere off in the trees caused us both to jump and turn in the direction of the sound. It came again, muffled this time, a strangled moan, though whether of pleasure or pain was impossible to say.

The masked man took advantage of the distraction to drop his torch and break away into the trees at a run. I grabbed the light, but already the crunch of his footsteps had almost vanished into the wood; I would be at a double disadvantage in pursuit, since he was now armed and I would be lit up like a bonfire if I tried to go after him. I cursed my stupidity aloud; I would not have been so slow if I had stayed away from the drinks as I had intended. Now I had lost Circe, who had as good as confessed to some plot when she mistook me for her fellow-conspirator, and I had also lost my knife to the mysterious man in the Greek mask, who had certainly been spying on me with the King earlier and was apparently intimate with the woman I assumed to be the Duchess of Montpensier. He had seen me, but he must have been satisfied that I had not identified him, or he would not have let me go so easily. From his height and build he could have been the Duke of Guise, or Charles Paget. Or someone else entirely.

I shivered, cursed again, pulled my mask down – too little, too late – and made my way by the light of the torch back to the formal gardens with their illuminated paths and the great ornamental fountain in the centre, where I broke the thin skin of ice on the surface and plunged my burned hand into the freezing water. The pain flared briefly and began to subside. I sat on the stone rim of the fountain until my hand and right arm grew numb with cold. I was about to withdraw it when I heard brisk footsteps behind me.

'This is the one.'

I turned to see two armed men pointing halberds at me.

'Show your face,' said one.

'Are you Italian?' said his companion.

I looked from one to the other without speaking, while I shook the water from my hand and dried it on my cloak. The first man lowered his weapon until the point touched the bottom of my mask, lifting it a fraction. One slip of his hand and the tip would pierce my eye. I clenched my jaw and tried to stop shivering.

'Take the fucking mask off, whoreson, or I'll take it off for you.'

I leaned back and lifted the mask. He nodded approval.

'Come on, then.' The second man pulled me to my feet while the first kept his halberd lowered in case I tried to run. 'Hold your arms out.'

I did as I was told. He pulled open my cloak and grabbed at the belt with my empty scabbard. 'Where's the dagger?'

'I didn't bring one.'

'Horseshit. Why else would you be wearing that? Doublet and boots off. I'll find it, even if you've hidden it up your arse.'

I unclasped the Doctor's cloak with clumsy, frozen fingers and removed my doublet, carefully palming the gold medallion from the inside pocket as I did so. I took off both boots and felt the damp of the frost seep up through my hose. The guard shook out the garments I had given him before feeling roughly up and down my torso and legs.

'Hurry up, mate, they're waiting,' said the first man, stamping his feet against the cold. 'You don't have to grope him all night.'

249

'Shut it. He's got a weapon somewhere, I know it.'

'Usually I have to pay for this kind of attention,' I remarked.

The first guard sniggered; the one patting me stood upright and struck me in the face with the back of his hand.

'All right, let's go.' He handed me back my boots. 'See how smart your mouth is when we get inside.'

'Where are we going?' I asked, stretching my jaw from side to side to ease the bruising. I knew the question was redundant.

'Private reception,' he said, while the first man let out a gurgling laugh which offered no comfort. 'For the honoured guest.' He nudged me none too gently towards the palace with the shaft of his weapon.

At the top of the steps to the terrace, a dwarf suited in black velvet waited for us, arms folded across his barrel chest, a thin smile just visible beneath his mask. Someone had betrayed me after all.

FOURTEEN

I was led through the Grande Salle and along a series of corridors, some of which seemed familiar in the way of landscapes in dreams. At the top of a handsome marble staircase we traversed a receiving room papered in violent green; the dwarf pressed onwards into a long, oak-panelled gallery set with window seats at intervals and lined with glass-fronted cabinets of curiosities: Venetian crystal, fine as spun sugar; shelves of polished rocks and minerals; porcelain from Delft, glazed in cornflower-blue; small stuffed rodents posed in tableaux and wearing tiny, hand-sewn clothes; china dolls in elaborate costumes, and one case devoted to the display of reliquaries and minute silver-cased prayer books. In the centre of the gallery stood a large Florentine mosaic table bearing an armillary sphere in brass and silver. Every inch of space on the walls above the cabinets was occupied by portraits of Valois ancestors, creating the air of a family shrine; the King's father, Henri II, cast a baleful gaze over the room from his canvas in prime position over the fireplace.

The gallery ended in painted double doors; at the dwarf's knock they were opened to reveal one of the strangest chambers I had ever seen. A reception room of generous proportions, though the sheer quantity of furnishings and clutter which filled it contrived to make the space feel crowded. Tall windows on three sides pointed up to high ceilings, where seven stuffed crocodiles hung in formation by silver chains. A fire roared and crackled in the hearth. On the far wall, opposite the doors, hung a vast portrait of Catherine de Medici as a young queen, her face even then severe and unsmiling. Beneath it, on a raised platform covered by a woven Turkish carpet, the original sat bolt upright in a high-backed chair wearing an identical expression; some of the nymphs from the masque had arranged themselves at her feet, still in their flimsy costumes. Gabrielle was not among them. I was relieved to see there was no sign of Ruggieri either.

The dwarf bowed and swept an arm towards me; I heard the doors shut behind us and the guards step away to either side, leaving me standing before Catherine, my gaze fixed firmly on my boots. When I dared to raise my head I encountered her black eyes boring into me, fierce as a raptor. She was not a physically imposing woman – she was almost as broad as she was tall – but the force of her presence could unnerve a strong man. I understood why Henri had said Guise quaked before her like a child caught stealing sweetmeats.

'Here is a face I hoped never to see again,' she announced, in French, for the benefit of her entourage. She had a voice made for speaking over men in halls and council chambers, and age had not weakened it. 'Our little Neapolitan heretic,' she continued, leaning forward and clutching the carved arms of her chair. 'I suppose my son smuggled you in with the players, or some such ploy?'

I hesitated. She let out a sigh. 'Don't bother to answer. That way you can say your loyalty to him remains uncompromised. He always was inexplicably fond of you.' She tilted her head to one side as if trying to comprehend this aberration.

'Not in any improper way, madam,' I said, lowering my eyes again to the floor.

'No, I never thought you posed that danger. You are not

252

his type. Too Italian.' She gave a short, barking laugh. 'But your *ideas*.' She tapped her temple hard with an arthritic finger. 'You lead him into sins not of the flesh but of the intellect.'

'With respect, Your Majesty—' I looked up and met her stare once more; in the corner of my vision I caught the women exchanging glances – 'from where I am standing I can see volumes on your shelves that are named on the Index of Forbidden Books. Your library is renowned for its collection of works on the occult sciences. Whatever was said of me, I taught His Majesty the King nothing he could not already have discovered among your own manuscripts—'

'Then he wasted his money employing you, did he not?'

A titter of laughter rippled through the group of women. Sweat prickled under my collar and armpits. The fire was stoked high and the room had begun to seem stifling.

Her gaze travelled pointedly down to my mud-spattered boots.

'I see you have been enjoying my gardens.'

'Yes.' Then, because she was still looking at me expectantly – 'I needed to take the air.'

'Is that what we call it now?' She cocked an eyebrow and the women giggled again like schoolgirls. 'Were you in company?'

'Only the company of my own thoughts.' But she had caught my hesitation, I was sure of it.

'Something of a wasted opportunity, then, with all this for the taking.' She gestured carelessly at the girls and sniffed. 'Dreaming up more heresies, I suppose?'

'Madam, my memory system—' I began, but she held up a hand.

'I am not interested in your memory system. Walk with me in the gallery. And take that ridiculous thing off your head.'

I did as I was told and removed the mask. Two nymphs leapt up and helped Catherine rise effortfully from her chair, holding her arms as she stepped down from the platform. As soon as she was standing she shook them off and snapped her fingers until another attendant handed her a silver-topped walking stick. The armed men and a couple of girls made as if to escort us, but she turned and froze them with that piercing black stare.

'You—' she pointed at the guards – 'wait by the doors. The rest of you, stay here. I wish to speak to Doctor Bruno in private.'

She set her face, but she walked stiffly and I could see the lines of pain at the corners of her mouth with every step. I glanced up as we neared the doors; overhead, one of the crocodiles cast a sad eye over the room, his jagged little teeth protruding either side of his jaw like the blade of a handsaw. I shuddered; teeth like those, and he still ended up as Catherine's trophy.

'They weep, you know,' she remarked, following my gaze. 'Have you heard that about crocodiles? Imagine such a thing – a killer who weeps for his victims.'

'I have seen it happen,' I said, thinking back to my time in England. 'Though not, I confess, in crocodiles.'

She shot me a sharp look. 'I suppose a soldier may do his duty in war and still feel sorrow at the shedding of innocent blood.' We walked on a few paces in silence, accompanied by the clicking of her cane and the rustle of her skirts. I wondered if she was thinking of the massacre of Saint Bartholomew's. 'Though, of course, there are no true innocents in war,' she added firmly, pre-empting any argument. 'Even a babe-in-arms belongs to one side or the other, and will grow up a danger to his enemies.'

I decided it was wiser not to contradict her. The doors closed behind us and we were left alone in the gallery, save for the two armed guards who pressed themselves against the wall and tried to look invisible.

'And now we may speak in our own tongue,' Catherine said, falling back into her Florentine Italian with a nod towards the guards. 'More convivial and more discreet, no? Hold this.' She handed me the cane.

From a jewelled purse hanging at her waist she withdrew a small silver box and took from it a pinch of brown powder, which she spread on the back of her hand and sniffed vigorously up each nostril. When she had wiped her nose delicately on a lace handkerchief, she replaced the box, held out her hand for her stick and addressed my curious expression.

'Tobacco. Most beneficial for the health. Have you tried it?'

'Not like that. I thought one smoked the leaves?'

'I dislike that method. Makes me cough. Powdered like this, it is efficacious against headaches. In Paris, the people call it *l'herbe de la reine*, on my account. You might benefit from it. You do not look well, Doctor Bruno. Perhaps it is the strain of meddling in affairs that are not your concern.'

I looked away to catch sight of my hollow face reflected in the glass of one of her cabinets, superimposed on the mad-eyed stare of a china doll inside.

'Tell me what you know about Circe,' she said, the conversational tone just as suddenly vanished.

'I never saw her before tonight.'

'That was not my question. Tell me what you told the King earlier.'

I paused, weighing my words before I answered. She banged her stick on the floor in her impatience; one of the guards snapped his head up and started forward, but she held up a peremptory hand and pointed him back to his post.

'Henri came to me before the masque like a frightened hind, shaking all over and gibbering that Circe planned him harm tonight,' she hissed, pinning me with the force of her glare. 'Demanding we cancel the entertainments, evacuate the palace and lock the poor girl away while he shut himself in his chamber with his armed men. He was already issuing orders to that effect, though he barely took heed of what he was saying. Do you know how much money I paid out for tonight's ball?'

'I—'

'Of course you don't. More than the treasury can afford to throw away, is the answer. Nor did I wish the cream of Parisian nobility and the ambassadors of half Europe to be turned out of my gates before the festivities had even begun, whispering to one another that the King of France is afraid of a dancing girl. We would be a laughing stock.' She paused for me to appreciate the gravity of the situation. 'So,' she continued, resuming her slow pace towards the doors at the far end while I walked alongside. 'A little judicious soothing of my distraught son, and he confesses it was you who planted this idea in his overheated brain. Complete with some fanciful tale about a murdered priest.'

'Your Majesty, I—'

'What kind of a fool are you?' She rounded on me, the silver head of her stick thrust towards my face. 'Do you not know Henri better by now? He has a weak constitution – all my sons were cursed with it. Any threat of discord makes him ill.'

'He is ruling the wrong kingdom, then.'

I should have held my peace; I feared she might strike me for that, but after a moment she merely inclined her head with regret.

'True. He would have been a happier man if Fate had spared him the throne, I grant you. But our duty is God's will, and we must fulfil it as best we can. I could get no further sense from Henri, though thankfully I talked him out of scattering our guests to the four winds. Now you will tell me everything you know about this Circe business. But I warn you—' she raised the cane again – 'I am more than ready to believe there are plots against my son's life and his throne, but not from within my own household. That is plainly absurd. So explain yourself.'

Feeling that my options were limited, I related as we walked a carefully edited version of the story, including the letter I had found in Paul's fireplace and the connection with Joseph de Chartres, but leaving out my first-hand experience of Joseph's murder. Catherine's face remained impassive throughout. When I had finished she halted and leaned on her stick, looking at me for a long time without speaking.

'Why has it taken you so long to tell the King about this so-called threat from Circe?'

'Your Majesty, I did not wish to alarm him without good cause. He had asked me to find out who killed the priest and there was no evidence that letter was ever sent. At the time I had no idea who or what Circe might be.'

'Hm.' She considered. 'Léonie de Châtillon has been in my household since she was fifteen years old. Thirteen years altogether, and in that time she has been nothing but loyal. I find it hard to credit that she could have been turned by our enemies.'

She was either too trusting or too arrogant, I thought, if she imagined the intelligence acquired by her bevy of lovely informers flowed only one way.

'Was she ever intimate with the Duke of Guise, or his sister?'

Her expression clouded and the flesh around her lips turned white as she clenched her jaw. 'Guise . . . Devil take him. Yes, there was a time I sent her to Guise, and she proved herself useful. Le Balafré is not apt to give much away to my women – he is too canny. That's why I only deploy the most skilled with him. As with you.'

I bowed my head in acknowledgement, even as I guessed it was Gabrielle who had betrayed my presence here to her mistress. Catherine dabbed her nose with her handkerchief.

'But that was years ago. She has not been near Guise for over a decade. It could not be that.'

'Could they have renewed their liaison without your knowledge?'

'Impossible.' She spat the word. 'My women do not have liaisons behind my back. They have too much to lose. Léonie de Châtillon most of all. She plays for higher stakes.' Her gaze swerved away from mine as she said this, but I caught her knowing tone. I was tempted to ask if she meant the King, and wondered again if Léonie was the mistress Henri had mentioned with his nonchalant swagger. The way they had looked at one another during the masque spoke of something between them. But that did not preclude Léonie also being Guise's lover, whatever Catherine wanted to believe; in fact, what better way to get close to the King than to subvert the woman who shares his bed? A suspicion began to form in a dark corner of my mind.

'Well, if you are certain of her loyalty . . .'

She smiled, showing her teeth. I thought of the crocodile.

'I have been playing this game since you were a barefoot child in Nola, Doctor Bruno. This is what Guise wants, of course – to sow mistrust among the King's supporters. Be assured – my women have better discipline than most armies I have seen. Those I cannot trust absolutely do not last long in my service. If there were a traitor among them I would know it before they had even formed the thought. Never imply to me that I cannot govern my own household.'

'I did not mean—'

'Nothing happens in this palace or the Louvre that does not reach my ears. I knew when Henri brought you here for your little midnight summit. What I cannot fathom—' here she made a moue of irritation – 'is why he came to you with the matter of the priest's murder, rather than seeking my help, as he should have done.'

'I have some experience in that area.'

'Oh, I know it. I know what you were up to in England. Tell me – do you still correspond with your friends there?'

Her tone was light, but there was no mistaking the threat beneath it. I tried to keep my face as neutral as hers.

'My friend Sir Philip Sidney now commands a garrison at Flushing. I write to him from time to time.'

She snorted. 'Do not talk to me of the war in the Low Countries. My youngest son's involvement there was nearly the death of me, God rest him.' She paused to cross herself before fixing me with an appraising look, her head tilted. 'And what do you make of Stafford, Elizabeth's ambassador here? You are in touch with him, I believe.'

There seemed little point denying it, though I wondered how she could have come by that information. 'I find him to be a gentleman.'

'Hm. Still fond of the card-table, is he?'

'If so, he has not invited me to join him.'

'You should. You would come out of it a richer man. I hear his judgement is somewhat flawed when it comes to a hand of cards. Perhaps not only cards.' She leaned towards me, one bent forefinger raised in admonition. 'I give you this advice, Bruno, since you are a man whose life depends on judging whom to trust: never put your faith in a man who cannot temper his appetite for gaming.'

'A man who cannot temper his appetite for anything is not apt to be trusted,' I said.

'True. Obsession is a malady that consumes all reason. I know that too well.' Her eyes flitted to the portrait of her husband over the fireplace and I sensed she spoke from the heart. 'Well – Elizabeth of England is deceived in her ambassador. There is my counsel – heed it if you will, though I suppose you will not, since Stafford must be lining your pockets.'

'I don't know what you mean.'

She gave a mirthless laugh. 'Elizabeth favoured you, it seems. She gave you licence to publish your heretical books. Four of them in three years. You must have done something to please her.'

'You have seen my books?'

'Of course. Those you sent to the King via Jacopo. I told you, there are no secrets from me.'

'And did you read them?' I realised I could not quite disguise my eagerness. I should have realised Henri would not keep anything from his mother.

'I read enough.'

A long silence unfolded. One of the guards coughed. From beyond the double doors I heard the women laughing.

'You wish to know what I thought, I suppose,' Catherine said, when the silence had grown unbearable. She shifted her weight from one hip to the other. 'I will tell you. I think you are a very dangerous man, Doctor Bruno. All the more so because your arguments appeal so persuasively to reason. And reason is frequently the enemy of obedient faith.' She pinned me again with that frank stare, a half-smile on her lips. 'If our first mother Eve had obeyed the Lord's command in the garden without question instead of allowing the serpent to reason his way around it, how different the story of mankind might have been. We would be spared all this.' She gestured toward the window as if to encompass the general predicament of France.

I was denied the chance to contest this, because at the same moment the doors at the other end of the gallery crashed open and Balthasar de Beaujoyeux appeared as if he had been harried out of Hell, wringing his hands, his face white and his eyes wild, his hose and his velvet dancing slippers all spattered with mud and leaves. He flung himself to his knees before Catherine, shaking his head and snatching gasping breaths.

'What is it, man?' she said, her tone growing more imperious, as if to counter Balthasar's evident distress.

'Majesty, she is dead.' He looked up at her, imploring. 'Circe is dead!'

FIFTEEN

Catherine blanched, but did not lose her composure; only her free hand flailed, clawing the air in search of support. I stepped to her side and she grasped my arm.

'Where? How?'

'In the gardens – she was found – all bloodied – oh *madonna santa*, what shall we do?' Balthasar was struggling to form sentences between snatched breaths. He pressed his hands to his face. Catherine inhaled sharply, her eyes calculating. Only I could feel how hard her fingers were gripping my arm.

'This must be kept quiet,' she said, at length. 'Get up. Have her brought in through the back door by the kitchen, down to the cellar.'

Balthasar rose unsteadily to his feet, shaking his head. 'Too late for that, I fear – the people who found her made such a commotion it drew others to the site. Someone ran for the guards. They are bringing her to you now. They didn't know what else to do,' he added, spreading his hands to show his helplessness.

Catherine's face tightened. 'Through the palace? For all to see? God save us – does no one here *think*?'

'You must have all the gates barred immediately,' I said. 'If she has been killed, the murderer must be here in the palace.

He – or she – will most likely try to leave as soon as possible, if they have not already done so. Your guards should detain anyone attempting to escape in a hurry. If we are fortunate, we may even catch them with blood or a weapon on their person.'

She turned to look up at me with slow amazement, as if she had only now remembered I was there.

'Do you give the commands here? We do not yet know what has happened. If these fools have sown panic, people will naturally rush to leave. I cannot keep them against their will while accusing them of murder. That will only make matters worse.'

'Even if one among them is guilty of it? In the light of our conversation before . . .'

Her eyes hardened and I felt her hand clamp tighter. 'Have I not just impressed upon you that I know how to govern my own household?' She spoke through her teeth. 'We must impose order on this situation immediately. Balthasar, mobilise the guards, make sure they prevent—'

But her orders were interrupted by a further crash and judder of the doors as two men barged their way into the gallery bearing a limp body between them, a curtain of dark hair hanging down and swaying with the motion. In their wake surged a crowd of guests, shrieking and shoving one another for a better look.

'You!' Catherine roared, pointing at the guards flanking the doors to her chamber. 'Get those people out of my private apartments. Call your fellows and make sure the guests are confined to the public rooms downstairs. Find the captain of my household guard and send him to me. Keep the doors barred.'

Her armed men jumped to obey and after some struggle the spectators were pushed back and the outer doors to the gallery closed. The two guards carrying the body laid her down gently on the wooden floor, her hair and white cloak spreading around her. Smears of blood stood out bright crimson against the white. Balthasar turned his face away, shielding his eyes, just as the air was shattered by a chorus of women's screams, as the nymphs burst from Catherine's inner chamber and skidded to a halt before the corpse of their friend.

'Get back inside,' Catherine ordered, in a voice that brooked no argument; howling and clutching one another, the girls obeyed. Their laments could be heard loudly after the doors had closed behind them.

Left alone, Catherine looked from me to Balthasar. Her face was pinched but she kept her bearing erect. 'Where is my physician? Fetch him here.'

'I believe he did not attend tonight, Your Majesty,' Balthasar whimpered, unable to take his eyes from Léonie's body.

'Send for him at his house, then. And find Ruggieri. Anyone who can tell me what happened here. And, Balthasar – fetch the King to me immediately. Whatever he's doing, drag him from it bodily if you have to.'

Balthasar shot me a brief glance, lowered his eyes to the corpse and scurried away, a hand pressed over his mouth to stifle his grief. If he were not Italian and theatrical, I might have said he was overdoing it.

Catherine let go of my arm and walked around the body. The girl's eyes bulged in terror, her face drained white, the lips peeled back in a grimace. Her wrists and arms were smeared with blood and dirt. Dead leaves had tangled in her curtain of hair.

'Well. Whatever threat you thought she posed to the King, she is none now,' Catherine remarked quietly. She did not seem particularly distraught by the murder of a young woman who had served her for thirteen years, but that did not necessarily mean anything; she belonged to an age when a queen was expected to conceal her private feelings at all costs.

'No. Someone has made certain of that,' I said. We looked

at one another. I suspected we were both wondering the same thing. There was a long pause. I cleared my throat.

'Your Majesty,' I ventured, 'I have some knowledge of anatomy and a little experience in instances of unnatural death. Might I be permitted to make a cursory examination?'

Her brow creased. 'It would not be seemly for you to handle the body of a young woman. You are not a physician.'

'Neither is Ruggieri. He is an astrologer.' *And a charlatan*, I wanted to add, but held my tongue. 'With respect, Your Majesty, I would not be seeing anything she did not already show to three hundred spectators this evening.'

Again, I had the sense that her first instinct was to slap me, but instead she regarded the body in silence, her jaw working from side to side. At length she prodded Léonie's limp arm with the end of her stick, turning it to expose the inside of the wrist. 'See here. I am no physician either, but this has the appearance of self-slaughter, would you not say?' I caught a note of supplication in her voice; she wanted me to confirm her conclusion.

I had already registered the slashes to the wrist, but I had also observed Léonie's face. I crouched by the body and looked up at Catherine.

'The appearance, yes. If I may?'

She pursed her lips, then nodded a grudging agreement. I lifted the right hand to show her. 'These wounds are too superficial to have bled out. They are made horizontally across the wrist. The vein is not severed – see? These cuts could not have killed her.'

'Then – what?' For the first time, I glimpsed the mask of control slip a fraction. Catherine de Medici was frightened. I could not blame her; we both knew the person who had felt most threatened by Circe that night was Henri, and that it was I who had planted that fear.

'Look.' I lifted the coils of hair that had draped across her neck. 'See this bruise at the throat, and the flecks of blood in the eyes? She was strangled, with a ligature by my guess. I think the incisions were made afterwards.'

Garrotted, I thought, by someone who knew what they were doing. Just like Joseph de Chartres. It must have happened quickly, before she could scream for help; there had been enough couples seeking out a private spot in the wood for someone to have heard something otherwise. I recalled the cry that had echoed through the trees while I was tussling with the man in the Greek mask, that I had taken for a woman in the throes of passion; could that have been Léonie? My stomach knotted at the thought that I might have been close enough to save her.

Catherine appeared to be digesting this.

'It is an interesting theory, Doctor Bruno. But as you say, you are not a physician. I suggest we do not leap to any conclusions. I will reserve judgement until I have heard an expert opinion.'

'But you must have the clearing and the woods searched for any traces the killer may have left behind. The knife that was used, for a start. If she died by her own hand it would still be there.'

Catherine shifted her weight again and looked at me with a curious intensity. In the same instant I realised my mistake.

'Clearing?' she said, raising an eyebrow. 'Woods?'

'Or wherever she was found. Balthasar mentioned—'

'Balthasar said she was found in the gardens, as I recall. You are the one who has introduced this clearing in the woods.' Her gaze drifted again to my boots. I had a sudden dread that Gabrielle might have told her I was asking questions about Circe and that even now Catherine was drawing her own conclusions, pleased to have found a ready scapegoat.

But I was spared the necessity of responding as the door opened once again to admit a figure like a great crow, black wings flapping the length of the gallery. As he drew nearer I realised he was wearing the same costume as me, the Dottore from the Commedia, in black gown and sneering beaked mask. When he untied the mask and lifted it, the face beneath wore a remarkably similar expression of contempt.

Cosimo Ruggieri still wore his white beard long and forked, in emulation of some long-ago fashion of the Florentine aristocracy which he supposed gave him the look of a magus. He had developed more of a squint since I last saw him, presumably because he was too vain to admit his eyes were failing. He had always claimed to be older than his years in order to seem more venerable, but he must be at least of an age with Catherine; where she had grown stout, Ruggieri seemed to have shrivelled, his skin stretched tight over the bones of his face, dry and lined as one of his alchemical parchments.

'Gracious Queen,' he began, in his grandiose manner, offering her a sweeping bow but keeping his greedy little eyes trained on me, 'it can be no accident that such black misfortune should befall your noble house on the day this Neapolitan sorcerer dares to show himself uninvited at your feast.'

I could not hold my tongue. 'Sing a different tune, Ruggieri. At least no one has ever accused me of keeping a child's severed head on an altar to speak prophecies.'

He gave a dusty laugh that rattled in his throat. 'What need have you of an intermediary, when it is known you commune with the Devil face to face?'

Catherine rapped her stick hard on the floor. 'Gentlemen! A woman is dead. I did not call you here to bicker like children.'

Ruggieri looked briefly chastened, which gave me some satisfaction. 'Tell me how I may be of service, Majesty,' he said, holding out his hands in supplication.

'I want you to look at this girl. Tell me what you think happened to her.'

His eyes darted nervously to me; clearly he feared it might be a trick question. He made a great show of pacing around

266

the body, pulling at the twin points of his beard in contemplation. When he could delay no longer, he addressed Catherine.

'It would seem she has dispatched her own soul to Hell. A sin against God and nature,' he added, adopting a suitably sage expression. I snorted.

'Doctor Bruno says otherwise,' Catherine said, watching me carefully.

'Doctor Bruno says the universe is infinite, but he has no proof of that either.'

Catherine allowed a flicker of a smile, but it did not touch her eyes. I considered confessing to her that I had encountered Léonie in the copse and repeating what she had said to me in error, but instinctive caution told me I would not help my own cause by placing myself at the scene of yet another murder, particularly after my ill-judged comment about the clearing, and in any case, the moment had passed; I should have spoken before Ruggieri arrived.

I glanced across at the old sorcerer. Léonie had been waiting for someone. She had been in a state of considerable distress, but had steeled herself to tell that person she could not go ahead with a task they had evidently demanded of her – a task she was terrified of carrying out, something so grave she believed it would damn her soul. I could think of few sins that would appear so terrible to a woman steeped in the casual debauchery of Catherine's court, except murder. To my ears, Léonie's wild words had as good as confirmed Paul's letter and his dying warning: that she had been part of a plot to kill the King.

The more I turned over her outburst in my mind, the more tantalisingly this hypothesis took shape: she had been charged by some unknown person to assassinate Henri and had lost her nerve. The conspirators manipulating her realised she had become a danger to them – especially if they learned that she had confessed her treasonable plans to a priest – and decided

267

she needed to be silenced. I could go so far as to speculate that, since she had once been Guise's lover, the Duke may still have some hold over her; it seemed the most likely explanation. Although there was always an alternative possibility that could not yet be discounted: that the King, alarmed by my warning, had acted on impulse to disarm the threat of Circe for good. I could see full well that this was the fear behind Catherine's reluctance to accept that the girl had been murdered. I wondered if Ruggieri had reached the same conclusion and scrambled to support his mistress with the verdict she wanted to hear; no one with even a passing knowledge of anatomy could seriously suppose the girl to have killed herself. But one other question troubled me: had Léonie mistaken me for the man she was expecting, *because I was wearing the same costume?*

Ruggieri shivered and wrapped his Doctor's robe closer around him, the empty mask swinging from his hand.

'We do not usually hear you so quiet, Bruno. Is it because you dislike being told you are wrong?'

'I was only wondering,' I said, 'why you are so certain she took her own life? Did she have particular cause that you know of?'

Catherine made a gesture that seemed to imply the question was redundant. 'Young women. Thwarted affair of the heart or some nonsense. She would not be the first to fall into despair because a man had cast her aside.'

'But you just said your women do not involve themselves with men except at your command,' I said. Her eyes narrowed. 'I wondered,' I continued, keeping my tone light, 'if perhaps it could have been because she was with child?'

The silence that followed this was so profound I could hear the ice cracking on the window panes.

'What makes you say that?' Catherine asked, in a voice like a knife on a whetstone.

I was about to answer, but at that moment King Henri

268

burst in, distraught and dishevelled, his doublet unlaced and his cream silk stockings caked with mud. He threw himself to his knees beside Léonie's body and manoeuvred her torso clumsily into his lap.

'*Mon Dieu*,' he moaned softly, rocking her back and forth, her head hanging limply in his arms like a grotesque doll. He repeated this lament, the words muffled as he pressed his lips against her hair. The rest of us stood awkwardly watching this performance until Catherine clapped her hands and ordered her son to get up.

'Have you been drinking? You know what the physician said about your constitution – you are not supposed to touch wine. Put the girl down, Henri,' she added briskly, as if talking to a dog, though the King appeared not to hear. He remained folded over Léonie's body, his face wracked with pain, but I could not have said for certain whether it was grief or remorse. Henri was prone to dramatics either way.

'I will speak to the King in private,' Catherine announced. 'Ruggieri – take Doctor Bruno to the library and keep him there until I send for you again. Have the servants bring you meat and drink. And *you*—' she raised her walking stick and pointed it towards me with finality – 'will not repeat to anyone what you said just now. If that idle speculation finds its way into common gossip, I will have you arrested for slander. Do you understand me?'

I nodded. I, too, would have liked to speak to the King in private, but there was no question of that at present. Catherine meant to manage this situation in her own way. I tried to catch Henri's eye, but he would not raise his head from the corpse in his arms.

I followed Ruggieri along the corridors, empty now of guests but with a noticeable increase of armed guards, halberds bristling at every set of doors, though they parted swiftly for the astrologer as he strode towards them with his hand raised like Moses before the Red Sea. When we reached the library, he bade me take a seat at a table in front of the fireplace, on which large star maps and charts of the heavens lay unfurled, curling at the edges, held flat by several measuring instruments. Though the papers were upside down to me, I leaned across and peered at them with curiosity while he bustled about lighting a sconce of candles. It looked as if Ruggieri had been plotting a natal chart; the margins of the map were filled with gnomic scribbles in his cramped handwriting. In the top right-hand corner I saw that he had drawn the figure of a dolphin.

'Whose chart?' I asked, tapping the map.

He blew out the taper and leapt across with surprising speed, gathering the papers and rolling them tightly together. 'No business of yours.'

The way he pursed his lips, all puffed up with the importance of his confidential knowledge, made me determined not to give him the satisfaction of pressing him any further. He paced behind my chair while I ignored him. 'Whatever made you say the girl was with child?' he asked, at last. I swivelled to face him.

'You did not observe her during the masque tonight?'

He made a derisive noise. 'I did not. I was in here all evening, working. I don't need to see those girls writhing about. Give me a seizure, at my age.'

'Nonsense. I knew a man in Nola older than you, fathered twins.'

'Well. No idea of continence, you Nolans. What would I want with twins?' He raised his hands in retreat, as if someone were threatening to hand him a pair. 'Tell me about the girl, then. I have seen her recently – I did not remark that she had a big belly.'

'Not especially big at this stage. But there was a tell-tale sign, visible only because her gown tonight was so thin. She had the line on her belly, though very faint – she was still in the early months.'

'Line?' He frowned.

'The dark line that forms on the skin from the navel to the pubis. Have you not observed this in a woman expecting?'

'I am not a midwife, Bruno,' he said, with a little shudder of distaste. 'Your experience of looking at pregnant women unclothed is clearly broader than mine, but then you are a Dominican. Ah. I see that amuses you.'

I could hardly tell him I was nodding because it was true that my only previous experience of seeing a pregnant woman naked had been as a young novice at the convent of San Domenico Maggiore in Naples, though not in the way Ruggieri imagined.

'Of course, I may be mistaken,' I said, conciliatory. The suggestion that Léonie might have been pregnant had clearly caused Catherine further anxiety; I could guess why.

His shoulders relaxed. 'You would do well to say so to the Queen Mother. Bad enough that this dreadful business has occurred during an event that was supposed to increase good-will toward the royal family. She does not need you spreading malicious lies as well.'

'Not lies. Merely speculation.'

'Based on the scantest evidence and likely wrong, by your own admission. Like all your other theories, in your books which no one reads.'

I reminded myself silently not to rise to it. Fortunately I was distracted by the arrival of a boy in livery bearing a tray loaded with two plates of roast pheasant and large silver goblets of spiced wine. Ruggieri swept the remainder of his books from the table, not without a good deal of muttering, and the boy set the tray down with a bow, closing the door behind him.

Ruggieri and I looked at one another.

'After you,' I offered, indicating the plates.

'But you are our guest,' he returned, mirroring my gesture.

I smiled. 'I find I am not hungry after all.' It was a lie; my stomach growled, empty and sour from my earlier drinks, and the hot scent of roasted meat was making my gut cramp with hunger, but I would be a fool to ignore the advice I had given the King earlier, especially in these circumstances.

The old man gave one of his dry, rattling laughs. 'Are you suspicious of our hospitality? Do you suppose she means to poison you?'

I said nothing. It was rumoured that Catherine had plotted to poison her own daughter not so long ago; she was more than capable of dispatching me without a second thought.

'It is like a fairground riddle, is it not?' Ruggieri continued, enjoying himself. 'If I choose first, you will assume the other glass is poisoned. If I allow you to choose first, you will assume both are. If we were to drink at the same time, however—'

'I don't have time for your games,' I said, irritated.

'Pardon me, but you have all the time in the world. You are to remain Her Majesty's guest here until further notice.'

I turned away and slumped back against the chair. 'Drink or don't drink, Ruggieri, it's of no interest to me.' I pressed my sleeve against my face to try and block out the scent of the meat.

'Let this reassure you, then.' He pulled up his chair again, picked up one glass and drank from it, followed by the other. He did the same with a piece of meat from both plates, smiling with what I assumed was meant to be encouragement, though it still looked menacing. Warily, after a few moments, I reached across and took one of the plates from his hand. The meat was tender and savoury, and I devoured it in a hurry.

'There was a book,' I said, licking the last of the juices from my fingers. His head snapped up, immediately alert. 'About a year ago, Queen Catherine bought it from an English girl. I see you know the one I mean.'

He sat back, nodding. 'Yes, I thought you might come sniffing after that sooner or later. The girl was keen to insist on her acquaintance with you. She seemed to believe that would lend the book veracity.'

'And on the strength of that, Catherine bought it. Fifty écus, I heard.'

'She asked me to examine it first, naturally,' he said, ruffled. 'I thought it might prove a worthwhile addition to her collection. I wanted to pay less but the girl bargained hard. You clearly schooled her well. I do wonder, though, that you should have allowed such a book out of your hands.'

I chose to ignore the implicit question. 'You know what it is then.'

He folded his hands together on the table. His fingers were long and spindly with swollen joints, the tips stained purple from one of his concoctions, I presumed, though for a moment I had an image of him in his private room, picking through entrails to divine the future like an ancient Roman.

'I can see what it purports to be. The lost book of the Egyptian sage Hermes Trismegistus. Last rumoured to have been stolen from a bookseller in Venice, though that was two decades ago. You will know, of course,' he said, tapping a discoloured fingernail on the table as if instructing a child, 'that that book was salvaged from the ruins of Byzantium and brought to Italy at the command of Cosimo de Medici. So, if it is the same one, it rightly belongs in the hands of his great-great-great-granddaughter. Though it is considered a dangerous book, and forbidden by the Church.'

'Have you read it?'

He leaned forward, screwing up his face further to scrutinise me with his rheumy eyes, trying to divine whether I meant to catch him out.

'Have *you*?'

I merely smiled in a manner I hoped he would find enigmatic. The truth was that the book had only been in my possession for less than a day before it was stolen from me (even now the memory of Sophia's betrayal could make me grind my teeth involuntarily), but I already knew that the heart of it was written in a complex code as yet unbroken by scholars.

273

Let Ruggieri believe I had cracked the encryption. Catherine would want to know the book's content, after paying so much; it might enhance my value if she thought I was the only one who could read it. Besides, I felt confident that, given the time to make a proper study, I would succeed in deciphering the cramped handwriting that filled the ancient pages.

'I would not profane its secrets by discussing them with a man such as you,' he said loftily, after a hesitation long enough to reassure me that he had not managed to penetrate the book's mysteries.

'A man such as me?' I laughed. 'Oh, come, Ruggieri – if you did not have Catherine's protection they would have burned you for a witch long ago. You call yourself a scholar, but you are little better than a village wise-woman. Love-philtres and divination by guesswork, that is the extent of your occult wisdom.'

He half-raised himself out of the chair, leaning on both hands across the table. 'Do not think yourself so far above me, Giordano Bruno. For all your degrees in philosophy and theology, I know you have studied natural magic too. Why else would you want that book? And do not think to mock me – my prophecies have shaped this kingdom—' He broke off suddenly, as if stricken by a terrible premonition, and stared at the rolled charts in his hand until I coughed, bringing him back to himself. He squinted hard at me. 'We are two sides of the same coin, you and I. Look – we are even wearing the same costume tonight. People would be hard pressed to tell between us.'

'If I had known, I would have worn something different. I would not wish to be mistaken for you,' I said carefully. 'By some woman you had made a tryst with, for instance.'

He gave a dry laugh. 'Hardly a danger these days. I always come as the Doctor to a costume ball, everyone knows it. You should have recalled that. You being the one who professes the art of memory,' he added, unable to resist the barb.

I was too preoccupied with the thought of my encounter with Léonie in the clearing to respond in kind. It had been almost completely dark, and I was standing outside the reach of her lantern; I could not know for certain whether she had seen my costume and spoken as she did because she had been waiting for a man dressed as the Doctor from the Commedia and assumed I was he. But it made no sense to think she had been expecting Ruggieri; he was Catherine's man to the bone, he would be the last person to incite anyone to harm the King. I pressed the heels of my hands into my eyes; I was tired and still blurry from drink, and my mind was making wild leaps without the aid of reason. I needed to rein it in and proceed logically.

'Speaking of memory,' I said casually, 'do you remember the girl's name? The one who sold you the book.' I scratched at a splinter of wood on the table so as not to look overly interested.

'She was trying to present herself as a boy, I recall. No one was fooled by that.' He paused to pick a shred of meat from his remaining teeth. 'When she finally admitted her deception, the name she gave was very ordinary. Something that made me suppose it was a false name too. Anne, perhaps? Jane? Mary?'

I tried to suppress my irritation. 'Well, which?'

He shook his head. 'I never had the benefit of your lessons in memory, of course,' he said, with a malicious little smile. 'Might have been Mary.'

'And the surname?' I asked, already knowing this was pointless.

'Something like Gifford,' he said, unexpectedly. 'One of those peculiar English names.'

I sat up. 'Mary Gifford. You are sure?'

'Not how you knew her, I take it?'

'She has had many names since I've known her.'

Ruggieri pulled at the points of his beard. 'She sounds like a handful of trouble, Bruno. You must be made for each other.'

I stared into the fire, my thoughts scattered. Sophia Underhill. A boy called Kit. Mrs Kate Kingsley. And now Mary Gifford. At least I had a means to begin looking. Made for each other. There were times when I feared that might be true, and not in a comforting way.

Bells chimed the hour from a distant part of the palace. The candles burned low. I must have dozed a little, listening to the fading crackle of the fire and the sound of Ruggieri sucking the bones for the last scraps of meat. Eventually the chewing gave way to the rhythmic gargling of an old man's snores. I roused myself and saw that he had fallen asleep, his head lolling on to his chest like a hanged man. I pushed my chair back and stood, as silently as possible. We were alone in the vast space of the library, wooden stacks filled with books stretching away into the darkness in both directions. I had no idea how much time had passed, but I decided that, whatever the consequences, I would rather not wait for Catherine's summons. I picked up my mask from the table and tied it tight around my head again, flinching at the clamminess inside. Ruggieri might be deep in the arms of Morpheus but I supposed the guard was still outside and I was unarmed since the loss of my dagger. I cast around for anything I might use as a weapon and my eye fell on a poker in the fireplace. Tucking it behind my back, I tiptoed across to the door and turned the handle. Ruggieri shifted and snorted in his sleep; I froze, my throat tight, but he settled himself like an old dog and slumbered on. I slipped out, closing the door behind me and keeping my back pressed against it.

The guard looked surprised at my appearance; he gripped his halberd with both hands and demanded to know what I was about.

'It is time for me to return to the Queen Mother's apartments,' I said.

He frowned. 'I was given no orders.'

'No, but I was. She told me to return at this hour.'

He glanced along the corridor to left and right, as if some explanation might be waiting. I suspected this one was not overburdened with wits.

'We don't want to keep her waiting,' I added, with a warning note. 'She will be angry if she hears you stopped me.'

He hesitated. 'I will have to accompany you.'

'Of course. Is it down here?' I took a step forward in the wrong direction.

'This way.' He moved to usher me along, turning as he did so to point ahead; in the same moment I swung the poker with both hands to catch him on the back of the skull. He was a tall man, but not heavy; he fell on his face with a thud like a sack of flour dropped from a height, narrowly missing the blade of his weapon as he toppled forward. I murmured an apology as I fumbled at his belt for the short knife he carried there. It was a poor substitute for the beautifully crafted Damascus steel I had lost, but at least I felt a little better prepared. I ran along dim corridors where the sconces had burned down to one wavering flame on a mound of melted wax, winding my way through the now-deserted palace, keeping close to the walls, until a draught of cold air led me to a side door that opened on to the gardens.

A brittle dawn light was spreading slowly up from the horizon, the sky cold and smooth as glass, the air charged with the metallic taste of frost. A lone seagull drifted above me with a mournful cry, wings motionless, floating like a sheet of paper on the wind. Ahead, the gardens were emerging into a patchwork of shadows, the detritus of the night – abandoned masks, gloves, lanterns – outlined on the whitened grass. The bowl of the great fountain loomed out of the retreating darkness. The gardens too seemed abandoned; I guessed the night's revellers had been packed off into boats before panic and scandal could spread too far.

I set out briskly on the path towards the copse, my feet so quickly numbed by the cold that it hurt to walk. The torches that had lit the way a few hours earlier had all burned to blackened stumps or been appropriated by couples seeking the shelter of the wood. I had no need of a lantern to find the place now, though when I reached the clearing where I had encountered Léonie, I wished I had thought to bring one; the trees overshadowed the ground and the frail light barely penetrated here. I walked carefully around the fallen trunk where she had been sitting, crouching to sift through piles of dead leaves with my fingers. After a few minutes, I sat back on my haunches and blew on my frozen fingers. It was still too dark to make out footprints clearly and in any case, so many lovers seemed to have made their way through the clearing I was unlikely to find anything that would show who had encountered Léonie here.

I stood, hearing my knees crack, and followed the direction she had taken in such haste when she realised she had said too much to the wrong person. She had run wildly into the trees where there was no path, but by proceeding slowly I could see from the broken branches and traces of her white fur cloak snagged on twigs the course of her panicked flight. Some fifty yards into the wood, my eye was caught by a pale streak on the ground. I pushed through the thicket of branches and bent to pick up a white silk scarf, sown with tiny pearls and embroidered with silver thread and tassels, now trampled and muddied. A knot had been tied midway along. I stared at it, recalling Léonie's body, the bruise at her throat. Whoever killed her had known this trick with the knot, just like Joseph de Chartres's murderer.

I tucked the scarf inside my doublet and stumbled back into the clearing, wrapping my hands inside the folds of my cloak. The sun had almost risen above the horizon; in the chilly light I saw a figure moving among the trees on the other side, by the path back to the palace. I froze, but a twig snapped beneath my feet and it was too late to hide; I drew the small dagger I had stolen as he whipped around and I realised he was not wearing a mask.

278

'Jacopo!' I sheathed the weapon with relief and pushed my own mask on to my head.

'Bruno?' He took a step towards me, frowning. The pouches under his eyes were deeply shadowed; he had evidently been up all night too. 'What on earth are you doing out here?'

'Looking for anything that might tell us what happened to the girl. You?'

'The same,' he said, after a pause. I noticed that he looked past me towards the trees as he spoke. 'I thought Catherine had you under guard in the library?'

'I thought I might spend my time more usefully.'

He glanced fearfully in the direction of the gardens. 'She will be angry when she finds you gone.'

'Ruggieri can take the blame for that. Though he will probably claim I bewitched him.'

'Did you find anything?'

I unbuttoned my doublet and reached into the inside pocket. 'I cannot tell you how glad I am to talk to you, Jacopo. There is something I must show you.' I told him briefly of my earlier encounter with Léonie and what she had said, then handed him the gold medallion she had left behind. 'She dropped this when she ran from me. I suppose it is valuable – she was worrying at it like a holy medal when I interrupted her.'

He started visibly as I laid the disc flat on his palm, the side with the dolphin engraving uppermost, and the colour drained from his face. 'Dear God. Do you know what this is?'

'A piece of jewellery, I guessed. But I do not understand its significance.'

'Better you do not.' He pressed his lips together and closed his fist over the medal. 'Leave it with me – I will see it returned to its rightful owner. You must not be found with it on your person. In fact, you should not be found at all.' He checked quickly in both directions. 'Come with me. I helped smuggle you in – the least I can do is show you out. And God help us both if we run into anyone.'

I followed him back to the path, but instead of turning towards the palace, he led me in the other direction, along the edge of the wild part of the gardens in the shadow of the riverside wall, until we reached a small gate tucked away at the far end. Jacopo took a bunch of keys from his belt and unlocked it.

'You can get a boat across the river from the steps at the Tour du Bois, there should be boatmen about at this hour,' he said, chivvying me through. 'And Bruno – tell no one else of what the girl said to you. Do not even mention that you saw her in the clearing. I told you before – it is safer for you to keep your distance from all this.'

'All this? So you know that this murder is connected to the others?'

He laid a hand on my arm. 'I know you believe so. Catherine told me what you said to Henri tonight, about Circe.'

'I heard the girl, Jacopo, only minutes before she died, protesting she could not go through with it or she would damn her soul. What else could she have meant? Someone had corrupted her to their cause to kill the King, I am certain of it. She must have confessed to Paul Lefèvre, who wrote anonymously to the King to warn him. Henri never received the letter, but whoever was behind the plot found out by some means. Paul was killed to silence him, so was Joseph. When it became clear that Léonie had lost her nerve, she too was silenced.'

Jacopo looked at me with great weariness in his dark eyes, his face grave. 'It sounds a wild theory to me, Bruno. But these deaths should be reason enough to leave the business alone. Let Catherine deal with it now as she judges best. Léonie de Châtillon was a member of her household.'

'Guise and his sister are behind it, I am certain. It is just a question of finding proof.' I felt my fists clench as I spoke; I had almost forgotten my obligation to Guise. But I still could not fathom why he had set me on to investigate the previous murders if he knew the trail would lead back to his associates.

'Then you must certainly leave it to Catherine. She is practised in negotiating with the Duke of Guise – if he is responsible, she will find a way to have satisfaction.' He darted a quick glance over his shoulder and squeezed my arm. 'Now I must go. Promise me, Bruno, that you will not put yourself in any further danger?'

I laid my hand over his. 'I can promise you that I will not take undue risk.'

'That is not the same thing,' he said, his eyes stern.

'I have been given a task by the King, and until he releases me from it I consider myself under royal command.'

He sighed. 'Too stubborn, Bruno. One day it will be the end of you. The King is hardly himself at the moment, surely you can see that?' When I said nothing, he shook his head with an air of paternal disappointment. 'Go, then. But come and dine with me this week. I will send you word when I am free.'

'Thank you, I will.' I pressed his hand. 'One more question – are the *Gelosi* staying at your house this week?'

'They will be there for today, collecting their belongings. Tomorrow they move to the Hotel de Montpensier – they have been offered rooms while they entertain the Duke tomorrow night. After that I believe they are bound for Lyon.'

'Good. I want you to pass a message to Francesco. Tell him I need to take him up on his kind offer to join the company.'

SIXTEEN

I arrived back at my lodgings in the full light of a winter dawn and removed only my boots before wrapping myself in a blanket and falling on to my bed. The combined effects of wine and exhaustion overcame my racing mind and I slept until almost noon, when I was awakened by a furious hammering on the door to my chamber. I jolted upright, convinced it must be Catherine's armed men come to escort me forcibly back to the Tuileries to account for having absconded the night before. While I debated whether it would be feasible to escape out of a second-floor window, the knocking came again, and with it the voice of my landlady, Madame de la Fosse, frostily informing me that a man in a friar's habit was downstairs to see me. She made this sound vaguely reprehensible. I wondered how she would respond when a brace of armed guards eventually did turn up to arrest me.

I broke the skin of ice on the jug of water by my bed and splashed my face, ran my hands through my hair, straightened my clothes and pulled on my boots. When I was certain that Madame was downstairs again, I dragged a stool to the edge of the room and lifted the loose panel under the eaves that hid the cavity where I kept my most secret writings and correspondence, together with other items I would not wish to be found if anything happened to me. Through the small gap I eased out a cloth bag where I had stowed the silver penknife I had found by the body of Joseph de Chartres, and stuffed into it the embroidered scarf I had found in the wood, to examine later. I pushed the bag back and replaced the panel before snatching up my cloak and gloves and racing down the stairs to the front door, where Madame stood eyeing young Frère Benoît from Saint-Victor with her arms folded across her scrawny bosom, blocking his way in case he might be tempted to make off with her best candlesticks. He looked relieved to see me, his breath smoking around his face as he stamped his feet on the doorstep, his hands tucked into the sleeves of his habit.

'Thank you, madame,' I said, graciously. She gave me one of her looks and retreated into her own quarters, though it was clear she had not fully closed the door to the entrance hall. She disliked my notoriety, but that did nothing to dampen her interest in my business in the hope of some gossip.

'Come,' I said to Benoît, nodding to the street, 'let's walk.'

The rutted mud underfoot had frozen to hard peaks and troughs, as if the ground had been turned to stone overnight. I pulled on my gloves as we set off in the direction of the rue Saint-Jacques and the colleges of the university. 'Have you news?' I asked, when we were beyond the reach of Madame's eavesdropping. Benoît blew on his hands.

'Frère Guillaume sent me with a message. He needs to speak to you.'

'Why? Did he say?'

The boy shook his head. 'He said only that it was important. He had found something he thought you should see urgently. He wants you to meet him at the back gate to the abbey this evening before Vespers.'

'No hint of what it might be? No letter for me, perhaps?' I tried not to show my hesitation. I wanted to trust Benoît but this would be a laughably easy trap to spring; Paul Lefèvre had died because he had walked trustingly to a rendezvous on that deserted river path behind the abbey. The Abbé of Saint-Victor was a League supporter and had already had me thrown in gaol once; outside the city wall I would be under his jurisdiction, and I would not be surprised if he found a kind of poetic justice in luring me to the same end. On the other hand, if the message were genuine, I was curious to know what Cotin might have found that he considered so important. Something to do with Joseph? I looked at Benoît. His habitual manner was so jittery that it was difficult to judge whether he was lying.

'Tell him I will be there,' I said, slowing as we reached the cloister of the Mathurins. I would need a better weapon than the knife I had taken from the guard at the Tuileries, though; it would be folly not to prepare myself for an ambush. I wondered if I could persuade someone to go with me, even if only for the sake of appearances; no one looks so vulnerable as a man alone. Francesco and some of his players, perhaps, or even Paget? But I could not justify dragging the *Gelosi* into possible danger – I had too much need of them the following night – and there was always the chance that Cotin had genuinely found something connected with the murders, in which case Paget was the last person I wanted as a witness.

'Well, this is where I must say goodbye,' I said, offering my hand in the English style more as a hint than a farewell, since Benoît still lingered at my side, hopping from foot to foot.

'Where are you going?' he asked, his eyes eager.

'To collect my laundry from a washerwoman,' I said, stepping back, afraid that he might offer to come with me. He seemed well-meaning but I could not discount the possibility that he had been sent by his abbot to report on me. To pre-empt any such suggestion, I gave him a curt nod and set off up the street; he looked disappointed, and stood watching me for a few minutes as if making up his mind whether to follow, so that I was obliged to turn the corner and loiter in the shadow of a doorway until I was sure he had gone on his way. God, this city! I pushed both hands through my hair and leaned against the wall. So many factions, so many plots; everyone an informer with two faces, playing one party off against the others. At least in London my enemies had been more visible, and I had known who my friends were. Here, I could rely only on Jacopo, and even then I knew that if he were forced to choose between the various loyalties he owed, Catherine and the King would trump me every time: that was mere self-preservation.

When I was certain that Benoît was no longer watching my movements I hurried down the rue du Fouarre, reminding myself that at some point I really would have to collect my clothes from the laundress, and tip her well for her trouble. I wound my way along narrow back streets until I saw the sign of the Eagle hanging above a narrow doorway. Entering, I found myself in the low-beamed tap-room of a tavern, broad and well furnished with a wide hearth along one side. The place was half-full, the customers all men, mainly young, though by their coats and boots they crossed all divides of class. Most striking was the rhythm of their talk, the unmistakable flat cadences of English; before I had even closed the door behind me I felt I had been transported back to London. The tables nearest the fire were occupied and the conversations tailed off as the drinkers turned to look at me. I met no one's eye and slipped into a seat in a poorly lit corner. After a while, the other customers appeared to lose interest and the low hum of talk resumed, though they leant in closer and spoke more quietly than before, casting the occasional glance over their shoulders in my direction.

I ordered a bowl of stew and a jug of wine from a surly serving girl and tried to observe the young men by the fire without being noticed. Perhaps it had been a mistake to come here in daylight; I was more obvious alone, and less likely to fall into easy conversation. It was clear they were wary of a

285

stranger; hardly surprising, if this was where the disaffected English Catholics gathered to boast of their plans for taking back their homeland. But as Paget had said, the hot-headed plots cooked up here by angry students over a jug of cheap wine need not disturb Walsingham's sleep; the truly dangerous conspiracies were brewing in more richly furnished rooms than these. In any case, I had not come for Walsingham, but for a purpose of my own. That knock on my chamber door this morning had been a warning; I knew it was only a matter of time now before soldiers arrived to arrest me on some imagined charge – whether sent by Catherine de Medici or the Duke of Guise seemed almost irrelevant. I did not like to leave unfinished business, not when I was so close, and I had waited over a year to conclude this particular matter. But now that I was here, I no longer felt sure of myself. My name, if not my face, would be familiar to many of these young Englishmen thanks to the Throckmorton business two years ago; I would need to approach softly if I were not to rouse their suspicions.

I dipped a heel of dry bread into the stew – it was as well my expectations on that score had been low – and strained to catch any of the exchanges around me, when the door opened and a man entered, clapping his hands against the cold. He pulled down his hood and stood for a moment looking around uncertainly, until a barrage of protests at the draught from the open door prompted him to shut it in haste, with muttered apologies. I recognised him as the young man with the freckles I had seen at Brinkley's print shop, the one who had delivered the package that Paget later collected. He was still casting around the tap-room as if expecting to meet someone. Evidently whoever it was had not arrived; he pulled off his gloves and took a seat at the next table from mine, his eyes on the door.

'Turned colder today,' I said cheerfully, lifting my cup of wine in a manner of greeting. I recalled how fond the English were of talking about the weather. 'We might have snow before the week is out.'

The young man stared at me as if I had insulted him. Too late, I also remembered how affronted the English are at being addressed by a stranger in a public place. After a moment, his face creased into a frown. I could see he was trying to place me.

'We met at the printer's shop last week,' I said, to help him out. He nodded, though his face grew guarded.

'I remember. You were asking for illegal books.'

'I was advised by a friend – God rest him – that Brinkley might be one of the few brave souls to print the truth about the persecution of the true Church in England. Books the Valois regime do not want the people of France to read, while they plot their alliance with the heretic queen.'

His eyes widened at this, but he remained cautious. 'You said it was the priest who was killed. The friend you spoke of, I mean?'

'Yes.' I assumed an appropriately sombre expression. 'Père Lefèvre. We used to lecture together at the university. Did you know him?'

Instantly his gaze swerved away, guilty. 'No. But I had heard him preach. It was dreadful, what happened to him.'

I nodded sadly. 'He has still had no justice, despite the protests.'

'Nor will he,' the boy said, suddenly animated, 'unless the people take justice into their own hands.'

'Rise against the King, you mean?'

'Why should they not, when the King scorns true religion and murders those who defend it? He will fall, just like our heretic queen at home, who spills the blood of faithful Catholics. It is written in scripture. *The wicked have drawn out their sword; they have bent their bow, to cast down the poor and needy, to kill the upright of heart,*' he quoted solemnly. 'But the Lord says, *Fret not thyself because of the wicked men, for they shall soon be cut down like grass, and shall wither as the green herb.*' He nodded an emphatic full stop. I looked impressed.

'No doubt they shall be. But how soon, is the question?'

'Sooner than they think,' he said, with the satisfaction of one whose inside knowledge gives him an advantage. His manner reminded me of Paul's hints to me in the confessional that the King was not long for his throne: not quite able to resist a tacit boast.

I was considering what more to ask without putting him on guard when the serving girl slumped her flat-footed way towards us again and demanded to know what my companion wanted to eat. He shifted uncomfortably in his seat and mumbled about expecting to meet a friend. From his clothes and his general demeanour, I guessed he had little money. I wondered if he was there to pass over another package, and who he might be meeting.

'Take a drink with me while you wait,' I offered. He shot me an anxious glance from the tail of his eye and returned his attention to his fingernails. 'No obligation. You look as if you could do with something warm.'

He acknowledged this with a rueful nod, but still he hesitated.

'You are worried about talking to a stranger,' I said, with a nod of understanding. 'Perhaps you fear I am a spy.'

He glanced up with an expression caught between guilt and apology. 'This is Paris, after all.'

'Quite. You are probably one yourself.' I thought of the package I had seen him hand to Brinkley. At this he coloured so violently that I knew I had struck a nerve. 'Don't worry, I am only teasing you. Let us not discuss politics, then,' I said. 'We could talk about women instead.'

His face suggested he found this even more alarming. He was reprieved by the arrival of the wine. I poured a cup for him and lifted my own.

'We are two foreigners, far from home – let us at least take a drink together. What is your name?'

He hesitated, then relented. 'Gilbert. Gilbert Gifford.'

I tried to keep my face composed. 'Pardon me, but your name seems familiar?'

His jaw clenched and I saw his hand tighten around his cup. 'If you have heard that name, it is probably because of the insults and injustices that have been heaped on my family these past years. The pretender Elizabeth Tudor has made us a byword for disgrace.'

'Ah. Then your father is . . .?'

'John Gifford of Staffordshire, imprisoned in London for recusancy with all his goods forfeit.'

'That is hard indeed,' I said.

'There is worse. Two years ago, my cousin was hanged and quartered at Tyburn.'

'God have mercy. That is a terrible death. What was his crime?'

'No crime at all, unless it be a crime to say the Mass and bring the comfort of the sacraments to the faithful.'

'Ah. He was a secret priest, then.'

'Aye, and martyred for it. And if that be made treason under English law, why then I say we owe no loyalty to the law of heretics, only to God's commands.' He thumped his fist on the table as he spat the words; some of the men by the fire turned with reproachful glares and he subsided, embarrassed. Though he fell silent, anger still burned in his face. He would be a gift to the cause of the English exiles, I thought; a young man so alive with fury and the desire for righteous vengeance was ripe for their purposes. I nodded in sympathy. I did not tell him I had watched his cousin die.

'And your sister?'

He snapped his attention back to me, puzzled. 'I have no sister.'

'Your pardon, I must be mistaken. But I thought there was a Miss Mary Gifford living among the English here in Paris?'

'You know Mary?' The high colour that suffused his cheeks betrayed his interest. Poor boy; I feared he would not last long as an agent for the Catholic cause. His every feeling was written on his face as it occurred. Though he was hardly a boy any more; I guessed him to be in his mid-twenties. Perhaps he would learn discretion, if he lived long enough.

'I have only heard her spoken of as a most accomplished young woman. She is a governess to one of the English families, I believe?'

'Yes, to the daughters of Sir Thomas Fitzherbert in the Faubourg Saint-Germain. I take lodgings in his house. But she is not my sister. How do you know of her?'

'We have a mutual acquaintance in Paris. She is some relative of yours, though?'

'I suppose she must be. But from no branch of the family I ever heard of. I did not even know we had relatives in the West Country. So she must be a very distant cousin, if she is one at all. It gave us much amusement when I first met her at Sir Thomas's house and we discovered we had the same name.'

'I imagine it did.' Sophia most of all, I thought; she had blithely taken the name of the man she once loved, as if she had been married to him, never supposing she might have to explain herself to another Gifford here in Paris. She must have smoothed it over, though; she was always good at talking her way out of trouble. 'Well, if you wed her, at least she will not have to change her name,' I said, with a smile, raising my cup in a mock toast.

He spluttered, spraying wine across the table. When he had recovered, he fixed me with an outraged expression. '*Wed* her? What put that in your head? I mean to say, I *admire* her, who would not, but I have not presumed to think . . . Besides, how could I wed her,' he continued, interrupting himself, 'when I have no estate left and no means to support a wife?' The bitterness had crept back into his tone. 'And in any case, she would not look at me now.'

'Ah. She has another suitor, then?' Really, the boy was so

transparent the Queen of England would not need to make a window into his soul – his face was one giant window already.

'She affects to spurn him. But women are weak.' Gifford curled his lip. 'How can I compete with a French duke? And I must travel to England again before Christmas. I fear he will corrupt her virtue while I am away.' He took a long gulp of his wine and wiped his mouth on the back of his hand.

Corrupt her virtue? Was she presenting herself to the Catholics as a pure maid? I almost laughed aloud, but it was choked by a hard bud of anger in my throat at the memory of Guise so smoothly using Sophia to threaten me. Paget too, taunting me with the mention of her and refusing to tell me her new name or how to find her; I had supposed he wanted her for himself, but now it seemed he was only procuring for Guise. I had no proof of this, and perhaps my jealous mind was too quick to leap to conclusions, but I could think of no other French duke who would be so familiar with the house-hold of an English Catholic family. I looked down at my hands gripping the pewter cup and realised I too was in danger of allowing my feelings to show, as if I were a green boy. I finished the wine, stood abruptly and reached for my purse.

'Listen, my friend – she is said to be a young woman of unusual intelligence. You must trust, then, that she is clever enough not to judge a man's worth by his titles, or lack of them.'

He gave me a look of such puppyish gratitude I was almost sorry to deceive him. I threw down some coins on the table.

'And now I must go. Thank you for passing the time with me. When do you go to England?'

'In a fortnight. To take some money for my father from his friends in Paris,' he added, quickly. So that was his cover story. I wondered what else he would be carrying for Paget and the other Catholics here, and what he might intend to bring back. More martyrs' fingers or teeth, perhaps? Well, that would be uncovered soon enough.

'Then I pray God you have a safe trip and find him in good health.' I smiled and made a little bow as I turned to leave. 'My name is Filippo, by the way. I hope we meet again.'

He nodded, though he did not look as if he welcomed the idea. And now I had a name for Walsingham, I thought, as I closed the door behind me. Poor fool. He was right – Sophia would not look twice at him, unless she thought she could use him to her advantage.

In the street outside the tavern I walked straight into Charles Paget.

'Bruno!' He sounded, as always, as if it was a delightful surprise to bump into me – a sure sign he had known very well where to find me. 'We do not often see you frequenting such disreputable places. Wouldn't have thought they were your kind of people, in there.'

'Englishmen?'

'*Papists.*' He said it in a theatrical whisper, as if sharing a dirty secret. 'Did you find good company?'

'I found a hot meal, Paget, which was all I looked for.' I shouldered past him in the narrow street and began to walk away.

'Yes, you must have needed sustenance, after last night. An eventful evening all round, I understand. Catherine's entertainments can usually be relied upon to provide some drama, but rarely after the show is over.' Paget kept pace with me easily with his long legs; I could not hope to shake him off.

'Were you there?'

He merely smiled. I supposed the answer was yes – it would have been unlike Paget to miss an occasion such as last night's – but with a girl murdered I could understand why he was unwilling to confirm his presence.

'Where are you going?' he said, as we reached the Mathurins. 'I'll walk with you.'

'I thought you were going to the Eagle?' I nodded back towards the tavern.

'Oh, that will keep. Tell me what happened with the girl. You were there.' He took hold of my arm to pull me to a halt, his grip firm enough not to be argued with. 'I know Catherine sent for you. What are they saying about the death? Is it connected?'

I hesitated, weighing my answer. It was never easy to judge how much Paget already knew. If Léonie de Châtillon was killed because of her part in a conspiracy against the King, it could only lead back to Guise, or someone acting on his behalf. I looked at Paget, trying to size him up. He and Guise were of a similar stature, both tall and broad-shouldered; either could have been the man in the Greek mask. I presumed it would serve their purpose better to think the death were not being treated as murder. I wondered what he had meant by saying I was there – was he hinting that he had seen me, or just trying to frighten me into giving more away than I intended?

'They seem to believe the girl took her own life.'

His eyes grew shrewd. 'But what do *you* think?'

'I saw nothing to suggest that was not the case.'

'Hm.' He let go of my arm. 'Guise says she was murdered.'

'*Guise* thinks so?' I could not keep the surprise from my voice. 'Then he clearly knows something I do not.'

Paget rolled his eyes. 'He didn't *do* it. He thinks it must have been someone at court – it would explain why they want to cover it up. That's why he's keen to know what you might have observed, at close quarters. I should not need to remind you that you made an agreement with him.'

I thought back to the scene in the gallery: the way Catherine and Ruggieri had closed ranks to deny that Léonie had been murdered. Perhaps Guise had a point. But I was less afraid of his threats after my conversation with Gilbert Gifford. If Guise wanted Sophia for his mistress, he was hardly likely to hurt her in order to spite me. At least, not until after he had had her, and if Gifford was to be believed, she was still holding out. For a better deal, I thought, bitterly.

293

'If it were the case that she was murdered, I ask myself why the Duke should care? Did he have some vested interest in her?'

'I believe she was a mistress once, years ago. He's been through most of Catherine's girls at one time or another. But he remained fond of her. Besides, he thinks her death is connected to the others. The priest and de Chartres.'

'Why does he think that?' My palms had begun to sweat, despite the cold. I reminded myself that there was no possible way Paget or Guise could know that I had seen the Circe letter or told the King about it.

'She was observed visiting the church of Saint-Séverin recently.'

'How do you know that? From Lefèvre?'

'No. He never mentioned it – that is the strange part. Another helpful party saw her leaving his confessional.' He shook his head. 'Curious, isn't it? One of Catherine's women choosing a League church for her confession? What did they *talk* about?'

'I suppose we will never know, since they are both dead.'

'Both murdered,' Paget said, darkly. 'Remarkable coincidence. Guise wants to know why. And you are supposed to be finding out for him.'

'I am doing my best,' I said, needled. 'He will have to wait a little longer.'

'You don't *have* much longer,' he said. Before I had a chance to ask what he meant by that, he laughed abruptly and clapped me on the shoulder. 'Dine with me this evening. I am having a small gathering at my lodgings on the rue Neuve. Gentlemen only, but we'll make an exception for you.' He chuckled again, to show that the insult was only half-intended.

'Will Guise be there?' I asked, apprehensive.

'Not tonight. Exclusively Englishmen and Scots. And friends of England,' he added, with an inclusive sweep of his hand towards me. 'Stafford is coming. My neighbour Sir

Thomas Fitzherbert. Archbishop Beaton. You might find the conversation interesting. Some supper, wine, a few hands of cards.'

'Alas, I am not a gambler,' I said, backing away.

He answered with an arch smile. 'I beg to disagree, Bruno. Your entire life is a gamble. I recognise it all too well.'

'Let us say, then, that I do not have the appetite to play with you and your friends. I suspect the stakes will be too high.'

The smile widened. He was a man who appreciated a double meaning. 'Let that not hinder you. I could always extend you credit. You would not be the first.'

'I thank you, but I am occupied this evening.'

'Pity. You would have added much to the entertainment. Well, I hope you will spend your time profitably making enquiries about the de Châtillon girl. Guise is losing patience with you. His sister the Duchess wants you arrested for murder and I can't hold them off forever.'

I was not sure how to respond; the image of Paget standing bravely between me and the Fury of the League was hard to swallow, but I could not deny that my continued liberty was a surprise to me, given what a gift I would make as a scapegoat for Joseph's murder, so I had to conclude that someone must be speaking for me and could not discount the possibility that it might be Paget. The question of *why* was another matter, and one I preferred not to dwell on for the moment.

'I shall come and find you tomorrow,' he called after me, as I crossed the rue Saint-Jacques. His tone was jaunty, but to me it carried an implicit threat.

'I hope Dame Fortune smiles on your cards tonight,' I replied, looking back.

'She always does.' He tilted his hat to a rakish angle. 'I make sure of it.'

SEVENTEEN

I returned to my rooms, locked the door and sat down to write a brief letter to Walsingham. This was a more laborious process than it sounded, thanks to Master Secretary's devilishly complicated system of encryption, but at length it was complete: a warning to look out for Gilbert Gifford's arrival in England and keep a close eye on his contacts, since I believed he would be entrusted with packages that might prove interesting. I hesitated with my quill over the page, wondering if I should pass on what Catherine had told me regarding Stafford's gambling habit. I decided against it; Walsingham would know the ambassador's vices better than I, and there was no proof beyond an old woman's insinuations. Besides, there was every chance that Stafford would attempt to read the letter first, since I would have to send it through the diplomatic courier; I did not have time to wait for this messenger of Walsingham's to make himself known. I signed my name, dusted the ink with sand and sealed the paper with plain wax, adding to the outside corner my customary symbol, the astrological sign for Jupiter, to let Walsingham know the contents were urgent.

Before I set out again, I took down the cloth bag from its hiding place in the roof and tipped the contents on to my bed. All these items – the love letter from Frère Joseph's mattress, the silver penknife found by his body and the scarf from the clearing last night – connected the three murders in some way that I could not yet comprehend. It was another kind of code, but one to which as yet I lacked the key. The manner of Joseph's and Léonie's deaths – both garrotted with a knotted ligature – suggested the same killer, one with some experience of murder. If Joseph was found naked because he was killed – or at least lured to his death – by his lover, then it was a question of identifying the author of that letter, and that meant finding a match to the handwriting. I pushed my hands through my hair and sighed; it would not be easy, but it was my only firm idea of where to start. I left the letter and turned the penknife over in my hand. To my unskilled eye it offered no obvious marks of identification save the hallmark of the tower on the blade. I would need to take it to an expert, someone trained in reading the language of the silversmiths' symbols. Finally, the scarf. I smoothed it out on the bed and noticed again the faint smudge of blood on the ivory silk. I was still dogged by the lingering sense of guilt that I might have been close enough to save Léonie last night. If I had not frightened her by revealing my face, or if I had pursued her when she fled, perhaps her attacker would have been denied his opportunity, at least for that night. 'Will you not release me?' she had begged. But from what? What had bound her to the man she had arranged to meet in the clearing, for whom she had mistaken me?

With some effort, I forced my attention away from these unanswered questions, and held the scarf up to examine it more closely. The border was delicately embroidered with a pattern of curling vines and leaves, recurring emblems worked into them at intervals: a double-barred cross and a small crest, a gold shield crossed with a band of crimson showing three white eaglets displayed. I did not recognise the crest, but I was familiar enough with the court to know it was not the arms of the House of Valois or the House of Guise. Jacopo would know; he could identify the devices of most of the French and Italian nobility at a glance. The cross was more of a puzzle; the double horizontal bar was the emblem of the Templars, but could also denote the rank of archbishop. There were senior churchmen in the Guise family, though it seemed unlikely that an archbishop had been wandering the gardens in costume waiting to strangle a half-dressed girl. Although by the standards of Catherine's spectacles, nothing was impossible. I replaced the items in their hiding place, picked up the bundle containing the clothes Stafford had lent me and tucked my letter to Walsingham into the pocket of my doublet.

On the way to the Quai des Bernardins I stopped at a barber's for a shave and a haircut. I asked him to cut it short; it seemed prudent to look as little like myself as possible if I wanted my plan for the following night to work. A blast of icy air whistled across the back of my neck when I came out; I ran a hand over my cropped skull and jammed my hat down hard over my ears. The barber must have done a good job; when I knocked at the door of the English embassy it took Stafford's steward a few moments to recognise me. When he finally realised who I was he tried to claim the ambassador was busy, but I had my foot inside the door by then and insisted my business was urgent, so that eventually he was forced to let me pass.

Stafford glanced up from his desk with a frown as I entered his study.

'I would prefer it if you didn't come here in daylight,' he said, by way of a greeting. 'People might see you.'

'Last time you told me not to come in the middle of the night.' I pulled up a chair, though none had been offered. I was aware that I ought to show more deference but his manner riled me. 'How much light would be proper, Ambassador? Dusk? Dawn?'

'What is it you want?' He tapped a knuckle on the papers before him. 'I'm very busy and I have an engagement this evening.'

'Of course.' I placed the bundle of clothes on his desk, followed by the letter. 'I came to return these, with thanks to your clerk. And I need to send this message urgently to Master Secretary with your next courier. In the next day or two at the latest – can that be done?'

Gifford had said he was travelling in a fortnight; it could take at least a week for my letter to reach Walsingham, and he would need time to alert his people at the ports along the south coast.

Stafford placed the clothes on the floor and eyed the document with suspicion. 'What is it?'

'A reply to the letter he sent me.'

'The one in cipher?'

'That's right.' We looked at each other, unblinking.

'Fresh intelligence?'

'Observations. Rumours. That is all.'

He put down his quill and steepled his fingers together, but he appeared twitchy.

'Any observations you have for Walsingham should pass through me. I am the one who needs to know most immediately what direction events may take in Paris.'

'With respect, Ambassador,' I said, with a polite smile, 'those were not my instructions. I work for Master Secretary.'

'With *respect*, Doctor Bruno—' he half rose from his chair, leaning towards me across the desk – '*my* instructions are to pay you from the embassy coffers when you bring me intelligence I deem worth the price. Then I will decide what to pass on to Master Secretary. That is how the system works here. Now, I will ask again – what news does your letter contain?'

I hesitated. Stafford continued to fix me with a glare that he meant to be intimidating, but I could read the strain on his face, in the red-rimmed eyes and the tiny muscle that jumped under the right one, the shadows from lack of sleep. I had to tread carefully, or he could simply refuse to send my messages to Walsingham in order to make a point. But I still did not know the extent of his collaboration with Paget, and if Paget was involved with Gilbert Gifford and his deliveries, I could not run the risk of Stafford putting them on the alert.

'A girl died at the Tuileries last night during the ball,' I said, after some consideration.

His eyes registered a brief flicker of interest. 'I heard. One of Catherine's attendants.'

'You were not there?'

He made a noise of contempt. 'I do not care for that sort of display. Vulgar Medici crowd-pleasing. And everyone knows it always descends into the worst kind of debauchery.'

I wondered what Stafford considered to be the worst kind of debauchery. I could not imagine he had much experience; I would put money on Catherine exceeding even his wildest expectations. It was also clear from his tone that he was trying to cover the fact that he had not been invited.

'I heard the girl killed herself,' he added.

'So it was said. But I have reason to believe that she was connected to the plot against the King. She was known to Père Lefèvre, the dead priest.'

One eyebrow raised a fraction above his glasses. 'So she was murdered too? By whom?'

'I don't know. Some associate of Guise, I would guess.'

'And why does Master Secretary need to know this so urgently?'

'I am only passing on what I know. You said yourself, the priest's murder has the city on the knife-edge of an uprising. I thought he should be kept abreast of every development.'

He pointed a finger at me. 'You see, this is exactly the kind of information I expect you to bring to me first. What does Henri intend to do about the girl?'

'Find the murderer and bring him to justice, I would imagine.'

'Ha. Henri couldn't find the laces of his breeches without his mother's help.' He moved some papers from one side of the desk to the other, to make himself look busy. 'He will not hold Guise to account, he is too afraid. How is the Queen?'

I shrugged. 'Her usual bullish self. She seems keen to put it out that the girl took her own life, but I suppose that is to avoid a scandal.'

Stafford narrowed his eyes. 'Actually, I meant Queen Louise. I had heard she was quite gravely ill.'

'She did not appear well last night, it is true. I have no idea how serious it might be. The King did not seem overly worried.'

'No, I don't suppose he would.' He paused, waiting for me to pick up on his meaning. After a moment he clicked his tongue impatiently. 'Think about it, Bruno. I know what is said of Henri and his courtiers, but it is generally accepted that when there are no children in a marriage, it is the woman's fault.'

'With respect, that has never been conclusively proved,' I said. 'Medical science remains divided on the process of gener-ation, since—'

'I don't have time to debate the science of generation now. And stop saying *with respect* when it is clear you have none. I am merely pointing out that Henri's throne would be a good deal safer if he could produce an heir of his own. That is obvious to everyone, and therefore perhaps it would be no disadvantage to him if he were obliged to find a new wife. It would be useful to know if Louise takes a turn for the worse, and who he or the Queen Mother might have in mind as a replacement. It could certainly make England's position more secure if there were a legitimate Valois heir.'

'I'm sure that will be of great comfort to Queen Louise if she falls into a decline,' I said. But his words had set faint alarm bells ringing in the back of my mind.

He gave me a sour look. 'I must get on. But anything else

301

you find out from the palace, you bring straight to me and I will sift it for Walsingham. Understood? And I want your cipher. The one he uses with you. I do not like the thought of information passing through this embassy without my knowledge.'

'The cipher is very complicated,' I began, but he cut me off.

'I am a highly educated man, Doctor Bruno, and experienced in diplomacy, I'm sure I can manage to familiarise myself with its workings.' He smiled, showing his neat little teeth.

I nodded, and rose to leave. 'But you will send that letter with all urgency?'

'I will, this time.' Behind the bluster, I could see he was afraid, torn between his need to feel in control and his anxiety lest he be responsible for withholding vital information from Walsingham. 'But in future, everything comes through me.'

I inclined my head in a bow. 'But not at night or in daylight. I understand. There was talk of payment, I recall?'

His mouth twisted. 'You try my patience, Doctor Bruno. I do not know yet how useful your information may prove to be.' When I did not move, he blew out his cheeks in exasperation and reached into a compartment of his desk for a purse. He flicked a quarter écu d'argent across to me, as one might throw a tip to a stable boy. 'Take that for now. Geoffrey will see you out.'

I pushed my chair back and stood. 'I will leave you to enjoy your evening.' At the door I turned. 'I hope your losses are not too severe.'

'*What?*' Stafford was out of his chair and across the room to me as if a dog had bitten him, his face inches from mine and white with anger. 'Explain your meaning?'

I stepped back, surprised. I had meant it as a light-hearted parting jest, but the man looked ready to punch me. 'I meant only – at the card table. Paget said you were joining him for a game with friends.'

'What else did Paget say? My *losses*?'

302

'I was joking, Sir Edward,' I added gently. 'It is customary to wish a man luck at his card game, where I come from. That was all.'

He stared at me, quivering with emotion, while he processed this. Eventually he subsided, straightening his doublet.

'Well. Yes. Of course.' He passed a hand across his brow. 'I hope Paget has not given you the wrong impression. I would not wish you to think I was often at the gaming tables, Doctor Bruno. A few hands among friends for modest stakes now and again is quite proper entertainment for a gentleman, I think.'

'Absolutely. No one has said otherwise.' I offered an indulgent smile.

'Well, that is my limit. Give you good night.'

Struck a nerve there, I thought, as he closed the door swiftly behind me. Catherine de Medici, shrewd as ever, had been one step ahead.

It was already dark when I passed the Porte Saint-Victor and crossed the bridge over the channel to reach the towpath behind the wall of the abbey. I carried the short dagger I had taken from the palace guard drawn under my cloak, lamenting again the loss of my beautiful Damascus steel to the mysterious man in the Greek mask. I had begun increasingly to suspect that he was the man Léonie had been waiting to meet in the clearing. He was a confederate of the Duchess of Montpensier, and I had seen him walking alone in the wood before Léonie was killed – though if the scream we heard from the trees had indeed been Léonie, he could not have been the one who killed her, since he had been tussling with me at the time. Though I knew my chances of finding him were small I was determined to try, not only because I was sure he was involved in the conspiracy somehow, but because I could see it had amused him to best me and take my dagger, and I was not prepared to let it go without a fight.

For now, I had to make do with the stubby knife I held in freezing fingers as I sidled my way along the river path, pressed into the black stone of the abbey wall with no light but the moon behind a tracery of cloud, until I reached the small gate opposite the jetty. It was close to six; the bells would soon ring for Vespers and I would learn whether I had been lured into a trap. The air was biting, sharp with the promise of snow; I could almost fancy my breath turning to ice crystals before my face. After perhaps ten minutes I heard the crunch of footsteps on the frosted ground and the low murmurs of muffled laughter; from the direction of the city I saw the faint bobbing glow of a lantern and behind it, two figures lurching towards me. I waited until they were close enough and stepped out in front of them, knife drawn; a woman screamed, a piercing note that cut through the still night. I caught my breath and leaned back against the wall; it was only a weathered-looking prostitute and a boy draped across her shoulder who looked young enough to be her son, and so drunk it was doubtful whether he would get his money's worth. She began to protest that they had nothing to steal; I shooed them away irritably.

'Find somewhere else for your business. Back the way you came, or I will come after you.'

She dragged the lad away with her; I was still watching the small disc of light recede along the path when I felt a hand on my shoulder. I stifled a cry of my own as I whipped around, knife raised, and almost impaled Cotin, who had appeared out of the darkness with a lantern.

'Steady, boy – how many ways are you trying to finish me off?'

I sheathed the weapon, my legs weak with relief.

'It *is* you. I didn't hear the gate open.'

'I've learned to be stealthy. Pity you didn't – you might have saved us both a lot of bother.'

'Are you all right?' I peered at him. Shadows loomed and

ebbed on his face in the wavering light but I could see that he looked haggard.

He fluttered his free hand. 'Never mind me. We haven't got long. After you were carted off from Frère Joseph's cell last week, I reckoned I'd better have a look among his papers.'

'But I took everything that was there,' I said. And lost the most valuable part of it to Paget, I reminded myself, bitterly.

'From his cell, you did. But he had a little office above the bursary where he kept all the account books and ledgers connected to his work as almoner. I reasoned that if he didn't turn up soon the Abbé would make it his business to go through whatever documents he could find there and remove anything that might cause embarrassment to the abbey. While the place was in uproar over you, I thought I'd take the opportunity to have a look before anyone noticed I was not where I was supposed to be.'

'But a man with secrets to hide would not have left his private papers lying around for anyone to find, surely?'

He looked away with a modest cough. 'There was a small locked casket hidden behind the ledgers on a high shelf. I'm afraid the lock might have smashed when it accidentally fell on the floor.'

'Cotin, you are a genius.' I grabbed him by both shoulders and kissed him on his shiny pate, while he grumbled about Italians and emotion. He rummaged inside his habit and brought out a sheaf of papers.

'I'd have got these to you sooner but I was indisposed. The Abbé felt that a period of solitary prayer and fasting might help me to focus on my duty and obedience.'

'Jesus. He locked you up and starved you.' I laid a hand on his arm.

'Well. That makes it sound worse than it was. He questioned me hard about you when they found Joseph killed, though – God rest him.' He crossed himself out of instinct, I supposed, rather than any respect for the dead man. 'All I could do was

305

to keep repeating that I had no idea what you wanted in Joseph's room, until he gave up.'

'Thank you.' I squeezed his arm and nodded to the papers. 'What did you find?'

'There are notes in there for polemics, in Joseph's hand. Inflammatory stuff – arguments in support of a coup, calls for an uprising, that sort of thing. But the letters . . .' He gave me a sidelong look with a quirk of the eyebrow. 'Well, I'll let you read those for yourself. Rather spicy. He'd not be the first man in holy orders to keep a woman, but I'm surprised he didn't have the sense to burn the evidence.'

'Perhaps he liked to re-read them. Was there a name?'

'No name that I could see. Not that I've read them in detail,' he added, hastily. 'There are things in there an old friar hadn't even heard of, in fifty years of celibacy. Any case, that's not the point. Look here.' He handed me the lantern, peeled a sheet of paper from the bunch he held and smoothed it flat under the light. 'This is what I thought you should see.'

I recognised the hand immediately; the same neat, confident lines, the characters with their bold strokes and tails. There was no question that this was the same correspondent who had written the passionate letter I had found in Joseph's mattress. I peered in closer to examine it.

. . . the priest Lefèvre has discovered us, I know not how. He threatens to denounce you as a spy and expose us for what we are. Beloved, you know we would not survive the damage if all this were to be made public. You must ensure he does not speak, for all our sakes. And when you are assured of his silence, make certain he has committed nothing to paper on the matter. When you have made arrangements, send me word and my messenger will come to you. Do whatever is necessary and I give you my assurance, in the name of one who is able to protect you, that you will be immune from

*any consequences. As for your immortal soul – you and
I know that was lost long ago. Do this, and we will not
be parted. Burn this paper with all the rest.*

I glanced up at Cotin. 'But he burned nothing. You're right,
it's curious.'

'Perhaps he didn't entirely trust his lady to protect him. He
might have kept this as insurance to bring her down with
him, if he was caught and accused.'

'He didn't get the chance,' I said, grimly.

'He was right not to trust her, then. But this is damning
evidence that he killed the priest, it seems.'

'I never doubted it. Thank you for this.' I took the letter
from him and tucked it into my doublet. 'When we have the
identity of this mistress, we have them all. What do the other
friars say of him? I heard there was talk of a married woman
– any rumours as to who she might be?'

Cotin glanced up at the wall behind us. 'There's always
talk in an abbey, you know that. Especially now the man is
dead. What they say—' he shifted uncomfortably from foot
to foot – 'is that he had close ties to his family. Too close,
perhaps.'

'The Montpensiers?'

He nodded. 'Spent a lot of time at their house, apparently.
The Duchess has made generous donations to the abbey since
her husband died. There is the usual lewd speculation about
how Frère Joseph coaxed the money out of her.'

'So it all points back to the League,' I said. 'She mentions
this person who can protect him from the consequences. It
would have to be someone with significant power to defy the
law. That would fit, if she meant her brother Guise.'

Behind us, the bells of the abbey church struck up their
melancholy summons to Vespers. Cotin started like a spooked
horse.

'I must go.' He thrust the remaining papers into my hand.

307

'Make of these what you will. And take care of yourself, Bruno. I fear you are coming too near the heart of this business for your own safety.'

He gave me the kiss of peace on both cheeks and fumbled with his keys before disappearing through the gate in the wall. I was left alone in the darkness. A faint gleam of moonlight rippled on the water. Behind me, over the abbey orchards, an owl hooted. I clutched the bundle of Joseph de Chartres's letters and set off for home with the sinking sense that I was still nowhere near the heart of the business.

EIGHTEEN

'Just promise me you are not going to get us arrested,'
Francesco Andreini said, hefting a crate on to the cart.

There was a long pause. He finished tying off the rope that
held the box and turned to look at me. 'Oh Jesus. What are
you planning to do – steal something?'

I lifted another bundle and passed it up to him. 'Nothing
valuable.'

'I am serious, my friend. Whatever you are involved in is your
business. But if it puts my company in danger, I cannot help you.'

'You will not be in danger. All I need is to get inside the
building.'

'If you are caught it will be assumed we are all part of
your scheme.'

'I will not be caught.'

'How can you guarantee that?'

'Because I am good,' I said, with a grin, clapping him on
the shoulder. He returned the smile, but his eyes remained
unconvinced. I tried not to think about Joseph's cell and my
subsequent visit to the Conciergerie.

The Hotel de Montpensier stood behind high stone walls
topped with ornamental battlements on the rue Saint-Antoine,

a broad, tree-lined avenue leading out towards the city gate and the fortress of the Bastille to the east of the Marais, a district favoured by the nobility for their imposing residences. Though it was not much past four o'clock in the afternoon, dusk had already crept over the sky, another clear, bitter night almost fallen, when the company of the *Gelosi* were ushered through a set of heavy gates into the courtyard and instructed to unload by an outbuilding. I walked along with the others, keeping my head down, my hood pulled around my face, reminding myself that there was no reason anyone in this house should recognise me. I was just another Italian player, come to entertain the Duke of Montpensier and his guests. The pale façade of the Hotel was lit by burning torches in wall brackets, a curious confection of conical towers and delicate crenellations, pointed gables and high arched windows that belonged to a previous century.

A steward came out to greet us and show us to a side door. Francesco and Isabella walked ahead with him, discussing the arrangements for the evening; the rest of us followed, lugging boxes of costumes and properties from the cart. Though the Andreini spoke fluent French, a number of the other players barely managed a few words; I intended to be one of them, but as I was crossing the courtyard I noticed a boy of about fourteen leading a horse over to the stable block, and the sight caused me to stop dead. I peeled away from the group and approached him, still clasping a trunk to my chest.

'That is a fine horse you have there,' I said, blocking his path. The boy looked surprised, but he acknowledged the compliment with a nod and made as if to lead the animal around me. A handsome black charger, muscles rippling under its glossy coat, with four white socks and a scar down its cheek. It was the same horse I had seen tethered in the yard outside Stafford's house the night Paget brought me there from the Conciergerie, the scar left no doubt. 'I have seen him before, I am sure of it. What is his name?'

'Charlemagne,' the boy said, with a flush of pride, patting the animal's neck. 'He has been to war, this one.'

'He has the bearing of a warhorse,' I said, smiling encouragement. 'Does he belong to your master?'

The boy shook his head. 'He is the Duke of Guise's horse.'

'Of course. He has the scar to match.'

The boy giggled, pressing a hand over his mouth and glancing around hastily. I kept the smile rigid, but my skin prickled with fear; if Guise was here, I had put myself in a far more dangerous situation than I had anticipated. I was a dead man if I were to be caught, and there was no knowing what might happen to my friends. *Charlemagne.* You had to admire the man's audacity.

'The Duke of Guise is a guest here tonight, then?'

The boy nodded and patted the horse again; it was growing restless, its nostrils flaring and steaming in the cold.

'Filippo!'

It took me a moment to realise it was I who was being called; I turned to see the others waiting by the entrance to the house, Francesco glaring at me pointedly and jerking his head towards the door. I bowed to the stable boy and hurried back to join them, keeping my cloak over my face, afraid to look up and catch a glimpse of anyone watching from the windows.

The steward led us along servants' corridors until we reached a wide oval salon hung with tapestries. A dozen chairs had been set out in a semi-circle. Francesco and Isabella stood aside with him, debating the dimensions and position of the playing space while the rest of us piled up the boxes at one side, until they had agreed on a suitable arrangement and the steward discreetly retired to allow us to prepare. I was given various menial tasks – mainly holding poles and the end of strings – while the members of the company moved swiftly to rig up a wooden frame across the far end of the room. When this was erected, curtains of black material were draped across to make a partition behind which the players

311

could retreat to change costume between scenes. From the space behind this curtained-off area it would be possible to watch the guests unseen as they entered the room from the door at the other end and took their seats. The partition also gave the players access to a smaller door which opened on to the corridor outside; behind the curtain, no one in the audience would be able to see who came and went through this door. It was perfect for my purposes.

I was helping Isabella hang the costumes on a stand in the correct order when this door behind us opened to admit a large man in a dark blue velvet doublet and breeches, a glass of wine held loosely in his hand. I did not recognise him, but from the hush that fell and the way Isabella dropped immediately into a curtsey, I assumed this must be their host, the Duke of Montpensier. I bowed low and kept my eyes down.

'Good evening, good evening,' he said, waving for everyone to straighten up. 'Will this do you?' He gestured to the room. 'It's where we do the musical recitals. The sound's rather good, I think. Something to do with the walls. Just came to make sure you've got everything you need.'

The players murmured their deferential thanks. While his attention was fixed on Isabella, I took a long look at the Duke. He was loud and affable, in his early forties, with a head of tightly curled hair, a neat pointed beard, and a paunch and broken veins that spoke of good living and a fondness for claret. The glass in his hand was clearly not his first of the evening.

'Now listen,' he said, sounding apologetic, 'I like a bit of bawdy as much as the next man, but my *stepmother*—' his voice curdled on the word, as if it could only be said with sarcasm – 'is currently in mourning and I don't want to give her cause to make a fuss. So – keep it just the right side of obscene, eh?'

Francesco inclined his head in assent.

'I mean, I'm not saying make it a performance for novice nuns,' the Duke added, quickly, 'but on the other hand, there

312

are things she doesn't need to see simulated on a stage. Bestiality, sodomy – none of that. And there's a young lady of delicate sensibilities among my guests tonight and I don't want her to take away the wrong impression of me. Ideally something suggestive enough to put ideas in her head and bring a maidenly blush to her cheek, but not enough to make her think I'm a complete degenerate. Are we clear?' He grinned and raised his glass to Francesco, who smiled back politely.

'Absolutely no bestiality, Your Grace,' he said, with his most earnest expression. The Duke nodded, satisfied, and turned to go.

'I'm very sorry for your loss, Your Grace,' I said, appearing smoothly at his side while folding a cape.

'What?' He stopped, squinting peevishly as if trying to place me.

'You said your household was in mourning.'

'Oh, that. Not *my* household. Just my stepmother,' the Duke said, with distaste. '*She's* the one carrying on as if she's lost her first-born child. He was only a distant cousin, and he was my cousin at that, not hers. I never really liked the fellow much, if I'm honest. Is that uncharitable? I don't recall her making this much fuss when my father died. In any case,' he peered into his glass as if trying to comprehend how it could be empty, 'this is *my* bloody house now, whatever she wishes to believe, and I'm not going to shut the place up in mourning for a man I had no time for in life just because she demands it.'

He looked aggrieved. I made sympathetic noises.

'A man wants to feel he is master in his own house. Not to be commanded by a woman.'

'You have it exactly,' he said, widening his eyes and wagging a finger at me, as if I had offered him a revelation. 'I mean, she has her private apartments upstairs, that should be enough for one dowager and her servants, wouldn't you say?'

'Quite. Upstairs,' I murmured, in a tone of mild interest. God bless the loose tongue of a drinker.

313

He pointed at the ceiling, in case I was confused. 'Up there. Whole suite of rooms in the east wing.' He drained the last dregs from his glass and turned to go. I moved neatly between him and the door.

'Why didn't you like him?' I asked casually. 'Your cousin?' Across the room, Francesco shot me a warning look from beneath lowered brows.

The Duke flapped a bejewelled hand, apparently untroubled by the impertinence of my questions. 'Oh, those Holy Leaguers – they're all the same. She collects them, you know. Little entourage fawning around her, doing her bidding. With all their talk about the purity of religion, it's just jostling for power when it comes down to it. Always is. Guise wants the throne for his family in the end, however he dresses it up. She's frantic for me to throw in my lot with the League, but I say this—' he pointed an unsteady finger in my face – 'Henri of Valois may be a useless sybarite, but he's a prince of the blood and as such I owe him my duty. If that makes me a royalist, so be it. Better than a traitor, however holy you paint yourself.' He paused, peering closer at me. 'I haven't seen you before, have I? What's your name?'

'Filippo, Your Grace.'

He leaned down; I could smell the wine on his breath. 'What part do you play?'

'Oh, servants, messengers, that sort of thing. I am still learning the trade.'

At the edge of my sightline, I saw Isabella getting ready to intervene; she was afraid I would give myself away.

He waved his glass towards Francesco. 'Get him to give you a bigger part. You have, what do you call it? Presence.'

'Thank you, Your Grace.' I offered a little bow. He seemed pleased. I realised I might have cause later to wish I had made myself less memorable, but the Duke had been remarkably helpful.

It was only as he turned to leave that I caught sight of the

314

ornamental dagger he wore in a sheath at his belt and felt myself flush hot and cold in the same instant. The design wrought on the handle was unmistakable.

'Excuse me, Your Grace.' I insinuated myself between the Duke and the door again and saw a minute twitch of pique around his lips. I pressed on, regardless. 'I couldn't help noticing – that is a very fine knife you carry. May I see it?'

'Well. I suppose so. Here.' He unsheathed it and held it out towards me. The mottled silver-grey of the blade, as if water-marked, was as familiar to me as the patterns of my own fingerprints. I reached out to touch it and he whisked it out of reach.

'Careful. It's very sharp. Damascus steel. It will cut—'

'—a human hair dropped over the blade,' I said. 'I know. It is a beautiful piece of work. Have you – had it long?' I sized him up as I spoke. He was the right height, but he was too broad, too solid around the middle to have been the man in the Greek mask, I was certain.

The Duke blinked, frowning. He seemed unaccustomed to such direct demands from an inferior and therefore at a loss as to how he should respond. 'Since you ask, I was only given it today.'

'By whom?'

His face registered open irritation now; for all his hearty manner, this was not how a travelling player spoke to a duke and we both knew it. I lowered my eyes immediately.

'You ask a lot of questions, don't you, Federico?'

'Forgive me, Your Grace. My father was a master bladesmith – I get carried away when I see such fine craftsmanship and I forget myself.'

'Was he really?' Montpensier looked mildly interested. 'Oh. We must talk about blades one day, then – it is a passion of mine. I collect them. That's why Guise gave me this – he knew I would appreciate it.'

Guise? So he must have been the man in the Greek mask.

315

I was considering whether I dared press Montpensier further when the door opened and the steward's head appeared through the gap.

'Pardon the intrusion, Your Grace, but Sir Thomas Fitzherbert and his party have arrived early.'

'Ah.' The Duke's doughy features lit up briefly and he rubbed his free hand on his thigh. 'Take them into the blue room. Say I will be there presently. Where is the Dowager Duchess?'

'Still attending to her toilette, I believe, Your Grace.'

'Good. Keep her away from my guests for as long as possible. Don't let her harangue them before they've even had a drink.'

When the door had closed behind the Duke, Francesco appeared at my side with a face like stormclouds and grabbed my arm in a pincer grip. 'You promised me you would be discreet,' he hissed.

'Sorry. But I needed to ask him—'

'Listen.' He wrenched my arm up, tightening his hold. 'Maybe the great philosopher Giordano Bruno can get away with speaking to kings and dukes as if he were their equal, but a humble player cannot, and you need to remember that's what you are tonight, if you are not to drop us all in the shit. You asked me for a favour. Fuck this up for us and I'll kill you myself. With one of your imaginary father's knives,' he added, releasing me with a ghost of a smile. 'Master blade-smith my arse.'

'I thought you would appreciate the improvisation,' I said, rubbing my arm. 'I have presence, apparently.'

'You'll have the presence of my boot in your balls if you don't watch yourself.' He cuffed me around the back of the head and returned to his warm-up stretches.

Two hours passed while the Duke and his guests dined in another chamber. Servants brought us plates of meat, bread and two jugs of wine, though Francesco forbade his performers

316

from touching the drink before the show. I too abstained, knowing I would need all my senses sharp. Eventually, as we were growing irritable and quarrelsome from boredom, the servants returned to replenish the candles and we heard the sound of conversation carrying along the corridor. Through a gap in the curtain I watched as the guests made their way into the salon. Montpensier's loud, bluff voice boomed into the room well before him, his laughter swelling like the bass notes of a great sackbut. I shrank back from the curtain when I saw the Duke of Guise enter, unsmiling, his face craggy and impassive in the candlelight. By his side, her white hand resting lightly on his arm, was a thin woman dressed head to foot in black, her face hidden by a black lace veil. I supposed this must be his sister, the Duchess of Montpensier, Fury of the League. From her bearing she appeared remarkably self-contained for someone wracked by grief for a lover, but perhaps that was the most dangerous kind of fury. I could not judge without seeing her eyes.

She took a seat next to her brother and behind them came an older couple: a distinguished-looking man with a concerned frown and extravagant moustaches, his grey hair swept back from a high forehead, and beside him a small woman of about the same age wearing a neat crescent hood and hairnet. Montpensier bounded into my line of sight, unnecessarily fussing about this couple and ushering them to their seats, so that for a moment my view was blocked and it was only when his bulk moved aside that I saw her.

I don't know what I had expected to feel. She had not changed much in a year, except that her hair had grown long again and she was wearing it unbound down her back under her small hood as if she were a virgin, so that the chestnut and gold streaks caught the candlelight and glowed as if lit from within. She was less gaunt, too, though still slender, her waist neat inside a plain dove-grey bodice, but her cheeks were not so hollow as the last time I had seen her, in England,

and her skin was restored to the sheen of youth and vigour. She turned and lifted her head in response to something Montpensier had said, so that I could see her in profile, her throat stretched up, her mouth open in laughter, tawny eyes dancing, and all the rage and rejection of our last meeting surged up to my throat in one great flood of emotion and threatened to burst out in a roar, so that I had to turn away and bite hard on the edge of my hand until the urge had passed. So this was Sophia Underhill, now Mary Gifford, making her way in Paris, firmly ensconced in the world of the Catholic émigrés and doing very nicely out of it, by the look of the jewelled necklace that glittered on her delicate collarbone, despite her avowed hatred of all religion. But then what did I know of her beliefs now? Everything else she had avowed to me had been false; there was no reason to suppose she had kept her integrity in matters of faith.

Montpensier had settled himself next to her like a large, over-friendly dog, solicitous in proffering drinks, sweetmeats, a shawl. Every time he leaned in to speak to her, he rested a meaty hand on her wrist or her shoulder; though I had no right to feel possessive, I bristled at every touch. Sophia kept her composure; she smiled and declined his offerings with impeccable politeness, but I could see the effort of forbearance in her face. As I watched, it occurred to me that I may have jumped to the wrong conclusion about Gilbert Gifford's words; when he had mentioned a duke pursuing 'Mary', perhaps he had not meant Guise after all but Montpensier. The thought gave me some relief; Guise was dangerous to women, but a man like Montpensier would be of no interest to Sophia, with or without his title. I wondered if he had given her the necklace; it was an unlikely adornment for a governess. Though how foolish, I reprimanded myself in anger, how shamefully weak that I am still thinking in those terms, as if even now I were competing for her affections. After everything that had passed between us. I tore my gaze away and breathed hard, eyes fixed on the floor. At a gentle touch on my wrist, I lifted my head to see Isabella looking at me intently with a mixture of curiosity and concern.

'Are you all right, Bruno?' she whispered.

I forced a smile. 'A little tired. That's all.'

'Don't mind him.' She nodded towards Francesco. 'He doesn't want you getting into trouble. These people are no friends to you.'

'And I don't want to make trouble for you. When I have found what I came for, I promise I will wait quietly until it is time to go home, and I will not ask for your help again.'

'But you know we will offer it whenever we can. Now I must get ready – we begin in a few minutes. Good luck.' She kissed me lightly on the cheek.

'And to you. No sodomy, mind.'

She made a lewd gesture and poked her tongue out. I waited until Francesco stepped out from behind the curtain to a smattering of applause before slipping silently out of the door and into the dim light of the corridor.

The house was hushed, though far from silent; the Duke's guests may have been contained in the salon but servants still moved about, quiet and efficient, their footsteps tapping on the old stone floors. From the far reaches of a corridor came the clinking sounds of the meal being cleared away, curt exchanges in low voices. Away from the fire in the salon, the high passageways held the mineral chill of a cathedral. I was still wearing my outdoor cloak; I pulled the hood down around my face and turned right into a broader corridor lit at intervals by candles in iron sconces. Almost immediately I was forced to duck into a window embrasure as a man in the Duke's livery hurried past carrying a silver ewer. I held my breath until I was sure he had gone and continued my stealthy progress. For now, if I were caught, I could claim I was going out for a piss or to fetch something from the cart; that would be harder to argue once I was upstairs. Laughter gusted from the direction of the salon, Montpensier's distinguishable by its volume. At least they seemed to be enjoying the performance. I would be safe, I thought, as long as Guise did not set eyes on me.

The corridor opened into a grand entrance hall with a vast chandelier suspended above the centre. Decorative cabinets stood around the walls; a wide staircase swept in a curve to the upper floor. Though there was nowhere to hide, I realised I would be less conspicuous here than trying to sneak up the servants' stairs, which would be busy. I took a deep breath, waited until I was certain no one was coming, and ran up. On the first landing, I tried to orientate myself to work out which way would take me to the east wing. While I was calculating, I heard someone coming and had to dive into the nearest doorway. The footsteps veered away, echoing down the passage to my right. I turned in the opposite direction, peering into rooms, trying the latches of doors, less certain now that this had been a good idea. If I were caught up here, it would be assumed that I was a thief, and the rest of the *Gelosi* would be punished with me. It was imperative that I found what I came for without being seen, for everyone's sake.

The corridor dog-legged around to the right and I noticed that here the starkness of the house was softened by more feminine touches: tapestries on the walls, fresh rushes strewn over the floor. I tried one door; it opened into a prettily furnished bedchamber with a fire burning low in the hearth. In the next room, though, my pulse quickened; it was arranged as a study, with cabinets and shelves for books along the walls, two chairs with embroidered cushions by the fireplace and an escritoire of carved walnut in the corner. The room was dark and cold, suggesting no one intended to use it that evening. I lifted a candle from the sconce in the corridor and closed the door behind me.

The writing desk had two drawers set into the wood. Before

I attempted to open them, I checked the room for possible places to hide if I should be interrupted. Velvet drapes hung over two tall windows reaching from the floor almost to the ceiling; these were covered by wooden shutters on the outside but on trying the latch I found they opened to reveal a small stone balcony overlooking the courtyard. I pulled the shutters and the windows almost closed again, shielding the flame from the draught, and turned my attention to the desk.

The drawers were locked, as I had supposed. The knife I had with me was not fine enough to work into the keyhole – I thought bitterly of my own dagger, hanging at Montpensier's belt – but it was solid, and I had risked too much now to go home empty-handed. I jammed the blade into the gap at the top of the drawer next to the lock; fortunately it was decorative rather than substantial and with a little force I managed to bend it until it snapped. There would be no disguising that the lock had been broken, but I hoped we would be long gone before the Duchess noticed.

I drew out a leather folder from the drawer and opened it to reveal a sheaf of letters. With all my senses alert for the slightest sound from outside, I brought the light closer so that I could read them. The first sheet was addressed to Don Bernardino de Mendoza, the Spanish ambassador in Paris; skimming it, I gathered that it was a delicately worded plea for further funds from King Philip of Spain for the League's armies. But it was not the content that troubled me. Tucked inside my doublet I had brought the love letter I had taken from Frère Joseph's mattress, but I hardly needed to look at it to know that the handwriting was no match for the letters in this folder. I flicked through the papers; these were all written in the same small, round hand, neat and compressed, no sign of the bold flourishes that characterised the note I had found in Joseph's cell or the one Cotin had passed on to me the night before. I turned over the sheets in the folder to be certain. They all bore today's date – the 8th of December – and were

321

signed with the Duchess's name, Catherine de Montpensier, in the same careful writing; I presumed these had been written earlier and were waiting to be sent. I offered up a silent curse. I had been willing my theory to be true; if the Duchess of Montpensier had been Joseph's lover, everything would tie up tidily and I would be able to take proof to the King in the form of these letters. But unless she was adept at disguising her hand, it seemed I must accept that this was not the case. Joseph's lover – and murderer – remained unknown.

I was unbuttoning my doublet, thinking to compare the letters even though I already knew my conclusion, when I caught the sound of footsteps and the exchange of low voices from the corridor. I bundled the papers back into the folder, replaced them in the drawer and slipped between the curtains, quietly opening the window and edging my way on to the balcony just as the chamber door opened. I pushed the windows and shutters almost closed and crouched outside, straining to hear and hoping the thin draught would not be noticed.

'You can't leave now, don't be ridiculous,' said a woman's voice, sharp and peevish.

'No one will care. I have better things to do. I can't sit through another hour of this nonsense.' A man's voice; gravelly, tired. I recognised it at once as the Duke of Guise.

'You can and you will. Montpensier will notice. You can't afford to offend him at this stage. We need him too much.'

A mighty sigh from Guise. 'I have said it before – if he will not support the League through the prompting of his conscience, I fail to see why he should be moved to do so by my attending a few dinners and watching Italians pretending to fornicate.'

'Because that's how he is.' She sounded obstinate, as if they were retreading an old argument. 'You have to flatter him on his terms. It would be a great triumph for us to win him away from the King. But he is a bon viveur at heart and he fears

322

that puts him at odds with the League. He does not want to see France governed by joyless clerics.'

'He prefers to see power in the hands of heretics and libertines?'

'Those are his words, Brother, not mine. You must help me allay his fears by proving you know how to be good company, both now and in any future office you may hold.'

I could not see Guise's expression, but I heard the snort he made in response. I knelt and tried to squint through a gap in the shutters. A sliver of a gap offered me an occasional glimpse of the Duke's tall figure crossing in front of the window.

'An hour more, then. After that I must attend to other business. The money is downstairs with my bodyservants – how much do you want?'

'Paget says three thousand écus will do it.'

Another murmur of discontent from Guise. 'That is more than I expected.'

'You will recover it from the Spanish when you pass the material on.'

'They will want to be sure it is a worthwhile investment. As do I, for that matter. We don't even know what's in those papers. You should not have agreed such a sum in advance without consulting me.'

'If I had not, he would have taken the intelligence direct to Mendoza and we would know nothing of it. We cannot afford to be excluded from any developments at this stage. And Paget has assured me he would not dare cheat us. He is too indebted.' She gave a dismissive little laugh. A long pause elapsed.

'You should not encourage Paget,' Guise said, eventually, in a reproving tone. 'It is imprudent, in your situation.'

'He is useful. He is another who needs to be flattered.'

'Yes, but you go too far. He has hopes of you – and not without cause, from what I observe. Even you, with your fabled chastity, must see it.'

'You are mistaken. Charles hopes only to see a Catholic sovereign on the thrones of France and England, and in that common cause we support one another. In any case—' her tone sharpened – 'it is not *my* liaisons threatening to bring trouble on our heads at the present time.'

'Keep your voice down. The girl is dead. She can bring no trouble on anyone now.'

'I wish I had your assurance, Brother.' I heard brisk footsteps across the room. 'You still have no idea who else she confided in, admit it. Not the first time you have placed your trust unwisely in a woman.'

'The court is saying she died by her own hand. As long as it suits them to say that, we are safe.'

'You are deluded,' the Duchess said. 'Well, you had better get rid of the husband, now. You have probably told him more than was good for him, if I know you.'

'He knows nothing. He lost his wits long ago. Leave him – he is near death already. He will oblige you soon of his own accord.'

'Yes, but all the time he is rotting away in the Conciergerie he is costing you money.'

'Hardly. It's not as if they're keeping him in luxury.'

'But you pay the gaoler for his silence, do you not? Well, then. Why waste that money? The world thinks Saint-Fermin has been dead these thirteen years.' A pause. 'Send the order tonight. I don't know why you're being squeamish about this – it's not as if you baulk at death when it suits you.'

'I will do it tomorrow. Other matters demand my attention tonight.'

'Oh, other matters. Some doxy from the Tuileries, is it? I don't know why you don't run the other way when you see those Medici whores coming. You make their job child's play.'

'Perhaps that's what I want them to think.'

'Ha. If only I could believe that. You are not as shrewd as you would like people to think, Brother.'

'Nor you as chaste,' Guise said, with a soft laugh. 'All the talk at court is of how you murdered de Chartres over a lovers' quarrel.'

The Duchess clicked her tongue.

'God, have these people nothing better to do? Give me the name of everyone you heard say so and I will see them whipped for slander, whatever their rank.'

'That would only serve to confirm the rumours, dear Sister.'

'Then we should make haste to have the heretic Bruno arrested and charged with his murder. That would solve two problems with one stroke.'

'I have told you to leave that in my hands,' Guise said, his tone severe again. 'I have other uses for him yet. By God, this room is freezing – have you left the window open?'

I had only a moment; quickly I climbed over the parapet at the side of the balcony and clung on to the outside, crouching low, hanging perhaps twenty feet over a border of shrubs below me. I could only pray that there was no one in the courtyard who might glance up and see me clinging on. The shutters were flung wide, though fortunately the left one obscured me from the view of the Duchess, who stepped out on to the balcony and surveyed the ground directly below.

'Must have been the wind. The latch on these shutters is loose. Come – we should return before they begin the next performance or we will be missed. And this person will be here with the package soon – I do not want Montpensier's servants to encounter him first.'

I let out a shaky breath; my fingers had grown numb with cold and I was not sure how long I could go on gripping the stone balcony.

'Are you sure no one's been in here?' Guise's voice shocked me with its proximity; he had joined her on the balcony. I hoped he had not noticed the drawer of the escritoire. I could see his shadow as he leaned forward to look over to the ground. If he should think to pull the shutter back . . .

325

The stone under my hands was icy; I felt my fingers beginning to slip.

'Who would be in here?' the Duchess said, impatient. 'Come, I am freezing – let us not waste any more time.'

Guise muttered something I could not catch. The shutter hiding me moved; I held myself rigid, not daring to breathe, but they were pulling it closed from the inside. I heard it firmly shut and the windows bolted. Though I was relieved they had not seen me, I was now left with a different problem: there was no latch on the outside of the shutters and I was stuck on this balcony. I had begun to haul myself back over the parapet to relieve my arms while I considered the situation, when I heard footsteps on the frosted ground below. Glancing down, I saw a woman walking across the courtyard, a heavy shawl wrapped around her shoulders; she paused by one of the torches in the wall long enough for me to glimpse her profile and the recognition sent that same jolt through my gut. Sophia, alone outside; who was she meeting? Without allowing myself time to think, I let go of the parapet, dropped into a bush below, rolled out and on to my feet, ignoring the dart of pain in my left leg; she had whipped around, startled, at the noise, but she barely had a chance to react before I had grabbed her by the arm and dragged her into the shadow of an arched passageway at the side of the house. We stared at one another, our faces inches apart, for the first time in more than a year. It gratified a streak of cruelty in me to see that she looked afraid, her lips parted as if she were on the verge of crying out.

'You owe me fifty écus,' I said, through my teeth.

NINETEEN

'I could scream,' she said, her voice low. 'There was a groom over there just now.'

Before she could attempt it, I had whipped the knife from my belt and pressed the tip against her stomach. 'You would be dead before he could cross the courtyard.'

It pleased me to see that she flinched, though she held her nerve, jaw clenched. It was I who was trembling.

'You are still angry with me, then,' she said, after a pause. I thought I could detect a faint smile hovering about her lips, which only enraged me more.

'What did you expect?' I pressed the blade home a fraction and heard her gasp.

'You were always a man of strong feeling.'

'You have no idea.'

We held each other's gaze, so close I could feel the heat of her breath on my mouth; I searched her eyes for some sign of remorse, affection – any nuance of emotion would do, anything beyond the calculating pragmatism I now feared had always coloured her dealings with me. Her face seemed to soften; slowly she reached up and brushed the back of her fingers against my cheek. Our breath clouded and dissolved together in the raw air. I let the arm holding the knife slacken.

A horse whinnied across the courtyard and the moment was broken; I slapped her hand away and she dropped her gaze.

'I thought I would run into you sooner or later,' she murmured. 'I did not expect it to be in this place, though. I had thought you might come looking for me.' I was almost sure I heard a wistful note in her voice that suggested she had hoped so.

'You knew I was in Paris?'

She gave a brief nod. 'Charles Paget is a neighbour of my employer, Sir Thomas. He speaks of you often.'

'With great affection, I suppose. Paget found you the position, didn't he?' When she didn't answer, I put my face closer to hers. 'You must be greatly in his debt.'

'Seems I owe everybody,' she said, with a studied carelessness.

'And how do you repay him? On your back?' I could hear the rising pitch of my voice; I seemed unable to rein in my anger and jealousy, and that only made me more furious with myself.

Sophia blinked calmly. 'How does anyone barter with Paget? I keep my eyes open for him. Not that it's any of your business,' she added.

'Then you have not – with Paget?'

She gave a mirthless laugh. 'I assure you, Charles Paget sets his sights higher than an English governess.'

'And you? Where do you set your sights? This is pretty.' I flicked the jewelled choker at her throat. 'What did you do in return for this? Do you have hopes of being a duchess now? Or is being his mistress profitable enough for you?' Stop now, stop yourself, the voice of reason clamoured in the back of my head, but I seemed powerless to heed it.

'Jesus, Bruno. Now I know you have lost your senses.' She looked at me with an expression that was hard to read, but might have been disappointment. 'If you mean Montpensier, he is a flatulent idiot. I only came out here to escape him for a few minutes. I tolerate his attentions because Sir Thomas needs his goodwill, and I need Sir Thomas's goodwill to keep my position. And if you really think it is my ambition to become a rich man's wife again, you have a short memory.' She said this last with a flash of anger. She too had buried a great deal of feeling below the surface in order to survive; I should pity her for what she had suffered at the hands of her wealthy older husband in Canterbury, the man her father forced her to marry, but I was struggling to look beyond my wounded pride.

'Perhaps I have had to erase my memory,' I said, in a tight voice.

'Well, you would do well to remember this.' She drew herself up a little taller here, to fix me with a direct stare. 'I do not have to account for myself to you. You have no right to make those accusations about men. I owe you nothing.'

I risked my life for you, I wanted to say. I was the one you came running to when you were accused of your husband's murder, begging me to find the real killer; I saved you from the gallows then, and almost ended up there myself for my trouble. And you took me to your bed; you let me believe you loved me in return, while all along you always knew you would be leaving. Don't try to tell me there is no debt between us.

Instead I said, stubbornly, 'Apart from the fifty écus for the book you stole from me.'

She made a small noise of contempt. 'If it will make you feel better, I'll find half the money, and then we are even. Not that it was actually your book in the first place, was it?' I did not reply. She sighed, relenting. 'Look, I'm sorry I took it. But you understand that I had to leave England. It was all that was to hand of any value. I thought only of surviving.'

'Well, you appear to have survived and thrived admirably,' I said icily. 'And I see you are a good Catholic now, *Mary*. I suppose you attend Mass dutifully every day.'

'I am whatever it is expedient for me to be in the

329

circumstances,' she hissed in my face, her eyes flashing. 'I thought you of all people would understand that.'

'Then you are mistaken,' I said, through my teeth. 'You and I are not the same. I am at least true to myself.' Even as I spoke, I knew I sounded ridiculous; I could hear the disdain in her laughter.

'Well, how noble you are. I congratulate you on your unshakeable integrity. Except that's not even true, is it? Paget told Sir Thomas you were trying to get your excommunication lifted. So don't preach to me about pretending to be Catholic. You're not a travelling player either,' she added, as if this proved her case. 'And if you are, why are you jumping off balconies?'

We glared at one another, defiant, until I realised that a smile was twitching at the corners of her mouth. I would not give her the satisfaction of returning it, I thought. She raised an eyebrow. I pressed my lips together into a hard line. Eventually I could not help it; I laughed, despite myself, and she laughed with me. I held her gaze until the laughter faded and we were left, still looking into each other's eyes, the embers of something long-buried stirring into life.

'Mary? Are you out here? The players are about to begin.' A woman's voice, calling in English. Sophia started and glanced guiltily towards the house.

'Lady Fitzherbert. I should go.'

'Wait. Will you—' I left the question hanging; I could not quite bear to hear her tell me she would not see me again.

'I will get your money, never fear,' she whispered, the hard edge returned to her voice.

'That wasn't—' I let it pass. 'You live in the rue Neuve, I believe.'

Her eyes widened in horror. 'For God's sake, you can't come to the house, are you mad?'

'Mary?' Lady Fitzherbert called again.

'She will come looking for me if I don't go in.'

'Listen, I don't want the money. But there is one favour you can do me by way of compensation.'

Her face grew guarded; I could see what she was thinking. I shook my head to pre-empt her objection.

'Your admirer, Montpensier. He likes to give you gifts, yes?'

Her fingers strayed to the choker at her throat. 'What of it?'

'He has a dagger that belongs to me. Guise stole it and gave it to him. It's valuable. I want it back.'

I could see her weighing it up. 'Why would Montpensier give me his dagger?'

'I saw his manner with you. He'd give you the bells of Notre Dame if you asked him charmingly enough. Use your womanly arts. You're happy enough to use them when it suits you,' I could not help adding, with venom.

She pulled away, her mouth tight. 'I will not promise.'

'Rue du Cimetière,' I hissed, as she stepped out of the doorway. 'The far end from the Swan and Cross. Ask for the house of Madame de la Fosse.'

She registered this without comment. 'Coming, my lady,' she replied aloud, into the courtyard. She turned back and gave me a long look. For a heartbeat it seemed she was about to add something, but the moment passed and she was gone. I heard her footsteps quicken and fade as I leaned against the wall with my pulse hammering.

My immediate difficulty was how to get back into the house without advertising my absence. The only options were to try the servants' door where we had entered and pretend I had slipped out for a piss, but that might make it obvious I was lying. Or I could hide outside by the players' cart until they left, though that would mean avoiding the stable boys and anyone else moving around. I stuck my head out of the archway and looked around. I could see no movement in the stripes of shadow that lay across the courtyard. Over by the stable block, the only sound was the stamping of hooves and the occasional snort from the horses. I slipped out into the open and picked my way towards the far side of the yard. As I neared the stables I saw the boy I had spoken to earlier; he was lolling against the upright post of a covered shelter, talking to one of the serving girls. I froze, but the boy had his back to me and the girl, her arms piled with firewood, was laughing up at him; she had not seen me, but they were between me and the house, and I could not reach the servants' door without attracting their attention. I would have to wait until they moved. The cart stood in front of the stables. I decided to take my chance and dashed across the last few yards of open space just as I heard a pounding on the wooden gate in the outer wall. The stable boy and his girl whipped around in the direction of the noise; I barely had time to duck behind the cart, out of sight.

Crouching in the cart's shadow, I watched as the side door of the house opened and a figure with a lantern moved briskly down the steps and across to the gates. As the person drew nearer I realised it was a woman, wearing a hooded cloak. A servant followed her, carrying a wooden chest in his arms, which gave a metallic rattle with each step. I could not see the woman's face, but from her build I guessed it could only be the Duchess of Montpensier. The stable boy hastened after her towards the gate with mumbled apologies – I heard him call her 'my lady' – but she snapped back, shooing him away. The Duchess unbolted the gate and drew it open a fraction to admit a man, his features obscured by the brim of a hat worn low over his brow. Her lantern swung between them; by its lurching light I saw him draw out a packet from inside his cloak and pass it to her. She tucked it away out of sight and motioned for the servant to pass the chest to him. It was evidently heavy; the man staggered back a pace under its weight. They exchanged a few muttered words I could not hear and she turned to leave; as she did so, the man tilted his head and the light caught his face long enough for me to recognise him as Sir Edward Stafford's steward, Geoffrey.

The gate closed again and the Duchess strode back towards the house while I let my breath escape slowly and tried to piece together what I had just seen. I had been so thrown by the conversation with Sophia that I had hardly had time to process what I had overheard on the balcony between Guise and his sister. The three thousand écus he had mentioned, promised by the Duchess in return for papers containing information they intended to sell on to the Spanish ambassador. A deal brokered by Paget, but when she had said *he* owed too much to risk cheating them, I had assumed it was Paget she meant. Now, with the appearance of Geoffrey, I began to see the greater picture: Catherine de Medici's reference to Stafford's gambling habit; Paget's sly remark that I would not be the first to gamble on credit at his card table; Stafford's reaction when I joked about his losses; the exchange I had just witnessed. It was hard to find any other interpretation – Stafford was selling secrets to England's enemies to pay off gambling debts Paget was encouraging him to incur. *Dio porco.* Walsingham would have to be told – but how? Even with our sophisticated code, I could not risk sending that information by the diplomatic courier; there was always the chance Stafford's people would find a way to read it somehow, and then they would need to silence me. There was no knowing when this messenger Walsingham had promised was likely to turn up, if at all. Perhaps I would have no choice but to go to London myself. The thought of leaving Paris lifted my spirits briefly.

I was jolted from my thoughts by the sudden snort and stamp of a horse, close by; I turned and saw two handsome mounts tethered to a post a few feet away. The torches in the wall brackets gave out enough light for me to recognise the nearest one as Charlemagne, Guise's horse, the one I had seen at the English embassy that night. No wonder Stafford had been skittish about his secret visitor. I wondered how long the ambassador had been brokering deals with the Catholic League and the Spanish. The horse regarded me with disdain, mist rising from its flared nostrils. I straightened up and glanced around for the stable boy, but could see no sign of him; perhaps he was still skulking in the shadows with the girl. It was only as I leaned against the cart, debating what to do, that another snatch of Guise's conversation returned to me, with such a force of shock that for a moment my legs buckled and my stomach twisted with a pang of fear. Get rid of the husband, the Duchess had said. She had called him Saint-Fermin, and mentioned the Conciergerie; that poor blind wretch I had found in the oubliette must be Léonie de Châtillon's husband, the Comte de Saint-Fermin. He had told me Guise had been keeping him alive; now the Duchess wanted him dead. What did he know that was so important to them?

My pulse was racing. Whatever the Count knew, by tomorrow it would be too late to find out. There was still time to save him, and only one possible way of doing it. I looked back at Guise's horse. It had lost interest in me and returned its attention to the bale of hay that had been placed on the ground by the post, but it was saddled and harnessed; Guise must have given the boy instructions to have it ready in case he wanted to leave early. I peered once more around the courtyard for any sign of movement, but could see no one nearby. Crouching low, I crept the few paces out from the shelter of the cart and tried to untie the horse's reins from the post, my fingers clumsy with cold. It whinnied loudly in protest; I hushed it with a whisper, fumbling with the knot until, to my surprise, it came loose. I gripped the reins, jammed my foot into a stirrup and hauled myself up into the saddle with some difficulty as the beast reared backward. The clatter of its hooves brought the stable boy running from his dark corner, shouting for me to stop, but I had already wheeled the horse around. I leaned down – not easy, it was an impatient creature and did not like standing still – and unlatched the gate, trying to pull it open; the horse was in the way and for one terrible minute the boy was on us, lunging for the bridle, but the horse lurched back, almost trampling him, a gap opened up and I kicked the beast hard in its flanks, causing it to take off out of the gate so fast I was almost flung out of the saddle backwards. I could do nothing but cling on as we bolted down the rue Saint-Antoine, the boy's outraged cries giving way to the sound of the wind rushing past my ears and my own manic laughter at my audacity. It was only when it showed no inclination to slow down that I remembered I had relatively little skill or experience as a horseman, particularly with a strong-willed animal like this one.

'Come on, Charlemagne, do me this favour,' I muttered, pulling the reins and concentrating on remaining upright, one foot still flailing around for the other stirrup. Perhaps he responded to pleading, or perhaps he had lost interest in his dash for freedom, but he gradually dropped to a trot just as we neared the turning for rue des Tournelles. He seemed to have his own ideas of where he wanted to go, but I managed to wrench his head around and point him in the direction of Jacopo's house. As we approached, I could only offer a silent prayer that Jacopo was at home; if he were still at the palace, I had no hope. I did not dare risk showing my face there.

An armed watchman, freezing and bored, snapped to attention as I rode up the path, lowering his pike and demanding my business. I slithered down from the saddle, insisting I was a friend, and handed him the horse's reins while I hammered on the door. The watchman seemed too surprised to protest. Jacopo's steward answered. He was also startled to see me in a state of evident desperation.

'Is he home?' I said, without a greeting.

'He has only just come back from the Tuileries,' the steward began, 'and he has not yet eaten—'

'Thank God. I must see him. Please tell him it is a matter of life and death.'

The man hesitated, but behind him I could see Jacopo's silhouette move forward into the light. I almost wept with relief at the sight of him.

'It's all right,' he said, ushering his servant inside, 'I can always make time for Bruno. Now then. What has happened?' In the flame from his candle he looked drawn, as if he had not slept since the ball.

'Do you have the King's seal?' I blurted.

He frowned. 'No, not here.' He must have read my expression, because he stepped forward and laid a hand on my arm. 'I have Catherine's, though. I require it sometimes when I am sent on her business. Why do you need a royal seal?'

'You must come with me, right now. Bring the seal, and some money. We have to save a life.'

He hesitated; I could see he wanted to ask me more, but after a moment he merely nodded and turned back. 'Wait inside. I will fetch it, and a warm coat.'

I could have embraced him. 'Fetch a spare too, if you have one. And ask your steward to send for a physician, to be waiting when we return.'

'A physician?'

'I will explain on the way.'

When he returned, I gestured for him to mount. He turned to me, brow creased with concern.

'Where did you get this horse?'

'I borrowed it.'

'From whom?' He peered more closely at the saddlecloth. A spasm of alarm crossed his face, but he mastered it. 'Dear God, Bruno – these are the Guise arms. Please don't tell me you have stolen the Duke of Guise's horse?'

'Borrowed,' I repeated firmly. 'Come on – we can't waste time.'

'Where are we going?' he asked, clinging around my waist as we set off at a more sedate pace towards the river.

'The Conciergerie. We have to prevent a murder.'

I felt him tense behind me. 'Whose?'

'The Comte de Saint-Fermin.'

'But – that is absurd. He was killed thirteen years ago, on Saint Bartholomew's night.'

'No, he wasn't. But he will be killed tomorrow morning by Guise if we don't reach him first, and I believe he may hold the key to all the murders – including his wife's.'

Jacopo fell silent then, and did not ask me anything more until we arrived at the gates of the prison.

He showed Catherine's seal to the soldiers on the gates and we were waved through. The squalid gaoler was fetched, the growth on his face looking more malignant in the light. He squinted at me for a moment before recognition dawned. A curdled laugh escaped from his throat.

'I remember you. Homesick, were you? Missing the old place?'

'You will recall I mentioned my friends at the palace,' I said calmly. He blanched, and the laughter died on his lips. I gestured to Jacopo. 'This is Signor Corbinelli, secretary to the Queen Mother.'

Jacopo held out Catherine's seal again. 'You have been taking bribes to keep a prisoner here illegally. We have orders from the Queen Mother to release him.'

The mockery in his eyes gave way to fear. 'But – I can't allow—'

'We are also commanded to arrest anyone who tries to obstruct us, in the name of Queen Catherine,' Jacopo said, with the same steady air of authority.

'He's dead,' the man said, panicking.

'You're a poor liar,' I said.

'Honest to God – he died this morning.'

'I'd like to see for myself.' I tried to shoulder past him but

337

he blocked me, barring the entrance with his outstretched arms.

'Look, I'll lose my head if I let you take him.' His voice was shrill with fright now.

'You'll lose it quicker if you don't,' I muttered.

'No, he won't,' Jacopo said, behind me. 'Beheading is for the nobility. He won't be granted anything like that kind of dignity in the manner of his death. There'll be nothing quick about it.'

'Oh, Jesus.' The man crossed himself as he stepped aside. 'I only did as I was ordered, you understand – I didn't know he wasn't supposed to be here.'

'You can save that for later. Just show us where he is.'

He led us back through the warren of passageways leading through the old Palais, until we stopped at the hatch of the dungeon. A shudder passed through me at the memory of it.

'He's in no fit state to be moved,' the gaoler said, as he lowered a ladder down into the stinking darkness. His manner had turned ingratiating, as if he thought that cooperation was his best hope of immunity. 'You've seen him, monsieur. You take him through the streets this cold night, it'll kill him.'

'Because he is so warm and comfortable now?' I gave him a hard look. 'It will be better for his health than staying where he is, I assure you.'

I took the lantern, filled my lungs and climbed down into the oubliette, trying to hold my breath against the stench. I had not forgotten those minutes of blind terror when I had believed I might be here for good; the fetid air stung my eyes, sharp with ammonia, bringing the memory back all the clearer. The dungeon was freezing, a bone-deep, damp cold that seeped in through the skin. From a corner, a scuffling noise alerted me to the presence of the prisoner, somewhere in the shadows beyond the reach of the lantern. I held up the light and picked out the wasted figure of the Count, cowering in a corner and making that strange inhuman whimpering sound I had

338

heard before. He looked even more like a corpse than the last time I had seen him, if that were possible. Fighting my instinctive revulsion, I approached him slowly. He lifted his sightless sockets and appeared to sniff the air.

'Who is there?' he said, in that cracked voice.

'Monsieur. Don't be afraid. I have come to help you.' I reached out and laid a hand on his arm. He shrank away from me. It was like touching dead flesh. 'We are going to take you away from here, my lord.'

He tilted his head towards me. 'Why do you call me that?'

'You are a count, my lord. You are the Comte de Saint-Fermin.'

'No longer. I am a dead man.'

'Not if I can help it,' I said grimly. 'Do you remember me? I was with you here a few days ago. The Italian.'

He made an empty noise that might even have been laughter. 'Days, years. I cannot distinguish one from another. It is all just darkness. The mind longs for oblivion, but the body stubbornly endures, beyond all reason.'

I should have realised he would have no concept of time passing. After a pause I felt his bony fingers clutch at my sleeve. 'There was an Italian boy here,' he said, lifting his chin as if listening for some prompt from the past. 'He spoke to me of Circe.'

'Your wife,' I prompted, folding my hand over his.

'In name, perhaps. But she was never mine, in her heart.' I wanted to press him further, but he fell into a coughing fit that threatened to tear his fragile frame apart. When it subsided, I hooked an arm under his.

'Come with me. You will have food and warmth, and rest. You will be free.'

'Free.' That dusty laugh again. To my surprise, I felt him resist with what little strength he had. 'I am dying, boy. It no longer matters to me where I do it.'

'It matters to me, my lord. If I leave you here, you will be dead by tomorrow.'

'Then it cannot come soon enough.'

'Please, my lord.' I slackened my grip and bent closer to him. 'What do you dream of, in here, when you remember your old life?'

'The sun on my face,' he said, without hesitation. He lifted his ravaged eyes upward. 'Birdsong.'

'Would you not like to feel that again, before you die?'

The claws around my arm tightened their grip.

'I believe you would,' I persisted. 'I'm afraid it is December, so there are limits, but we will do our best. I can probably rustle up a seagull.'

He did not speak, but he stopped trying to pull away and I thought I saw him incline his head.

'This journey will hurt you,' I said, draping his skeletal arm around my shoulder. 'I cannot help that, and I'm sorry for it. But at the end, there will be a soft bed, and hot food, and rest.'

'Come, then,' he said, in a voice so thin it was barely the ghost of a whisper.

I do not know how he endured the journey without screaming; thirteen years in that dungeon must have taught him a stoicism I could not begin to imagine. His limbs were so wasted he could not stand on his own, much less walk; though he weighed less than a child when I lifted him, it set my teeth on edge to feel how I was jolting him in trying to climb the ladder and hand him up to where Jacopo and two of the Palais guard were waiting to haul him through the hole. It was Jacopo who cried out in horror when he saw the emaciated figure. We wrapped him in the spare cloak and with the help of a mounting block he was lifted into the saddle in front of me, where he slumped in my arms without a sound as we made our slow way back over the river to the rue des Tournelles, Jacopo walking beside us with the guards as escorts. I heard the chink of coins as he dismissed them at the door and sent them on their way, with instructions to return the horse to the Hotel de Montpensier and explain that they had found it running loose in the street. I watched them guiltily while they led Charlemagne away, his hooves ringing on the iron-hard ground as the blur of their lantern gradually faded into the night, and hoped that Francesco and his friends were not being punished for my rash decision to abscond with Guise's horse. After I had specifically promised him I would not steal anything of value.

TWENTY

Jacopo's steward appeared and between us we carried the Count upstairs to one of the guest rooms. He looked so broken when we laid him on the bed that even the physician turned pale; it would not have surprised me to learn that the journey had killed him. But the physician confirmed he was still breathing, and called briskly for hot water and clean linen to be brought before urging me and Jacopo from the room and promising to fetch us when he had examined the patient.

Jacopo asked the steward to bring us a jug of hot wine in his study. He gestured me to a chair near the hearth, while he hurried across to his desk and tidied away the book and papers lying there. Then he pulled up a chair opposite, threw another log on to the fire and poked it until the sparks jumped up like a furnace. When it was blazing higher, he leaned forward, elbows on his knees, chin propped on his fists, and stared into the flames, his expression unreadable.

'Thank you,' I said, when I could no longer stand the silence. 'I put you in a difficult position, I know.'

He did not shift his posture, merely turned his head to look at me.

'I can barely frame my thoughts into words, Bruno. How

could he have been down there for thirteen years without anyone knowing? Even the poorest wretch in the kingdom would not let his dog live like that.' He shook his head, gazing at the fire again.

'I suppose no one inspects the prisons,' I said. 'It was Guise's doing – all of it. He blinded the Count on Saint Bartholomew's night and threw him in that dungeon. He's been paying them to keep him there ever since.'

'But why? What use is the Count to him in that state?'

'I don't know. But it has something to do with Circe. Léonie de Châtillon. She was married to him.'

'So she was.' Jacopo stared at me, his face creased with concern. 'Why do you say that?'

I related the conversation I had heard from the Duchess of Montpensier's balcony.

'Guise distinctly said that now the girl was dead, she would not cause them any trouble. His sister then said the Count should die too. Guise was going to kill him in the morning.'

'So they had no further use for him without Léonie. But why, I wonder?'

'I am hoping the Count will be able to tell us.'

'I wouldn't depend upon it, Bruno.' He leaned forward and poked the fire again. 'Moving him like that almost finished him off, the physician said. He may not last the night. Even if he rallies, do you not think his mind will be as broken as his body, after thirteen years in that pit?'

'I think his wits are sharper than you might imagine,' I said. 'We can only hope.'

'What in God's name were you doing on the Duchess's balcony, anyway?'

'I was in her room looking for a letter.'

'What letter?'

'Any one. I needed to see her handwriting.'

I explained about the letters to Joseph de Chartres from

his mystery lover. Jacopo listened, his frown growing more entrenched.

'But now you think the Duchess is not the mistress after all?' he asked, when I had finished.

'Not as far as I can see. But Guise is behind all this somehow, Jacopo, I know it – all three deaths. I just cannot find one piece of evidence that will tie him to it conclusively. Still, perhaps we can take comfort in having saved one life tonight. Or at least making his death more dignified.'

'Poor, poor man. I cannot bear to think of what he has suffered. He was accounted very handsome once, you know. And a fine soldier.' He clenched and unclenched his fists. 'I sometimes think the Duke of Guise is the Devil incarnate.'

'It was Guise I saw in the Greek mask on his way to the clearing, around the time Léonie was killed. I got into a scuffle with him – he took my knife from me. Two days later, he gave it to the Duke of Montpensier.' I took a sip of wine and wrapped my hands around the glass to warm them. 'I am certain Guise must have been the one Léonie was expecting to meet, when she blurted out to me that she could not go through with it. He planned to use her to attack the King. It is the only explanation that fits.'

Jacopo let out a sigh. 'It is one explanation, certainly. But as you say, you have no proof beyond one overheard conversation that can easily be denied, and another with a girl who is now dead, and can tell us nothing at all.'

'The Count may know something.'

'He may, but who would take his testimony seriously, in his state?' He scratched the tuft of hair in the centre of his balding pate. 'All this is speculation.'

'But I have a feeling we are drawing closer to the truth than we have been all along,' I said.

'Still, only this mysterious lover can prove or disprove Guise's involvement.' He refilled my glass and his own and sat back, his hands folded in his lap, contemplating the flames.

'You say she persuaded Joseph de Chartres to kill Lefèvre for fear he – de Chartres – would be denounced as a spy? No mention of this conspiracy involving Circe that you thought was the reason for the priest's death?'

'No. That was odd, I grant you. Perhaps she feared to put that in writing.'

'Hm. A spy for whom, though? I thought de Chartres was a loyal League man.'

'Christ, I don't know.' I put my head in my hands. 'In this city it could be anybody. The young curate at Saint-Séverin mentioned that he'd heard Lefèvre calling Joseph *Judas*. Perhaps it was true that he had discovered a betrayal.'

'And I suppose you still won't heed my advice to leave this business altogether?' he asked gently.

'How can I? When I am so close. If I can give the King this, Jacopo – proof that will publicly condemn Guise and his associates for murder – he will be in my debt.'

'You think he will give you back your position at court?' I heard the scepticism in his voice.

'I would not expect that. I only want modest financial support and immunity from persecution for my books. A post at the University, perhaps.'

Jacopo ran a hand across his head and did not look at me. 'For himself, Henri might do that much, but I don't know if Catherine would permit it. In any case, you will not get much sense out of the King at the moment. Léonie's death seems to have affected him badly. He has fallen into one of his fits of melancholy and will see no one.'

'Then the surest way to lift him from it is to bring her killer to justice.'

'What do you propose? Break into the house of every woman who associates with the Catholic League and steal a sample of her handwriting?'

I shifted in my chair. The pain in my hip from my impetuous leap earlier was growing worse. 'If that is what it takes.'

He sighed. 'Ah, Bruno. Your stubbornness will be your undoing, one way or another.'

An hour ticked by. Jacopo returned to his desk to continue with his paperwork. I picked up a book and tried to read, but I could barely keep my eyes open. Overhead the boards creaked in different tones as the physician moved about the room. My clothes smelled of the gaol again, and from carrying the Count; I caught the stink rising from them in the heat of the fire. Eventually there came a discreet tap at the door and the physician entered, wiping his hands on a linen cloth.

'He is more comfortable now. I've given him a draught to help him sleep.' He shook his head, amazed. 'He must have the constitution of a lion, to have survived in that condition for so long. Man's capacity for endurance is remarkable.'

'Will he live?' I asked, standing.

He gave me a frank look. 'For a while. But do not expect too much. His health is in shreds. He will not get well again, in the sense that you might understand it. His body has been destroyed.'

'But, for now . . .?'

'I see no immediate danger. There is no trace of gaol fever that I can detect.' He turned to Jacopo. 'I will return in the morning. If he wakes, I recommend a thin chicken stock – nothing more substantial. His stomach will not cope with it. And – ah – if we might discuss the matter of the fee . . .?'

'I will sit with him, in case he wakes,' I offered, partly because I did not want to hear how much the Count's life was going to cost Jacopo. That was something else we would have to work out when – if – I eventually had any reward from Henri.

The bedchamber was warm and airless, hazy with woodsmoke from the fire that had been stoked high and now blazed fiercely. A faint vegetal trace of medicinal herbs lingered, but it was not enough to disguise the smell of decaying flesh. The Count lay stretched out under blankets, perfectly still, dwarfed and shrunken against the plump pillows. The doctor had bathed him and dressed his wounds, clothed him in a clean nightshirt and taken the worst of the filth from his face, but if anything this only made his wasted flesh seem more naked, the scarred tissue around his empty sockets more ghastly. He looked entirely bloodless, like a mummified corpse, as if you could snap off one of the desiccated limbs and nothing would spill out but dead insects and dust. But he was alive, I reminded myself, and free.

I fell asleep in the chair by his bed. I do not know how many minutes or hours passed, but I was awakened by a choking noise; I lunged forward and lifted him, holding his torso upright while his breath rattled in his chest like a handful of stones thrown down a dry well. When the coughing fit subsided, he slumped back into my arms. I thought he was asleep; I was about to lay him down once more when he drew a scraping breath.

'I dreamed I felt the wind on my face.'

'You did,' I said, amazed and delighted to hear him speak, though he was barely audible. 'I'm sorry I could not arrange the sun, but it's the middle of the night in December. Soon it will be spring, though,' I continued, trying to sound encouraging. 'When you are well again, you will be able to sit outside in the sun and hear the birdsong.'

'I do not think I will see the spring, boy.' His hand clawed for mine. 'I dreamed they gave me something to take away the pain. And that I was lying in a feather bed. I think I am still dreaming it.' His voice was faint and full of wonder.

'No, it is real.' I held his hand. 'You are safe now.'

'Such kindness,' he murmured. 'I never thought to hear a kind word again.'

Tears pricked at my eyes; I could not let go of his hand to brush them away.

'Why did you save me?' he asked, running his tongue around his cracked lips.

'You have been the victim of a terrible injustice,' I said, fighting to keep my voice steady. 'And—' I hesitated – 'he was going to kill you. The Duke of Guise.'

'Ah.' He nodded. 'Le Balafré. He killed them all, you know.'

'What?' I tried not to jolt him as I tensed. I did not see how this could be true – Joseph had killed Lefèvre, for a start – but I wondered what more the Count knew. 'How do you know?'

'I was there,' he croaked, trying to sit up. 'I saw it all, before he put my eyes out. Dragged them from the house, slaughtered them like beasts on the steps. My cousin, his wife, the little girls in their new gowns . . .' He tailed off into another bout of coughing. 'It was *her* doing,' he said, with sudden vehemence. I recalled he had said those words before, the night I was imprisoned with him. I closed my eyes and forced myself to be patient. He was not talking about the murders after all; he was tumbling back into the past, to the night of the massacre.

'Did Guise kill anyone else?' I asked, as gently as I could.

'Thousands, I heard. All the Huguenots . . . they came for the wedding of the Princess Margot to the King of Navarre. My cousin . . .'

'I mean – more recently? Did Guise ever visit you in prison?'

'Oh yes, he came. He could not resist. What has happened to my wife?'

'Your wife?' I was caught out by the question. 'Why do you ask?'

'If Guise no longer needed me alive, he must have married her or killed her. One or the other. He only kept my life to bargain with.'

'I don't understand,' I said.

'Water,' he rasped, his hand fluttering.

I passed him a cup and tipped it carefully to his parched

lips. Most of it was spluttered over the bedclothes, but at length he lay back against the pillow.

'It was my pride,' he said sadly, raising his head a fraction, just when I thought he had fallen asleep again. 'I thought I could have whatever I wanted. I chose her. I was forty-five, she was a child of fifteen. I was a powerful man. And the Medici woman needed my alliance. I demanded Léonie. Catherine granted her. It never occurred to either of us that she might have desires of her own.'

He fell back, as if the length of this speech had exhausted him. I did not want to press him too hard, but I felt he was on the verge of revealing something.

'She did not wish to marry you?' I prompted.

'She had no choice. But she was in love already and would never love me, she made that clear. I punished her for it.' A spasm jerked his face; I could not tell if it was pain or remorse.

'She loved Guise?'

'So she said. It was she who brought him to my house with his soldiers that night. She wanted me dead. She thought then he would be rid of his wife and marry her.' He gave a sigh that shook his frame with alarming force. 'Well, she learned that night not to trust Le Balafré. He did not give her what she wanted. She was not free, and she knew it. My life kept her bound to him.'

'So—' I hesitated, trying to work it out – 'by keeping you alive, he made sure she could not marry again?'

'I was the card in his sleeve,' he whispered. 'If she wished to marry, he threatened to bring me out to destroy the match. All this time, she was in thrall to him.'

'Did he ever hint that he had pressured her into anything? A plot to kill the King, for instance?'

'The King?' A vein trembled at his temple; his face twisted with the effort of remembering. 'Charles?'

'Henri. His brother. Henri of Valois is king now.' This was hopeless. Jacopo was right, I thought; the Count's memories

349

were so scattered that, though I believed there was truth in them, it would be impossible to sift through in search of anything solid.

'Henri . . .' His voice drifted away. 'He never mentioned Henri. But he did say—' He tried to raise his head again to cough; I slipped my arm beneath his shoulders and lifted him, trying to curb my impatience. 'More water.'

'What did Guise say?' I asked, when the water had been dealt with.

'He said she was going to put a Guise bastard on the throne. He laughed like a madman about it.'

'Circe was? I mean, Léonie?'

'That's what he said. I did not understand his meaning.'

No, but I was beginning to see a glimmer of light.

'When did he say this? Was it recently?'

The Count made a papery noise that might have been laughter. 'I could not tell you, son. Time had no shape in that darkness. It might have been yesterday, might have been years ago.'

I patted his hand and settled him back among the pillows. There was no use pushing him any harder tonight; I did not want to risk his fragile state any further. He lay very still again, his chest barely rising and falling, though with no eyes it was impossible to tell if he was asleep. I tucked the blanket closer around him and crept towards the door, when I thought I heard him murmur. I rushed back, laid my hand over his and bent my head close to his lips.

'God bless you,' he croaked. His fingers moved under mine, and he fell silent once more.

TWENTY-ONE

I stumbled home and fell into bed as a thin light began to spread over the horizon and a lone bird trilled its dawn song into the brittle air over the river. When I woke, the day was already advanced, the sky clear and pale. I asked for a bucket of hot water to be brought up and cleaned myself thoroughly, examining my new injuries from the night before; a purple bruise spread over my hip and there were fresh scratches on my face and hands from falling into the bush, but the damage was not as bad as I had feared. When all this was over, I thought, I would shut myself away in a library and never again complain of the lack of incident in a life of writing. Then I remembered that I might have to return to England with news of Stafford's treachery; in my present state of exhaustion I could not work out whether the idea excited or depressed me.

My immediate preoccupation was finding something to eat; I could not remember the last time I had had a proper meal. I dressed in clean clothes, ran a comb through my hair – a quick task now there was less of it – and climbed on my stool to retrieve the bag of items I now thought of as evidence that might link the murders. I slipped the silver penknife inside my doublet, swung my cloak around my shoulders and took myself to the Swan and Cross for a bowl of stew.

'Seen the latest pamphlets?' Gaston asked, as he slopped it down in front of me. I shook my head, as my mouth was crammed with bread.

'That girl that was killed up at the Tuileries the other night,' he continued, with the air of a professional opinion-former, resting one hand on the table. 'The pamphleteers are saying Catherine did for her by witchcraft.'

'Ah. And do they say why she wanted to do that?'

He sniffed. 'Witches don't need a reason, do they?'

'So she just killed one of her ladies for her own amusement?'

'Well.' He leaned in and lowered his voice. 'You know what they say about that Italian sorcerer – no offence – she favours. He has built a chapel to the Devil under the palace where he keeps the severed head of a Jewish child to prophesy for him. And he makes wax dolls of all the royal enemies and sticks them with needles when she commands him. They say he can call up spirits who aid him to walk forth out of his body so he can commit murder invisibly.'

'Trust me,' I said, tearing another hunk of bread, 'I know Ruggieri – he is much less interesting than that.'

'Anyway, the point is, they're saying he murdered that girl by mistake. Catherine meant for him to kill someone else.'

'Perhaps his spirit had trouble recognising people after he left his eyes behind. Who do they think he meant to kill, then?'

'Don't know. They say maybe her daughter, Margot.'

'Margot is not in Paris.'

'I'm just telling you what I read.' He held up his hands as a disclaimer. 'I thought you'd want to keep up with the tide of public feeling.'

'Thanks, Gaston. I can't help thinking these pamphleteers run ahead of the facts.'

He gave me a pitying look. 'It's a story about a beautiful

rich whore killed by black magic. Do you think anyone gives two farts for the facts?'

After I had eaten, I crossed the river and made my way up the old rue du Temple towards the north of the Marais district, where the silver and goldsmiths had their workshops. As I walked, my thoughts returned to Sophia. There had been a moment, the previous night, when I imagined I saw a spark of what had once been between us, but now, in daylight, I realised I was fooling myself. Perhaps there had never been anything beyond a superficial attraction. With a twinge of anxiety, I recalled what she had said about keeping her eyes open for Paget by way of payment. I wondered now if she meant within the Fitzherbert household, or in more general terms. Would she run straight to Paget and tell him about seeing me sneaking around the Hotel de Montpensier, jumping off balconies? Sophia was an opportunist, and I could not blame her for that; she had had no choice. Brought up in an Oxford college, educated equally with her brother, she had come of age with ambitions and expectations that far exceeded what society would grant to a young woman of her status. She had rebelled against the constraints placed on her, and she had suffered for it. I had been useful to her for a time, but that time had passed. There was nothing I could offer her in my present circumstances. And yet, for a fleeting moment as she looked into my eyes, I could almost have persuaded myself that I could win her back.

Dismissing these thoughts, I made for a narrow shop with no sign over the door. Inside it was clean and well kept, though dim, since the small windows allowed in little light. A skinny apprentice leaned against the ware-bench polishing a monstrance. He glanced up as I entered, his eyes suspicious.

'Is your master in the back?'

The boy jutted his chin out as if to argue, then thought better of it and disappeared through a door into the workshop.

A moment later an older man in a leather apron appeared, wiping his hands on a cloth.

'Help you?'

'You are the master silversmith?'

'I am.'

I removed my gloves and took the penknife from inside my doublet.

'What can you tell me about this?' I handed it to him.

He turned it over, running a finger along the carvings on the handle.

'Selling it, are you?'

'Possibly. I want to know more about it. Do you recognise this maker's mark?'

'Fetch my lenses,' he barked at the boy. He peered more closely at the blade, affecting detachment, but I had seen the gleam in his eye when I had mentioned selling it; clearly it had some value. The boy returned with a thick disc of glass, cut and polished to magnify objects, like one lens of a pair of spectacles. The silversmith fitted it to his right eye and examined the knife.

'Florentine,' he said, with satisfaction.

'You are certain?'

'No doubt. This symbol of the tower has been used by the guild of Florentine silversmiths since the last century. Fine piece of work, this. Fifty years old, I'd say, maybe more. Worth something though.'

'Could it have been bought in Paris?'

'I've not seen anything like this for sale here in all the time I've been working, and that's over forty years myself. No, I reckon this came out of Italy a while ago.' He removed the lens and squinted at my expression. 'Is it stolen, then?'

'No. It's been in my family for a long time.'

He shrugged, unperturbed.

'Not my business how you came by it. But I'll give you a good price, as long as the owner won't come looking for it.'

'I am the owner,' I said, holding my hand out for the penknife. 'And I thank you for your time – you've been a great help. If I decide to sell, I will certainly come to you.'

'Don't you want to know how much I'm willing to offer?'

'Next time,' I said, tucking it away again and rushing out of the shop before he could ask any more questions.

I hurried back towards the river, mulling over this new possibility. There were Italian merchants and traders in Paris, of course, as well as diplomats and couriers from Rome, but the majority of Florentines were to be found at court, orbiting around Catherine. Just as I had thought everything pointed indisputably to the Duke of Guise, the penknife seemed to tell a different story. I was so confused by this conflicting information that I stopped still in the middle of the Pont Saint-Michel to puzzle it out, drawing curses from those trying to pass through the narrow street around me. The letter Cotin had found among Joseph de Chartres's private papers made it clear that he had feared being exposed as a spy; he had feared it so much, in fact, that he had been willing to kill Paul Lefèvre to prevent such a denunciation. So the letter implied, anyway. The question was: who was Joseph spying for, and on whom? I pressed the heel of my hand to my forehead and tried to think clearly, as the crowds jostled past. Had I been looking in the wrong direction all this time? If Joseph's lover was not the Duchess of Montpensier, could she be someone within the court – someone with access to an antique Florentine penknife?

An elbow in the back from an impatient passer-by jolted me out of my reverie and I walked the rest of the way home thinking that perhaps Jacopo was right and I should make the decision to walk away. Too many powerful interests were pitted against one another for this to be resolved with anything as simple as identifying a murderer. It was folly to imagine the King would dare bring Guise to justice, even if I turned up with irrefutable proof against him. Henri was too afraid of the Duke's popularity and, as Gaston pointed out, people don't much care about the facts if the truth is less exciting. If they want to riot against the King because Guise tells them Henri killed a priest, they won't put down their weapons and go quietly home because someone like me turns up with the real perpetrator. They're rioting against the shortage of bread, the poor harvest, the endless wars, the instability, the failure of their leaders to tell them once and for all who God favours and who He will burn. None of them really cared who killed Lefèvre.

By the time I reached the Place Maubert I had almost convinced myself to heed Jacopo's advice, but I could not shake off the thought that, if someone within the court was involved in Guise's plot, the King was still in real danger. As I turned into rue du Cimetière and approached the front door, Madame de la Fosse shot out and launched into an attack as if she had been watching for me from the window.

'This is a respectable house.' She folded her arms across her chest, her eyes blazing accusation.

'Has someone suggested otherwise?' I asked, with wide-eyed innocence, though my stomach lurched; she would not forgive me if armed men had turned up to arrest me in full view of the neighbours.

'I'm not having fornication in here.' She drew herself up, bristling with indignation.

'I'm sorry to hear that,' I said, trying to edge past her. 'I wish you better luck in future.'

'It's not a joke.' She blocked my way. 'Some doxy appears on my doorstep, insists on seeing you, refuses to leave. Says if I don't let her in she'll wait outside until you come back. What would people say to that? Well, I couldn't have her hanging about where everyone could see her.'

'So, where is she now?' My heart was hurtling, tripping over itself in a mixture of relief that I was not being arrested and a fierce thrill that Sophia had come to find me so soon. I had been right about that frisson last night, I thought.

'Well, I had to let her in, didn't I? I told her she could wait on the landing outside your door. But I'm not happy.'

'Madame, you are magnificent.' I planted a kiss on her cheek before she could protest and bounded up the stairs two at a time, my spirits revived by optimism. I rounded the turn of the stairwell and had to fight not to let my disappointment show on my face when I saw Gabrielle de la Tour leaning against the frame of my door.

'Oh. This is an unexpected pleasure,' I said, hoping to sound sincere.

She offered a charming smile, which looked equally unconvincing, and kissed me awkwardly on both cheeks.

'Catherine wants to see you.'

'Is that an invitation or a summons?'

She arched an eyebrow to indicate that this was a foolish question.

'I was expecting her to send armed guards for me.'

'Oh, she will do that if you don't come willingly.' She nodded at the closed door. 'Can we go inside for a minute?'

I hesitated. I knew I had hidden away anything incriminating – I always did before leaving the house, as a precaution – but I did not trust her and the idea of allowing her inside my private rooms made me feel oddly vulnerable. Perhaps that was also because I did not wholly trust myself to resist her.

But I unlocked the door and let her step inside, closing it behind us. She dropped on to my bed and sat with her head in her hands. I hovered by the door, disconcerted; I had half expected her to pounce on me as soon as we were alone. I had not anticipated this complete deflation.

'Why does she want to see me?' I asked, more sharply than I had intended. 'Did you tell her I had asked questions about Circe?'

'What?' She peeled her hands away from her face and

stared up at me. She looked pinched and worn, her eyes bruised with sleeplessness; she appeared to be fighting to keep her mouth from trembling. 'I told her nothing, Bruno.'

'You told her I was at the ball. She sent soldiers to find me shortly after I spoke to you.'

'That was not my doing, I swear.' Her eyes widened in distress. I watched her with caution; I could not discount the possibility that this was all an act.

'Oh God. We are all so afraid,' she whispered, bunching her hand into a fist and pressing it against her mouth.

'Of what?'

'What happened to Léonie. In case it should happen to any more of us.'

'Why would you fear that? What do you think happened to her?' I crossed the room to sit beside her, softening my voice. If she were telling the truth, it may be that she knew something, though I was still wary of being manipulated.

'I don't know. But none of us – in the Flying Squadron, I mean – believe that she took her own life.'

'That is still Catherine's view?'

She nodded, pressing her lips together as if she were fighting back tears. 'So she says. I think she's trying to avoid any gossip. But we talk among ourselves – we all fear that someone killed Léonie as a way of getting to Catherine. As a warning, you see. We fear that he may pick off more of us if she fails to heed it. We're so scared, Bruno.' Her voice quavered and she reached out a hand for me, turning to bury her face in my shoulder. Tentatively, I put my free arm around her.

'Who do you suspect would do something like that?' I asked, into her hair.

She drew her head back and looked at me with blank, miserable eyes. 'Any of her enemies might.'

'But – forgive me – aren't you all sleeping with her enemies?'

'That's what makes it so frightening,' she said. 'We don't know who to fear.'

'Who was Léonie sleeping with?' I asked. Her gaze sharpened. 'You don't know?'

'I'm asking you.'

Her shoulders slumped. 'I suppose it hardly matters now. It was an open secret, anyway. The King had taken her for a mistress. I expect he fancied the novelty, with the Duke d'Epernon away at war,' she added, in a waspish tone that belied her mask of trembling anxiety.

'But did she have someone else? You can hardly suppose the King would kill her to spite his mother?'

She frowned. 'No – I didn't mean . . .' She stopped, rubbed her eyes, tried again. 'We hadn't seen much of her lately – Catherine sent her to serve in Queen Louise's household about a month ago, so I only saw her again when we were rehearsing the Masque of Circe for the ball. Léonie wasn't one to talk much about her business. We have all had to learn the art of discretion, but most of us have one or two close confidantes among the group – you'd go mad if you didn't, the things we have to endure.' She grimaced, then her mouth contorted with embarrassment. 'Not you, obviously. But some of the others.'

'I hope I wasn't too much of a trial for you. But you were talking about Léonie?'

She flashed me a soft smile, tracing her finger in a light circle over the inside of my wrist. 'She didn't seem to talk to anyone. She was always quite aloof. She had perfected discretion – I suppose that's why Catherine favoured her.'

'Did you think she was pregnant?'

'What?' She dropped my hand and sprang away from me, her face frozen in amazement. 'No – are you sure? The King's, you mean?'

'I only wondered if it was a possibility.'

'It's always a possibility with us,' she said frankly. 'I had not noticed anything with Léonie, and we all have sharp eyes for the signs by now. But then, we were not living with her

359

day to day, as I told you. Poor girl, if she was. Seems worse somehow, doesn't it? Taking two lives, I mean.' She cupped her hand over her mouth.

'What about Guise? Was Léonie his mistress too?'

'Oh, we have all had a go at Guise one time or another. Catherine keeps trying. She persists in the belief that there is one divinely gifted woman who will find his weak spot, while he uses each of us as he pleases – which is no pleasure for the girl, believe me – and laughs at his own cleverness. She sent Léonie to him years ago, when she first came to court, *virgo intacta*.' She enunciated the Latin as if it were self-evidently a bad joke.

'Was she in love with him, do you think?'

'She never spoke of it, if she was. But it is a hazard of our situation – more so for the young ones who come straight into Catherine's service, their first time away from home. They form attachments, especially when they're deflowered.' She let out a cold laugh. 'It's a habit one is quickly cured of.'

'The rest of you are pure cynics, then,' I said.

'Names on a list, Bruno. That's all you are, after a while.' She gave me a sidelong look with a knowing smile. Either she had forgotten her earlier distress or she was putting a brave face on it. Her hand rested lightly on my thigh. She continued to hold my gaze, her blue eyes expectant.

I stood decisively to pre-empt any sudden move. Though I had been tempted to revisit my liaison with her at the ball, driven by loneliness and the need for a familiar embrace, here in the fading light of the afternoon I realised what a mistake it would be – especially now that I had seen Sophia again. Not that she was any more to be trusted than Gabrielle, but at least my feelings for her went beyond a quick tumble.

'I had better not keep Catherine waiting,' I said. Gabrielle rose slowly and came to stand in front of me, snaking her arms around my waist.

360

'Can't we stay here a little longer?' she murmured, sliding her hands skilfully under my doublet. 'I don't suppose she'll mind.'

I felt her lips move lightly across my jaw, her breath hot on my ear. Her tongue darted out and caught my earlobe; her small teeth nipped it gently. I held my breath for a moment, battling the sudden awakening of my senses, the usual rush of blood, thinking how easy it would be to give in.

'I think she would mind very much,' I said, prising her arms off me with some effort.

She sucked in her cheeks. 'Ah, the legendary self-control. Which I happen to know is, like all legends, greatly exaggerated. Or perhaps I don't attract you any more? Now that I have had a child.' She looked at me from under her lashes to see what effect this had.

'Of course I am attracted to you. There was never any doubt about that.'

'You're right, it seems clear enough.' She wrested one hand free and placed it purposefully over my crotch. I closed my eyes for a moment, breathed hard, moved her arm with some force.

'My mind is on other things.'

'That's not how it looks,' she said, in her silkiest voice.

'Perhaps I don't want to be left wondering if I have scattered any more children around France. Do you even know who your daughter's father is?'

I had not meant to sound so harsh. I heard her draw a sharp breath through her teeth just before she slapped me in the face.

'Don't you dare presume to judge me, Bruno. You don't know what it is to live as we do.' She glared at me, nostrils flared, eyes hard as diamond. 'We know you think us no different from common whores when you've had what you wanted. But we are the ones who are laughing at you. Do you understand that?'

361

'I only wanted you to tell me the truth,' I said quietly, rubbing my cheek.

'I have told you all I wish to say on that subject.' Her tone was pure ice now. 'Let us go to the Tuileries, then. Catherine will be waiting, as you say.' She swerved past me to the door.

'At least tell me her name. Your daughter's.'

She hesitated, her hand on the latch.

'What harm can it do?' I persisted. 'Catherine may be about to have me arrested.'

Gabrielle turned back, surprised. 'Why would she do that?'

'Does she need a reason?' I thought of Gaston's pamphlet.

'That's not why she wants you.' She looked at me as if I were being deliberately obtuse. 'It's the King.'

'What about him?'

'He's locked himself in his private oratory and taken no food or drink for the past two days. He refuses to speak to anyone – none of his courtiers or his bodyservants. He won't even admit Catherine. She thinks you're the only person who might be able to get through to him. You're a last resort.'

'I don't doubt it,' I said grimly. As I unlatched the door, I heard the patter of quick footsteps descending from the lower landing. Madame de la Fosse could move swiftly when she chose. She should have picked up plenty of material to keep her friends busy for the next fortnight if she overheard even half of that, I thought.

We stepped outside into a raw December dusk, though it was not much past three in the afternoon. I glanced up at the sky; it would snow before nightfall. Gabrielle stopped and laid a hand on my arm.

'Béatrice,' she said, not looking at me. 'Her name is Béatrice.'

Catherine received me once again in her extraordinary *cabinet de travail*, sitting imperiously in her chair on the raised dais, the crocodiles looking down on us with their lidless, distant stares. Ruggieri stooped beside her, his eyes equally reptilian.

The Queen Mother appeared pale but composed, her face etched with tiredness under her black hood. I did not miss the questioning glance she darted at Gabrielle as we entered. I knelt and bowed my head, hearing the door close as I waited for permission to rise. Three of Catherine's young women sat listlessly playing cards on velvet cushions at her feet. She dismissed them with a word. I could feel the force of their curious stares as their satin slippers trooped past my line of sight.

'Get up, then,' Catherine commanded, in a voice that implied I was the one wasting her time with my obsequies. I noticed when I stood that Gabrielle had also discreetly disappeared.

'Your Majesty.'

'You disobeyed my orders two nights ago. I told you to wait until I sent for you.'

'I could not see that my presence was particularly useful, in the circumstances.'

'You fetched my guard a nasty injury, and then you ran away. Slipped out like a rat down a hole. This old fool is partly to blame for not keeping his eyes open.' She nodded towards Ruggieri, who cringed and twisted his beard. 'But those look to me like the actions of a guilty man.'

'Guilty of what, Your Majesty?'

'You tell me. A young woman died in my gardens. You were seen in the woods where her body was discovered. You knew she was found there. Then you escape before you can be questioned.'

'But—' I tried to stay calm, offer a logical defence – 'I was here with you when she was found. She was still warm. And you decided she had taken her own life.'

'Whereas you seemed most determined that she did not.'

'I would hardly draw attention to that if I had killed her.'

'Perhaps you were trying to be clever. You have a reputation for that, after all.'

We looked at one another. Before I could speak, she held up a hand to pre-empt me.

363

'That was not why I brought you here. I mention it only to let you see that there would be grounds to have you arrested, if at some future time I should change my opinion about the manner of the girl's death. I dislike having my orders disobeyed. Let it not happen in future. Have I made myself clear?'

I inclined my head. 'Your Majesty.'

'Good. Walk with me.' She lifted an arm, Ruggieri lurched forward to help her laboriously to her feet. When she had stepped down from the dais, she extended her arm to me and told him to wait. We proceeded as before, at the same painful pace. 'The King is indulging one of his black moods,' she said, when we reached the gallery, in a tone devoid of sympathy. 'He refuses all food and drink and will not speak to anyone. I fear he means to destroy himself. He is certainly wilful enough to try it.'

'For love of Léonie?'

She stopped and turned her most withering expression on me. '*Love*. God in Heaven. Henri falls in love twice a week. It is not *love* you are about to witness, nor grief – it is the tantrum of a spoiled boy who did not get his own way. We have seen all this before, you know.' She resumed her halting progress along the gallery. 'He was obsessed with another woman, before he married Louise. He became determined to make her his wife, against all my counsel, never mind that she was entirely inappropriate, not to mention married to someone else. He intended to have her existing marriage annulled but she inconveniently died of a fever before he could arrange it.' She gave a dry laugh. 'He responded with the same conspicuous display of mourning. Ordered silver death's heads embroidered all over his black suits. Refused to eat, scourged himself. The physicians had to hold him down and force food into him in the end.'

'Have you tried that this time?'

'Not yet. I hope it will not be necessary. It irks me to acknowledge this, as you may imagine, but he has always respected you. I am hoping you will talk some sense into him where we have failed. In the present climate, we simply cannot afford for the last Valois king to starve himself to death over a courtesan.'

'If she was a courtesan, you made her one,' I said. There was a long silence while her black raptor's eyes bored into me. Men had been executed for less insolence, I reflected.

'That little theory you voiced the other night,' she said eventually, glancing back to the far doors where Ruggieri and the guards stood waiting, out of earshot. 'I trust you have kept your word not to repeat it to anyone?'

'That Léonie was with child?' I thought of my conversation earlier with Gabrielle, the stunned astonishment with which she had greeted the idea. 'No. Not a soul.'

'Good. Keep it that way. Above all, do not breathe a word about it to Henri.' Her nails dug into my arm. 'If he ever gets wind of that notion, I will know where it came from and I swear before God, I will have you locked up on the instant.'

'Was it his, then?' I stared at her, as the ramifications began to multiply and expand in my head. All of Europe had drawn the conclusion that Henri was not capable of fathering a child. But what if he had managed it, just not with his wife? Even a bastard Valois was better than nothing; Catherine had enough lawyers and theologians in her pay to make the case for legitimising a son born outside marriage. Then I recalled the Comte de Saint-Fermin's words to me the night before: how Guise had boasted that Léonie was going to put his bastard on the throne. The idea was extraordinary – had she been pregnant with Guise's child and tried to pass it off as Henri's?

'Close your mouth,' Catherine said tersely. 'You were mistaken. Two physicians examined the girl and concluded there was no sign of pregnancy. I would not expect you to have any experience in judging such matters, but you should be very careful about voicing your opinions before they are substantiated. Now you must go to the King before any more time is wasted.'

I nodded and made a small bow. I was certain she was lying. She grasped my arm harder and pulled me close, her voice an urgent whisper.

'One more thing, before you leave. My book. The one I bought from the English girl. Can you read it?'

'I have not had the chance to try. Part of it is written in code.'

'Why? What does it contain?'

I hesitated. 'It is supposed to be the lost book of the Egyptian sage Hermes Trismegistus. There are scholars who believe it holds the secret of how to recover man's lost divinity. How to become like God.'

She released her grip, her expression thoughtful. 'An extremely dangerous heresy, then.'

'There are men who would kill for the chance to read that book. Others for the chance to destroy it.' Some have tried already, I thought, recalling my time in England.

'I do not hold with books being destroyed, whatever lurks within them.' She set her chin in a posture of defiance. 'Ruggieri is trying to decipher it, with no success so far.'

'He will not do it,' I said, unable to hide my scorn. 'The cipher is beyond his capabilities.'

'You think you could do a better job?'

'I am sure of it,' I said. There seemed no point in false modesty.

'Hm.' She nodded. 'Very well. Bring my son back from this pig-headed self-destruction and I will employ you to translate the book. On the condition that you do not mention a word of it to anyone.'

'I am practised in discretion,' I said, bowing.

Catherine fetched up a sliver of a smile. 'Not as much as you think, Bruno.'

TWENTY-TWO

She instructed Ruggieri to take me to the King. 'Try not to fall asleep on the way and let him escape,' she added drily.

'You caused me a great deal of trouble,' the old sorcerer snapped, as we crossed the great courtyard that separated the palace of the Tuileries from the Louvre.

'Consider it payment for all the trouble you have caused me,' I said. 'You want to keep your wits about you, old man.' I did not feel inclined to soothe Ruggieri's ruffled feelings. The conversation with Catherine had lifted my spirits a little; she had been forced to acknowledge that she needed me, both with Henri and with the book. Even so, I did not doubt that, if I failed her or made a misstep, she would not hesitate to carry out her threat of having me arrested.

'At least I have lived to be old,' Ruggieri said, with a shrewish expression. 'Somehow I doubt you will see seventy winters, Giordano Bruno, unless you can learn to say what people wish to hear.'

'Speaking of which – how is the prophecy business? Did you predict the girl's death, I wonder?'

'What?' He stopped dead and levelled a bony finger at me. 'Are you implying I had some knowledge of it?'

I held my hands up. 'I am merely asking whether, with your

famous gift of divination, you foresaw this chain of events? The girl's death, the effect on the King, your own failure to persuade him back to reason? Can you predict how it will end?'

'The only thing I would venture to predict with any certainty,' he said, loftily sweeping his cloak around him and setting off again, 'is that you will not be in Paris for much longer.'

'I look forward to proving you wrong,' I said, but I was discomfited by the knowing curve of his smile.

We passed under the great gate of the Louvre and into a smaller, inner courtyard.

'You do realise he won't see you?' Ruggieri said, as we crossed to the royal apartments. 'We have all pleaded with him, even his own mother, and he refuses to come out. I don't see what you think you can do.'

'It was not my idea,' I said. I suspected that his own mother might be a strong reason for Henri to prefer being locked in his chapel.

Ruggieri sniffed. 'She is clutching at straws,' he said, as an armed guard held open a door into the most private wing of the palace.

As I entered, I glanced to my left at the adjacent façade and was startled to see a woman's pale face at one of the windows on the second floor, watching me. I strained to look – the figure was distorted by the glass and the flickering lights of candles, but I was sure it was the King's wife. Whoever it was, she jumped back when she realised I had seen her. I stood, waiting to see if she would reappear, but the guard holding the door coughed impatiently, and I hurried inside after Ruggieri.

The King's private oratory was tucked away in a corner on the first floor, adjoining the royal apartments. Outside the door we found two weary soldiers, a white-haired man in the robes of a physician and Balthasar de Beaujoyeux, pacing and twisting his hands. He had an unusually frayed air about him, as if he hadn't slept, and his collar was awry.

'Thanks be to Our Lady that you have come, Bruno. We didn't know what else to do, save force the door, but if he is in a fragile state, who knows what that might cause him to do? We think he has a dagger in there with him. Her Majesty says you may be able to bring him back to himself. You're our last hope.'

'So I understand. Has he spoken at all?'

'Only once, and that was to say that if we break the door down, he will cut his own throat.' He passed a hand over his close-cropped hair. 'I have been here all night. His chaplain has tried to reason with him, and a couple of his gentlemen, as well as his mother. No one can move him.'

'He has not taken food or water in over two days,' the physician said, his face grave. 'I feel bound to point out he will die sooner or later if we do not intervene.'

Balthasar clasped his hands together and closed his eyes. His anguish appeared genuine, and I began to grasp the severity of the situation. Anyone who had spent time with Henri was familiar with the way his moods pitched between extremes, often calculated to win attention, but in his most violent dark episodes he was more than capable of harming himself. His attendants knew it; they also knew that their own livelihoods – and perhaps even lives – were in jeopardy if the King did not rally. There were no more Valois sons left.

'Call to him,' Balthasar urged, gesturing to the door.

I knocked firmly. 'Your Majesty. It's Bruno.'

Silence.

'I have some news that will interest you, Your Majesty,' I called, in what I hoped was a buoyant tone. 'Touching the matter we discussed before.' I did not miss the way Ruggieri's sharp eyes brightened with interest.

Still no answer, but a faint shuffling from inside. Encouraged, I tried again.

'I have made progress. In the business of the priest. But I need your advice.'

The movement stopped and the room fell silent again.

'Keep trying,' Balthasar hissed. He pressed his fist to his lips; it seemed he was praying under his breath.

'Your Majesty, I think I have answers, but they are only for your ears. Please let me speak to you.'

The shuffling began again, to no obvious purpose. At least he was still alive in there, I thought. Just as it seemed we would have to admit defeat and risk forcing the door, I heard the rattle of a key in a lock. I held my hand up to prevent anyone else coming closer.

'Bruno alone,' said the King's voice from within, hoarse but menacing.

'On my oath, Your Majesty.'

The door opened a fraction of an inch. Balthasar sent me a questioning look, gesturing to the guards; I shook my head and slipped through the gap. The door was slammed and locked almost before I had whisked the hem of my cloak inside.

I could have been forgiven for thinking myself back inside the oubliette at the Conciergerie. The small room was almost completely dark and at once both cold and stuffy, rank with the smell of unwashed bodies and human waste and overlaid with a more sinister odour, the faint scent of decay. The windows had been covered with thick black cloth, the only light burned from two fat tallow candles on the altar, where I saw the source of that strange, sepulchral smell: a row of human skulls, some with the earth of the grave still clinging to them, had been lined up in the place of a chalice or crucifix. The King backed away to lean against the altar, watching me like a beast cornered in its lair. He was naked from the waist up, shivering, his chest and shoulders scored with red lashes. His cheeks looked sunken and his eyes unnaturally bright, but though he appeared worn down by his extravagant display of emotion, I was relieved to see that he did not seem to be

370

on the brink of death. I approached him cautiously, trying to calculate which words might best draw him out.

'Your Majesty.' I took off the cloak I was wearing, knelt beside him and draped it around his shoulders. He did not protest. The smell rising from his body was feral. 'I understand how hard it is to lose someone you care about, but—'

'You understand nothing.' His voice emerged hollow and flat. He wrapped his arms around his knees. 'I deserve to be punished. I beg God's forgiveness but all I see is endless night. He has turned His face from me.'

'You cannot blame yourself,' I said gently.

'But I killed her,' he said frankly, looking at the floor. A long silence unfurled. I balled my fists tightly, concentrating on the knuckles of my thumbs while I tried to steady my thoughts. I had not expected this confession. It had been my immediate fear on the night of the ball, but in the heat of the discoveries about Léonie and Guise I had all but forgotten the idea. No wonder Catherine was so determined the girl's murder should not be investigated. I wondered if she had guessed from the beginning.

'Why?' I asked.

'You should not have said what you said, Bruno. About Circe intending me harm. You knew nothing about it.'

I shifted position; my knees were beginning to ache. I knew I needed to navigate this carefully; Henri was quite capable of trying to shift the blame by claiming I had encouraged him to murder.

'I was thinking only of Your Majesty's safety. I believed she was part of a plot against you. The priest Lefèvre believed it too, and wanted to warn you.'

'But you did not know the whole truth,' he said again, more forcefully this time. 'She would never have harmed me, I would swear to it. Now she is dead.' He hugged himself, rocking back and forth. 'And it is all my doing. And Ruggieri's.'

'Ruggieri?' I sat back against the altar, trying to comprehend.

371

The old sorcerer was robust for a man of seventy, but I could hardly believe that he had the strength to subdue a young woman for long enough to strangle her with a scarf. 'Was it he who—'

'It does no good to talk of this now.' Henri rubbed both hands over his face. 'God will punish me. He has told me.' He tapped his temple and dropped to a whisper. 'I have heard His voice in here, saying He will tear my kingdom from me and scatter it among my enemies.'

I looked at him. If he were not the King, someone would have given him a good slap by now. I had to fight back an urge to shake him myself. He had just admitted to killing a young woman, and now he was sitting here in his own filth like a sulking child, pouring forth biblical laments as if he had not brought it all about himself.

'He won't have to if you persist in this course, Your Majesty,' I said, losing patience. 'If you don't come out, dress yourself and rule like a sovereign, you will throw your kingdom to Guise and the League with your own hands, and there will be civil war. Another massacre, perhaps. Is that what you want?'

Henri blinked at me. He seemed taken aback by my tone. 'But how can I be absolved for what I have done?'

'You could atone by discharging the duty God has placed on your shoulders as King of France. Do your people not deserve that? And trust in God's mercy.' Strange, I reflected, how easily all the pat answers of faith tripped off my tongue when they were useful.

'But I loved her, Bruno,' he whimpered, his fingers scrabbling at my sleeve. 'And I have brought about her death as surely as if I had opened her veins myself.'

'What do you mean?' I grew still, holding my breath.

He frowned at me, puzzled. 'That it was I who killed her, in the end, as surely as if I had held the knife in my own hand. I drove her to it. I was too quick to credit your theories – I accused her of treason. I spoke cruelly to her – told her I knew everything she was planning. She broke down, swore she was loyal, begged my forgiveness.' He shivered violently. 'The look she gave me when she danced for me, Bruno – it cut me to my heart. I meant to find her and take back my heated words but I was too late. She took her life, convinced I thought she had conspired against me, and I can't forgive myself.'

'Wait.' I knelt up again so I could make him look me in the face. 'Is that what you believe?'

'How could it be otherwise? Why are you staring at me like that?'

'Because . . .' I hesitated, allowing my breath out slowly. Relief sluiced through me. 'Your Majesty, Léonie did not kill herself. Whatever the physicians told you.'

His eyes widened and his mouth fell slack. 'What are you saying?'

'She was not killed with a knife, nor by her own hand. She was strangled, with a scarf. Someone murdered her,' I said, to clarify, since he was still gaping at me as if I were speaking another language.

'Who? Why?'

'I don't have those answers yet. But I believe it was as I told you – because of her part in a conspiracy against you.'

Henri doubled over, pressing his thumbs into his closed eyes; he stayed like this for a few minutes. I crouched beside him, one hand resting on his arm.

'Why did you mention Ruggieri?' I asked.

He raised his head and looked blearily at me. 'Because it was he who said – oh, no matter now. I can hardly credit it. I will find whoever did this and have him tortured.' He sounded more robust already. With a concerted effort he shook off my hand and reached for the edge of the altar, pulling himself unsteadily to his feet. 'So she did mean to kill me after all,' he murmured.

'I fear so, Your Majesty.'

'And they all lied to me. My mother swore stone-faced she had died by her own hand.' His expression hardened. 'You were the only one who told me the truth, Bruno.' He leaned heavily on my shoulder and heaved a sigh that juddered through his bones.

'I think your mother was trying to protect you,' I said. 'She wanted to spare you a scandal.'

'I'll give her a fucking scandal.' He lurched towards the door.

'Your Majesty,' I caught him by the arm. 'You are weak – for the sake of your health you should not exert yourself until you have taken some food.' While Catherine would no doubt be pleased to see her son emerge, I suspected she would not consider my intervention successful if he exploded out of the oratory spitting accusations in her face, and I could say goodbye to my chance of studying the Hermes book.

He shoved me away with unexpected force. 'Exert myself? I tell you this, Bruno – I am sick of being manipulated by women. Damn them all. Never again.' He took another staggering pace towards the door, uttered a small, sharp cry, teetered for a moment and crumpled to the floor like a marionette dropped from a height. My heart caught in my throat; if Henri had died here alone in my company, there was no way out for me but the scaffold. I shook myself, checked his breath and pulse, muttered a prayer of thanks and unlocked the door.

'He fainted, I think from lack of food,' I said to the anxious faces gathered outside. 'He should see the physician now.' I noticed that Ruggieri had disappeared.

Balthasar nodded, flinching slightly at the smell creeping out from the open doorway. 'You go in, do not waste time,' he urged the doctor. 'I will send for water and lights.' He looked at me uncertainly. 'What did you say to him?'

'He unburdened himself of his distress at the death of the

girl. In his weak state he was overcome by emotion and passed out.'

He eyed me warily. 'I hope you have not made him worse.'

'I did what I was asked to do. The door is now open and the King is alive.'

'Well, this guard had better take you back to the Tuileries so you can report to Catherine. She will want to know everything the King said. Will he rally, do you think?'

'I am sure of it. It is not the first time, after all.'

'No.' He sighed. 'It is Catherine who suffers most through all this. I know we should not question the Almighty's ways, but one can't help wishing over and over that He had seen fit to send her better sons. She has worn herself out in the service of France – she deserves an easier life in her old age, poor lady.'

I could not help thinking that Balthasar's image of Catherine was heavily romanticised, but it was not the time to contradict him.

'I'm sure the Almighty has His purposes,' I said blandly.

'I don't know if that is a comforting thought or not.'

'Depends whose side He is on.'

He pursed his lips. 'Yes. If only He had thought to make that clearer. Sometimes I wonder if He doesn't just look down on our petty strife and laugh.' His face turned sombre again. 'It is probably blasphemy even to think that.'

'Don't worry – I don't think it counts if you blaspheme to a heretic.'

He gave me a tired half-smile. 'Go on, you had better not keep her waiting.'

One of the soldiers gestured towards the corridor; I inclined my head to Balthasar and followed the man out.

The inner courtyard glittered with frost; torches had been lit in the wall brackets, chasing shadows into corners. The King still had my cloak; in the bitter air I felt the lack of it, but I could hardly ask to go back now. We were almost at the far side when a young woman appeared from our right with silent steps and planted herself in our path. By her clothes and hair it was clear she was a gentlewoman; she wore a crescent hood and huddled into a thick fur cape. She addressed my guard.

'This man is to come with me.'

He frowned. 'My instructions were to take him to the Tuileries.'

'Your instructions have changed.' She was as brisk and imperious as a dowager duchess, though I guessed she was not yet out of her teens. 'We will see him delivered to Queen Catherine shortly. Go on,' she said, shooing him away with a flap of her hand, 'about your duties. This is not your responsibility now.'

His eyes flitted anxiously between us. 'Will you be safe alone?' he asked.

'I'm sure I can fight her off if she tries anything,' I said. The guard grinned; the girl's expression remained stony.

'We will be perfectly fine,' she said. 'Come along.'

The guard looked back to me, shrugged, and returned the way he had come. 'You. Italian. Follow me,' she said, setting off towards the adjacent wing.

'Where?'

'You'll see. No more questions. Remember your place.'

TWENTY-THREE

She led me up a staircase and through a series of lavishly furnished rooms until we came to a door at the end. The girl knocked and was summoned by a female voice; I found myself ushered into a circular chamber in one of the towers. Queen Louise stood by the fire, her eyes fixed on the flames. I dropped immediately to my knees.

'Your Majesty.'

'You can get up,' she said, in her soft voice, with its oddly flat intonation. 'Thank you, Charlotte. You may leave us.'

I stood as the girl closed the door behind her, to find myself alone with Henri's wife. I had barely spoken to her, even in the days when I was a regular visitor to the court; she had tended to keep to herself, and showed a marked suspicion of anyone the King favoured. Not without reason, I thought. She had been pretty in her youth, though never with the striking beauty that turned heads; she still had her looks, but the years of increasingly extreme treatments for her childlessness had faded her. She appeared drained; at thirty, the lines around her eyes gave her a look of permanent anxiety, though I noted that she had more colour in her cheeks than when I had last seen her on the night of the ball. She crossed the room, skirts susurrating behind her. Her gown was exquisite;

shimmering green silk embroidered with silver thread and sewn all over with seed pearls, but she seemed ill at ease inside it, as if she had been made to dress up as a queen for a costume ball. I noticed, as she approached me, that her fingers were constantly in motion; plucking at the cloth of her cuffs, the rosary at her belt or the dry patches of skin on the backs of her hands.

'Did you see my husband?' she asked, without preliminary.

'I did, Your Majesty.'

'How is he?'

'The physician is treating him now. He is weak but not in danger. I believe if his spirits recover, his body will follow.'

She nodded, wrapping her arms around her narrow ribs as she crossed to the window. 'I heard she had sent for you. He would not see me. Nor any of his advisors. He would not even see Catherine.'

'Perhaps he wanted some peace.'

She whisked around, her eyes darting over my face, trying to assess me.

'Are you close to my husband?'

I hesitated. 'I was his tutor for a time, in the art of memory.'

'I remember. He used to shut himself away for hours with you in the library. Ruggieri said you were teaching him black magic.'

'I hope Your Majesty knows that is not true.'

'Oh, I am inclined to believe you. Every word that man speaks is a malicious lie.' She said this with unexpected vehemence. 'But Henri confides in you, I think?'

'On occasion, he has done me that honour.' I could not gauge the direction of her questions. 'But we are not – intimate, Your Majesty.'

'I did not mean that. Though I would not much care if you were. I am not afraid of his *mignons*. Does that surprise you?' Before I could answer, she continued, 'Henri's sins are his own business. You know he designed my wedding dress and insisted

378

on arranging my hair himself for the ceremony? Hours, he spent. Twenty minutes before I walked to the altar he was still fiddling, sewing precious stones on to my bodice while I was wearing it. Do you think I did not understand him then?' She cracked a dry smile. 'It was a work of art, though – see for yourself.' She gestured to the wall behind me.

I turned to see an imposing portrait of Queen Louise posed in one of the great rooms of state in her wedding finery, ten years younger with a sparkle of hope in her eyes, though still outshone by the brilliance of her gown, so crowded with gems that it looked rigid as armour. But the detail that caught my eye was the pendant she wore around her neck in the portrait: a gold medallion engraved with the symbol of a dolphin.

'You look radiant, Your Majesty,' I said, with a small bow. 'That is an unusual necklace, in the picture.'

A shadow crossed her face. 'Catherine had it made by Italian goldsmiths for Henri to present to me on our wedding day. As a symbol of my duty to give him a Dauphin. Not especially subtle.'

I looked back at the painting. Of course – *Dauphin* meant 'dolphin' in French, but it was also the title of the heir to the throne. So the medallion was to celebrate the future Dauphin, the prince who never came. Had Léonie stolen it, then?

'Do you still wear it?' I asked.

'That would hardly be appropriate,' she said bitterly. 'Catherine made me give it back to the King for safekeeping. She said he would return it and I could wear it again when I had fulfilled its promise. So you see why the men are no threat to me. It is the women I fear.'

'What do you mean?'

She laid a hand flat across her abdomen. 'What do you suppose? Ten years of marriage and no Dauphin. I have done everything humanly possible, but it seems all the saints are deaf to me.' Her face pinched, as if with a sharp pain. 'And what of Catherine – are you close to her?'

I hesitated. 'I think Catherine would gladly see me dead, Your Majesty. Except for the rare occasions when she finds I can be useful to her.'

'Hm. That makes two of us, then.' She turned her attention to a loose thread in her sleeve. 'Since the King's brother the Duke of Anjou died last summer I feel I have been teetering on the edge of a precipice, waiting for her to push me. I am no longer useful, you see.'

I looked at her, beginning to understand. 'You think the King wants a new wife?'

'For himself, I don't think Henri would cast me off. He feels too guilty. But *she* controls everything. She will not see the House of Valois lose the throne without a fight. I knew it had begun when Ruggieri pronounced his new prophecy. So I wondered if Henri had said anything to you?'

'His Majesty did not mention any prophecy,' I said. She watched me with a clear, level stare.

'Nothing you say will go beyond this room. I will give you my word, if you will do the same.' She pointed at the wall, tracing a circle around her with her finger. 'Day after day I am trapped here, knowing there are plots being woven all around me, and no one will tell me anything. Do you know how that feels?'

'I know what it is to feel friendless,' I said. She regarded me for a moment and nodded; her eyes suggested she was struggling with her desire to confide in someone. 'What did this new prophecy say?' I prompted, gently.

'That the King would have a son within the year.'

'But that speaks in your favour, does it not? If one believes Ruggieri truly has a divine gift,' I added, in a tone that made my own view clear.

'He did not say it would be with me,' she said. 'He predicted a son born to a fertile union – those were his exact words. It was carefully ambiguous. But I know, because Balthasar told me in confidence, that around the same time Catherine held a private audience with the Papal nuncio. I am sure it was to discuss the possibility of annulling my marriage.'

'You think she would do that?' I was surprised not by the suggestion of Catherine's stratagems but by how astute the Queen was in guessing at them.

'No, I don't,' she said, shortly. 'I think such a process would be drawn-out, diplomatically fraught and expensive. Catherine would not want that. And why should she go to all that trouble when there are easier ways to remove me?' She toyed with her cuff again. 'Then she sent that Circe woman to join my household. To spy on me, I supposed at first. She would not have been the first. I thought then it had begun. And I have been so ill these past weeks, I feared she was already practising against me. I had good reason to believe it, too.'

She pressed her lips together and turned back to the window. I watched her, the pent-up agitation making her thin frame quiver with nervous energy. It was impossible to know how far her fears were exaggerated by loneliness and her sense of isolation at court, but with Catherine de Medici, everything she was saying sounded entirely plausible.

'But – if you will forgive me, Your Majesty, you are looking better. I pray that your health is returning.'

She glanced at me over her shoulder. 'I thank you. Yes, I feel a little more like myself these past couple of days.' She gave a short laugh. 'Coincidence, isn't it – that woman dies and immediately I begin to recover. Perhaps the priest was right after all.'

'What?' I fought to keep my voice level. 'Which priest?'

'I don't know. I received a letter, almost a month ago now. Anonymous, of course. But the author said he had good intelligence that Circe meant me harm. He spoke of the confessional, so I assumed it came from a priest. And the de Châtillon girl was silly and superstitious enough that she would seek absolution for murder even before she committed it.' Her fingers moved to pick at the beads on her belt. 'No doubt you think I am full of absurd fancies. But if you lived as I do, knowing Catherine, you would be afraid for your life too. Don't be deceived by these clothes—' she held out the fabric of her skirt – 'I am a prisoner awaiting execution like any in the Bastille. So I am pleading with you to tell me if Henri has said anything to you that would confirm my suspicions. Because I would go quietly – you can tell him that. To a convent, if he wished it. There is no need to kill me.' I could hear the desperation in her voice, even as she tried to keep her face stoical.

'*Dio mio*,' I said forcefully. I had misunderstood everything from the beginning. '*Your Majesty*.'

'Yes?' She looked at me expectantly.

'No, I meant—' I could only stare at her, wondering how I could have made such an obvious mistake. All along, I had assumed that Paul Lefèvre's letter had been intended for the King; it had never occurred to me that the same form of address, *Votre Majesté*, might refer to the Queen, or that she might be in danger. Like everyone else, I had barely given her a thought.

'Do you still have the letter?' I asked.

She shook her head. 'I burned it.'

'Did you tell anyone?'

'No. Who could I tell, in this place? I did not think anyone would take it seriously. They would tell me it was the ravings of a madman and I should ignore it. They would say that especially if there were any truth in it.'

'Who brought you the letter?'

'I don't remember. It just arrived with all the others. I suppose any of the servants.'

'Could anyone have read it before it reached you?'

A small crease appeared in her brow. 'It was sealed, I do remember that, because I recall looking to see if there was an insignia. But the wax was unmarked.'

'Did you ever confront Circe? Léonie, I mean?'

'Yes. I began refusing any food or drink she brought me. When she asked why, I made a joke of it. I said, "You would never do anything to hurt me, Léonie, would you?" She burst into tears.' Her lip curled with contempt. 'Fell on her knees, swore to me her love and duty were all mine as long as she lived and she would give her life for mine. I have never seen such a performance. She didn't realise I knew she was fucking my husband, of course.'

I gaped at her.

'Don't look so shocked, Doctor Bruno – I am not a child, though everyone treats me as if I were.' She hitched up her skirts and crossed back to the window. This time I came to stand beside her. We looked down over the courtyard. A few flakes of snow had begun to drift into the light of the torches. 'She was bursting into tears a lot these past few weeks,' Louise mused, touching her fingertips to the glass. 'At everything and nothing. I suppose one becomes emotional in her condition.'

'Condition?' I said faintly.

'She was pregnant. I am sure of it, though I lack experience.'

'I am certain of it too.'

She turned to me, amazed. 'Did Henri tell you?'

'No. I don't think he knows. I observed it for myself. That Circe costume did not leave much to the imagination.'

She made a face. 'The costume was Catherine's idea. My original design was much more subtle. You see?' She indicated the table to her right. I moved closer and saw that it was spread with sheets of paper covered in brightly coloured sketches of women showing the various costumes from the Masque of Circe. The drawings were beautifully executed, with an artist's eye for the human form; the women had been rendered as if in the midst of the dance, so that the drape and movement of the fabric appeared charged with energy. Each one had been carefully painted, the colours suggesting the play of light and shadow as the dancers whirled. I recalled that Queen Louise had been involved in the *ballets de cours* in the past, but I had not realised the extent of her creative talents. Beside each dancer was a brief note on her place in the masque and how she would move.

'This was how I pictured Circe,' she said, pointing to a sketch that was clearly a likeness of Léonie, in a more modest Grecian gown of deep azure.

'These drawings are exquisite, Your Majesty,' I said. She flushed with pleasure and I was moved again with pity for her. 'Did you contribute to the choreography too?'

'Not really. A few suggestions. Balthasar added the notes but the costumes are all mine. It was Catherine who wanted Circe to look more titillating. I could not understand it – I would have thought in the circumstances she would have preferred to conceal the girl's condition until the timing was more favourable.'

'Favourable – how?' I thought of how swiftly Catherine had dismissed my suggestion that Léonie was pregnant.

'Catherine was deceived if she thought it was Henri's,' the Queen whispered, half to herself, watching her wavering reflection in the window. 'Ten years of being probed and scraped by doctors and not one can find anything wrong with me. But it is always said to be the woman's fault if she cannot conceive a child. To suggest it is the man's failure casts doubt on his virility. And it is easier to replace a wife than a king, is it not?'

'You mean you don't think Henri can father a child?' I asked.

'To say so would be treason,' she replied carefully. 'I am saying I did not believe Léonie de Châtillon's child was Henri's. So I had her followed. I wanted to see if she met other men. I could not see the King so grossly deceived. I still care for my husband, you see. And I was terrified.'

'Of what?'

'That if Catherine believed Léonie was carrying the King's child, it would hasten her plans for me. I had to do *something*.' She spoke so softly I could barely hear her. She remained by the window, her gaze unfocused, toying with the lace of her collar.

I crossed the room and studied the wedding portrait hanging on the wall opposite the fireplace. In the lower right-hand corner two coats of arms had been painted to symbolise the joining of the two houses. One was the Valois arms, the other a gold shield with a crimson band showing three white eaglets displayed. I closed my eyes briefly and felt a cold sensation spread from the nape of my neck along the length of my spine. I realised now where I had seen the emblem sewn on the scarf I had found in the copse where Léonie was killed. This was the arms of the House of Lorraine; the Queen had been Louise of Lorraine before she married.

I turned slowly to find that she too had moved from the window and was looking at me across the room. I tried to keep my face steady but my mind was racing. She had seemed so ill the night of the ball, barely able to hold her head up during the masque. Could she have been feigning?

'I want you to do something for me,' she said. 'I will pay you.'

'I am your servant, Your Majesty.' I dipped my head, watching her; the nervous movements of her hands, the way she bit the corner of her lip. She did not look like a killer, but then a desperate woman might defy anyone's expectations. Even so, if I had been forced to guess, I would have supposed a more detached method, such as poison, to have been her preferred choice.

'Take a message to the King. Tell him I need to speak to him alone. Ask him to grant me a private audience.'

'I'm not sure they will allow me to see him again, Your Majesty. His physicians are with him now, and he is very weak. Perhaps, when he is better, one of your servants might—'

'They will not let any of my servants near him,' she snapped, and I caught a sudden flash of steel in her eyes as she advanced a pace. Perhaps I had underestimated her. 'That is why I sent for you. They will admit you. Tell the King he must see me as a matter of urgency. Say he owes me that, at least. But do not let *her* know that I sent you.'

'I can try, but I fear—'

I was interrupted by a sharp knock at the door. Without waiting for a summons, it opened to admit Balthasar, who looked from me to the Queen with puzzled consternation, as if trying to unpick a mathematical sequence.

'Your Majesty, forgive me—' he made a brisk bow – 'but this man is expected at the Tuileries by Queen Catherine. He should not be in your private apartments alone.'

'Peace, Balthasar. I sent for him, it is not his fault. I only wanted to hear from the horse's mouth how my lord husband does. You know I have been praying for his well-being.'

'You could have asked me, Your Majesty,' Balthasar said, with gentle reproach.

'But you did not speak with him. I am the King's wife – I have a right to hear the news of his health directly.' She drew herself up, bravely facing Balthasar down, but his expression was one of pity.

'Of course, Your Majesty. I hope Doctor Bruno's report was encouraging. I am pleased to say the King is now resting in bed and his physicians are attending to him. With God's blessing he will soon be restored to vigour. And now, pardon me but we must not keep Queen Catherine waiting any longer.'

'No, God forbid she should be inconvenienced,' Queen Louise said, her face tight. 'I thank you for your time, Doctor Bruno. I know that you are a loyal servant to your sovereign.'

She shot me a meaningful look as I bowed and backed towards the door. I could not help a final glance towards the wedding portrait as I left.

'What was that about?' Balthasar hissed, as he hurried me down the stairs.

'No more than she said. She wanted me to tell her about the King. She is frantic with worry over him. I believe she really loves him,' I said, shaking my head.

'I know. Remarkable, isn't it? After everything he has put her through. I never cease to be amazed by the tenacity of women. I suppose she doesn't have much choice. So what *did* Henri say to you in there?'

We emerged into the courtyard. The snow was falling heavily now and a wind had picked up, causing it to swirl and eddy. I shivered.

'He believes God has forsaken him. The usual. Most of it didn't make sense.'

Balthasar nodded, sympathetic. 'But you mentioned that you had news for him. That was what prompted him to open the door to you. Something about a priest?'

'Oh, that.' I hesitated, knowing every word would be repeated to Catherine. 'There was a League priest killed a fortnight ago, the curé of Saint-Séverin – you remember? Henri was afraid Guise was going to find a way to blame him and incite the people to riot. He asked me to see if I could discover anything.'

'I remember – there were reports of unrest. Catherine was worried. I didn't know he had you looking into that. But you found something?'

'No. I only said that to make him open the door.'

'Ah. I suppose there is no doubt Guise ordered it, though you will have a job finding proof of that.' He quickened his pace, muttering curses at the snow. We made our way across the open space between the two palaces, bordered on each side by buildings housing the vast complex of royal adminis-tration. 'So Henri still has you working for him in secret?'

'He thought so. But Catherine knew all about it.'

He laughed. 'Of course she did.'

'Queen Louise showed me her designs for the Masque of Circe,' I said, to change the subject. 'She has quite a gift for drawing.'

'Extraordinary, isn't it? She conceived of all those designs from her own imagination. And she can draw anything from the life too, with no training,' he added. 'It's the one time I see her truly animated, when we are planning the grand ballets. I sometimes think she would be happier making costumes for a company of travelling players than being Queen of France, poor creature. It's a pity her health is so fragile.'

'Is she as bad as she looks?' I thought of what Louise had told me. She had suspected Léonie of plotting to kill her and deceive the King; she said she had had to do something.

'Oh yes. She missed most of the ball the other night. She was so ill she had to retire to her chamber directly after the masque. May I confide something in you, Bruno?' He stopped abruptly with a hand on my arm as we approached the vast façade of the Tuileries.

'Of course.' I clenched my teeth to keep them from chattering. He fixed me with his solemn dark eyes, though he seemed jittery.

'I am afraid for Catherine's health too. She is as stubborn in her way as Henri – she barely sleeps now, and she will not delegate to anyone. She feels she must oversee every bit of state business while the King is indisposed, or the kingdom will fall apart.'

'She is probably not far wrong.'

'True, but she stays up all night writing letters, she sits in war councils all day, she plans to travel south to meet Navarre before Christmas, if you please – she will not listen to reason, and she is in such pain, all the time, but she refuses to rest. And I am obliged to be at the Louvre so much now that I can't watch over her as I would like.' He appeared to be on the verge of tears. 'I really fear she will drive herself into her grave, and then we will all be at the mercy of Guise.'

'But the Queen Mother is tough. She has endured worse times than this.'

'Not as tough as people think,' he said, his voice heavy with implication. 'And Léonie's suicide has affected her deeply. She has taken it very hard.'

'She seemed more inconvenienced than distressed when I

saw her,' I said, thinking of Catherine's callous remarks about the girl.

'That is because you do not know her. She keeps her feelings hidden. So you must be careful what you say to her.'

Snowflakes had begun to settle on his hair and shoulders. I wondered why he was telling me this; perhaps he just needed to unburden himself.

'I do not think she will take notice of me, if she will not listen to her advisors,' I said, blowing on my fingers and hoping he would take the hint.

'I didn't mean that. I only meant – try not to upset her. Every time she has spoken to you recently she has come away angry and agitated.'

'I have that effect on people. I can't help it.' I smiled, but he did not return it.

'*Try*,' he said, with a stern look. 'Tell her what she wants to hear.'

'Doesn't she have enough people to do that already?'

'*Madonna porca*.' He lifted his gaze skywards and back to me, his eyes harder this time. 'You take such pride in your defiance, don't you? You think you have special licence to speak the truth to power, and that great princes respect you more for it?'

'I never met a wise ruler who respected empty flattery,' I said, needled.

'I am just asking you to put aside your pride for once,' he hissed, bringing his face close to mine. 'Have some human decency – she is not an opponent you need to best in the debating chamber. She is an old lady who is exhausted and in pain. Say her son is feeling better. Do not put any more ideas into her head that will give her further grief and sleepless nights. She is the only thing holding France together at the moment, and she cannot continue as she is without destroying herself and the kingdom. Let me put it bluntly – if anything happens to her, we will all be lucky to escape with our lives.'

389

I could no longer feel my hands or feet, so I assented dumbly and allowed myself to be led inside.

There was a great flurry of activity around Catherine's apartments; women bustled past with armfuls of furs as a sedan chair was carried in by six large men. Balthasar left me in an antechamber while he went to announce my presence and eventually returned, looking even more preoccupied.

'It seems you have had a reprieve,' he said, his eyes distracted by the movements of servants around us. 'Your detour to Queen Louise means you have arrived too late – Catherine is already preparing to spend the evening at the Louvre by the King's side. You should return home.'

'That will be a relief to everyone,' I said. 'I was afraid I might say a wrong word and find myself single-handedly responsible for the downfall of France.'

He didn't smile. 'I'm glad you find it all such a joke. She asked me to thank you for restoring the King to her, and to tell you that she has not forgotten her promise. She will send for you tomorrow to discuss terms.'

I nodded, realising that at this stage, a little humility would serve me better. 'Tell her I am grateful. I will try not to put ideas in her head.'

He gave me a wry look in parting, as his boot heels clicked away over the marble floor. I wondered what ideas he meant; I had not missed the fact that he had referred pointedly to Léonie's suicide. But Catherine knew full well that the girl's death was murder without my insisting on it. Perhaps that was one of the causes of her sleepless nights. Balthasar was not wrong to fear the consequences of Catherine's demise, though; without her, Henri would be easily toppled and there would be no one left to protect those of us who had depended on his favour as the country fell into civil war.

I allowed myself to be escorted to the gatehouse arch by two armed guards, but as I was ushered through, I heard a woman's voice calling my name from across the courtyard. I turned to see a swaddled figure hurrying towards me and recognised Gabrielle somewhere inside the fur hood.

'I saw you leaving Catherine's apartments from the window,' she said, breathless, eyes bright and her cheeks flushed with the cold. 'How is the King?'

'He'll live. Can I ask you something?' My teeth rattled. She nodded, though her eyes had grown cautious. 'How well do you know Queen Louise?'

She looked surprised. 'Not so well. I served in her household for a time – Catherine makes us all take a turn.'

'To spy on her?'

'What do you think?'

'Why? What does Catherine suppose she might do?'

She shot me a pointed glance. 'Don't be obtuse, Bruno.' When I continued to look blank, she sighed and drew me over to a far corner of the archway where the guards on the gate could not hear. 'A woman who cannot conceive a child with her husband might be tempted to try a little subterfuge. When that woman is the Queen of France and any child of hers the heir, it is essential that there be no hint of any such tricks. Do you see?'

I recalled the gossiping woman at the ball who had said she would bed the nearest courtier if she were the Queen.

'So Catherine sends members of her Flying Squadron to police the Queen's fidelity?'

'Ironic, isn't it?' Gabrielle gave me a tired grin.

'Is that why Léonie de Châtillon was sent to the Queen's household?'

She glanced away. 'I presume so.'

'But wasn't the Queen jealous? If it was known that Léonie was Henri's mistress, I mean? Surely that would be adding insult to injury.'

She shrugged. 'I don't suppose Catherine would care about that. Louise must have learned to live with it by now. She would tear herself apart if not. Why are you so interested in the Queen suddenly?'

'She called me in to see her just now.'

'Really?' Her eyes glittered in the torchlight. 'What did she say?'

'She asked after the King.'

'Nothing else? She seems to have excited your curiosity.'

'She strikes me as a very unhappy woman.' I paused to breathe on my fingers and rub my hands. 'And with good reason.'

Gabrielle held my arm and leaned closer, so that I could feel the heat of her breath on my ear. 'I will tell you this in confidence, and you must promise not to repeat it. I have often wondered if Catherine keeps her drugged.'

'How?'

'She has Ruggieri concoct philtres that are supposed to encourage conception and Louise is made to drink them with the promise that the King will come to her that night. My guess is they are no more than sleeping draughts. She always seems a little – how can I put it? – *slow*. Dazed. Her eyes don't focus. I noted it when I served her and I have heard the same from other girls. Didn't you notice? I think they keep her subdued so she won't protest or assert herself.' She grimaced. 'I would not be her, poor bitch, for all the jewels in the Louvre and the Tuileries combined.'

I nodded, thinking again of the women at the ball and the one who had said she would drink poison if she were the Queen. How simple it would be to slip something deadly into one of those philtres. But it seemed to me that Queen Louise had grown wise to the tricks used against her.

Gabrielle slipped her arms around my waist and pressed herself against my side.

'Such a cold night, Bruno. No one should sleep alone on a night like this. Let me come home with you and keep you warm.'

392

I smiled, and prised her away. 'I have a lot of work to do.'

Reluctantly, she released me and bent her head towards mine again, her hand pressed to my chest, lips against my ear. 'I recall you always used to say that, until the night you didn't.' She smiled. 'Well, if you change your mind, there's a little gate in the back wall that leads into the gardens. The man who guards it at night is called Rémy. He's very obliging. He would bring you to me, if you made it worth his while.'

I shook my head. 'Thank you, but when I get into bed tonight, I intend to sleep like a dead man.' As soon as the words were out of my mouth, suspended in the frozen air, I wished them unsaid.

'You might get your wish,' she said, mock-stern, plucking at the buttons of my doublet. 'You don't even have a coat. You'll freeze to death.'

'I gave it to the King. He had more need of it at the time.'

'Well, you won't see that again. Here, take my cloak. I have another. You can return it when Catherine sends for you again. Which I'm sure she will, now that you have succeeded in drawing Henri out of his despair.' She shrugged off her fur-lined cape and swung it over my shoulders. 'There. Now it will be as if I am wrapped around you all night. Perhaps soon I won't have to imagine that.' She wriggled closer and kissed me on the mouth. I closed my eyes and briefly considered taking her up on her offer, before reminding myself sternly that she was almost certainly reporting on me to Catherine. Besides, there was a small chance Sophia might come looking for me. I allowed myself to wonder for a moment how she would react to finding Gabrielle in my room, before answering my own question: she would simply turn around and walk away. She was not the sort of woman whose interest would be piqued by competition. I eased Gabrielle off me, thanked her for the cloak and stepped out into the falling snow. I did not look back, but I knew she was watching my steps as I walked down the street towards the river.

TWENTY-FOUR

I lowered my head and pressed forward into the falling snow as I made my way along the Right Bank. Above me the sky sagged with layers of grey cloud like wet wool; the snow had begun to settle already, smoothing over the ruts in the frozen mud underfoot. I was glad of Gabrielle's cloak, though it was a strange sensation to pull the fur hood close around my face and catch the scent of her perfume, oddly familiar. Once or twice instinct caused my skin to prickle and I ducked into the shelter of buildings, convinced that someone was following me, but the snow had muffled all sounds and reduced my vision to a few yards in either direction. If anyone was tailing me, they must have watched me come from the palace. I quickened my steps. The Duke of Guise would be looking for me, of that I was certain; he would surely have learned by now that I had robbed him twice over, of his horse and the Comte de Saint-Fermin, not to mention the business of breaking open his sister's private escritoire, and he might well feel it was time for a reckoning. I did not want to find myself intercepted by him before I had had the chance to speak to Jacopo.

I turned into the rue des Tournelles, keeping close to the shadows where I could, and saw that there were now two armed guards outside Jacopo's gate. I stated my business and one of them held me at bay while the other knocked at the door and exchanged a few words with the steward, who beckoned me in with a marked lack of enthusiasm.

'Brought any more dying men for my master to tend at his own expense?' he asked, peering past me into the night.

'Not today.' I ignored his tone and shook the snow off my boots. 'How is the patient?'

'Sleeping, mainly. He took a little broth this afternoon. One of the maids is sitting with him.' His manner softened a fraction. 'It would make a stone weep, to see a man reduced to that state. Signor Corbinelli is not yet back from the palace. With this weather it may be that he decides to stay. Do you want to wait?'

'For a while. If I may.'

He showed me into Jacopo's study and offered to bring me some warm bread and fresh candles. The fire had burned low but I threw on another log and huddled on a chair by the hearth. When the food had been brought and the steward had closed the door behind him, I took off Gabrielle's cloak and paced the room, trying to gather my thoughts. As I passed Jacopo's desk, my eyes fell on the heavy volume he had left open there. This was the book he had been in such a hurry to clear away when I arrived the night before. Curious, I pulled it towards me and found that it was a copy of the *Summa Theologica* by Thomas Aquinas, with sheets of paper poking from it at intervals. I turned to the pages Jacopo had marked with his notes and felt my throat dry as I began to see the import of what I read.

He had been underlining passages in the *Supplementum Tertiae Partis* where Aquinas addresses questions concerning matrimony and the legitimacy of children. I picked up one of the sheets of notes in Jacopo's handwriting.

Aquinas clearly states that a child conceived and/or born out of legal marriage can be legitimised in one of six ways, the first two according to the canons if the man marries the mother of *the child, and by special dispensation and indulgence of the Lord Pope, <u>providing the child was not conceived in adultery</u>,* he had written. Below he had noted: *He may also be legitimised if the father designate him legitimate in a public document signed by three witnesses, if there be no legitimate son.*

There were further notes and jottings, half-formed sentences peppered with question marks, but the gist seemed clear enough.

I sat down at the desk, hands pressed to my temples, my thoughts racing. More than once I considered leaving and taking my chances in the streets, but I realised I had nowhere else to go. There was no one in Paris save Jacopo that I could talk to about any of this, except perhaps the King and he was in no state to discuss anything. Perhaps I could rely on the old scholar to deal frankly with me, though I was less certain of that than I had been when I arrived.

An hour passed before I heard the front door and the muffled exchange of voices in the hall. I arranged myself calmly behind the desk so that I had a clear view of Jacopo as he entered the study, brushing snow from his coat and rubbing his hands.

'Bruno! How good to see you – what about this weather! Are you warm enough? I shall send for more logs – the snow looks as if it means to stay.' He stopped when he saw my face. 'What is it? Has something happened?'

I tapped the book with a forefinger. 'You have been studying Aquinas.'

He looked down at the papers and back to meet my eye. 'There is always fresh wisdom to be found in the writings of the good Doctor,' he said carefully.

'Why – are you expecting a child out of wedlock? My congratulations.' My voice was flinty.

His brow creased; he tilted his head and looked at me a little sadly.

'Bruno, you are always welcome as a guest in my house, you know that. But as a courtesy – my private papers . . .'

He gestured to the desk. 'I would not go through your note-books in your absence.'

'You could, if you wished. You would not find any evidence that I had connived at *murder*.' I half rose from the chair as I spoke; I saw a flash of anger in his face.

'Think what you are saying, Bruno, before your words do too much damage. Do you not know me better than that?'

'Tell me I am wrong, then. This is about Léonie de Châtillon, isn't it?' I jabbed at the book again. 'You knew what Catherine was planning all along.'

He drew breath to speak, just as there was a knock at the door and the steward entered with a tray bearing a jug of hot wine and two glasses. He squinted from one to the other of us with mild interest, noting the tension in the room, before backing away quietly and closing the door. Jacopo lifted his head, listening for the man's retreating footsteps before he spoke.

'Catherine asked me to find any legal and theological precedents for legitimising a child conceived outside marriage,' he said in a low voice. He poured two drinks and stood by the fire, hands wrapped around his glass, watching the flames. 'This was around a month ago. She did not explain her reasons. I presumed it was connected to her ongoing schemes for Henri, but I did not question her.'

'You have underlined this sentence about adultery,' I said, pointing to the sheet of notes. I sat back in the chair. 'Don't tell me you didn't know she was asking about his mistress. The dolphin medallion – you realised then, didn't you?'

He sighed, passing a hand over his bald patch. 'I understood better, yes. I took it to Catherine and said it was on the ground where the girl's body was found. She confessed then that Léonie had believed herself to be carrying Henri's child. Catherine gave her the medallion as a promise that her child would one day be Dauphin, if she did as she was told.'

'Did you ask Catherine what she planned to do about Queen Louise?'

397

'She said she had intended to have the King's marriage annulled in time to legitimise the child by a new marriage before it was born. But it was all moot by then. The girl was dead.'

'Catherine wasn't looking for an annulment. Not when there was a quicker way to be rid of the Queen. You must have guessed at that.'

'Your imagination is running wild now, Bruno.' There was a warning note in his voice.

'On the contrary – I have never understood the matter so clearly. Everything is connected. When Catherine found out that Léonie was pregnant after she had become Henri's mistress, she had to accelerate her plans. There was no time for legal procedures. Did you not see how ill Queen Louise was on the night of the ball? One of them was poisoning her, little by little – Léonie, perhaps, or Ruggieri. Louise was convinced of it. But Léonie was eaten up by guilt over this plan she had become entangled in – she confessed to Père Lefèvre, who was moved by his conscience to warn the Queen in an anonymous letter. But I think someone at the palace read that letter. Paul had to be silenced and so did Léonie.' I pushed the chair back and joined him by the fire. 'No wonder you kept telling me to leave it alone.' I could not hide the resentment in my voice.

'I had no idea the priest was anything to do with this business, Bruno, you must believe me. I only thought it wiser for you not to be involved, especially if Guise was behind it. But when Léonie died and you seemed determined to prove that all the deaths were connected, I knew you were going to march straight into trouble.'

'Because you knew the killer was inside the palace, you mean?'

He hesitated, weighing his words, not meeting my eye.

'I know nothing about the other two, the priest and the friar. I give you my word. When Léonie was found and you showed me that medallion, I confess I had misgivings. It seemed

398

easier to believe she had taken her own life.' His voice had grown quiet. He drained his glass and turned away.

'You had misgivings,' I repeated flatly. 'But there was a further twist to the story, you see – Léonie's child was very likely not even Henri's. She was still sleeping with the Duke of Guise.'

He raised his head and stared at me. '*Gesù Cristo.* Do you think Catherine found out?'

'Someone found out,' I said. 'Queen Louise took the priest's warning seriously. She also guessed that Léonie was pregnant. She had one of her servants follow her to see if she met other men. I think she knew about Léonie and Guise.'

'And you think she told Catherine?' He frowned. 'But that would have meant admitting she believed Catherine was plotting against her.'

'I think she found her own solution.'

Jacopo rubbed a hand slowly over his beard and stared at me. 'What are you saying, Bruno?'

'I found a scarf with Queen Louise's device embroidered on it in the woods where Léonie was killed,' I said. 'I believe it was the one used to strangle her.'

'You think Queen Louise murdered Léonie? Have you gone quite mad?'

'It fits. Louise knew her life was in danger from this woman who planned to take her place, marry the King and give him a supposed Dauphin that was most likely a Guise bastard.'

'That's impossible,' Jacopo said.

'But she had every reason to want the girl dead,' I persisted. 'She may not have been as ill as she looked that night.'

He shook his head. 'I'm afraid she was worse than she looked. She sat bravely through the masque, but she was overcome by a terrible fit of vomiting immediately after and had to be carried to a guest room. I accompanied her, along with two of her ladies. She was given a draught to settle her stomach and help her sleep and the women remained there with her, along with a nursemaid, for the rest of the night.

She certainly wasn't dashing through the grounds strangling anyone, that much is beyond question. Though I do not deny her symptoms could be consistent with poisoning,' he added, as if this might make me feel better.

I fell heavily into a chair, pressing my fingers to my eyes. 'You're right. It was an absurd idea. I couldn't make it fit with my theory that the same person killed both Léonie and Joseph de Chartres. But, Jacopo, I am still convinced the killer is inside the palace.'

He laid a hand on my shoulder. 'Then do you not think it is time for you to follow my advice and walk away? If Catherine is the author of it, what can you do?'

'I could tell the King,' I said, defiant. 'He is the highest authority in France, not her, and he wants the killer found.'

Jacopo laughed softly. 'Think what you are saying. You saw for yourself the state he worked himself into over the girl's death. As far as I know, he had no idea about the child. How do you think he will react when he learns your theory that she was pregnant with a child that may or may not have been his, and that his mother intended first to kill his lawful wife and then ordered the death of his mistress? Do you think that will spur him to a speedy recovery, the quicker to take up the reins of government again? Or do you want to make him worse, hm?' He searched my eyes, his mouth compressed into a grave line, until I was forced to look away.

'I think he would want to be told if his mother was practising against him.'

'Do you really?' He let his arm fall to his side and crossed the room to pour another drink. 'You know Henri by now, Bruno. He is a weak man, governed by lust and fear in equal measure. He could not survive without Catherine, and he knows it. He may rail against her, but in the end he will accept her rule, whatever it involves. If you try to set him against her you will only succeed in losing everyone's favour, and you cannot afford that. Ask yourself – can you?'

'But he set me to find a murderer,' I insisted, hearing myself sound like a petulant child.

'And you almost did. You uncovered a conspiracy that, unfortunately, you can do nothing about. Now let it go. Your friends have suffered enough for your meddling already.'

'What do you mean? Are you in trouble?' His tone sent a prickle of anxiety up my spine; I thought of Cotin, sentenced to solitary confinement because of me.

'I'm talking about the *Gelosi*,' he said, grimly, sitting down at his desk and closing the Aquinas book with a decisive thud. 'I have only just heard that they are being held at the Hotel de Montpensier because apparently one of their number is accused of theft and spying. They managed to slip a message out with a servant. They are supposed to leave for Lyon tomorrow, but the Duchess refuses to release them until this man returns and hands himself in with the stolen goods.' He gave me a meaningful look from beneath lowered brows.

'*Merda*.' I pinched the bridge of my nose between my thumb and forefinger. 'I didn't think she would imprison them. I should go there now.'

Jacopo shook his head. 'That would be extremely unwise. I am about to write to Catherine asking her to intervene with the Duke of Montpensier, but there is not much I can do without her approval. It will require a show of force, I suspect. Our friends will be all right – I don't suppose the Duchess would dare to harm them. But this would not have occurred if you had listened to me sooner, Bruno.' He spoke gently but firmly, a father to a wayward boy. I nodded. A wave of tiredness crashed over me and I buried my face in my hands again.

'Why don't you stay here tonight?' Jacopo said, picking up his quill. 'You don't want to go out in that again. Get some rest and you can find your way home in the morning.'

I stood, watching him sharpen his nib for a moment before my eyes focused clearly on what he was doing.

'May I see your penknife?' I asked.

He glanced up, surprised, but held it out to me. I reached inside my doublet and took out the one I had been carrying around since my visit to the silversmith's that morning. They were almost identical.

'Where did you get this?' I asked.

'A gift from Catherine, years ago now. They were made by a master silversmith under her patronage back in Florence, I believe. The work is quite distinctive. She has given them to some in her service as a mark of favour. They are worth a bit by now. Where did you find that one?'

'By Joseph de Chartres's body.'

He eyed the knives as I handed his back. 'I mean it, Bruno. Let it go. For everyone's sake. And any time you wish to apologise for accusing me of conniving at murder, I will be glad to accept it,' he added, with an edge to his voice, returning his attention to the paper before him.

I lowered my eyes. 'Forgive me, Jacopo. I spoke in haste.'

He nodded, mollified, and the conversation appeared to be at an end. But you *are* conniving at murder, I thought, tucking the penknife away in my pocket. And so am I, if I agree to leave this business unfinished.

I took a bed in one of the guest rooms as Jacopo had suggested, but I could not sleep. Thoughts of Queen Louise, Paul, Léonie and the *Gelosi* tumbled through my mind as I lay there in my clothes, staring at the ceiling while my candle burned lower and listening to the sounds of the household preparing to turn in for the night, until silence settled over the house. From a nearby street I heard church bells tolling twelve. I rose as quietly as possible, pulled Gabrielle's cloak around my shoulders and tiptoed to the door. When I was certain no one was stirring, I crept downstairs and found my boots in the hallway. I could not let Francesco and Isabella and their friends remain incarcerated and lose their livelihood because of my recklessness when it was me that Guise wanted. Privately

I thought Jacopo over-optimistic in his assertion that the Duchess of Montpensier would not harm them; the rule of law had deteriorated so far in Paris that the Guises seemed to believe they were no longer subject to it. I doubted Catherine would make the players a priority while she was preoccupied with the King's health, but Jacopo was right that it would be folly to hand myself over to Guise or his sister alone. That left me with only one possible avenue. I would have to ask Paget for help.

The prospect of it stuck in my throat. I had no idea if he would consider it in his interest to do me another favour and I was all the more reluctant to ask now that I knew the truth about his relationship with Stafford, but it seemed he was close to the Duchess of Montpensier and he was my best hope of reasoning with her. I took a lantern, unbolted the front door and slipped out silently. Outside, the snowfall had slowed, a few stray flakes still drifting from the densely packed sky, though the ground was now a uniform white, rippled with violet shadows where the drifts rose and fell. The men-at-arms still waited by the gate, rigid and glassy-eyed with cold; they looked surprised to see me, but their orders were to stop unwanted visitors from getting in, so they let me pass without comment.

I could hardly feel my feet by the time I had reached the end of rue des Tournelles. The streets appeared ghostly and deserted; not even a seagull cried over the river, and I walked on virgin snow, as yet unmarked by footsteps. As I turned right on to the rue Saint-Antoine I believed myself alone in this strange, blue-white world. Perhaps this belief made me less vigilant; perhaps the snow muffled the sounds around me. I had barely walked twenty yards when out of nowhere a blade appeared at my neck and a voice hissed in my ear,

'Nice and still, now. Try not to make a noise.'

TWENTY-FIVE

Before I could gather my thoughts sufficiently to react, a thick hood was bundled over my head, my arms were seized roughly and bound at the wrists, and I was lifted up and thrown over the back of a horse. It all happened before I had time to cry out, not that it would have done me any good. No one spoke while I was jolted along in darkness; the only sound was muted hoofbeats on snow for fifteen or twenty minutes before I heard bolts scraping back and a gate being opened. I was dragged from the saddle and set on my feet, then shoved between two men up a short flight of steps and into a building, conscious all the time of the knife-point held to my ribs. The hood was only removed when I was pushed into a warm room and found myself standing before a table where the Duke of Guise sat with his hands folded, his eyes wintry in the dim light. It was not the grand salon where I had first seen him, but a small study, furnished only with the desk and a row of bookshelves along the wall opposite the fireplace. I was not even certain whose house I was in.

'And how is our friend the Comte de Saint-Fermin?' Guise asked, without preliminary, as the door closed and we were left alone with the whisper of the fire.

'I think the change of air has helped him,' I said, fighting to keep my voice even.

'No doubt. Has Corbinelli told Catherine about him?'

'Yes. He is under royal protection.' I did not know if this was true, but I thought it might improve the Count's chances of survival.

'Much good may it do him. Catherine is the last person who would wish to start raking over the ashes of Saint Bartholomew's night with accusations.' He returned his attention to the papers in front of him for a few moments, leaving me to wait, before raising his eyes and fixing me with a reproachful stare. 'You stole my horse, Bruno. What will it be next? Sleeping with my wife?'

'I would stop at the horse if I were you,' murmured a laconic voice in English behind me. 'If you've seen his wife.'

I turned to see Paget leaning against a cabinet in a shadowy corner of the room, turning a letter round by its edges between his fingers. He offered a conspiratorial smirk, though I doubted now that I could rely on much support from that quarter.

'Quiet, Paget,' Guise said. 'Well?'

I turned back to him. 'I am sorry about the horse, my lord. I only meant to borrow him – I acted on impulse. I trust he was returned to you unharmed?'

'If he'd been harmed, you'd be dead by now,' Guise said, without emotion. 'He and I have been through battles together. He's worth far more than you are, even as dead meat. On top of that, my sister seems to think you have broken into her private study and stolen some letters.'

'I have stolen nothing from the Duchess, my lord.' I felt that deference was the best way to help myself and the *Gelosi*.

'You'll understand why we find that difficult to believe. What were you looking for?'

I hesitated. 'In truth, my lord, I was trying to find out if she had been the mistress of Frère Joseph de Chartres.'

405

'My sister?' The Duke's expression hovered somewhere between amused and incredulous. 'Did you hear that, Paget?'

'Bruno evidently does not know the Duchess's reputation for chastity,' Paget remarked from his corner, not without an undertone of resentment.

'I thought all Paris knew of it,' the Duke said drily. 'What on earth led you to that theory, Bruno?'

'The fact that she was close to him. There was talk among the other friars at Saint-Victor that he was involved with a married woman. And the way we found him – it seemed likely he had been intimate with someone before he was killed.'

'So you are accusing my sister of murder as well as fornication?' He arched an eyebrow.

'I was investigating a suspicious death, my lord, as you ordered me to.'

'I didn't mean you to start pointing at my family.' His voice had risen; he paused to bring it back under control. 'So, then. Did you find anything to suggest your theory was correct?'

'No. And I no longer believe the Duchess to have been involved with de Chartres in any sense.'

'Well, we are all mightily relieved to hear that, I am sure.' His eyes narrowed in scrutiny. 'But you must have found other letters of interest to you. Or to your associates.'

I thought of the letter to the Spanish ambassador. 'I do not recall anything I read, my lord. I was looking only for love letters and found none.'

He gave a tight smile and picked up a silver seal from his desk, running his fingers over the ridges of its design. 'No, I don't suppose my sister goes in for that sort of thing. Not that she would leave lying around, anyway. So if the Duchess was not de Chartres's killer, have you a new theory?'

I took a deep breath. 'I have an idea, my lord.'

'Really?' He sat back in his chair and folded his arms, watching me, his face expectant. 'You have my full attention.'

'I believe it was a young woman in Catherine's service,' I began, making my voice as strong and steady as I could. 'A member of her Flying Squadron. Léonie de Châtillon.'

I saw him exchange a glance with Paget. 'Interesting. And why did she kill him, in your view?'

'I believe she was his lover.'

Guise let out a snort of laughter at this.

'Busy girl,' Paget murmured. Guise silenced him and motioned for me to continue.

'She had persuaded him to pass on intelligence about League activities, which she conveyed to Catherine,' I said, warming to my theory as I extemporised it. 'But the priest Lefèvre found out and threatened to expose him. Léonie persuaded Joseph to kill the priest, and then she killed him in turn to keep his silence. But she was overcome with remorse and took her own life three nights ago at the Tuileries ball.'

Guise continued to watch me for a long moment, passing the seal from hand to hand. I remained there without moving, looking directly at him, afraid to blink in case my expression gave anything away. The shadows deepened around us. Eventually he set the seal down as if he had come to a decision.

'It's a neat hypothesis,' he said. 'What do you think, Paget? Credible?'

'Certainly no more implausible than any other intrigue in Paris,' Paget said, with apparent indifference.

'Hm. It was a good try, Bruno.' Guise pushed his chair back from the desk and stood. 'But I'm afraid I don't believe it any more than you do.'

'I don't know what you mean, my lord.' I tensed my jaw to avoid betraying any emotion.

'There is a flaw in your theory, you see. Joseph de Chartres was murdered on the 28th of November. Léonie de Châtillon was with me that day. Most of the day, in fact. So it could not have been her, and I think you know it. Which leads me

407

to wonder who you are protecting. Because I was right, was I not – everything points back to the Louvre?'

'I am protecting no one, my lord, I swear it. I concluded it was Léonie from the available evidence. If what you say proves me wrong, I will have to begin again.'

'There's no time for that. I've been indulgent with you, Bruno. I thought you might be persuaded to make yourself useful. And in a curious way I admire your bloody-mindedness. But my patience has run out.' He cracked his knuckles, causing me to jump. 'It's clear your loyalties will always lie with the enemies of the true Church. Although we're not even sure who you're spying for, are we, Paget? Henri or the English?'

'Perhaps both,' Paget said, behind me. 'Whoever is the highest bidder.'

'You would know about that,' I said, without turning around. I saw Guise give him a nod. He stepped forward into the pool of candlelight that surrounded the desk.

'Talking of letters, Bruno – we'd be interested to know what this one says.' He held out the paper he had been toying with. My stomach jolted with the sensation of missing a step as I saw that it was my letter to Walsingham about Gilbert Gifford, the one I had asked Stafford to send by urgent courier. The ambassador must have handed it over to Paget instead of sending it with the diplomatic packet, perhaps fearful that I had uncovered his situation.

'Could you not manage the cipher?' I said.

'Ah, Bruno.' Paget laid the letter on the desk and gave me an indulgent smile. 'Your arrogance is almost endearing sometimes. I shall miss it.'

'For the sake of your Italian friends,' Guise said, the mock-politeness vanished, 'it would be best if you stop wasting time and cooperate.'

'This has nothing to do with the players,' I said, my voice rising in panic. 'You must let them go – they have done nothing wrong.'

'Apart from smuggling a man into my sister's house to steal from her. Though I'm sure she'll feel more lenient when she has her letters back.'

'There were no letters taken, I swear to it. Please – you must tell her to release them. They need to travel tomorrow.'

The Duke's eyes grew cold. 'Never use the word *must* to me, Bruno. Perhaps I can do something for your friends, when you've told me what's in this message to Francis Walsingham.' He nodded to the paper on the desk.

'You see, we fear you may have said something disobliging about us,' Paget added, in a pleasant tone, standing close behind me so that I could feel his breath on the back of my neck.

'General observations only,' I said, keeping my eyes fixed on Guise. 'I mention the death at the Tuileries ball, the King's present illness. I say that the city is restless since no one has been brought to justice for the priest's murder. I ask him for money. That is all.'

Paget laughed softly at my back. 'I wish you luck with that last one. But it's hard to see why any of that should require such an urgent dispatch as you have demanded. We'd be happier if you'd copy out the cipher and then translate this letter in full, word for word, so we have a more precise understanding.'

'I do not have the cipher here. It's extremely complex.'

'No doubt,' he murmured. 'But you are an expert in the art of memory, so I'm sure you have committed it to the great map of your mind. You only wrote the thing two days ago, after all.'

'What does it matter? You are holding the only copy in your hand. All you need do is destroy it, if you fear its contents.'

'If only we could trust you in that regard, Bruno. But you are a slippery fish. You might have made a copy, or passed on the contents to some other messenger as a safeguard. That's why we need to verify what you have said.'

'I will give you some time to think it over,' Guise cut in, gesturing towards the door. I turned to see Paget open it to admit two men-at-arms. 'If I have a full and honest translation of that letter by dawn, your actor friends will come to no harm. Paget, accompany my guest to his quarters, would you? Reunite him with his old acquaintance.' He made a short, barking sound that might have been laughter.

I looked at him for some clue to his meaning, cold with fear at the suggestion that he had already brought in someone known to me, perhaps as another means of bargaining. Francesco, or one of the others? Sophia? Surely he would not dare detain anyone with connections, such as Jacopo or Gabrielle? But he had already returned his attention to his papers; he raised his head briefly to nod at the armed men, who closed in on either side and marched me swiftly back into the corridor. Paget followed, swirling a cloak over his shoulders.

'I rather fear your luck has run out, Bruno,' he murmured, in English, as we were led into a snow-shrouded courtyard lit by flickering torches. 'You'd be wise to tell him what he wants to know voluntarily – he will have it from you one way or another. I don't think I can help you this time.'

'I would not expect you to,' I said quietly, stumbling over a drift of snow as I was shoved forward. 'I was never persuaded that we were on the same side, Paget.'

'And yet, in a strange way we always were, despite our difference of religion,' he mused, quickening his pace so that he walked alongside me as we approached a row of outbuildings where I could see two more armed men stamping their feet outside a door. 'You are a spy, as I am. You should not take any of this personally—' he motioned to the guards. 'It's one of the hazards of the enterprise. We court danger knowingly, you and I. But I will tell you this.' He planted himself in front of me and pointed a finger in my face, bringing us to an abrupt halt; the guards exchanged glances, but decided to defer to his authority and waited. 'I know how you regard me, Bruno,' Paget said. 'You think me a mere mercenary, with no higher motive than profit, and that allows you to believe yourself superior to me – you who grub about in the sewers of intelligence work out of a lofty sense of principle. Am I mistaken?'

I said nothing, only returned his stare, impassive.

'I know more about honour than a man like you could ever hope to understand,' he continued, undeterred. 'I am the son of a baron. My father was secretary to Henry the Eighth, and since childhood I have watched my family name torn to shreds and ground into the dirt under the heels of Protestant councillors who were not worthy to empty my father's privy. If you think me a cynic in matters of religion, you could not be more mistaken. My faith *is* my honour. The two cannot be separated. I am an Englishman *and* a Catholic, and all the work I do here is so that one day I may stand on my native soil without being forced to choose between them.'

'I would applaud that moving speech if my hands were free,' I said. His expression hardened.

'Monsieur, we have to take the prisoner in,' one of the guards said apologetically. He, at least, had given up the pretence that I was being treated as a guest.

'Take him away. I have nothing more to say to him.' Paget gestured towards the low brick building where the guards stamped their feet and blew on their fingers outside the door. As we approached, I heard a low, wordless moaning from within, like the bellowing of a wounded bull. The men on the door pointedly did not look in the direction of this sound, save for the occasional darting glance, tinged with fear. I looked down and saw that the snow around the door was churned up and stained pink. Paget snapped his fingers towards the guards; the one who slid back the bolts recoiled as he did so.

The noise swelled horribly as the door swung open and the reek of hot blood hit my nostrils through the clean, icy air.

Inside, a lantern swung from a beam in the ceiling; though the candle inside had almost burned down, there was enough light to make out a series of shapes hanging from the rafters, swaying on their hooks as if with some slow rhythm of their own, lifeless limbs dangling like pendulums. My initial terror subsided as I saw that the room was a cold store, hung with the carcasses of deer for the winter. The channels cut into the floor showed that it was also a slaughterhouse, indeed had been used for that purpose very recently, as the drains ran scarlet with fresh blood. I clenched my teeth and prayed that it was an animal, but the sound had already led me to expect the worst.

'Oh, sweet Jesus,' I breathed, standing in the doorway, as my eyes adjusted enough for me to understand what I was looking at.

Hanging from the central hook, between the carcasses, was a person, or what remained of one. On the floor beneath him a pool of blood had spread from the stumps of his limbs where his hands and feet had recently been cut off and bound with dirty tourniquets. His face was also covered with blood, though I could see he had lost an eye, and when he opened his mouth to howl again, I realised his tongue had been cut out, so that all he could utter were those gurgling, inhuman cries. He was suspended by a rope tied around his chest and strung under his arms.

'You know this man, I believe,' Paget said, but his voice was quiet and tight; even his flippancy withered in the face of such horror. My stomach heaved and the guard to my right had to catch me and hold me upright as my knees buckled and I slumped against him, though this was largely from relief. I did recognise this mutilated creature, but it was none of the people I had feared to see. The crust of blood over his features did not disguise the growth on his cheek. I was looking at the gaoler from the Conciergerie.

'I fear this was meant as a cautionary tale,' Paget murmured, still subdued. 'Guise wants you to understand what happens to those who fail to do what he asks of them.'

'Don't put me in there.' My throat had dried and my words came out in a thin croak. 'Please, Paget. By all that is holy—'

The gaoler convulsed with the effort of his cries. Paget shook his head as if absolving himself of responsibility.

'This is Guise's house, and you are here at his pleasure. These are not my methods, but there's nothing I can do. It's up to you now, Bruno. I advise you to tell him everything he wants to know while you still have your tongue, and you may yet save yourself. It's too late for this one.' He gestured towards the gaoler with the toe of his boot. 'I told you there would come a day when you would wish you'd answered when I asked you nicely.'

'Is Guise letting him bleed out like an animal? Is that the idea?'

'He won't be allowed to die,' Paget said, without emotion. 'That would be too merciful. He'll be dumped before dawn at a leper chapel somewhere outside the city. Let the nuns take him in. Guise has left him one eye so he can see the disgust on people's faces for the rest of his life as he tries to beg for alms. See the children scream and run away at his approach.' He turned to me, his eyes unexpectedly candid. 'Don't be a fool any longer, Bruno. Guise could do the same to you without breaking a sweat, before the bells sound the next hour. He would make sure even your own mother wouldn't recognise your corpse. This wretch is here to make sure you know it. Swallow your pride and throw yourself on his mercy. It's all you can do.'

'But he will kill me anyway,' I said, my voice thinned almost to nothing.

'That is between you and him now,' Paget said. Then, to my amazement, he reached out and clasped my shoulders with both hands, a brief and thoroughly English attempt at an

413

embrace, more expressive in its reserve than any full-bodied Italian bear-hug; that one gesture told me with absolute certainty that he expected me to die.

Paget walked away towards the house without looking back, though I called after him; I was pushed, still protesting, into the storeroom with the mutilated gaoler and heard the bolt slide home behind me.

The sound he made was interminable; a raw moan with no accent or syllable, a low, shapeless, animal howl of pain that poured from his ruined mouth along with the flow of blood. I walked the edge of the room over bloodstained straw, shouldering past the headless bodies of animals, until I found a row of straw bales against the far wall. I sat down and tried not to look at him but it was impossible to wrench my gaze away; the way he swung back and forth between the swaying carcasses, fixing me with his one remaining eye every time he moved into view, trying to lift one bloodied stump of a wrist towards me in a gesture of pleading. I huddled into Gabrielle's cloak, breathing in its fragrance as a defence against the overpowering smell of blood and tried to gather my thoughts through the noise. I could tell Guise everything I knew about the murders, including my conclusions about Catherine and my belief that Joseph de Chartres's killer was someone at court, even if I did not yet know who. Would that be enough to appease him? I doubted it; I had defied him too many times for him to let me live, for the sake of his honour. Royal protection was the only thing that might save me, if Catherine or Henri were prepared to bargain for my life; Jacopo might guess that I had gone to plead for the *Gelosi* when he woke and found me missing, but that would not be until the next morning, and the day would be well advanced before he could get word to the Louvre and track me down. Guise had given me until dawn. No one was coming for me. I would have to save myself.

I cast my eyes around the walls in the dim light. There

were no windows, though a fierce draught blew in through the rafters from the thatched roof overhead. The only door was the one through which we had entered, now bolted on the outside and guarded by two armed men. My wrists were still bound, but the cord was thin enough that I hoped it could be severed, if only I could find something sharp-edged. The candle in the lantern guttered behind smeared glass and I thought I caught a flicker of movement in the reflection. I whipped around and craned my neck to see a pale shape above me, hunched and watchful, sidestepping on the rafters, piercing eyes in white feathers. I flinched at its talons, but after a few minutes the owl evidently decided there was nothing to hold her attention here and vanished into a corner of the roof before I heard her screech rising into the air outside.

I stood on a bale and peered up to see where she had disappeared. This was where the draught was coming from; there must be a hole in the thatch. My pulse quickened; if it was big enough for an owl, perhaps it could be worked on until it would fit a smallish man. I jumped down and kicked the bale until it was directly under an empty meat hook. When I climbed up again, I could just reach my arms high enough to catch the bonds on the point; it was slow work and painful – I tore my skin repeatedly – but eventually I had frayed the rope enough to pull one strand apart and loosen the others until my hands were free. I glanced at the door but it remained firmly closed. I could only hope that the ghastly sight of my fellow prisoner would be sufficient deterrent to keep the guards outside.

Before I could lose my nerve, I began to drag all the bales of straw together as quietly as I could and pile them up in the corner directly under the gap where the owl had vanished. Through the forest of hanging animals the gaoler glimpsed what I was doing and took up his keening with renewed force. I could not tell if he was shouting encouragement or trying to alert the guards, but the end result would be the same. I hissed at him to be quiet, though I was not sure he even heard me. I heaved the last bale up and judged the stack high enough for me to attempt to reach the roof beams, just as his pitch and volume increased to a frenzy and was answered by a furious banging on the door. I froze, dreading that the guard would open the door and see my makeshift steps.

'Shut that fucking noise or I'll come in there and shut it for you,' shouted a rough voice from outside.

'How? They've already cut his tongue out,' I called in response.

'I'll cut yours out as well if you don't pack it in,' the guard yelled back, through the door. It was an empty threat; he could do nothing without Guise, but it would not help me if he chose to relieve his boredom by coming in to remind me that he was in charge. I decided to do as I was told. I fought my way back through the carcasses to the grotesque body suspended from the central beam, forced myself to look up at his mutilated face and pressed a finger to my lips. But even in the fading light I could tell that he barely saw me; the stumps of his limbs were still bleeding profusely, despite the tourniquets that had been tied, I guessed, by men whose expertise was learned on the battlefield. Gradually his cries grew weaker and his spasms stilled as his head slumped on to his chest. I doubted he would last the night. Though I would not have wished his fate on any man, it was hard not to recall how the gaoler had used the same words to me when I was in the oubliette, nor the leering contempt in the way he had laughed at his prisoner's distress, with his tiny shred of power. How slippery our grasp on our position in the world, I thought. But I intended to hang on to mine a little longer. As I stood watching him, the lone candle in the lantern flickered and died, plunging the room into blackness.

I waited a moment for my eyes to adjust. The place seemed all the more sinister now, the dead deer solid black shapes against a deeper dark, their cold flesh thudding against me as

I stumbled back to the far corner and scaled my stack of straw bales until I could almost reach the roof beam overhead. I could just distinguish it from the surrounding shadows; I would have to jump to catch hold, and if I fell, the guards would surely hear. I screwed up my courage and launched myself upwards, managing to hook my hands around the beam, though the pile of bales tumbled to the floor with the force of the movement and I swung there for a few moments, afraid to move in case the sound had alerted the men outside. But the door remained shut; I released my breath, tensed and swung my legs up to fasten my ankles around the beam. I was fortunate that it was solid oak, made strong enough to bear the weight of dead meat. I pulled myself up until I was sitting astride it and shunted along by inches, feeling my way to the corner where the wall met the sloping edge of the roof. Here I could breathe in ice-edged night air through a hole where the thatch had rotted, though when I reached up and groped around I found that the gap was far too small for anything much bigger than an owl to pass through. But the roof was in poor repair, and a handful came away in my fist when I grasped it. Leaning in and gripping the beam with my left hand, I began to tear away at the reeds, ignoring the pain as they sliced my palm and my numb fingers, terrified that someone would see what I was doing from outside or that one of the guards would open the door to check on us. After a few minutes, I had pulled away a hole large enough to poke my head through.

Outside I could see nothing except the ink-blue of the sky above me and the snow on the sloping roof of the building all around. There was no way of knowing if anyone would see me emerge, but I had no choice left; at least this way I would die trying to save myself. But I realised I could not fit through the gap still wearing Gabriel's fur cloak; reluctantly I unfastened it and let it fall to the floor. I manoeuvred my legs so that my feet were braced against the beam and pushed hard against it, forcing one arm and shoulder through the hole as the wet reeds broke away. I had almost squeezed my torso through when I heard another shuddering groan from the gaoler below me, followed by the sound of cursing and the scrape of a bolt being driven back. I had only a few moments; I clawed frantically at the thatch around my chest, then pushed with the flat of my hand on the roof either side, using all my strength to lever myself through. I drew my legs up just as I heard the door open below me. It would take the guard a minute or two to realise in the darkness that one of his prisoners was missing – or so I hoped. I eased along the snow-laden roof towards the back of the building and saw that ten or twelve feet beyond it lay the boundary wall of the grounds. I dug my heels in, sliding to a precarious halt at the edge of the roof just as staccato shouts rang through the air below. I calculated; I would have to launch myself from the edge of the roof on to the wall and without the advantage of a running start I was not sure I could jump the distance – to say nothing of the difficulty of landing on a narrow wall that was visible only thanks to the pale line of snow along its crenellations. The shouting below grew louder; glancing down, I saw that one of the guards had appeared around the edge of the building and was calling to the other. Any minute now he would look up and see me. I took a deep breath, tensed every muscle into a crouch and sprang forward into the air, as a wild cry went up behind me. The snow on the wall glittered with extraordinary clarity as I hurtled towards it, legs flailing; in an instant, my fingers made contact with the stone and scrabbled for purchase, almost slipping as I clawed on to soft snow, but I clung on by my fingertips, bracing with my feet against the wall until I could pull myself up to the top and drop down on the other side.

Voices rang out through the hard-edged air; a dog barked, joined by another. I scrambled to my feet and ran blindly through the white street, not knowing which direction I was taking, my only thought to get as far away as possible before Guise sent his soldiers after me. I wove through unfamiliar roads lit with an eerie blue glow from the snow, hampered by the powdery drifts underfoot, hearing at my back faint cries and the frenzied yapping of the dogs. Fear lent me speed and numbed me to the pain in my leg and the cuts on my hands; I felt the cold burning in my lungs with every ragged breath, until I skidded around a corner and saw the black expanse of the Seine ahead. I slowed my pace, snatching breaths, trying to make a decision. I could not go home; Guise would know where to find me. Nor could I go back to Jacopo's – his thugs had followed me there already. There was only one place in Paris where I would be safe from the Duke of Guise, even if it did not guarantee safety from any other enemies. As I caught a chorus of dogs in the distance, I broke into a run again, heading along the Right Bank in the direction of the Tuileries palace.

TWENTY-SIX

I tapped discreetly at the small back gate but it had no effect. I tried hammering harder. At length this brought a tired face, raw with cold, to the grille in the door.

'Are you Rémy?'

'Who's asking?'

'I need to see Gabrielle de la Tour.' I glanced over my shoulder but it seemed I had shaken off my pursuers for now. Even so, bruised and bleeding, I could not have looked more like a fugitive; the manner of my arrival clearly did not inspire confidence. The gatekeeper observed me as you might an escaped lunatic.

'It's the middle of the night,' he pointed out.

'She told me to come to you.' I was shivering violently now that my burst of energy had subsided.

'Mate,' the man said wearily, 'everyone's tucked up in bed. Do me a favour and piss off, will you? Try again in the morning. Don't make me send anyone out to get rid of you.'

'Look.' I scrabbled in my purse for my last remaining coins. 'Could you at least get a message to her? Tell her I am here – if she won't see me, I have lost nothing and you have gained.'

He eyed the money suspiciously, then shut the grille in my

face. I stamped my feet, my gaze flitting anxiously back along the road, until a moment later the door swung open a few inches and I found myself staring at the point of a broadsword. This Rémy was a short man in a fur hat and gloves, his figure made almost spherical by the several coats he appeared to be wearing, but the man-at-arms who stood behind him was as solid and muscled as a warhorse. I was nodded inside to stand by a brazier burning behind the gate. The soldier lowered his sword and checked me over for weapons while Rémy inspected the silver écu in my palm before tucking it into the depths of his coats.

'Wait here with me,' he said. He pointed to the guard. 'You. Go and tell her ladyship she's got a visitor. What's your name?' He turned back.

I hesitated, but there seemed no use in subterfuge. 'Bruno. She's expecting me.'

Laughter gurgled deep in Rémy's layers. 'If you say so.' He jerked his head towards the palace and the other man stamped away into the dark. I huddled closer to the brazier, holding out my hands towards the flames, flinching as the feeling slowly returned and I became aware that my palms were cross-hatched with a hundred tiny cuts from the thatched roof and my wrists scored with gashes from the meat hook.

'Cold tonight,' I remarked, after a few minutes, tucking my hands into my armpits. The snow around us seemed to glitter with its own light. My teeth were clattering so severely that I feared I would bite my tongue.

'Mate.' Rémy leaned against the wall and gave me a look of infinite patience. 'I haven't seen you. Understand? We don't need to be friends.'

'Right.' I drew my chin into my chest and inched as near as I could to the flame without setting myself alight. After a while he sighed, levered himself off the wall and disappeared into the small wooden hut that served as his sentry box, emerging with a rough woollen blanket.

'Put that round you,' he said, 'or you'll freeze your bollocks off and you'll be no use to her then.'

I thanked him and wrapped the blanket around my shoulders. It smelled of dog. Twenty minutes or more passed before the guard returned and handed me a folded sheet of paper without speaking. I opened it to find a hastily scribbled note.

This man will take you to my maidservant. Do as she asks. I will be with you in an hour. G.

I stared at the paper for a few moments as a cold shiver prickled up my spine. Rémy nodded and I followed the guard past white trees and around the side of the nearest wing to a door where a young woman wrapped in the plain serge gown of a servant waited for us with a lantern. She led me inside the palace, up a flight of back stairs and along unlit corridors until we reached a door which she unlocked with a key from her belt and stood back, ushering me inside. I found myself in a modest bedchamber, dominated by a large carved bed hung with embroidered curtains. Under the narrow window stood a table covered with cosmetics, brushes, hairpins, vials of scent. An ivory undershift edged with lace had been draped casually over a chair. In the grate a small fire smouldered and the air smelled of perfume and spiced wine mixed with woodsmoke. The girl bowed out wordlessly, leaving me alone. As the door clicked shut I jerked around, suddenly afraid that she might lock me in, but I heard only the sound of her footsteps padding away down the passage. I dragged the chair over to the fire and threw on another log from a basket in the hearth, then took out Gabrielle's note and re-read it. I supposed the delay meant she was with another man, but I could not shake off a growing sense of unease.

I must have drifted into sleep; I jerked awake at the sound

of the door and turned to see Gabrielle lock it softly behind her and press a finger to her lips. Her hair hung loosely down her back and she wore a thick embroidered robe tied at the waist with a silk girdle.

'I'm glad you changed your mind, Bruno,' she murmured, gliding across to stand behind me, her fingers slowly kneading my shoulders. 'Did you decide I was a better option than work or sleep?'

I smiled. 'Something like that.' I could hardly tell her I had changed my mind because she was a better option than having my hands cut off by the Duke of Guise.

'Let me get you a drink,' she said, leaning over me and stroking her fingers down my chest.

'No,' I said, too emphatically. Her other hand stopped working the base of my neck. 'I mean to say, I have no need of anything.'

'I hope you don't think I would try to poison you, Bruno.' She moved around to stand in front of me, her eyes glittering.

'I would not put anything past you, Gabrielle.' I was still smiling, but she knew I was not joking.

'Well, then,' she said, in a lighter tone, 'let's not waste any more time.' She loosened the silk tie of her robe and let it fall to the ground. I let my gaze travel up the line of her naked body until my eyes met hers, frank and defiant.

'You'll catch cold,' I said feebly.

'Then you had better warm me up.' She took my hand and led me to the bed, blowing out the candles on the way. I tore off my doublet and felt expert fingers unfastening the laces of my shirt. The sheets were icy against my skin, but her body seemed to radiate heat as she wrapped herself around me in the dark.

'So,' she whispered, her tongue flicking at my earlobe, 'is it true that you are trying to find out who killed Léonie?'

'What?' I rolled over to face her. 'Where did you get that idea?'

'Catherine mentioned it. Henri told her he wanted you to find the truth, apparently.'

She kept her voice casual, teasing, but I tensed and I knew she felt it. I wondered if it was true that Henri had told his mother about finding Léonie's killer, or if Catherine had learned of it from Balthasar listening outside the oratory door. Either way, it was not good news for me; if Catherine feared I was drawing close to her plot against the Queen, she might take it upon herself to silence me before I could tell Henri. Perhaps, even now, I had unwittingly walked into her scheme.

'Does anyone else know I am here?' I asked.

She slid her hand over my chest and rested it on my stomach, tracing small circles with her fingers. 'Don't be absurd. Catherine would be furious if she knew. We are only supposed to grant our favours where she directs, and at present my attentions are engaged elsewhere.'

'Not with your husband, I presume.'

She laughed. 'Of course not. What purpose would that serve? One of Navarre's confidants, if you must know. But these great men don't like to feel they are sharing their mistresses with all-comers. Hence the need for discretion.' She allowed her hand to drift lower until her fingers folded decisively around my slumbering cock. 'So do you know yet who killed her?' Her voice was thick and smooth as honey. I closed my eyes.

'No,' I said, though this was a lie. Now I believed I did know. 'Do you?'

Her hair brushed my chest. 'I told you,' she said, her words muffled as she disappeared under the covers, 'all the girls are afraid. We don't know who to fear. We want to find this man as urgently as the King does.'

I lay still as she wriggled down and worked on me with her mouth, but my thoughts whirled, my senses straining for any tell-tale sound outside the bed curtains. Despite her best efforts, my body remained tense and unresponsive. Eventually she emerged, brushing her hair out of her face. I could just see the glint of her eyes in the dark.

'What's wrong?'

'Sorry. It's not you. I have a lot on my mind.'

'Your mind is never easy. Something troubling you?' She ran a finger along my upper lip. 'You know, you can always tell me. Perhaps I can help.'

'It's nothing.' I offered a wan smile. 'Nothing a good sleep won't cure, at least.'

She sank back on to the pillow beside me. I could tell she was piqued.

'That was a lot of effort to smuggle you in, if all you want to do is sleep.'

'Sorry to disappoint you,' I said coldly.

'Oh, Bruno.' She let out an extravagant sigh and flung her leg over my thigh. 'I shouldn't have started talking about murder. I don't suppose that helped. But I'm glad you're here. Get some rest. There's always the morning.' She kissed me lightly on the brow and burrowed her face into my neck.

'Good night,' I whispered, but I lay awake staring at the canopy overhead long after her breathing had settled into the gentle rhythm of sleep.

I woke into a chilly dawn, the room strangely lit by a gleam of snow outside filtering through a gap in the drapes. Gabrielle still slept, her limbs thrown out carelessly, one arm across my hips. I eased myself out from under it – she stirred, made a small animal noise in her sleep, settled back again – and slipped out through the bed curtains, scrabbling to find my clothes in the half-light. I dressed hastily, pulling on my boots, still damp from last night's snow. I had to find my way out of the Tuileries and across to the Louvre before the households awoke. Now that I was sure I knew who had killed Joseph de Chartres and Léonie de Châtillon, I needed to take that information to the King before Catherine guessed that I had

425

it; thereafter it would be in his hands. I also needed to beg for royal protection; Henri was the only person now who could stand between me and Guise. I had little doubt that the Duke would have someone waiting for me the moment I tried to return home.

I crept to the door and found, to my dismay, that it was locked; I remembered Gabrielle locking it behind her last night but I had been half-asleep and had not noticed what she did with the key. The robe she had discarded with such a flourish lay in a heap by the fireplace; I rummaged through its folds but found nothing. I cast around the room, trying to guess where else she might have hidden a key. The fact that she had not left it in the door only quickened my anxiety; had she wanted to make sure I could not leave? I heard the rustling of sheets as she turned over and an idea struck me; poking my head back inside the bed curtains, I slid my hand under the pillow beneath her head until my fingers touched metal. I tried to work in further so I could ease the key out, but at that moment she rolled back towards me, the weight of her head trapping my hand. I gripped the base of the key between the tips of my first and second fingers and, holding my breath, pulled it out in one swift movement; I saw her eyelids flicker as I did so, and just as I withdrew, I heard her sleepily mumble my name in a question.

I reached the door, unlocked it, was almost through when her tousled head appeared through the curtains, her expression somewhere between angry and puzzled.

'Where are you going?'

'Quick errand,' I said, the door already open. 'I'll be back.'

'No – you can't.' She spoke sharply; almost immediately she seemed to realise her error, and a slow smile curved across her face. 'I mean, you can't leave me unsatisfied, Bruno. Come back under the covers. I'll make it worth your while, I promise.'

But I had seen the flash of panic on her face that only confirmed my suspicions. She had already jumped out of bed with surprising speed. I glanced down at the key in my hand and in an instant made my decision.

'Sorry,' I whispered, as I slipped out of the door and turned the key in the lock behind me.

'Bruno!' She pounded on the door from the other side. 'For God's sake!'

But I was already halfway down the corridor. It was not ideal; she would probably wake the household before long, but if I had time to make my way between the palaces without interruption that would be enough.

I emerged into the cold light, into air that smelled of frost and smoke. Even at this hour, the courtyard was already bustling; men struggled to pull barrows stacked with firewood through the rutted snow; others rolled barrels towards the kitchens while women hauled buckets and sacks across their shoulders, bent under the weight. I kept my head down, chin tucked into the collar of my doublet, trying not to draw unwanted attention.

I crossed the rear courtyard of the Tuileries without incident and passed through the gate in the boundary wall that separated it from the Louvre. Here my task became more difficult; there would be several ranks of guards between me and the King's private chambers and I could expect to be swiftly detained as soon as I tried to get past them. As I edged around the chapel of Saint-Nicolas, I noticed that the door was ajar. I peered inside; there seemed to be no one about except an elderly priest lighting the candles by the altar at the far end for the early Mass. As long as he did not turn around and see me, my luck might hold. There was a closed door to my left; I tried the handle and to my immense relief it opened into a small sacristy, barely bigger than a closet, where vestments hung in rows on the wall. I snatched up a cassock, stole and biretta as quickly as I could, bundling them under my arm; as I was about to leave, I grabbed a prayer book from a table and dashed from the chapel just as I heard the old priest call out to ask who was there.

In the shadow of the porch I pulled on the cleric's garb, arranged the stole around my neck, and set off towards the King's apartments, praying I would not run into anyone who might recognise me.

But no one seemed to look beyond my clothes; at the sight of the priest's garments doors opened and I was waved through by guards until I found myself outside the King's private chamber, where a number of well-dressed young men lounged in an anteroom. None of them paid me any attention beyond an initial glance of boredom. By the fire, I noticed the physician who had been waiting outside the oratory the day before; I turned my face away, pulled the hat down and approached the soldiers guarding the door.

'His Majesty sent for me,' I said, with as much authority as I could muster. They looked at one another as if seeking confirmation. One tapped on the door. After a moment it was opened to reveal – to my dismay – Balthasar de Beaujoyeux, impeccably groomed, despite the early hour.

'Bruno? Good Lord. How did you get in here?' His eyes narrowed as he took in my appearance. 'The costume ball is over, you know.'

'I need to see the King,' I said, lowering my eyes and forcing myself to sound humble. 'Please, Balthasar. It's urgent.'

'He's not receiving visitors.' Balthasar glanced at the guards. 'What do you want?'

'It's a private matter.'

'Catherine has instructed that he is not be disturbed, especially with news that might upset him. You had better come and tell her your urgent business. She can decide if he is strong enough.'

'I can't do that.'

'I think you will.' He nodded to the guards. One stepped forward and took hold of my arm.

'Your Majesty,' I cried out, struggling as the soldier tightened his grip.

'Who's there?' came Henri's voice, from inside the chamber.

'It's Bruno,' I shouted, trying to wrench my arm away.

'Well, for God's sake come in, then,' the King called back, peevishly. The guard looked at Balthasar, who sighed and motioned for him to release me.

Henri was sitting up in bed, a book in his lap and a robe draped around his shoulders. He still looked pale and his eyes were ringed with purple shadow, though he seemed more alert than the previous day. I bowed; he beckoned me to approach his bedside, frowning.

'Why are you dressed as a priest?'

'It's a long story.'

'I'm sorry, Your Majesty,' Balthasar cut in. 'I told him you were resting. I have no idea how he managed to get into your private apartments.'

'Don't be ridiculous.' Henri shot him an irritable glance. 'It's only Bruno. Yesterday you couldn't push him into my presence fast enough. What are you doing here at this hour, Bruno?'

'I have more pressing news, sire.'

'Well, go on then.' He closed his book and drew himself upright, looking interested.

I glanced sidelong at Balthasar, who was standing at my elbow as if ready to wrestle me to the ground, should the need arise.

'It would be better done in private, sire.'

'Really?' Henri's expression grew more animated. 'You heard him, Balthasar. See yourself out.'

Balthasar gave me a wounded look, but he had the good grace not to argue with the King, and backed out of the room with a shallow bow. Henri took me by the wrist and drew me towards him. He had at least bathed since I was last this close.

'He'll be listening outside, of course,' he whispered, nodding to the door that had just closed. 'Scurrying back to my mother with snippets he's half-heard. Keep your voice down. Have you discovered anything? Do you know who killed Léonie?'

I dropped my voice so that it was barely audible. 'I believe I do, Your Majesty. It was the same person who killed Frère Joseph de Chartres, and coerced him into killing the priest Paul Lefèvre. And I also know who was behind all the deaths, and why.'

Henri grasped my wrist harder. 'Well?'

I hesitated. 'First, Your Majesty, I must extract a promise from you. I need your help.'

I did not miss the flicker of displeasure in his eyes. 'One does not usually bargain with princes, Bruno.'

'Nevertheless,' I pressed on, firmly, 'my situation is somewhat desperate. Since you asked me to look into these murders, I have crossed the Duke of Guise and now he wants to kill me.'

'Huh. That makes two of us.'

'In my case the danger is imminent. His men abducted me from outside Jacopo Corbinelli's house last night. I fear I won't elude him a second time unless you act in my defence.'

Henri's eyebrows arched upwards. 'Abducted? That does sound serious. I suppose I could ask my mother to have a word. He listens to her.'

'I was thinking more immediately of a bodyguard.'

He waved a hand, impatient. 'Yes, I'm sure we can find someone to see you home. But now tell me who this man is. I command you.'

I took a deep breath. 'It is not—'

But I was interrupted by the door opening to admit Balthasar again. He bowed low, but I did not miss the flash of malicious pleasure in the look he gave me.

'Your Majesty, forgive me,' he said, 'but a messenger has just arrived with all speed from the Tuileries. Your lady mother wants this man brought before her this instant.' He pointed theatrically at me. 'He broke into the palace last night, assaulted one of her ladies and locked her in a bedchamber.'

Henri's eyes widened. 'What an exciting night you've been having, Bruno,' he said. 'Breaking in, dressing up, assaulting ladies.'

'I did not assault anyone, Your Majesty.'

'Knowing the ladies of the Tuileries, Balthasar, I rather fear Bruno was the one whose virtue was in jeopardy there. They should be locked in their chambers more often.'

'Your Majesty,' Balthasar said, half-bowing to disguise the fact that he was attempting to give his sovereign orders, 'that may be, but the Queen Mother commands Doctor Bruno to appear before her immediately.'

Henri glanced towards the window, apparently deep in thought. Then, without warning, he swung his legs out of bed; I jumped back, startled, but he was already fully dressed.

'*You can tell my mother*' – he declared, in a voice that would have carried through all the anterooms; a king's voice, for once – 'that my friends are not hers to command. But – no—' he stopped, seeming to change his mind. 'Tell her we will come. You can deliver your news in her hearing, Bruno. See what she has to say about that.' He leaned heavily on my shoulder; despite his weakness, his face was lit by a perverse glee that verged on mania, as if the extreme melancholy of the past couple of days had metamorphosed into a frantic energy, darkly glittering and all the more dangerous.

'Your Majesty,' I began. From the corner of my eye I could see Balthasar twisting his hands together. 'I don't think that would be wise. Perhaps if you and I were to speak in private first, and you could acquaint Queen Catherine with the facts at your convenience, when you have had a chance to mull over—'

'Wise be damned,' Henri said, snapping his fingers. 'She is still insisting that Léonie's death was self-slaughter. I want to see her proved wrong to her face. Where is my sable cloak?'

'Your Majesty,' Balthasar stepped forward, his tone gently condescending, 'there is snow on the ground. Think of your

431

health. Your physician is outside, he will tell you the same. If you should take a chill and weaken yourself further—'

'For the love of Jesus, Balthasar—' Henri rounded on him, teeth clenched – 'I already have one mother. And that is more than sufficient, believe me.' He strode past us and picked up his cloak from a chair by the door. 'Fetch me my boots.' He turned to me. 'Come, Bruno. You can save your grand revelation for a bigger audience.'

I replied with a wan smile. As he had pointed out, only a fool would try to bargain with a king.

TWENTY-SEVEN

Though the sky was still barely light outside, we found Catherine formally dressed and seated expectantly on her high-backed chair with the crocodiles overhead. In the cold dawn, the stacks of artefacts and bric-a-brac surrounding her appeared worn and flat, like painted stage properties from another age. She gave a little cry of surprise as the King entered, supporting himself on my arm, and half-rose, a hand outstretched, her face creased in motherly anxiety.

'You should not be out of bed, my son,' she said, addressing him in Italian, as if maternal feelings expressed themselves instinctively in her own tongue.

'Sit down, Mother. Don't alarm yourself. I am much improved. Your doctor has purged me thoroughly.' Henri spoke in French, for the benefit of the rest of the company. Ruggieri sat beside the Queen Mother in an uncomfortable chair; his puffy features and drooping head suggested he had been hurried from his bed prematurely. Gabrielle perched on the edge of the dais at Catherine's feet, now dressed, her hair in artful disarray; she flashed me a look of pure fury as I entered. I found I could not meet her eye.

'I understand you wanted to see Doctor Bruno?' Henri

smiled pleasantly at his mother. 'I thought I would take the air and accompany him.'

Catherine glared at me, as if this were my doing. 'It was on a private matter.'

'It strikes me that there is too much private business going on in this palace lately. You know I don't like you having secrets from me, Mother.' Henri was still smiling, but there was steel in it. His fingers gripped my shoulder. 'Whatever you have to say, you may say it in the presence of your king.'

Catherine's face tightened almost imperceptibly at the subtle pulling of rank. 'You and I have spoken before about the company you keep,' she said, her voice taut. 'This man is a perfect example. He has been taking liberties. Twice in the last week he has found his way into my house under false pretences and absconded against my express orders. He has finagled his way into your wife's apartments. And now he has assaulted one of my women. The Duchess of Montpensier has written to me saying he broke into her house and took private letters before jumping out of a window and escaping on her brother's stolen horse. I say *enough*. A Neapolitan brawler, a thief and a known heretic, Henri. This is the man you choose as your confidant and your so-called tutor. What do you think people will say about you?'

'Blood of Christ, Mother! Bruno was out of Paris for three years – did people stop saying unpleasant things about me then? I cannot control what people say, not without closing every printing press in France, and that would not stop the ballads and skits in the tavern yards.' Henri let go of me and took a step towards her. Spittle flecked the corners of his mouth; his eyes bulged. 'I will not live my life in thrall to those fucking pamphleteers. Bitter little clerics truffling around in shit, with no—' he broke off, felled by an almighty coughing fit.

'Look to the King,' Catherine cried, rising effortfully from her chair. Balthasar and I dashed forward and caught Henri by the elbows, guiding him to an upholstered settle at the side of the room. Gabrielle rushed to bring him a glass of watered wine. When he had recovered, he raised his head and looked at me with admiration.

'Did you really steal Guise's horse?'

'I gave it back.'

He smiled, though it faded almost immediately. 'What were you doing with my wife?'

I glanced at Catherine. 'I was going to explain that, Your Majesty.'

'Listening to all manner of fanciful tales from a woman whose mind is clearly disturbed,' Catherine said, pinning me with her blackest stare. 'Barrenness can do that to the female brain, you know. Unbalance the humours. Tip women into madness, sometimes.'

'Well, you would know,' Henri said, heaving himself up again and crossing the room to stand before her. 'You were ten years married to my father before you first conceived, were you not, madam? While he was getting bastards all over France with his mistresses.'

Catherine gaped; her hand flew to her throat as if her son had struck her. I heard her attendants draw breath in shock.

'So do not be so quick to judge my wife,' he continued, in a voice like stone. 'Now sit down. Bruno has a story to tell, and I want you to hear it.'

'Really?' She looked back to me, a faint wrinkle of distaste forming across the bridge of her nose. 'I cannot help feeling the world would be a better place if Doctor Bruno learned to keep his thoughts to himself.'

'Not this time.' Henri held a hand out to me as if presenting me on a stage. 'Bruno has come to tell us who killed Léonie de Châtillon.'

Gabrielle gasped; I glanced over to see her pressing her hand to her mouth, wide eyes fixed on me.

'How clever of him,' Catherine said, with a dry laugh.

435

'When we already know. Two physicians have pronounced that she took her own life, God have mercy on her soul.'

'Madam,' Henri said, sounding tired, 'you pay your physicians to tell you what you wish to hear. Let us listen to Bruno's version.'

She snorted. 'Is he a doctor of medicine?'

'No, but he is a man of many subtle talents, one of which is probing into suspicious deaths, which is why I sent for him last month.' He gestured to me again. 'Speak, Bruno. Your audience is rapt.'

Catherine banged her stick on the stage. 'Clear the room. All of you – into the gallery. His Majesty the King may give credence to this Neapolitan fox but I will not have the rest of my household infected by his wild suppositions. Go on, out.' She thumped the stick again and her attendants hurried to obey. Gabrielle paused by the door and gave me a long look that seemed intended to communicate something, but I turned away.

When only the three of us were left in the room, Catherine motioned for Henri to sit beside her. 'I don't want you fainting again. Very well, then, Doctor Bruno – you have the floor. Tell us what you imagine happened that night.'

I cleared my throat and began.

'You asked me to look into the death of the priest Paul Lefèvre, Your Majesty,' I said, drawing myself up to face the King and trying to imagine I was presenting my case in a public debate at a university, as I had so often, in so many cities. But my palms felt sticky, my mouth gritty and strange. I folded my hands behind my back so Catherine would not see them trembling. 'You believed he had been murdered by the Catholic League, to incite a riot against you. But I had seen him on his death bed, after he was attacked outside the abbey of Saint-Victor. He managed to speak one word to me before he died. That word was "Circe".'

436

'From which you developed your far-fetched theory that Léonie de Châtillon was conspiring against my son,' Catherine cut in, her expression sceptical.

'Yes, eventually. Though I was mistaken.'

'I am glad you concede it.'

'But only in one particular,' I continued, and saw her mouth tense. 'Léonie did make her confession to Père Lefèvre. She told him she was part of a conspiracy that would involve murder. He tried to warn the party whose life was in danger. My mistake was in assuming that the person he addressed as "Your Majesty" in his anonymous letter was King Henri.'

The King started forward in his chair. 'Then whom? My mother?' He darted a fearful glance sideways at her.

'No, sire. Your wife, Queen Louise. And Lefèvre did send a copy of that letter, which she received. But I believe someone else at the palace saw it too. And that someone told the author of this plot against the Queen. That was why Paul Lefèvre had to die.'

Catherine clasped her hands together. 'This smacks of a League conspiracy. The girl had some residual attachment to Guise, even after all these years. I should not have trusted her.'

'It does seem the obvious answer, Your Majesty,' I said, inclining my head towards her in a show of deference. 'For a long while I assumed it must be an elaborate plan by the Duke of Guise. Especially when I found convincing evidence that Lefèvre was killed by Joseph de Chartres – the almoner of Saint-Victor and a League collaborator. But that was because I was working on the assumption that His Majesty the King was the target. Once I learned from Queen Louise that Paul Lefèvre's letter had been written to her all along, I had to revise my assumptions.'

'So – it was not Guise?' Henri sounded disappointed. 'But de Chartres was related to the Duchess of Montpensier. Who would he kill for, if not the League?'

'I realised that the answer lay not in his League connections but in another attachment. De Chartres was rumoured to have a mistress. I found a letter from his lover in his cell at Saint-Victor. My friend the librarian there found another in the same hand among his other papers – a letter telling him that Lefèvre was going to denounce him as a spy and must be silenced.'

'So . . .' Henri frowned. 'What does that have to do with Circe?'

'Nothing. That is precisely the point. There is no mention of this conspiracy involving Circe, which makes me think that Joseph de Chartres did not know of it. His lover used him. Joseph thought he was getting rid of Lefèvre for a different reason – to protect himself against exposure as a spy.'

'A spy for whom?' Henri asked. 'I am completely confused.'

'Bear with me – it will become clearer. We must suppose that he was afraid his comrades in the League suspected him of fraternising with their enemy. The curate at Saint-Séverin overheard Lefèvre calling him *Judas*.' I left a pause for him to work it out.

'There seems to be an awful lot of supposition here,' Catherine remarked, shifting her weight in the chair.

'I prefer to call it logical deduction,' I said.

'You mean, this mistress was someone from my household?' Henri stared at me as if the idea was preposterous.

'It was someone with royal allegiances, certainly. And I also believe the lover killed de Chartres not long after. Presumably he couldn't be trusted to keep quiet either.'

'But—' Henri shook his head as he struggled to make the necessary connections – 'if she came from inside the royal households, then the original conspiracy, the one involving Circe—'

'Also came from within the palace.' I took a few paces in front of them, as if speaking to a public gallery. 'Circe – Léonie – had confessed to a plot to harm Queen Louise. That made no sense if Guise was behind it – it would be no advantage to him to attack the Queen. Quite the reverse – it's in his interest that you continue in a childless marriage, sire. If your wife were to die, you would be free to find a new one who might give you a son, and his hopes of the throne would crumble. In fact, the only people who would obviously benefit from the death of Queen Louise would be the House of Valois.'

Catherine brought her stick down sharply again as if she were the presiding judge. 'I think we have heard enough of this nonsense. Banish this man, Henri. You have shown him too much familiarity – now he thinks he can speak to sovereigns as if he were their equal.'

'For courage and intelligence he is the superior of every prince I have known,' Henri snapped back, half-rising. He sounded unusually regal. 'And may I remind you, madam, that there is only one sovereign in this room, and he commands Bruno to continue.'

I had never seen Catherine shrink before. She pressed her lips together and folded her hands over the top of her cane, her eyes fixed intently on me as if daring me to finish my accusation.

'So you think Léonie was trying to kill my wife?' Henri formed the words slowly and carefully, as if their meaning was only now beginning to penetrate. Before I could answer, he turned to face his mother, understanding spreading over his face. 'You knew. Dear God – this was your solution?'

'The man is raving, Henri. He is saying the first thing that comes into his head because he is desperate for your patronage again.'

'With respect, madam, if I wanted to win royal favour this is not the story I would be inventing,' I said quietly.

'You spoke to me of a possible annulment, I remember that,' Henri said, still addressing his mother with the same incredulous gaze. 'I told you I would not countenance it. God knows Louise has endured enough – she does not deserve to be thrown aside so lightly. Then Ruggieri made his prophecy,

which I took as a sign that everything would be resolved . . .'
He let the sentence trail into silence as he looked back at me.
'Go on, Bruno. What further secrets has my mother been
keeping from me?'

My eyes flicked to Catherine; I saw her give a minute shake
of her head, her lips pressed so tight they had turned white.
If I spoke now, I would make a lasting enemy of the most
powerful woman in France, and despite the King's present
performance, I was not convinced he had the will to defy her
for long. I paused, breathed hard and plunged in anyway.

'One significant one, Your Majesty. Léonie de Châtillon was
in the early weeks of pregnancy when she died.'

'What?' Henri leapt to his feet, throwing his chair over
behind him. His nostrils flared as his gaze swung wildly from
me to Catherine. 'She was carrying my child? And you killed
her, knowing that?'

'Of course I didn't kill her.' Catherine smoothed her skirts.
'Do you imagine, at my age, I go stalking through woods in
the dark, garrotting young women?'

'Why would you say she was garrotted?' I asked, immediately. 'I thought you believed she killed herself with cuts to
the wrists?'

'I do.' She regarded me calmly; her expression told me I
would have to do better than that if I wanted to catch her
out. 'But I know that is your theory. You said so when her
body was first brought in. I presumed you had added it to
the many other foolish ideas you have been putting in my
son's head. Besides, Henri,' – she shifted to face the King – 'it
almost certainly wasn't yours. The girl was still Guise's whore.'

'But you didn't know that at first, did you?' I planted myself
before her chair. 'When she first told you she was with child,
you had to act quickly. You consulted Jacopo about the prospect of legitimising the child by marriage. And you sent Léonie
to serve Queen Louise. To poison her, little by little, so no
one would suspect foul play. But Léonie threw your plan into

440

disarray when she confessed it to Paul Lefèvre, who alerted the Queen. Then, when you learned the child might not even be the King's, you realised you had risked everything for a deception.'

'Where is your evidence for any of this?' Catherine still appeared admirably unruffled; it was I who was sweating. 'Henri, are you going to let this man interrogate me as if he were my judge and I a common criminal?'

'Yes,' the King said bluntly. 'And I would like to hear you answer his charges, madam.'

'I have asked him what proof he has beyond wild fancy.' She sat back and looked at me, eyebrows arched expectantly.

'The Queen's recent illness began when Léonie came to serve in her household, two months ago.'

Catherine waved her hand. 'That woman has always suffered from ill health, long before Léonie went near her.'

'Not with the symptoms of poisoning. Then there is the scarf I found in the clearing where Léonie was murdered. It was embroidered with Queen Louise's crest. I believe Léonie's killer dropped it there after strangling her with it.'

'Do you hear that, Henri? Louise's crest. He will be accusing your wife of her murder next.'

'No, but it was someone who has at some point had access to the Queen's apartments and could have taken it from her.'

'More speculation.'

'Then there was this.' I reached inside my doublet and showed her the silver penknife in my palm. I was gratified to see a flash of something – anger? fear? – twist her features. 'You recognise this, Your Majesty, I'm sure. Antique Florentine craftsmanship, rare in Paris. You brought them with you when you first came to France as a young bride, I understand? And you have given them as gifts to those who have done you special service. I know Jacopo has one.'

'What of it?' Her eyes narrowed. 'Where did you get this?'

'I found it by the naked corpse of Joseph de Chartres. He

441

too was garrotted. His killer – who was also his lover – used the knife to twist the tourniquet, but fled in too much of a hurry to take it.'

I could see the muscles working along Catherine's jaw as she considered her response. Henri's gaze rested on me with a kind of wonder.

'So – this lover killed both de Chartres and Léonie, at my mother's command?'

'I believe so, Your Majesty.'

'I train my girls in many arts, Doctor Bruno, but garrotting is not among them,' Catherine said, patting her hairnet into place. 'Do not listen to any more of this, Henri. My physicians assure me the girl was not even pregnant.'

'Then why did you give her the Queen's wedding medallion with the dolphin?' I shot back.

'I did no such thing. Perhaps she stole it from Queen Louise.'

'The Queen had already returned it to you, at your request. And you had Ruggieri draw up an astrological chart for the new Dauphin – I saw it in the library.'

'You must have imagined that.' She turned briskly to the King. 'You look tired, Henri. Let me send for some food. This is too much for you while you are still unwell.' She reached out a hand towards his face; Henri slapped it away.

'You are saying, Bruno, that this lover is one of my mother's women?' he asked.

'That seemed the obvious conclusion, Your Majesty. But I could not be certain until I found a match for the handwriting in the two letters I have from Joseph's lover.'

'And now you have?'

'Beyond doubt.'

'Tell me one thing. Is this lover among my mother's attendants today? Out there in the gallery?'

I nodded. The King rose, his face dark. 'Then bring them all in. See if she can keep her countenance with every gaze on her.'

'Do not do this, Henri, I beg you. Do not repeat these foolhardy accusations to people who have only ever loved and served you and acted for the good of your throne.' Catherine struggled out of her chair. She looked older suddenly, the emotion in her voice no longer within her control.

But Henri was already striding to the door; he flung it open and barked a command. They trooped in behind him, white-faced and anxious: Balthasar, Ruggieri, Gabrielle. I wondered how much they had heard. I caught Gabrielle's eye and held her gaze for a moment, trying to convey a wordless apology, but her face was rigid.

I reached into the inside pocket of my doublet again and drew out the love letter I had found in Joseph's cell.

'I had been looking for a woman whose hand matched this,' I said, addressing the King. 'But it was only very recently that I realised where I had seen this writing before. I said it seemed an obvious conclusion that Joseph's lover was a woman from the court. It would be logical – to seduce and win the confidence of a man with senior League connections. That is what your women do, is it not, Your Majesty?' I added, turning to Catherine. She neither acknowledged nor denied it. 'However,' I continued, with heavy emphasis, and I felt my listeners strain forward, 'once again, as with Lefèvre's letter and the phrase "Your Majesty", I realised that pursuing the obvious solution had made me blind.'

'What do you mean?' Henri said.

'It was only late last night that I realised where I had seen this handwriting. You will recognise it, I think, Your Majesty.' I approached Catherine and held out the letter to her, but she pointedly turned her head away. 'It was in Queen Louise's apartments,' I continued, undeterred. 'She showed me the drawings she had made for the costumes in the masque, and beneath them were notes on the choreography. Unmistakably in this same hand. It's not just your women who use the arts of love to spy for you, is it, Your Majesty?' I left a pause, while Catherine's face clouded with fury. 'Joseph de Chartres was clever – he was a frequent guest of the Duchess of Montpensier, he allowed rumours to flourish regarding their relationship, to disguise where his real interest lay.' I turned to Balthasar, holding out the penknife. 'Here – you left this behind in the priest's rooms with Joseph's body. Perhaps you should have sent your little go-between to look for it,' I added. 'The dwarf. The one you sent to search Lefèvre's lodging before, to see if he had left behind any other writings about the Circe plot.'

Balthasar stared at me, his mouth hanging open. The colour drained from his face. He turned fearful eyes on Catherine, waiting to be told what to do or say.

Henri stepped down from the dais, covering the distance between us in two long strides, and snatched the letter from my hand. His eyes skimmed the page; when he looked up at Balthasar they glittered with a cold light.

'You killed my child,' he said, with deliberate calm.

'Your Majesty—' Balthasar was shaking his head, holding his hands up, palms outwards, like a shield. Before he could complete his defence, Henri pulled his arm back and swung his fist until it connected with Balthasar's jaw with a sickening crunch. For a man in his state of health it was a surprisingly vigorous blow. The dance master was knocked to the floor, where he attempted to scramble backwards away from the King.

'It was not likely to have been yours, Your Majesty,' he pleaded, the words distorted in his bruised mouth. 'She was still seeing Guise. I was the one who found out – your wife had me follow her.'

'But it *might* have been. No one has ever proved that I cannot father a child, damn it. But no – I can see it would have been a lot of trouble to murder my wife, rush through another marriage and legitimise a bastard if you could not even be sure it was a Valois. Much simpler just to kill it off along with the woman who carried it.' He raised his leg as if to kick Balthasar in the ribs; with the quick reflex of an athlete he curled into a ball, arms over his face, begging for mercy.

'Leave him alone, Henri.' Catherine rapped out her command as if speaking to a dog. 'This is not justice. Conduct yourself like a monarch.'

'Like you, Mother?' The King spun around to face her, eyes blazing. 'Is it more fitting to poison people? Strangle them from behind when they are not looking? Is that how a monarch should behave?'

Catherine clicked her tongue. 'Be grateful you do not hold your kingdom in Italy, boy. You would see all that and more before breakfast, you would learn not to shrink from the smell of blood. Remember you are a Medici as well as a Valois.'

'You have never let me forget it, Mother.' Henri pointed to Balthasar, still balled up silent on the floor. 'Was that where he learned his assassin's tricks, at the Medici court?'

'Like all of us who make our home in a foreign land, Balthasar has learned the skills necessary to survive and be useful.' Catherine's tone was calmer now.

Balthasar peeled his arms away from his face and pushed himself up on his elbows to look the King directly in the eye.

'In Florence, Your Majesty, they kill men like us,' he said, his voice low and unsteady. 'The street gangs or the Church, it's all the same. We are easy targets. I was beaten so badly by youths one night that I could no longer dance. But at least I escaped with my life – my friend did not. After that – yes, I learned how to fight.'

Henri held his gaze, his fingers flexing as the conflict of emotions played out across his face. He turned back to his mother.

'What justice shall he have, then, your hired killer?' But he sounded more petulant than angry. Already, to my dismay, I could feel the balance of power shifting.

445

'Your *servant*, rather,' Catherine said firmly. 'Every decision I take is for the sake of your throne and your name, my son. If Doctor Bruno cared for you and for France as he claims to do, he would have understood this, and learned, as I suggested, to keep his opinions to himself.' She turned those black eyes on me for the briefest instant, with all the promise of Medici vengeance. 'Send the others out, Henri. You and I and Balthasar will discuss justice alone.'

The King havered, suspended between choices. Then he seemed to deflate, the raw fury ebbing away as suddenly as it had flared up. He sat heavily on the edge of the dais and hunched over, wracked by another bout of coughing. Catherine stood, wincing as she leaned her weight on her stick, and laid a hand on his shoulder. After a moment, Henri inclined towards her and rested his head against her hip. I knew then that I had lost, and she had won. It had all been for nothing. There would be no justice for the dead; the King would accept her justifications and my reward would be Catherine's lasting enmity.

'You may leave my son to my care now, Doctor Bruno,' she said, her voice gentler. 'You have done what he asked of you, with a tenacity none of us predicted. Now it is for the King to decide what he wishes to do with your hypotheses. You will wait in the gallery.'

I bowed in silence and turned to leave.

'And please do not leave the premises without permission this time,' she added, lightly. 'I am feeling less indulgent towards you today.'

As I passed Balthasar's prone form, he lifted his hands away from his face, blood still trickling down his chin. It disturbed me to see that the look he gave me was one less of hatred than contempt, mingled with pity. I would come out of this worse off than him, it seemed to imply.

Gabrielle slid in beside me on a window seat overlooking the courtyard below.

'For a moment there, I was afraid you suspected me,' she murmured.

I shook my head. 'Not of the murders. But I still accuse you of trying to detain me on Catherine's behalf last night. Sorry about locking you in.'

'It's not the worst that's happened to me in her service.' She breathed on the window and rubbed a small circle of frost away from the pane with her sleeve. 'I've decided I want to go home for Christmas,' she said quietly.

'Home?'

'To Ligny. To my husband and daughter. Away from this place.'

'Will Catherine allow that?'

'I don't suppose she can do much to stop me, if my husband demands it. I am his to command, after all. I have written to him already.'

'She might make it hard for you to come back.'

'I don't know that I want to.' She sighed and rearranged her legs beneath her. 'I have been thinking about it a lot since Léonie died. That could have been any of us. What I learned in there' – she jerked her thumb towards the closed doors of Catherine's room – 'didn't surprise me at all.' She tilted her head to look at me sidelong. 'I have always known Catherine was ruthless. She once offered to have her own daughter killed, as a bargain with Navarre, to release him from the marriage. If she was prepared to do that, how much more disposable are the rest of us? Our bodies are no more than a form of currency to be bartered, and one that is easily debased.' She sighed and rubbed the glass again. 'I shall be thirty soon. I want to see my daughter before she forgets me. Be a mother to her. Teach her not to live as I have lived, while there's still time.'

I heard the tremor in her voice. I laid a hand on her arm and she folded her fingers over it.

'Do that,' I said softly. 'Teach her to live well. Teach her to love, and be courageous, and she will grow into a fine woman. Like her mother.'

'Thank you, Bruno.' She squeezed my hand and turned her face away so that I would not see her blink away tears. We sat in silence as the minutes passed, the only sound the furious rise and fall of argument from the other side of the doors.

'What will you do now?' she asked, after a long time.

'That depends on what they decide in there,' I said, trying to sound unconcerned. 'I could be banished, executed or ennobled. It's anyone's guess.'

'Absurd, isn't it? You have done nothing except uncover a great wrong, and you are the one in fear of punishment.'

'That is Medici justice for you.'

An hour passed, marked by the chiming of the clocks, and still the sound of voices raised in accusation echoed from Catherine's chamber. My stomach growled with hunger, though I could do nothing but wait; guards stood at each end of the gallery, and Ruggieri had stationed himself in the window seat opposite, where he perched like an ancient raven, watching us, black eyes brooding. Eventually the doors opened and the Queen Mother emerged, her face strained, followed by Balthasar, clutching his swollen lip. He walked past without looking at me.

'The King will see you now,' she said, pausing to lean on her stick. Her tone was imperious as ever, but she looked exhausted. For once, her strength of purpose was not enough to hide the fact that she was old and tired, and had not had a moment's peace of mind in twenty-five years. I thought of my conversation with Balthasar, when he had urged me to respect her age and frailty. Impossible to know now whether he had been moved by concern for her or for himself. Perhaps they are the same thing, when you serve the Medici.

'You will follow Henri's instructions to the letter,' Catherine said. 'And keep away from the Tuileries from now on. I

448

sincerely hope not to cross paths with you again, Doctor Bruno. My advice is to stop meddling in the affairs of princes if you intend to keep your head attached to your neck for the long-term. As I said, you are a dangerous man. But the greatest danger you pose is to yourself, I fear.'

'It is a lesson I will take to heart, Your Majesty.' I scrambled to my feet and offered a hasty bow. I wanted to remind her about the book but I felt that might be stretching her patience too far, in the circumstances.

'See that you do. Come, Balthasar. And you, Ruggieri.' She flicked her gnarled fingers in his direction and the old sorcerer heaved himself up, looking at me with undisguised glee.

'Now we shall see my latest prediction come true,' he cackled, showing his broken teeth. 'When I said you should not be in Paris much longer.'

'Will you take a wager on it?' I drew myself up, defiant; whatever my fate was to be, I would not go down to the sound of this pseudo-magician's mockery.

He assumed an air of gravitas. 'One does not make wagers with the gift of prophecy.'

'Then what on earth is the point of having it?' I said, as I walked away.

Henri sat in his mother's chair, slumped like a straw effigy that had lost its stuffing. His skin looked grey, his eyes dim and unfocused.

'It's been a lot to take in,' he said, with uncharacteristic understatement.

'I know, sire. I'm sorry. Perhaps your lady mother is right – I should have kept my knowledge to myself.'

'God, no. Don't be absurd. She must realise she can't just go about disposing of people with impunity because they're in the way. This isn't Florence.' He pulled his gaze back to me with an effort. 'It's chilling, Bruno – to realise someone has manipulated every aspect of your life without your knowing.

449

With nothing but my best interests at heart, so she says.' He shook his head in sad amazement. 'This can never be made public, of course – you understand that? None of it.'

I opened my mouth to reply, but he pressed on:

'Because of Joseph de Chartres. If Guise or his sister ever learn that he was murdered by someone in my household, they would drive a mob on to the streets calling for justice. They would not rest until we were dragged from the palaces and torn to pieces. So these deaths must be whitewashed. Paul Lefèvre was attacked by thieves. De Chartres was killed in a gaming-house brawl. Léonie tragically took her own life. These will be the official verdicts, set down in the records.'

'Guise will not accept that.'

'I think he will, in the end. My mother intends to negotiate with him. She proposes to offer the League a number of concessions that will encourage him to forget about the priest and the friar. I have agreed and given her authority to do so.'

'What about Balthasar?'

'Banished from my household and my wife's. I have been firm about that. He was spying on me anyway. There was always something shifty about him.' Henri stretched out his legs and contemplated the buckles of his shoes.

'I mean to say – will he not be punished for the two murders?'

He let out a long sigh and shifted in his seat to look at me from beneath lowered brows. 'If you mean in the sense of tried and executed, then no. That would be impossible, for the reasons I have already explained. And because I have made a treaty with my mother. His freedom for yours.'

'Mine?' I blinked at him. 'I haven't murdered anyone.'

'You should know Catherine well enough to realise that is neither here nor there. You have seriously inconvenienced her. People who do that tend not to last long, as we have seen.' He sat forward and beckoned me to the chair beside him. 'I have told her that if any harm should come to you, I will strike her immediately from my royal council. That would be worse than banishment to Catherine, to be denied her say in the running of the kingdom. She knows I am deadly serious.'

You are deadly serious now, I thought, taking my seat. But she also knows well that you are a man of mercurial temper, and the righteous anger you feel today will soon be forgotten. You will not defy her to defend me for ever. Instead, I said:

'That is a relief. Now I need only worry about the Duke of Guise trying to kill me.'

'I've asked her to speak to Guise about you.' He pushed a lock of hair out of his eyes. 'Tell him you are under royal protection. Don't worry – you will be part of her negotiations.'

I did not find this greatly reassuring; Catherine was entirely capable of striking a private bargain with Guise to get rid of me in some way which would not implicate her, regardless of Henri's instructions. She might consider that an ideal solution. Even if, by some miracle, Guise agreed to leave me alone, that still did not solve the problem of Paget and Stafford and the fact that they suspected me of uncovering their dealings.

'Thank you, Your Majesty,' I said, without much conviction.

'I will lend you one of my bodyguards for the time being,' he added, as if he guessed at the tenor of my thoughts. 'And, Bruno—' he leaned across and rested a hand on my wrist. 'I know what you have risked for my sake, to do this thing I asked of you. Neither of us could have foreseen where it would lead. Some men would have chosen to make their own lives easier by keeping the information to themselves.'

'I have never perfected the art of making my life easier.'

He looked at me with a sad smile. 'That is because you are cursed with integrity. But I know you also did it in the hope of reward. You are neither a fool nor a saint.'

'Your Majesty, I—'

'No need to deny it. You want patronage. Of course you do. And I will keep my word. When I am well, I will think on what I may do for you. For now—'

451

'That book,' I blurted, before he could change the subject. 'The one she bought from the English girl. She said she wanted me to decipher it, but that was before. But I would still do it, without payment, if you could tell her—'

He nodded. 'I will see what I can do.'

'One more thing—'

A crease appeared between his brows; he did not like bargaining. I pressed on, quickly.

'The *Gelosi*. The Duchess of Montpensier is holding them in her house, as punishment for my breaking in – though I did not steal anything from her, as she believes. They are supposed to travel to Lyon today, but I fear she will not release them without a royal command.'

'Christ's wounds, that woman.' He grasped the carved armrests and heaved himself to his feet. 'She is another who has ambitions to rule France. Her brother should rein her in. Believe me, I know about wilful sisters,' he added darkly. 'I will send soldiers for the players right away – she needs to learn that she cannot make her own laws in my kingdom. God save us from women with dreams of power, eh, Bruno?'

I bowed my head in assent so he could not see me smiling.

'On that note,' he said, pulling his robe around him, 'I am going to visit my wife. There is one who has been nothing but obedient and kind to me.' A brief look of remorse passed over his face. 'I may not have been much of a husband to her, but by God, I will protect her from my mother's schemes while I still breathe. That much at least I can do.' He stepped down from the edge of the dais and paused, his eyes on the floor. 'Do you think, Bruno, if I had been more attentive to my wife, those three people would not now be dead?'

'You cannot blame yourself, sire,' I said, though it seemed unusually perceptive of him to say so. 'It does no good to speculate.'

'No. Look ahead, my mother always says. Still,' he said, brightening, 'there is always Ruggieri's prophecy. Perhaps, when my strength is recovered and the Queen is well again, it may yet come true.' He looked at me as if seeking confirmation.

'First time for everything,' I said.

He smiled briefly, though it didn't touch his eyes, and his expression darkened. 'I cannot help but wish it had been allowed to live, Bruno. The child. I know they say it was probably not mine, but it might have been, you see. That's the point. There was a chance.'

I cleared my throat. 'I suppose when it comes to the heir to the throne, a chance is not good enough. Besides, could you have lived with that – always wondering? Thinking every time you looked at it, that it might be Guise's?'

'Perhaps I am ignorant, but I always imagined a man would somehow just *know*. You would feel some . . . *instinct*. Don't you think?'

I closed my eyes briefly and tried to picture a two-year-old girl called Béatrice, running through a garden in Ligny. Would I just know, if I saw her? I could not imagine her as any more than a blur of colour; I hardly knew what two-year-olds did. 'I have no idea, Your Majesty.'

'No. No, I don't suppose you do,' he said, walking away, his mind already elsewhere.

TWENTY-EIGHT

'He died in his sleep, about two o'clock this morning.' Jacopo poured another glass of wine and pushed a bowl of hot chestnuts towards me. 'I was with him. It was a blessed release. I know that is usually said to make everyone feel better, but in this case it was the truth.'

I pressed a fist against my mouth. Two days since my ill-judged confrontation at the palace and I had heard nothing from the King, until a messenger had arrived from Jacopo on the morning of the 12th, asking me to call on him. I had meant to go sooner and see the Count – I was feeling guilty that I had not thought of him with the events of the past few days – but I had not expected to arrive too late.

'I should have acted as soon as I knew about him. I should not have left him there. Perhaps he would have had a better chance.' Tears burned at the back of my eyes, unbidden, though they were as much for myself as for him.

'Always so hard on yourself, Bruno,' Jacopo said gently. 'He was near to the end. A few days more would not have saved him. You gave him a great gift at the end of his life.'

'He never did get to feel the sun on his face.' I looked away, swiping my eyes with the back of my hand.

'Because of you, he died in a warm bed, with as little pain

as possible and a friend to hold his hand, instead of in that pit among the rats. It was nothing short of a miracle. He said as much. He said God would reward you.'

'I think God will probably take it as a downpayment against my considerable deficit.'

Jacopo laughed. 'Well, let's consider a more quantifiable reward.' He stood and rummaged in a dim corner of his study, returning with a small wooden chest that rang with the pleasing metallic slide of coins as he moved. 'The King sent this for you. In recompense for your troubles.' He shook the box for effect and placed it in my lap. 'There should be enough there to cover your debts and keep you comfortable for a while.'

I set it on his desk. 'Take from it what you need to pay the physician and funeral expenses for the Count.'

'Don't be absurd, Bruno. I am more than happy to cover the doctor's bill. As for the burial – Catherine has that in hand. She wants him interred quietly. His family think he died years ago – there seems little sense in disabusing them.'

I took a chestnut and began to peel it. 'She doesn't want to have to explain how he came to be in a royal prison at Guise's expense for thirteen years without anyone noticing.'

'In truth, it would raise awkward questions.' He sat down at his desk and unlocked a drawer. 'The King gave me something else for you. Here.' He passed over a slim rectangular object wrapped in crimson velvet.

My pulse leapt in my throat. I unfolded the cloth to reveal the dull and shabby leather bindings of the lost book of Hermes Trismegistus. I smoothed a hand over the cover as lovingly as if it were the head of a baby and looked up at Jacopo, a question in my eyes.

'He bought it back from Catherine. I don't know how he persuaded her – that is between them. But it is his gift to you. Because he cannot give you what he knows you really want.'

'No royal appointment, then.' I tried not to betray my disappointment.

'He says it would be politic for you to stay away from the court for a while. But he has secured you a teaching position at the Collège de Cambrai, if you want it. Lecturing in philosophy and theology.' He hesitated. 'I know it's not what you hoped for, but you would be paid well and I don't suppose the hours would be too exacting. It would give you a reason to stay in Paris, if that is still what you want.'

'I don't know.' I covered the book again and laid both hands flat over it in my lap. 'I had thought of going back to England. There is business I must attend to there.'

'Is that wise?' His great eyebrows knitted together with concern. 'Would you be safe there?'

'Probably safer than in Paris.'

'Really? Even with Simon?'

I gave him a tired smile. 'I can't have Simon following me around for the rest of my life.'

Simon was the bodyguard Henri had detailed to look after me, one of his own forty-five strong men and true; an affable six-footer from the Languedoc, of few words but reassuringly huge fists, who now accompanied me everywhere with his broadsword hanging ostentatiously at his side. He made me feel oddly claustrophobic, though he had charmed away the resistance of Madame de la Fosse, who had set up a temporary bed for him in the downstairs hallway so he could watch the door at night, and had taken to feeding him elaborate baked goods in return for odd jobs around the house. It amused me to see him jump up, looking boyishly guilty, whenever I came in and found him on a stool by the kitchen fire with his face full of cake.

'Well, give it some thought,' Jacopo said, draining his glass. 'Don't do anything hasty. And come for Christmas, won't you? I will be needed at the Tuileries on Christmas Eve, but I want to keep my Christmas Day feast here, with friends. I have invited the *Gelosi*.'

'Then I had better stay away. Francesco will want to give me a bloody nose for Christmas.'

'Well, he might take a swing at you to keep up appearances,' he said with a grin, 'but you know Francesco – he doesn't hold a grudge. Besides, he will have been dining out on the story all the way to Lyon and back. Though I suspect in his version, he will be the one who escaped out of a window and stole a duke's horse.'

I flicked the chestnut shell into the fire and fell silent for a moment.

'I'm sorry for my words before,' I said, after a while. 'When I accused you of conniving at murder. I should not have said that.'

'I did not understand what she was planning until it was too late.' He spoke quietly. 'But you were right, in a sense – even once I realised, I could not have stopped her. I have tried, over the years, to be the voice of her conscience, but she is a Medici.' He held his hands out, palms upward, to indicate helplessness in the face of such a legacy. 'Sometimes I have no choice but to turn a blind eye. That does not make me proud of myself, but I am not a brave man, Bruno. Not like you.'

I stood, brushing chestnut shell from my clothes as I clutched the book to my chest in the crook of my right arm. 'Some would say there is a very fine line between brave and foolhardy.'

Jacopo came around the desk and laid a hand on my shoulder. 'And I would say the difference is obvious. Bravery is doing something foolhardy for the sake of others.'

I smiled and he crushed me in a paternal embrace.

'Tomorrow is Saint Lucy's day, Bruno. The darkest point of the year. After that, the days will grow brighter.'

'I'll keep that in mind,' I said. I wished I could share his optimism.

'I will see you for Christmas, then,' he said, at the door, handing me my cloak that Henri had sent back from the palace, freshly laundered. 'You can bring Simon.'

'I will,' I said, as my large companion lumbered amiably into view from the kitchen. 'We're inseparable.'

We crossed the Pont de Notre-Dame under an iron sky. Occasional flakes of snow floated down half-heartedly; a crust of ice had formed over the mud-churned drifts in the streets. The church of Saint-Séverin loomed up ahead. I told Simon that I wanted to go inside, but that he could wait for me by the door.

I stepped alone into a reverent silence. The air smelled of cold stone and incense, just as it had on the day I came here to find Paul Lefèvre. I could almost believe that nothing had changed, that I might still find him there inside the confessional in the chancel, on the bench worn smooth by generations of penitents. How different the last few weeks would have been – for me, at least – if I had not decided to seek him out that day. I approached the confessional with slow steps and a heavy heart; even though I knew now that Paul had not been murdered because he was seen talking to me, still I could not escape the sense that my visit that day had set in motion everything that followed.

I reached out and touched the wood of the confessional with my fingertips. I closed my eyes, recalling his snide tone, his pompous certainty. Then I thought of that charred scrap of the letter he had written to save a life, and felt a wave of sadness. He had not deserved his death. None of them had.

'Are you making your confession today, Doctor Bruno?'

I spun round, startled out of my thoughts by a clipped English voice, impeccably polite. A small man with a reddish beard was standing a few feet away with his eyes closed, apparently praying to a statue of the Virgin in a wall niche. He was no one I recognised; my first thought was that Paget had sent him.

'Should I?'

'I think it would be a good idea,' he murmured, still without looking at me. 'The confessional is empty, after all.'

I glanced back up the nave to the door and jerked my head for Simon to come closer, holding my hand up to stop him when I thought he was near enough to respond if the man tried anything. Cautiously curious, I took a seat in the penitents' side of the confessional and drew the curtain across to close myself in.

I heard a soft rustle of cloth as someone settled the other side of the partition. The smell of the wood, the dust spiralling in the slats of light – all just as it was that day with Paul, the memory so sharp it almost hurt. While I was lost in thought, a piece of paper appeared under the gap in the partition.

'From a mutual friend,' said the Englishman, whose profile I could just make out through the wooden grille. I picked up the letter and turned it over. In the top right-hand corner someone had inked the astrological sign for Jupiter. The wax seal was intact, though that meant nothing. I tore it open and ran my eye over the streams of letters, meaningless to anyone but me. Though I had not admitted as much to Guise, he was right; I had committed Walsingham's complex cipher to memory and I raced through the apparent gibberish in the note as quickly as if it were a foreign language:

Bruno

This is Nicholas Berden, the only man in Paris in whom you should confide. You can trust him with your life – or at the very least your correspondence. Anything you give him he will put directly into my hands. Send to me soon.

FW

PS. My dinner table wants for wit and liveliness with you and Sidney gone. We are a sad company without you. Pray God we may see you again.

I folded the letter in my lap with a stab of anger. If Walsingham wanted to see me that badly, why wait for God to intervene when he could perfectly well make arrangements himself?

'All in order?' Nicholas Berden whispered, from the other side of the partition.

'Yes. Thank you for taking the trouble.'

'I sail for London tomorrow,' he continued, in his low, clipped voice. 'I'm a cloth merchant, you see. Constantly back and forth. Rather useful. So I thought, if there is anything you'd like me to take . . .' He let the suggestion hang in the air.

'There is. But I don't have it with me.'

'No matter. Let's meet for a drink tonight at the Swan and Cross.'

'But people know me there.'

'So much the better. Hide in plain sight. They know me too, so no one will remark on our presence.'

'I have never seen you there.'

'I'm easy to overlook.'

'Because you're hiding in plain sight?'

'Exactly.' He let out a merry laugh and I decided I liked him. 'Seven o'clock, then.'

I was about to reply when I realised he had already left. I rested my head against the wood behind me and closed my eyes.

As I prepared to leave the house that evening there came a knock at the door of my rooms which I knew, by its force and briskness, announced Madame de la Fosse. I cast a quick glance around to make sure I had not left anything incriminating in the open. All my dangerous papers, together with the

460

Hermes book, were safe in my hiding place in the rafters, the boards pulled tight so that it was impossible to see there might be a cavity behind them. Inside my doublet I carried two letters in cipher: a copy of the one to Walsingham about Gilbert Gifford that I had given Stafford, that he had handed instead to Paget, and a new document, setting out what I had learned about the ambassador's gambling debts and the secrets he was selling to Guise. I suspected the information would not come as news to Walsingham. His original letter to me had expressed a lack of confidence in the ambassador's judgement where Paget was concerned, and the fact that he wanted me to entrust my correspondence to Berden and not the embassy courier suggested that he had further doubts about Stafford's loyalties. I wondered what he would do now that he had confirmation: recall Stafford and accuse him of treason, or a more subtle approach – leave him in place with threats of disgrace and use his intimacy with the League to England's advantage, playing him against Paget? That would be the riskier strategy, but it might appeal to the old spymaster. For my part, I could not help a feeling of disappointment as I prepared to meet Berden; his appearance meant that I no longer had any pretence for returning to England. Perhaps that had been a foolish dream all along; there was nothing there for me to go back to.

The knocking came again, more impatient this time. '*Monsieur Bruno!*'

'*J'arrive*, madame.' I opened the door with a flourish, so that she almost fell over the threshold.

'What did I tell you about having women in this house?' she said, without preamble.

'What?' I stepped back from the doorway and swept my arm around the room to demonstrate its emptiness. 'No women here, more's the pity.'

'There's one downstairs asking for you. I don't like the look of her.' She wrinkled her nose.

'Did she give a name?' I felt a little stab of fear. Would Guise send a female assassin? It would be a clever move; a woman could more easily gain access, slip past a bodyguard. Then, a slim blade between the ribs . . . 'Where is Simon?'

'Having his supper. It's not the same one as last time. This one says she's an old friend. We all know what that means.' She leaned in. '*Foreign*,' she confided, in a stage whisper.

I stared at her for a moment, then bounded down the stairs two at a time to find Sophia standing on the doorstep, shivering despite the fur hat she wore pulled down over her ears. She looked at me warily, her eyes bright with cold.

'I have something for you,' she said, matter-of-factly.

'Come in.' I led her up the stairs, past Madame de la Fosse and her indignant spluttering, and closed the door behind us.

'Here.' Sophia reached inside her cloak and took out my Damascus steel knife in its scabbard. I was so delighted to see it – and her – that I darted in and kissed her impulsively on the cheek. We both drew back, alarmed.

'I am in your debt,' I said, turning it over in my hands.

'You certainly are,' she said, walking over to the window and pulling off her gloves. 'You don't know what I had to do for it.' She turned with an impish grin, enjoying my shock, leaving me hanging for a few moments. 'You're right to make that face. I had to walk in the gardens with the Duke of Montpensier for an hour, listening to his *poetry*. In this weather.'

'I'm so sorry,' I said, adopting a grave expression. 'I don't know how I can make it up to you.'

'Oh, you can never compensate me for that.' She leaned back against the wall and folded her arms. 'Shall we say we are even now? For the book, I mean?'

'Agreed. The slate is wiped clean.' I strapped the knife on to my belt and immediately felt more like myself with its familiar weight resting against my hip.

'To start over,' she said thoughtfully, looking back to the

window. Her reflection rippled as she moved, distorted in the bubbled glass. A long silence unfolded. Neither of us seemed to know quite what to say, but I had the sense that she was not in a hurry to leave. I poked at the edge of a rug with the toe of my boot. She looked back to me and held my gaze with a questioning look. I watched her, trying to find the right words, the ones that would make her understand without scaring her away. I thought about Jacopo's distinction between brave and foolhardy.

The silence was broken by the bells of Saint-André striking seven. I started, glancing guiltily at the door.

'Do you have to go somewhere?'

'No. Well, yes.' I rubbed at the back of my neck. 'I'm supposed to meet someone. But it can wait.'

'A woman?' She raised an eyebrow.

'No! A colleague.'

'You're working in Paris, then?'

'I may be. I have the offer of a job, anyway. At the Collège de Cambrai. Lecturing again.'

She nodded. 'Sounds like a good position.'

'It is. The King arranged it.'

'But you don't sound as if you want it.'

I hesitated. 'I'm not sure whether I should stay in Paris.'

A flicker of anxiety crossed her face. 'Where else would you go?'

'I don't know. I was thinking of Prague, perhaps. The Emperor Rudolf is more tolerant of free thinkers at his court. He collects them. My friend John Dee is there now.'

'Prague.' She rolled the word around her mouth like a strange delicacy and gazed into the distance, as if she might glimpse new worlds beyond the black rooftops of the rue du Cimetière. 'How lucky you are, having the freedom to travel anywhere you choose.'

'It's not exactly luck. More necessity. And I'm not free to travel to the one place I really wish to go.'

'Where is that?'

'Home.'

She looked at me as if searching for something in my face. 'Still. If you were a woman, you would think it enviable.'

'What about you? Will you stay in Paris?'

She shrugged. 'For now. There are fewer options available to me.'

'But this is not enough for you, surely? Living here, being a governess?'

It was the wrong thing to say; her expression hardened. 'How would you know what is enough for me? There's no shame in honest work. I came to Paris with nothing.'

'Apart from my book.'

A faint hint of a smile. 'Yes, all right. But things could have ended very badly for me. I have been fortunate. Sir Thomas is a generous employer, who doesn't try to take advantage, which sets him apart from many. His daughters are pleasant enough children. I'm paid reasonably, I have a comfortable room and I am allowed to use the library. What other life is there for a woman like me, except to become someone's wife?'

'And that is not an option you would consider?' I asked carefully.

'That is a mistake I would not make again in a hurry,' she said, in a voice like a blade.

'But you must have suitors,' I persisted, though I knew I should let the subject drop. 'Young Gilbert Gifford seems keen.'

'Gilbert Gifford?' She let out a burst of laughter, eyes wide with incredulity. '*Please.* Such an earnest boy. He is going to save England for the Catholic faith, you know.'

'Is he really?'

'Oh yes.' Her eyes danced with mischief. 'He's going back soon. He claims he's been entrusted with important letters for the Queen of Scots.'

'He told you that?'

She brushed a loose strand of hair out of her face. 'I thought he was probably showing off. He wants me to think he's an important player in the crusade against Elizabeth, like his hero, Paget.'

'You're right – it sounds like an idle boast to me,' I said, carelessly, while thinking I would need to add a quick post-script to the letters in my pocket.

'But in answer to your question, no,' she said.

'No what?' I frowned; my mind was still on Gifford.

'There are no suitors.' She fixed me with a level stare, the wide-set amber eyes cool and knowing, revealing nothing but a hint of challenge. I was not sure how I was supposed to respond, so I remained silent.

'Well, you should not keep your colleague waiting,' she said quickly, after a pause, her gaze swerving away, and I had the sense that I had somehow missed an opportunity.

'You could come to Prague with me,' I said, startling myself. The words seemed to be in the air before the thought had even formed in my head.

She let out that same laugh of disbelief. 'Are you mad?'

I tried to cover my embarrassment. 'Why not? I saw the light in your eyes when I mentioned it. You crave adventure, you know you do. This life – it may be comfortable enough but it will stifle you in the end. Travel with me. We can leave Paris and start again.'

She put her hand on her hip, cocked her head to one side. 'And what would I do in Prague? How would I earn a living?'

'The Emperor Rudolf is a generous patron of philosophers and alchemists,' I said, warming to the idea as it took shape. 'John Dee says there is money to be gained from the kind of books I write, and prestige. I could find a place at his court, I am sure of it.'

Again, her face closed up. 'I asked you what *I* would do. I have told you, Bruno – I will not be dependent on a man ever again.' Seeing my expression, she peeled herself away from the wall and crossed the room to me, taking both my

465

hands in hers. 'It is one of the things I have always liked about you,' she said, her smile edged with regret. 'You dream something and you see no reason why it should not happen the way you dream it. But life has dealt me too many blows for me to share that view.'

'Jesus, Sophia. You're only twenty-one. Do you think I haven't seen my dreams broken into pieces, over and over? But you have to believe in the possibility of a different life, otherwise you just . . .' I shook my head, let the sentence drift.

'What?'

'Give up and get a job teaching in Paris, until you grow old and die of boredom.'

She looked offended at first, but gradually her face softened and I saw the twitch of a smile.

'Given the state of things in Paris, growing old and dying of boredom might be considered a luxury.'

'True.' I thought briefly of Paul, lying on the table in the abbey infirmary, and Léonie's limp body carried into the gallery by soldiers. I squeezed her hands. 'We could make this work, I believe it. Don't be afraid of being dependent. We would be equals. We wouldn't even have to get married, if you're set against the idea.' My words tumbled out in a rush, but I could not read her expression.

'Ah, Bruno,' she said, after a pause. She bent her head forward until it was resting on my shoulder. I slipped my arms around her waist and held her, hardly daring to breathe, tense with the almost-certain knowledge of what she was going to say next. She drew her head back so that she could look me in the eye. 'If I was going to run away to Prague with anyone, it would be you. And I don't suppose I will ever find another man who would treat me as an equal. But . . .' she paused and dropped her gaze to my chest, her fingers plucking distractedly at the buttons of my doublet. 'It's not about Prague, or marriage, or even you, in the end. There is a greater claim on me. You understand that. I am saving every

466

penny I earn here. If I go on working, in a year or so I will have enough to return to England.'

'To find your son?' I said, my throat tight.

She nodded. 'He will be two years old now. I *need* to see him, Bruno. I'm his mother. I can't bear to think he doesn't know me. It's like an ache, here, that never eases.' She balled her fist and struck the base of her ribcage. I could hear the desperation in her voice.

'But . . .' I left my objection unfinished. The son she had borne from her forbidden love affair in Oxford had been given away to a respectable family at birth; she had no way of knowing how to find him, or whether he had even survived infancy – so many children did not – but she did not need me to tell her that.

'It's the one thing I cling to,' she whispered, as if reading my thoughts.

I nodded and took a deep breath, arranged my face. This is bravery, Jacopo, I thought, as I made my voice light-hearted. 'Think, though. Another year of Montpensier's poetry.'

She laughed again, but it did not disguise the sadness. 'No. I only did that for you.'

Then she leaned in and kissed me, her mouth warm and yielding as I remembered it, but it was a valedictory embrace, I could not deceive myself.

'I should go,' I said, when she eventually broke away. 'I hope you find what you are looking for, Sophia.'

'And you, Bruno. I hope you find your way home.'

'If I do, I will come back for you. And your boy. You would love the Bay of Naples.' I could not speak through the tightness in my throat.

'Do that, then.' I saw the glisten of tears in her eyes. 'Come back for us, one day.'

Sometimes, I thought, the stubborn clinging to an improbable hope is just enough to keep your head above the tide of despair. I held her a while longer, reluctant to let go.

TWENTY-NINE

I returned from the Swan just as the bells were striking midnight, stumbling into the darkness of the hallway with Simon, one lantern between us. I was a little drunk, he was reassuringly solid and sober, taking the candle from the lantern as I leaned against the bannister, lighting his own and then handing it to me while he settled himself in his makeshift bed. Berden had been brief and efficient in exchanging the letters, but I had stayed on at the tavern after he left, buying drinks for Gaston and the students from the money Henri had given me, trying to hold that hollow sense of loss at bay with noise and empty camaraderie, until eventually Gaston had bellowed that it was time to lock up and Simon had taken me gently but firmly by the arm and steered me home.

I wished him goodnight and climbed the stairs to my rooms, where I fumbled with the lock and stumbled inside, kicking the door shut and crossing as I always did to light the candles in the window.

'You're out late tonight, Bruno,' said a smooth, English voice behind me. 'Celebrating something?'

I started, dropping the light, and let out a cry as I whipped around to see Charles Paget sitting calmly in a chair, his feet resting on my desk, a sheaf of papers in his lap. I stamped on the candle and drew the dagger from my belt, my hand shaking with shock.

'Oh, put that away, Bruno. If I'd come to kill you I'd have been waiting behind the door with a knife, wouldn't I?'

The realisation of how easily this could have happened sent goosebumps prickling up my spine. I tried to keep my composure, wishing I had drunk less.

'How did you get in?'

'I waited until dear Madame had popped round to her neighbours while you and your dancing bear were out drinking. You're not the only one who knows how to break a lock, you know.'

I watched him flick the corners of the papers in his lap. I hoped it was something he had found on the desk. It took all my self-control not to glance up at the ceiling to see if my hiding place had been violated.

'What do you want, then?' I lowered the dagger, but did not sheath it.

'I have brought you some news I thought you might appreciate.' He swung his legs to the floor and tossed the papers back on to the desk as if they were of little interest. 'I dined at the Hotel de Guise last night.'

'How is the Duke?'

'Surprisingly mollified. He's had a productive parlay with Catherine. Apparently the King has promised to field three armies against the Protestants in the south by the summer, though God knows where he thinks he will find the money. More Italian loans, I suppose. But by curious coincidence, Guise seems to have forgotten all about the murder of Joseph de Chartres.' He gave a dry laugh. 'So the world turns. Anyway, one of the other guests was Girolamo Ragazzoni, the Bishop of Bergamo. You might know of him.'

'The Papal nuncio?' I stared at him.

'That's right. Your name came up in conversation.'

'I can imagine.'

469

'Ah, but can you? I told him you and I were old friends. He asked me to pass this on.' Reaching inside his doublet, he drew out a letter on thick cream paper, with a heavy wax seal. He held it out to me, then snapped it away at the last minute as I stretched out my fingers. 'Sir Edward Stafford really is terribly anxious about what you might have said in that letter to Walsingham.'

'Does he have reason to be anxious? Besides, the letter was not sent.'

Paget laughed. 'There's not a man in Paris who doesn't have reason to be anxious about what others say of him, you should know that. Especially when it's being said to someone like Walsingham. That copy wasn't sent, but you're a resourceful man, Bruno. I dare say you'll find another way, if your news is urgent.'

I gave him a thin smile. If he had been hiding in my room all evening, he could not have seen me meeting Berden, but you could never take anything for granted with Paget. I had to hope he would not manage to decipher the letter before Gilbert Gifford left for England; if the boy really was carrying letters to Mary Stuart, it was imperative that they should be intercepted.

'Are you going to give me that letter? Or was there something else? Because I'd like to go to bed now.'

'Don't let me keep you.' He pushed the chair back and stood. 'Nothing else for now.' But I did not miss the way his eyes flitted around the room; I was certain he must have been searching for papers, though he had left no sign of his efforts. He held out the letter and nodded for me to open it.

I turned it over. The seal on the thick wax showed the two crossed keys and crown of the Papal insignia. I felt a cold punch of dread to the stomach; even now, the symbols of the Church's authority could leave me mute with fear.

Doctor Giordano Bruno, it began, in the neat hand of an Italian clerk.

Before his untimely death, Père Paul Lefèvre wrote to me on your behalf to convey your penitence with regard to the events that led to your excommunication, namely your abandoning holy orders without permission and your many heretical writings, together with your wish to be reconciled in humility and obedience to Holy Mother Church. I have, accordingly, written to Rome to acquaint His Holiness with your desire and I ask you to call on me so that we may speak further on this matter.

I have also informed the Catholic League in Paris that, while your excommunication is under review, your safety is Rome's concern and until His Holiness has considered your situation, you must be regarded as a penitent and not an enemy.

It was signed *Girolamo Ragazzoni*, with a flourish. I allowed my breath to escape slowly. For all his self-righteousness, Paul had kept his word. I did not like the part about humility and obedience, but it had at least bought me a temporary reprieve from Guise, or so I hoped.

'I wouldn't expect too much, if I were you,' Paget said, with a wolfish smile. 'Ragazzoni's already been recalled to Rome.'

'What? Why?'

'He was appointed by the last Pope. Now the new Pontiff is having a clean sweep, replacing all his legates in Europe. He's a much less forgiving man, Pope Sixtus, in matters of religious orthodoxy. I doubt Ragazzoni will have much clout with him.'

'Then I will have to pray hard.'

'Yes. That would be wise.' He made no move to leave, his eyes shining dangerously. I was still holding the dagger. One lunge, I thought; he appeared to be unarmed. One stroke and I could incapacitate most of the plots against England and Queen Elizabeth; without Paget they would all collapse, at least for the near future. We watched one another in the leaping candlelight, that smile still playing around his lips as if he knew exactly what I was thinking.

I sheathed the knife. I could not kill a man in cold blood, and in any case I would be signing my own death warrant; no Vatican emissaries would protect me from Guise's revenge if I did that.

'You would have let Guise kill me that night, wouldn't you?' I said through my teeth.

'I couldn't have stopped him, if that's what you mean,' he said frankly. 'I'm rather pleased you escaped, though. I begin to think Paris would be terribly dull without you, Bruno.'

We both turned at the sound of thundering footsteps on the stairs outside, followed by a hammering on the door.

'You all right, sir?' Simon called from outside. 'Is someone there?'

'Oh look, your dancing bear has woken. Did you pull on his chain?'

I opened the door. Simon's jaw dropped when he saw Paget.

'How the fuck did he get in here? I was by the door the whole time.' He seemed to take the intrusion as a personal affront. It was the most words I had ever heard him speak in one go.

'Master Paget was just leaving,' I said. 'Show him out, would you, Simon?'

Paget turned halfway down the stairs. 'I shall see you soon, Bruno,' he said. 'Be sure of it.'

'Not if I see you first,' Simon replied, with grim resolve, giving him a little nudge in the back with the handle of his sword. I would not wish to understate the pleasure it gave me to see Paget stumble and miss his step, all his poise forgotten as he hurried for the door.

As soon as I heard the front door slam behind him, I locked myself into my room and stood on a chair to check my secret cavity above the rafters. Relief washed through me as I examined each bundle of papers and found nothing missing or apparently disturbed. The book was still where I had left it, wrapped in its velvet cloth, though I knew I needed to find a safer home for it, away from damp or mice or prying eyes and quick fingers. The fact that Paget had broken in so easily once meant he would do it again; though I was sure he was looking for copies of ciphers or letters that might be of interest to Guise, he would not fail to realise that the very act of hiding the book away in the rafters proclaimed that it was either illegal or valuable, or both. I thought of Berden's advice and wondered if it would be safer hidden in plain sight, among the other volumes on my shelves, where its worn calfskin binding would not catch anyone's eye.

I sat on the bed and opened it in my lap. This book had been brought to Italy out of the ruins of Byzantium in the last century by a monk working for Cosimo de Medici, who had commissioned a translation into Latin by the great philosopher Marsilio Ficino. I had searched for it in Oxford; found it, lost it, tracked it down to Canterbury, lost it again and now I could hardly believe I held it in my hands. People had murdered for this book. This was a copy of Ficino's translation of the fifteenth and final volume of the writings of the ancient Egyptian sage and magician Hermes Trismegistus, the only one of his works as yet unknown. I had been told by an old Venetian bookseller, for whom the book was no more than a legend, that when Ficino read the manuscript, he feared that the secret knowledge it contained was so dangerous he could not make it public, in case it should fall into the wrong hands. Instead he had translated it into a cipher no one but initiates could read.

I had drawn on the writings of Hermes in creating my memory system, but this was the book that had eluded me. It was supposed to contain the secret of man's divine origin, together with the knowledge that would allow him to regain that divinity. Some said it contained a magic that would bestow the secret of immortality. I could not credit that, but I did believe that the secrets locked within its cryptic pages must be powerful enough to threaten the established church, for why else would it have been suppressed, and sought for over a century by men who pursued occult knowledge? My friend John Dee had once been in possession of this book for less than a day when he was beaten almost to death by hired thieves, who had stolen it for a rival.

Although I had assured Catherine that I had the skills to break the cipher, I was growing less sure now that I was able to examine the book more closely. The more I considered it, the more convinced I became that I would not be able to solve this mystery without Dee's help. I had two clear choices before me, it seemed: the lonely life of a university teacher in Paris, with a steady income but excluded from the world of the court, and always looking over my shoulder for the blade of Guise or Paget flashing in a dark street – or the future I had proposed to Sophia, albeit without her. I could travel to Prague, find Dee, offer my services to the Emperor Rudolf with this book as my means of introduction; no other ruler in Europe would recognise its value as he would, or so I had been led to believe. Sophia was right; there was no guarantee of a place for me there, but at least there was a hope, and perhaps that was enough.

I held the book to my chest and walked to the window. All the lights were out, across the city; I could distinguish nothing except the faint white rise and fall of the snow-covered rooftops stretching out into the black distance. Maybe my future lay beyond these streets now, I thought. Perhaps this book would open the door to a new chapter in my life – one that would make it worthwhile to leave everything behind once again. Perhaps another journey would bring me one step closer to home.